I0714177

HOLLOW EDGE

FRANKIE CAMERON

Hollow Edge
Copyright © 2021 Frankie Cameron
All Rights Reserved

Hollow Edge is a work of fiction. Names, characters, places, and incidents either are the product of the author's imagination or are used fictitiously. Any resemblance to actual persons, living or dead, events, or locales is entirely coincidental.

All rights reserved. No part of this book may be reproduced or used in any manner without the prior written permission of the copyright owner, except for the use of brief quotations in a book review. To request permissions, contact the publisher at support@funnyfacefiction.com

Hardcover: 978-1-7776603-0-7
Paperback: 978-1-7776603-3-8
Audiobook: 978-1-7776603-2-1
Ebook: 978-1-7776603-1-4

First paperback edition

Edited by Jackie Brown Books
Cover art by Chealsy Dale
Layout by Owen Carless
Author Photographs by Sheldon Isaac Images

Published by Funny Face Fiction Ltd.
3852 Larose Crescent
Campbellcroft, Ontario, Canada L0A 1B0
www.funnyfacefiction.com

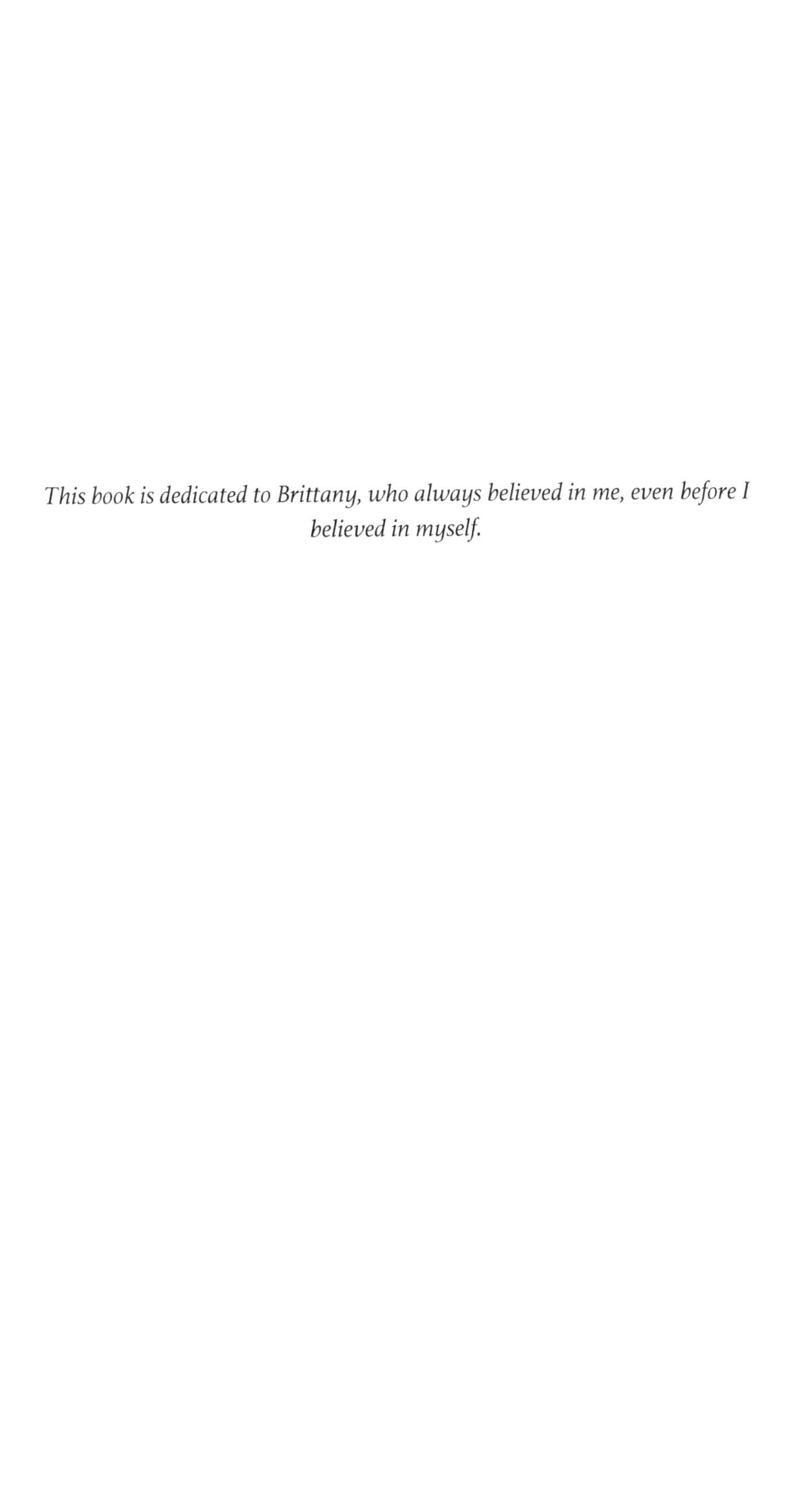

This book is dedicated to Brittany, who always believed in me, even before I believed in myself.

PROLOGUE

JUNE 27, 2049

When the lights flickered back on, Sofia pinched herself to make sure she was still alive. She felt her husband, James Cutter, the President of the United States, squeeze her shoulder. With difficulty, she raised her head. Her eyes lasered on to her boys; the rise and fall of their chests proof they were safe. Sofia pressed her palm against her bullet wound, relishing the pain because it meant they had survived. The bunker had withstood the blast—but now what?

As predicted, an asteroid, code named Attila, hit Earth. It was an astronomical disaster, not a political one, that almost wiped most life forms from existence. James immediately resumed his duties, rising to speak with the Secretary of Defense despite wobbly legs. Sofia knew she should do something as First Lady to comfort those surrounding her, but she didn't have the strength to move.

She looked around the command center, wondering how long they would have to remain there, two thousand feet below the Earth's surface. She breathed deeply, trying not to dwell on the reality of the situation and its effects above ground.

The Cheyenne Mountain Complex, designed in the 1960s to house the government in case of a nuclear war, was located just outside Colorado Springs, Colorado. Deep underground, it spanned just under five acres. She wondered how many people were alive in the other shelters or if anyone survived outside this self-sustaining city. The complex was built to withstand the horrors like the ones that had just obliterated civilization.

NASA's Planetary Defense Coordination Office tracked Attila long before impact. Slowly the governments of Earth's major nations had stockpiled weapons, gathered seeds, collected irreplaceable art, and prepared for the unthinkable. Sofia and her family, and the other VIPs, moved into primary warning centers. The VIPS included top government officials, doctors, engineers, and specialists of every kind. People that would be useful in helping society to rebuild while working with the materials they had stockpiled. VIPS, but not their families. Some of them were taken against their will, wanting to stay with their families instead. The government didn't share the news with the public until the last minute, not wanting to start a panic, but word eventually leaked out.

The TV screens were nothing but static. Like it was scripted, everyone in the control center hurried back to their tasks, trying to contact the outside world or what remained of it. How could they go back to work when everything had just changed? How could they function knowing their families were left outside?

The experts predicted the planet would be in rough shape. They expected the asteroid would land in the Atlantic Ocean, causing massive tidal waves and tsunamis that would eradicate the North American east coast. Dust from the impact would block out the sun, killing most life on Earth and push the planet into a deep freeze after smaller fireballs set the planet on fire. They had already seen the damage one fireball could do when half of Colorado Springs disappeared.

Earlier, those trying to approach the fence had been shot at, not stopping until several people had been killed. Not even stopping then, but the fence had held. Both soldiers and civilians had died in the skirmish. Had Sofia done the right thing when she showed mercy and snuck civilians into the bunker? When she saw people suffering, how could she not help? They could share the space.

Already she had heard rumblings that the more senior of the VIPs weren't happy. They were asking for the establishment of a commission and a fence to divide them from the subordinates. Looking around her at the hustle of those in duty mode, trained to do their jobs above all else, made her wonder if her rebellious act of kindness would doom them all. Only time would tell.

1

APRIL 22, 2167

Sparks flew around my head while the monotonous popping and hissing of the welder drowned out everything else surrounding me. Lost in my thoughts, the acidy smell of burning metal fusing together flooded my nose, becoming all I could taste. The vaporizing steel invaded my lungs, my pores, every cell of my body. I couldn't wait until I could scrub the day away. Even then, after the regulation four-minute lukewarm—though forceful—spray of the shower, there was always some residue left behind.

"Useless," I muttered as a large drop of water gathered, then dropped from the pipe mere inches away from the spot I had just fixed. Welding in the water plant was an endless job. The galvanized steel pipes sprung leak after leak as the bunker's infrastructure was old and worn. The welding torch in my right hand felt like a part of me, a metal extension of my body that I used twelve hours a day, six days a week. I loosened my grip, then stretched each finger individually to relieve the pain and stiffness.

Why couldn't I be ambidextrous?

Bundles of pipes and cables in various shapes and sizes ran along the sides and top of the walls. Once painted in brilliant colors, the years faded them until they became the same shade of dull. Knocking twice on the cold rock wall, I gave thanks the Hollows was still sustainable since the alternative was unthinkable. The lights flickered. Was there a problem with the generators? The underground whispers claim the diesel-filled lake is almost dry.

"Charlie. Hey, Charlie!"

My concentration broke. I released the trigger of the welding torch when I heard my name called, cocking my ear toward the sound until I heard it again. Flipping up the visor on my helmet, I spun around, catching a glimpse of Callahan striding towards me. His footsteps in the cavernous room were muffled by the sound of the welder.

I raised a hand in an uncertain greeting, and he waved back uneasily. Glancing around, I checked to see if anyone from the Authority lingered nearby. My heart pounded so hard it threatened to burst from my ribcage. My hands became slick with sweat inside the thick leather gloves that were two sizes too big.

What would possess Callahan to visit me while I worked? If they discovered us on an unsanctioned break, there would be consequences, severe ones. Thunder—thank goodness, there was no one in sight. Various scenarios played in my mind as he walked towards me. What had happened that he has shown up here? Why would he take such a risk? I checked my tag—forty-five minutes before the final horn. Not that long. I shuffled my feet, wondering if I should risk talking to Callahan or ask him to wait until the final horn sounded?

Against my better judgment, I turned off the welding torch, slipped off my gloves, and removed my helmet. My hair spilled out halfway down my back. Hurrying to throw it up in a ponytail, I pulled on the hat stuffed in my back pocket. I poked up all the loose strands into my cap, so my hair wasn't visible. I couldn't chance the paint wearing off.

"Whatcha doing here?" I swung down from the scaffolding, unsure whether to smile or frown. A visit with Callahan would usually put me in a better mood, but my stomach was queasy at the thought of someone noticing and reporting us.

"How did you find me?"

Callahan mouthed the word "blind spot." He pointed towards a black security camera anchored to the arched cement wall, motioning for me to bend down. The feeble lighting reflected off the camera lens, creating moving patterns on the opposite wall. Its mechanical whirling and clicking noises reverberated in the room. We would only have a few seconds until the camera swung back our way.

I dropped into a crouch, creeping towards the blind spot where those watching couldn't see. Cameras observed us twenty-four hours a day, seven days a week. Those of us from the eastern part of the bunker, the laborers, or Subs as the Elites called us for subordinates, learned how to stay out of sight as much as possible. It had taken years to discover and map all the blind spots in the Hollows.

Big fat drops of water plopped down on our heads from the leaking water pipes. The overhead fluorescent light barely reached the edges of the corridors, enabling us to get lost in the dimness. I felt the cold, rough rock wall against my back. A shiver ran through me as I thought of all the spiders and creepy crawlies that could easily touch my skin and get in my hair. A pitfall of living underground. I detested bugs.

"How's the welding going?"

Callahan wasn't acting like himself. He seemed fidgety. Restless, like he was about to jump out of his skin. His eyes darted from side to side, his head twisted over his shoulder, as if he waited for something to hop into the shadows with us.

"Still holding together so far," I replied with a half shrug. Experience taught me he was working up to telling me something else. Something I would not like.

"Good, that's good, right? Because we've been down here a long time, longer than we should have been?"

"Yup, they built this place for thirty days, not 118 years." I sighed as I checked the time, 5:15 pm. The workday would soon end.

I wasn't in the mood to rehash the history of the bunker with this senseless small talk. I monitored the camera. It swung back this way, but we should be safe here for now. "Is that what you came over here for, to discuss things we both already know? Why are you here? I need to get back to work. This can wait until the end of shift." I pointed to my tag.

His demeanor changed, as if by the flip of a switch. I watched as the pinched expression left his face. His head tilted to the side, and a ridiculous grin spanned from ear to ear. He rubbed his hands together then before I could react, splayed out his fingers, and ran them down my face, something he did from an early age when he discovered how much I hated being touched. Most times, I never reacted quick enough to move out of the way. If you told Callahan not to jump, it would be the first thing he did.

Callahan wore his sanitation uniform: black boots, gray baggy coveralls, covered with a bright orange vest. My uniform was green for maintenance, but otherwise the same. Callahan's clothing did nothing to take away the fact he was gorgeous, with jet-black hair, big brown eyes, light- brown skin, and chiseled features. His short strands stood straight up, spiked like an old punk rocker, a type of music he tried to make popular again. On anyone else, his hairstyle would look ridiculous, but somehow it seemed perfect on him.

My security tag beeped. I slipped it from the holder on my left arm to read the message. I noticed Callahan's tag missing.

"An alert?" he asked.

"Just a reminder about tomorrow's assembly."

"As if we could forget with all the daily alerts and notifications they send."

"Hey, where's your security tag?" I fumbled around the sleeve of my uniform until I returned the thin black metal tag covered in plastic to its proper place. My fingers ran over the smooth cover, clutching it closer.

"Don't worry, I've got it." He gave me a flippant wave of his hand, then flashed another mischievous smile. He pulled his tag out from the inside pocket of his uniform, reattaching it to its proper place on his left arm. "I wouldn't get caught without it . . . know better than that, right?"

"If you say so. You are breaking Code 7A-1421 not being in your proper work area just being here."

Callahan glanced at the camera. "Never mind that. Guess, what? You'll never believe what I've found. Like never, ever, ever, ever, ever, ever!" Callahan pulled something out of his back pocket, then stood with his hands behind his back. "Guess!"

"What are you? Twelve?"

"Just guess!" Callahan shifted his weight back and forth, unable to stay still.

His enthusiasm felt contagious. Despite my nervousness, I found a smile on my face without realizing how it got there. I was horrible at guessing games, but it meant a lot to him, so I tried. At each guess, he shook his head no. His eyes glinted. What had he found to make him react this way? I hadn't seen him this excited in a long time. Searching my brain for something, anything, I came up blank. I raised my arms in surrender. "Gees, I don't know."

Callahan dropped his hands to his sides. An apple floated out from behind his back, hovering just below his shoulders in front of his chest "Surprise!" Callahan made every simple act into a performance—although this time, an actual apple, made it worthy.

My jaw dropped. An apple, not just a picture of one. It was rumored apples grew in the restricted section of the food plant, but I had never even hoped to see one in my lifetime.

Callahan's twin sister, Gibson, and our friend, Reese, both worked in the food plant. They had never seen an apple either, probably because they couldn't access the restricted area. We chalked their existence up to a myth or an urban legend. But they actually existed. The shiny red color drew me towards it like a magnet. I couldn't look away. My hands trembled as I reached forward to touch it; but then I froze. Shrinking back, I dropped my hands, interlacing them behind my back.

My head swung to check the camera even though I knew it couldn't have caught Callahan's performance. The other camera, though, must have recorded I wasn't working, that I was not standing where I was supposed to be. Interlinked with the computer system, someone would have added a note to my file.

"Jumping jeepers, Callahan Malone, are you crazy?" I swallowed down a gulp. "What are you doing with that, you'll get us both sent to the vault? Don't you know how long you could get locked up just for touching one of those?"

"Overreact much? Can you believe my good luck? I still can't." Callahan's eyebrow raised slightly. "Anyway, they wouldn't send me to the vault for a tiny infraction like this, right?"

"You sound so sure." I wanted to shake him. How could he be this reckless? My head whirled; another headache was forming. I rubbed my temples to ease the pain. "You know if you break any of the commission's codes what will happen... getting caught with contraband breaks Code 3A-2933. Not to mention using your abilities... in *public*. You need to stop doing stupid stuff or you will get both of us killed."

"I'm careful. The TCC won't catch me. Besides, they'd never blame you as you've never been in trouble before."

I looked around and whispered, "You'd better not get caught calling the commission that name."

"What are you saying?" he pretended innocence, then grimaced, "TCC stands for 'Totally Corrupt Commission' and that's what they are, right?"

"Don't repeat it." I swatted his arm. "I have to get back to work."

"Charlie, listen... I know what you are thinking, but I didn't use my powers to get the apple; I swear I didn't. I found it... honest." He crossed his hand over his chest.

"Well, you are using your powers now, aren't you? Holy Attila... hang on to the apple with your hand." My words rushed out faster than normal. "Callahan, you know better than to use your telekinesis.

What if they caught you, and with the apple on top of that? Then it wouldn't just be the vault, would it? Do you want to get exiled?"

The vault meant incarceration, but exile was a sure death sentence. Nothing could survive outside of the bunker, in the frozen wasteland.

Callahan snatched the apple out of the air and spun it around on his index finger. "What's with you lately? You are even grumpier than usual."

"You—that's what!" I wiped my sweaty hands on my pant leg. "You are stressing me out right now. I don't want to get caught up in this. Why are we even friends? You live your life on the edge, and I know—I'm a boring rule follower. It's so... crazy. I can't breathe, I feel like I'm going to have a heart attack."

"Overreact much?" He raised an eyebrow.

I stared at the ceiling, trying to avoid the apple's allure. Steel netting covered the rocks overhead, anchored by over 115,000 rock bolts to keep pieces of rock from falling. Workers had hammered the bolts chaotically into the granite, so it looked like a crazy rock-climbing wall. Sometimes I imagined pictures in the design, shapes like stars and animals.

Callahan laughed at me throughout my tirade while polishing the apple on the sleeve of his coveralls. He'd seen me spin out-of-control plenty of times; it wasn't anything new.

"Um well... because you have enough fear for both of us, scaredy-cat," Callahan teased. His smile made him appear younger than his seventeen years. Callahan made big loops with his finger beside his head, like I was crazy.

I made a funny face at him, but Callahan's cheery mood immediately made me feel better. Callahan had an endearing habit of saying "right" after every sentence, as if he needed confirmation of everything he said.

"Whatever." I couldn't stop my lips from quirking upwards. "Rules make life easier. I don't know why I've always liked them, but I do. I think it's because it makes everything black and white, right or wrong, truth or lie. I liked absolutes better than maybes."

"Do you want the first bite?" Callahan motioned to hand me the apple. Callahan embodied generosity: always willing to share what little he had. He didn't have a selfish bone in his body. Others would have saved the apple for themselves and savored it in private, but not him.

I wanted to grab the apple from his hand and discover what it felt like, smelled like. The apple shone so red and glossy—my eyes had never experienced that color before. I couldn't even imagine how it would taste. My mouth watered at the thought.

"I'll pass," I answered after a long deliberation with myself. No matter how much I wanted to taste the apple, I knew I would never let myself try it. It wasn't a risk I would take.

Callahan taunted me with a twisted half-smile. He ran his hand through his spiked hair before he took his first bite, his face lighting up with delight. He barely swallowed the first bite when he took another. Did it taste as good as it looked? My mouth salivated and I tore my eyes away from him. "Charlie, you have to live a little. Take a chance, right?" He focused on the apple, mumbling and drooling as he took a bite. "When will you ever get an opportunity to try an apple again?"

He wasn't wrong. I might never get the opportunity again, but I just couldn't do it. Fear kept me from taking a bite. Fear stopped me from doing most everything. The thought of the consequences kept me in line. They were too severe; I took a big enough chance just sitting here while he ate the apple. It was out of character for me to do something this risky.

"Yeah..., no." I rubbed my temples as my headache pulsed. The initial low throb developed into a raging pain. The headaches began a few years ago, one every month or two, but lately, they were more frequent and intense.

"Headache again?"

I nodded. "If you didn't use your abilities, how did you get the...?" I motioned toward the apple, still too afraid to say the word.

"It fell off a cart coming back from the food plant." Callahan lit up as he explained. "It rolled into the corner without the Authority noticing. I snatched it, tossing it in with the trash because they never look in there when I'm cleaning. I couldn't believe my good luck."

Hiding contraband in with the trash became one method of moving things around from place to place without the Authority noticing.

"Hmm, sometimes, I guess you're lucky you have the worst job in the Hollows."

"Cause my job picking up everyone else's garbage is a dream, right?" He adjusted the collar on his uniform as if he were wearing a three-piece suit. "I'll trade you, sanitation for maintenance. You can get stuck with all the dirty jobs nobody else wants to do."

"Yuck, no thank you." My nose wrinkled at the thought.

"Are you positive? Not even to see the control center?" he nudged his shoulder against mine.

"Big deal. You've only gotten to see it once, it's not like it's an everyday event."

"That's still one more time than you saw it, right?" he continued in a singsong voice. "You could see more of the Hollows. I have access to move around almost everywhere."

"Not the West End. Plus, it's against the code 2A-9831 to access places you don't have clearance for."

"No, not the West End. Not yet, anyway." Callahan lowered his head. A wistful look appeared on his face. "Charlie, don't you ever wish you were an Elite? Imagine. You could eat amazing things like this all the time."

"Do you think they do? Or are they rationed like once a year?"

The juice from the apple trickled down his chin, washing the filth of the day from his face. I had to look away. He wiped the back of his hand across his mouth.

"Plus," I added, "what would be the point of wishing? You know things never change around here. Life is never so bad that it can't be worse."

"Damn Charlie, same old story, every time. Why are you so negative?" He glared at me, his jaw clenched, and a vein throbbed in his neck. "Life's not so bad... you're still alive, aren't you? Tomorrow is another day; you never know what could happen. Look at me: yesterday I had never even seen an apple and today I have tasted one. Life can change from moment to moment."

"I . . ." His tumultuous mood swings drove me crazy. "Expect nothing and nothing will disappoint you. You'll never get hurt."

"Unbelievable! You never look on the positive side of things." There was nothing left of the apple. He put the remnants in his pocket and licked his fingers before wiping his hands on his uniform. He dragged his hands through his hair as we stood in silence. His spikes bounced right back up.

After a few seconds, I reached over and tapped his arm. "I'm sorry, I wish I could be more like you, but... I don't know how. I'm emotionally backward."

"Um, maybe you choose pessimism, so you are never disappointed when you expected something good to happen and it doesn't, right?

"Whoa, that's deep. When did you get so poetic?" I tried to cajole him back to a better mood. He wouldn't stay mad at me for long; he never did. He always burned hot but cooled off quickly. How could he stay mad when he found an apple? Jumping jeepers—that might be the best thing that has ever happened to him.

I slide down the wall to sit on the rough concrete floor and Callahan plopped down beside me. "Did you ever wonder why the walls, floors, everything is gray; there is not a single drop of color in this place?" I asked. "Everything is so drab. Why can't we use color?"

"Nope," Callahan answered. "Never thought about it."

"Well, don't you think it would be better to see painted murals or pictures on the walls instead of stone and cement? Someone with artistic talent must live in the bunker. Maybe there could even be a modern-day Picasso or Monet."

"Who?"

"Don't you remember anything from our time at Voco?" I admonished him for forgetting. "Picasso and Monet, painters in the old world that painted famous pictures that hung in museums... I think there is a portrait hung in the assembly hall. The one with the bridge and water lilies—."

"They don't even give us enough to eat what makes you think they would give us paint for the walls... the TCC would never allow that."

I bumped his shoulder with mine. "I am fully convinced you never graduated from Voco."

"Guilty." A shadow passed behind his eyes.

I nodded. I shouldn't have brought up Voco. I knew Callahan hated talking about school. It had become a sore spot with him because of his dyslexia. The teachers didn't have extra time to spend with him, so he fell behind. We all tried to help him, but we didn't know how.

We sat together without speaking, content with the lack of words. Why weren't more people fluent in silence? I checked the location of the camera, estimating I had about ninety seconds before it would swing back around. I needed to get back to my post. The computer would have logged every minute it stood deserted.

Before I could leave, I felt my heartbeat pick up; I dropped down beside Callahan again. I sensed we weren't alone.

2

———

"The Authority is coming," I whispered a mere moment before six guards strode by in military formation followed by a soldier wearing fatigues. They walked in unison, their rhythmic footsteps timed. The reverberation from their stamping feet echoed in the room, causing my heart to continue to beat at a faster pace than normal. Although hidden from the cameras, we stood in plain sight should they happen to look in our direction.

Callahan shrunk back. His face flushed red like a neon sign. I hoped the Authority wouldn't notice how guilty he looked. "Thunder—."

"Don't curse. Shh! The Authority doesn't like it."

Dressed in black from head to toe, armed with bulletproof vests, automatic weapons, and clubs, among other weapons; complete overkill. No one else had weapons. The light bounced off their black opaque shields.

The Commission kept the identities of Authority members secret. They never addressed each other by name, just by six-digit numbers, like the 073169 that was displayed across their chest protector of the officer nearest us. Kept in an unknown part of the bunker, the members of the Authority interacted only with each other and only came out to patrol and arrest.

They noticed us so I repositioned my feet to rise. A captain, I knew by the number of red stripes on his uniform, motioned for us to stay seated on the ground. What was happening? Captains never went on raids.

The captain said something and one guard turned. He carried a locater; they were tracking someone. His voice, like all Authority members, broadcast too loudly and sounded like a robot or computer, devoid of emotion, inhuman. I cringed when they spoke; their voices had an element that sounded like microphone feedback. They continued on their way, marching around the corner until they disappeared out of sight.

"Do you think they found a deviant?" Callahan whispered into my ear.

Deviant... I hated that word, used to describe people like Callahan, those with powers or special abilities. The word tasted sour in my mouth. Swallowing hard, I leaned back into the wall, wishing it would absorb me, trying to make myself as small as possible should they return. How much trouble were we in? Would we get demerit points or worse?

Jumping jeepers, wasn't I under enough scrutiny because of Zander? Long ago, I promised myself I would do whatever it took to stay out of trouble. Making it a practice to fade into the background. Just one of the nameless Subs from the east end.

Callahan knew me so well I didn't have to say what I was thinking out loud.

"It's better than the word mutant, right? I consider it a gift."

"It's not a gift or a curse. It's the same as being born with blue eyes, totally out of your control." I felt trapped here; I wished I could be somewhere else, anywhere else. I pulled on my collar, struggling to find more air. The pain in my head exploded hard and fast.

"True. I think it's all the toxic chemicals and nuclear material released into the planet that caused babies to be born with abilities. Don't you?"

"Hmm, maybe, that's still not proven. Does it even matter how they originated?"

His leg bumped up against my thigh. I moved over an inch. He moved over again.

"Can you stop touching me?"

Callahan laughed before he flicked his finger against the end of my nose.

"I read in the archives that after the asteroid struck, it showered the entire planet with intense infrared radiation. That may have contributed to the condition," I said.

Babies were born with powers, starting with telepathy and telekinesis, after we had been in the Hollows for generations. My grandparents' age group developed them first. Children reached school age; they'd be four or five before parents noticed their abilities.

"You spend too much time reading."

"Books are way better than people."

"Yeah, no."

"Well, either way, if they discovered you have powers, I would never see you again, Callahan, would I? That's what happens. Code 1A-9966 Deviancy. The TCC signs a warrant. The Authority takes you into custody. Then your life is over."

"Do you think it's true what the underground whispers say?"

"Probably not. What are they saying now? I heard they run experiments on the prisoners. They say the TCC treats them as lab rats. And then..." I elbowed him in the side. "Hey, are you listening?"

"I'm listening to you. I'm just not paying attention." Callahan made a silly face, then he pushed lightly against my shoulder. "Relax. You worry too much. I'll be fine. I'm too slick to catch."

"Arghh. Trust me, you're not slick."

"Anyway, when's the last time they caught a deviant? Months? Years? How long ago?" Callahan got up and punched at the air, shadow boxing against an invisible opponent. He couldn't stay still. What was the matter with him? The Authority could come back at any moment.

"Pinky swear." I met his gaze and felt better; he had that ability, no matter the circumstances. I stuck out my little finger so he could intertwine his finger with mine. Something we hadn't outgrown since childhood. Our secret pact. "Why would anyone hide in the water plant anyway? Look around."

Callahan tilted his head. "Even if the Authority didn't find you, where would you eat or sleep? Dumb plan."

"There is nowhere to hide, here or anywhere. With them and the cameras. Finding a way outside is the only chance of escaping. But that's just suicide."

The two blast doors to the outside had the tightest security. I had never seen them, but they were rumored to be three-foot-thick and weighed twenty-five tons. Even if you could get close to the hatches, rockslides sealed all but one of them shut years ago. On the day the asteroid hit, the blast doors saved our lives. Even now, they protected us.

"Yeah, but there is no chance of surviving out there? Outside the walls. It won't be safe out there for at least another hundred years, right?"

"Well, that's what the TCC says. Do you think they always tell us the truth, though?" I stretched out my legs, adjusting a bit; my butt felt sore from sitting on the hard cement floor.

Every year, the commission sends someone to investigate the surface. We call it the jaunt. Outfitted with a decontamination suit and a set of scuba tanks, the volunteer, usually a guard from the Authority, checked the air quality and the frozen environment.

"Not likely. Just lies and more lies."

The readings suggest the radiation levels are still too high to leave. Diminished sunlight from the thick asteroid dust is made it impossible to breathe outside without a respirator.

"Shush," whispered Callahan as he sat with a thud. "They are coming back."

The Authority returned with a prisoner, stopping just down the corridor from where they had ordered us to sit. His hands were zipped-tied behind his back. The captain told the others to stay and left the area.

The prisoner turned his gaze toward me. He smiled and winked, his eyes glistening wickedly. Was he insane? It didn't matter. He had a one-way ticket to the vault. His life had already ended. I shared a look with Callahan, who thought the same thing.

"Who do you think he is?" Callahan whispered.

"An Elite for sure. The khaki pants and blue-collared button-up shirt are a dead give-away." He appeared to be around our age, seventeen.

Callahan nodded his agreement. "Yeah, he looks like one of those prep kids. He sure didn't go to Voco with us."

"He looks just like you, but he is better dressed." I winked at him, mimicking the prisoner. The prisoner's arms were enormous, causing his shirt to bulge over his muscles. He must work out all day long.

"This old thing, it's all the rage in the sanitation department." Callahan pretended to dust off the shoulder of his uniform. He looked at the prisoner again. "Guess so. Plus, there aren't that many brown Elites."

I estimated the prisoner was the same height as Callahan, around six feet tall, but he was muscular rather than lean. No one grew over-weight in the bunker since there wasn't enough food to eat. The shape of their faces was the main thing that set them apart. Callahan possessed an angular face while the prisoner had a square jaw. The prisoner's hair hung longer than Callahan's, falling to his shoulders. When he turned, I noticed a tattoo under his right ear.

"Do you see his tattoo?" I asked. "That's a strange symbol. Do you know what it is?"

"No, what tattoo?"

"It's under his right ear. Can't you see it?" The symbol felt famil-iar, and I could not tear my eyes from it. Why did I know that symbol? Something tugged at the memory, but it proved just out of reach, an elusive grasp of recollection that slipped through my fingers.

"I don't see it; those green eyes of yours are like x-rays."

"Oh, no, you discovered my secret power." I rolled my eyes at him as I tugged at my hat to make sure none of my hair escaped; a subconscious reflex I performed a hundred times a day. My coloring, white-blond hair and green eyes, made me an anomaly in the East

End. In the old world, only two percent of the population had fair-hair. In our world, it was an abnormality that only existed in pictures.

I had brown hair at birth. It didn't turn blond until I turned three. Samantha, one of Zanders' followers, who had eluded detection in the exile, started painting it then. She thought it would keep me safer. She found employment at the orphanage to have close contact with all the children left behind. When I was ten years old, the TCC exiled Samantha from the bunker after she took part in an assassination attempt on Joseph Cutter. I still miss her.

Even now, I painted my hair and covered it with a hat because it raised too many questions. Sometimes people wanted to touch it because of the color. To me, it was a reminder of my connection to Zander, something I didn't want to bring attention to.

"Oh no." Callahan's eyes flickered from me to the prisoner. "He wouldn't dare try, right…"

In a frozen second, the prisoner elbowed a guard in the throat, causing him to gasp for air. The others flew at him, but he danced around, dodging their attempts to subdue him. Their sluggish movements were far too slow to contain him. I saw him drop something and then kick it towards the corner.

"Protect it."

His hands were suddenly free of the restraints. The prisoner punched the guard he had elbowed. wrestling him to the ground. He slammed his fist into the guard's stomach, avoiding the hard helmet on his head.

The four remaining members of the Authority stood there motionless, completely immobile. How strong were his powers that he could subdue four guards while fighting another? I think he could have restrained the guard he fought, but he appeared to be having too much fun. The grin on his face spanned from ear to ear. I thought I might have even heard him laughing.

I turned to Callahan, noticing his clenched fists and flushed face. I knew it was taking every ounce of his self-control to stop himself from jumping into the fight. He bit his teeth into his lower lip until it bled. Drops of blood spotted his chin. I shook my head from side to side, then grabbed his arm to prevent him from doing something foolish. I wouldn't have the strength to stop him if he jumped into the fight.

Without warning, the captain returned and hit the prisoner in the back of the head with the butt end of his rifle. He fell to the ground like a rock, ending his control over the remaining Authority members. They moved as if they were unsure of what had happened and then helped their companion off the floor. Two of them picked up the prisoner's legs and dragged him along behind them as they left.

The captain strode in our direction. He punched something into the minicomputer strapped to his arm, then waved it over our security tags. My face fell when I heard the beep. I swallowed hard, trying not to react. Without a word, the captain spun on his heels and walked away without looking back.

I grabbed my tag to confirm what I already knew. Two demerit points. Two freaking Sundays I would have to give up working off the points. I slammed my fist on the floor.

"Ow!"

Callahan jumped to his feet and yelled at the empty hall, throwing up his middle finger, braver now that the Authority had disappeared. "Same to you."

Shuddering, I tried to pull myself together. I twisted my mother's ring around on the chain where it hung around my neck while taking deep breaths. The ring and watch were the only belongings I had left from my family. I should have thrown the watch away, but something always stopped me every time I tried. I put a reminder in my tag to schedule the Sundays.

"Charlie, are you okay?" Callahan asked. He unclenched his fists and wiped the blood from his chin.

"Yeah, guess so, you..." I exhaled loudly. I didn't realize I had been holding my breath. "I thought I would have to restrain you back there."

Casually, I walked to the corner to see what the prisoner kicked over there, discovering a small black metal box not much bigger than my thumb. The symbol on the box matched the prisoner's tattoo. I turned it over in my hand, trying to find a latch or mechanism to open it, but couldn't. I stuffed it into my pocket.

Callahan yelled over. "What did you find?"

"Nothing, I thought I saw something over here." I showed him a rock I picked up from the ground, careful to guard my thoughts about the box in my pocket so he couldn't read them. I would share my discovery with Callahan at some point, but for now, I selfishly wanted to keep it to myself. Just until I figured out what that symbol meant.

"They caught another one. Damn it, they caught another deviant." He simmered, pacing back and forth. "But did you see him fight? He was awesome."

Even though we didn't know the prisoner, deviants were all on the same side.

"If they caught him, what's stopping them from catching us?" I transmitted to him.

Callahan acknowledged my thoughts and nodded in agreement. *"I don't know. Strange Though? An Elite deviant? I didn't think that was a thing. And what was he doing here in the middle of the day?"*

3
____

A tone sounded at 6:00 pm, signalling the end of the workday and the workweek since it was Saturday. Our world revolved around tones for lights out, meetings, and meals. Callahan's tag beeped, so he checked it. "Gibson and Reese might be late."

"What else is new?" I walked over to pick up my welding helmet and torch, placing them in the beat-up brown satchel I left lying there earlier.

"Thunder! Why do you bother lugging all your stuff around with you?" Callahan asked. "You know no one ever steals anything. The punishments are too harsh."

"You stole an apple."

"Aaah! You're such a pain. I didn't steal it: I found it, right? I told you that already."

"The equipment is my responsibility. If I lost it, I'd get more demerit points, that's all I need." I shook my head, thinking of the demerit points we had just earned and the lost Sundays it would take to work them off. Slamming the bag shut, I flung it over my shoulder.

"I thought you hated speaking telepathically." Callahan massaged the back of his neck, twisting his head from side to side until it cracked, then he sighed in relief.

Although we are both telepathic, I don't have telekinesis like Callahan does. We don't read minds, just current or recent thoughts. It is like having a conversation without words. Blocking thoughts turned out to be the first thing we learned to do. Otherwise, we would never have a moment of peace. It worked like an open or closed door. To communicate with another telepath, you both need to have your doors open.

"I do, and I don't. Sometimes it's simpler . . . less work. Don't you think, it would be easier to get caught if they notice us all sitting around, and no one talked? It's an unnecessary risk."

"Maybe."

If no one stole anything, where's the stuff from the bazaar from?" I asked, getting back to answering his original question.

"True enough. It has to come from someplace."

The bazaar was the only place in The Hollows where people could get items like jewelry, books, clothing, and other tidbits leftover from the old world. After work and on Sundays, sellers set up shop in the bazaar, trading whatever they could get their hands on. Although not "officially" sanctioned by the TCC, they allowed it to operate with no restrictions.

"How do you think your uncle collects all his stuff?" I asked. Callahan's uncle, Jagger Malone, and the Kings, his associates, operated the bazaar and had the biggest trading area. If I saw the Kings coming, I would turn around and walk the other way to avoid them. So would most Subs.

Jagger had wanted to raise the twins, Callahan and Gibson, after the exile of their parents after in the Revolt of 2152, but the Commission wouldn't let him. It worked out just as well since he was an intimidating person, not at all compassionate or loving like Samantha had been in the orphanage. The twins hated to admit their relationship to him because of his reputation, even if they had no other family left.

"He has his ... ways," Callahan said. "His people bring him stuff they find. Other people make deals with him and his crew. I think he pays bribes to someone up high in the West End, right?" Callahan caught sight of his reflection and worked to tame one of his spikes.

The bazaar operated strictly on the barter system; strictly trade for trade, no TCC credits permitted. If a person had nothing to trade, the Kings would ask for a favor, usually something against the code. I wouldn't risk asking the Kings for anything, ever. Plus, the only time you could wear anything besides coveralls was on Sundays anyway.

The Kings also used the bazaar as a front for the black market. A way to get those things not sold in the open, such as medicine, electronics, or anything else the TCC wouldn't want us to have. You only needed to ask the underground whisperers, then they would get in touch with the Kings. They also controlled and manufactured the drug "synth." There were other fractions within the bunker, the Sparks, the Quakes, and the Dreamers, to name a few, but the Kings were like the mafia or a street gang while the others were mostly social groups.

Two brothers, Axel and Abel, kidnapped Gibson when we were eight years old. Callahan almost lost his mind with worry. Me too. Callahan couldn't sleep or eat the entire time she was gone. Jagger didn't worry at all. He put a bounty on the kidnappers, waiting until the underground whisperers brought him the information he needed. After four days, the Kings retrieved Gibson, then brutally executed the brothers as an example of what would happen to anyone else that attempted the same scheme.

The brothers had traumatized Gibson. They didn't hurt her physically, just mentally. They took her down one of the three horizontal passageways that led into the mountain for access or drainage and chained her there, stuffing her in a box. The box was shoved into a hole in the damp tunnel. They left her in the dark for days with nothing to eat, only checking on her sporadically. The sound of rats nearly drove her crazy.

"You set?" I asked Callahan. We started the brief walk back to the East End. I shifted the weight of my bag, so the helmet didn't dig into my hip. The contents weren't heavy, just awkward.

Stopping first at the checkpoint at the exit of the water plant, we scanned our security tags. Silence ensued when my profile appeared on the enormous screen over the gate. I should be used to the stares. The way people looked at me when they found out my identity.

Sometimes I wanted to scream, YES, LOOK AT ME! EVERYONE LOOK AT ME! I AM THE DAUGHTER OF ZANDER EDGE, LEADER OF THE REVOLT OF 2152. TAKE A GOOD, LONG LOOK. But I said nothing, swallowing the words. Almost choking on them.

The checkpoints were a colossal waste of time. No one had tried to resist the TCC since our parents had staged the revolt almost fifteen years ago. They exiled over a hundred citizens from the Hollows for that crime.

"I hate this part." Callahan removed everything from his pockets and placed them in a container to go through the x-ray machine.

"Who doesn't?" I mirrored his moves, tossing my satchel on the conveyor.

We took off our boots and stood with our arms raised over our heads, stepping into the body scanning machine that searched for suspicious items. The Authority waved us through the checkpoint; we stopped to put our boots back on. Callahan dumped a rock out of his boot. He put the boot up to his nose, then acted like he died from the experience. What a clown.

We merged into the congested corridor, continuing towards the residential blocks, with hundreds of others, all going in the same directions at the same pace. After a twelve-hour shift, we were exhausted. The weariness of all was visible both from the pace and by the hunched shoulders of people in coveralls of varying colors.

I saw the only colors of the East end, maintenance greens, Callahan's colleagues in sanitation grays, water plant reds, food plant blues, and power plant oranges. The pinks that worked for the Elites would come through the West End gate. I wondered if we wore colorful coveralls so those who watched the cameras could easier categorize and identify us.

The stuffy air had a trace of bleach and sweat. The chattering of the crowd was deafening, and although I could close myself to their thoughts, I braced myself against the emotions of the horde.

The corridor was painted gray, walls, ceiling, and floors. A labyrinth of cables, pipes, wires, and cords ran along the sides of the wall. In some areas, giant sheets of white plastic covered the towering rock walls, to keep the dust down.

"Do you ever wish you could work in the West End as a maid, cook, or something? It would be better than working for maintenance, right?" Callahan nodded and fist bumped a few of his friends as they passed by.

"Never!" I gathered my thoughts "No... it would be worse to work in the West End and come back home every night than to never see the West End and not know what you were missing. You can't miss what you don't know exists."

"Do you even listen to the things that come out of your mouth?" He stopped walking, causing the man behind him to curse. "You can't look at life that way."

Arriving at the bridge that spanned the mountain springs, we paused while the throng rushed past. The natural underground stream generated all the water needed to run the facility along with the 4.5 million gallons reservoir of water that served the people of the bunker.

The drab concrete and steel bridge had one lovely feature: a ledge that was big and wide enough to sit on. We saw it was empty and rushed towards it. We dangled our feet over the edge while listening to the water flow past. This must be how it felt to be outdoors in the days before Attila.

"Guess who?" Gibson sneaked up behind Callahan, covering his eyes with her hands. Gibson and Reese's approach had blended with all the noise from the tunnel. Startled, I almost toppled into the shallow water, but Callahan gripped me around the waist.

"Gibson, when you do the same thing every day, it kinda takes the thrill out of guessing." Callahan dropped his hands once I regained my balance.

Why was I so jumpy? We met at the bridge every day before going back to the residences for the evening. Maybe it was this painful headache that refused to leave that was throwing me off.

"Pfft, you're no fun, big brother." Gibson stuck out her tongue at her brother. That he was born fourteen minutes earlier seemed to annoy her.

Gibson and Reese were a matched set, identically dressed in their designated blue food plant uniforms. Gibson had the same light brown coloring as her twin brother. She was much shorter. She barely reached his shoulder if she stood on something. They have a running joke where Gibson teases Callahan about stealing her height.

Reese Wang stood taller than Gibson by a few inches; she had beautiful brown, wide-set eyes fringed with long lashes, giving her a unique look. She claimed to have a mixture of Chinese and Irish heritage.

"What's new today, ladies?" I asked. "Work good?"

Gibson rolled her eyes and made a silly face. "Lame as usual." She pulled herself up on the ledge beside her brother, Reese followed.

"You know, I'm so over working for a living." Reese inspected her raggedy chewed up nails. "I'm so sick of having dirty fingernails. I should apply for membership in the Toni Tango Club."

"Oh yeah, sure, send her a friend request on Hollowpic, right?" Callahan joked.

"I've looked at it. It's all pictures of her, with Slade Cutter, the next Commissioner and the other celebrity couples and Elites hanging out doing nothing, looking fabulous," Gibson said.

"They don't accept friend requests from Subs. They don't even work, do they?" I looked at the burn marks on my uniform from random welder sparks. "They certainly don't weld."

"Holy Attila, at least you don't have to touch the type of stuff I do," Callahan said. Gibson and I squealed as he tried to cover our faces with his hands.

We had been friends since forever. After the exile of our parents for the revolt, we grew up together in the orphanage with all the other kids who lost their parents. They called our group the Six Pack. The number of kids overwhelmed the number of staff, leaving us on our own most of the time. A less than excellent experience, although it taught us resourcefulness and independence at an early age. It became a game of how to evade the staff and, later, the Authority.

"Working is still better than going to Voco. Don't you think?" I shifted my weight, trying to get comfortable, but it seemed impossible against the unbreakable concrete bridge.

"I'm surprised the TCC educated us at all. They could have put us to work at five or six," Reese said. "You know, dumb people don't cause as many problems as smart people, duh."

"They barely taught us to read and write." Gibson dug in her pocket, searching for something.

"I wonder what they teach the Elites at Prep." A slow smile spread across Callahan's face. His eyes gleamed. "Rocket science."

"That would be funny if it wasn't so true," I said. After graduating Voco, the TCC tested aptitudes that placed us in job categories. That job became our occupation until death.

"And Prep goes longer, too, doesn't it?" Callahan added. I knew he was thinking of the Elite-prisoner we had seen earlier who seemed to be our age. "If we were over there, we'd still be in school now, right? What do they get tested for?"

"Government Occupation and Treating Subs Like Dirt," I offered.

"I'm the Boss 101." Reese fluttered her lashes mockingly.

"How to Do Nothing but Look Fancy and Busy? Aha found it." Gibson pulled an MRE from her pocket. It was beyond recognition, smashed and twisted. She closed her eyes as she chewed off a piece. A satisfied smile lit up her face. "Mmm, peanut butter."

"You actually like that, right?" Callahan said.

It must be the dessert part of the MRE because eating one had never made me smile. They tasted like eating cardboard. MRE stood for meals-ready-to-eat. They allocated us one every day for lunch. Anything but yummy.

"We only graduated from Voco a year ago; it feels like a lifetime now," I said. "Stuck in maintenance for life."

"Better than sanitation. How dumb am I that my aptitude test placed me in sanitation?" Callahan tossed some loose concrete pieces into the water, causing it to ripple. A look of great bitterness swept across his face.

"Don't say that," I said. "You have dyslexia, it's a learning disorder. You aren't dumb. You are good at lots of things."

"You aren't dumb. You're special." Gibson squeezed her brother's hand.

"Somehow the way you said it, Gibson, doesn't make me feel better." Callahan flicked her hand away.

"You know, there are other ways of being smart," Reese said. "Who cares about being book smart? I don't. Besides, none of those supposedly brainiacs can do the things you can do."

We knew what she meant. Reese was the only one of the Six-Pack without special abilities. She had a soft spot for Callahan.

Reese had been born a year after the rest of us. When we went to Voco without her, she caused a fuss for weeks, until the people at the orphanage let her join us. It meant she would work full time a year earlier, but that suited her. Reese screamed so long and so loud her voice became permanently hoarse and it still has a gritty edge.

Callahan related today's adventure to Gibson telepathically. As a clairvoyant, Gibson could perceive or predict future events. A great ability, but most times she had little a warning. I told her repeatedly, if she ever found out anything about me, not to tell me. I hated spoilers.

I noticed Callahan didn't tell Gibson about the apple. She would be furious he didn't share it with her if she ever found out. I smiled just thinking about the tantrum that would come. Plus, it gave me leverage to tease him, at least until he could no longer keep his own secret and he told her.

I relayed the same story to Reese in as few words as possible. With no powers, she didn't have to spend her days hiding abilities like the rest of us. We discussed the deviant for a while and his futile effort to free himself. The hopelessness of living in a society where we weren't free to live our lives in the open remained depressing. "Can we change the subject? I don't want to talk about it anymore."

"But how did you know he was an Elite, then?" Reese stubbornly would not let the topic go.

"He wasn't wearing coveralls on a workday. What other information do you need? Plus, he dressed fancy, like they do."

"Why was he in the East End?" Reese pushed a strand of glossy hair behind her ear.

"When did you start working for the Authority?"

"Yeah Reese, when did you start working for the Authority," Callahan taunted.

"So, he just ran into your station? Why were you two together?"

"No, the Authority dragged him past my station." I exchanged a look with Callahan. I wouldn't tell his secret.

I jumped down and was about to head back on my own. I put my hand in my pocket and rubbed the strange box. Her questions were making me wonder more about that Elite. Why had he chosen to run into me, ask me—and not Callahan—to protect the box? My head pounded. I had to get away from Reese as her emotions were turning to anger, and I just did not want to feel them. Sensing she pushed too far, Reese finally let go.

"Are we still going out tonight?" Reese asked loudly.

"Yup," Gibson and Callahan spoke at the same time, then laughed.

"Not me. I'm going to the archives. I need to do more research," I said. Maybe I could find out more about that symbol on the box.

The archives held all the remaining books and computerized records from the past. The Subs only had access to it a few times a month and I didn't want to miss my opportunity to visit my favorite place in the Hollows. I could spend hours with books soaking up their knowledge. The TCC digitalized everything in the Hollows, but there was still something fascinating about holding an actual book in my hands.

"Again," Gibson snorted. "You always go there. Why don't you come out to the Stone with us tonight?"

The Stone, a nightclub near the food plant, was the place where people went to drink and dance. The TCC approved it years ago, since people needed somewhere to go to break up the monotony of everyday life. Only open Saturday night it was a weekly must.

"I don't know." Spending time around lots of people was not my idea of a good time.

"Why do you go to the archives, Sunshine? I'll never understand." Callahan jammed his hands into his pockets. "You know you'll never find out what you want to know, right?"

"Don't call me, SUNSHINE!" I mustered up the best dirty look I could fathom. The people at the orphanage said Zander used to call me that. I wish I could erase all traces of him from existence. If it wasn't for him, my mother would be alive.

Callahan put his hands up in surrender and backed away.

"Charlie, you need to let it go... move on." Gibson brushed a strand of hair behind her ear "If the TCC did anything wrong, they would have gotten rid of any evidence a long time ago. There's nothing left to find."

I don't know how my friends could be so blasé about everything. It affected them too. Didn't they want to know what happened? Know the truth? I bit my tongue. The symbol on the box was a clue. The first new bit of information in a long time.

"You know, you never come out with us anymore." Reese made a noise in her throat and gave an exaggerated sigh. "When was the last time? I don't know why we bother to keep asking you."

"I..."

"What?" Reese noted the looks on Gibson's and Callahan's faces. "You know I'm not rainbows and sunshine. Don't expect me to sugar-coat anything."

Reese had zero patience and less of a filter, always blurting out whatever crossed her mind regardless of how it affected other people. What you see is what you get with her. Sometimes I envied that. I wished I could vent my thoughts, but I usually stuffed them down.

"Yeah, Charlie, why do we bother anymore," Callahan mocked. He twisted his arms behind his back until he heard a crack, then sighed in relief.

I rolled my eyes. His cracking drove me crazy. "Jumping jeepers, will you stop doing that!"

"Bite me." Reese swatted him.

I used to love going to the Stone, drinking, and hanging out with my friends all night. The alcohol they served tasted awful, but it did the job, enabling us to forget for a while that we lived trapped below ground. Recently, I hadn't been going because I sensed everyone's frustration, loneliness, anger, and desperation. Their hopelessness weighed on me and caused me too much pain since I am an empath.

Feelings cling to me like they are metal, and I am a magnet. It's hard to describe how this happens, but the best I can do is compare it to a chameleon. A chameleon changes colors to match its surroundings. I change emotions to match the people surrounding me.

Most people project tangible energy. If I walked by a group of five angry people, I could feel their anger. Likewise, if all five people had different emotions, I would feel happy, sad, angry, embarrassed, or whatever the strongest person experienced. Even if someone didn't project their feelings, I could physically touch them to discover their sentiments. If I wanted to. But I don't like to touch others or to be touched.

Unlike with telepathy, I don't have an internal door to shut off emotions like I can thoughts. Instead, it's like living on an emotional roller coaster, experiencing people's highs and lows. Exhausting! It also made me a natural lie detector.

"Come on Charlie, please." Gibson wagged her eyebrows. "Just come out with us tonight and we won't bug you anymore for at least a week... I promise."

"Please!" Callahan chimed in.

They ganged up on me. "Okay, I guess I can go to the archives another day." I gave in, even though I itched to do more research on the revolt and the symbol.

"You know, you might want to turn down your excitement level." Reese rolled her eyes.

The 6:40 pm dinner horn sounded, signalling dinner would start in twenty minutes.

"We gotta go before all the good food disappears," Callahan said.

"Hilarious, using 'good' and 'food' in the same sentence." Gibson grabbed Reese's hand, intertwining their fingers. They had been in a relationship for a long time now. The most stable couple I knew in the East End, not like the celebrity Elite couples who broke up then hooked up with others all the time.

"It's oxymoronic."

We laughed because nothing is funnier than the truth. Hopping down from the ledge, we hurried to the dining hall. As bad as the flavorless food tasted, hunger pains felt worse.

4

—————

Rush hour traffic at the checkpoint delayed our entrance into the residences. Fifteen buildings two and three stories tall housed the population of the bunker, which had grown from its original eight hundred or so. Nine buildings for the larger East End population, while the remaining five buildings were on the West End. The buildings rested on over 1300 springs, each weighing more than a thousand pounds. The springs kept the buildings safe should there be earthquakes or nuclear attacks. Navy engineers fabricated them using three-quarter inch rolled battleship steel.

One shared building in the center comprised the cafeteria and medical facilities. A fence spanned from floor to ceiling, physically dividing the East from the West. The checkpoints to get into the West End from the east were the hardest to get through and few from the East End were authorized, anyway. The only exception being the Pinks who performed services in the West End.

A series of hallways and ramps interconnected the buildings. The faded trim color changed from building to building, helping us to navigate the maze of corridors and walkways, the only items of colour in the East End. The original store had been transformed into an assembly hall after we consumed the supplies. Different religious groups took turns having services on Sundays. Except for the first Sunday of every month, which the TCC reserved for assemblies. They changed the original smaller, non-denominational chapel into a parts factory, reconditioning used parts. Everything in the Hollows served a dual purpose. We recycled, reused, and repurposed everything until it turned to dust.

"Home sweet home," Callahan pressed his fist against his mouth and puffed out his cheeks.

"There's no place like home," I recited a favorite line from an old movie.

"Hurry! You know, we need to get to the cafeteria and get into line." Reese pulled Gibson along. Callahan and I hurried to catch up.

We passed a case displaying photos of the original employees. Soldiers used to have button-up bags containing personal items when on duty; they carried them in case they were ever stranded away from their homes. Sofia Cutter, the original First Lady, set up the display in a tribute to the soldiers who had left their families behind and remained in the bunker to protect them when the asteroid hit. I used to spend a lot of time staring at those photos, wondering how they felt leaving their families outside the gates, knowing they would die.

The sign above the double doors to the cafeteria read "Granite Inn". A play on words because of the granite surrounding the bunker. The sizeable open concept room had structural pillars placed every few feet. Long tables and chairs were scattered throughout. Strips of fluorescent lights ran along the ceiling. The furniture, while clean, had become old and shabby, set to the commission's standards. The dry-walled room painted the same boring gray.

"There must have been a sale on gray paint before the asteroid hit."

"What?"

"Nothing, never mind."

We lined up behind the others, waiting for food. There must have been fifty people ahead of us, even though we had gotten here as fast as possible. Others quickly filled in behind us until the line stretched out the door and down the corridor. We grabbed tattered brown plastic tray when we got to the front hoping they wouldn't run out of food before we were served. The Authority stood in every corner, even though the security cameras scrutinized everything. What a boring job watching digital feeds all day long must be.

Steam rose from the kitchens behind the long stainless-steel food-serving counters. A cafeteria worker ladled out portions to everyone in turn. I nodded to people passing by. My friends chattered about what they would wear and whom they would see that night, but I tuned them out. It was one of the few times that we could wear something other than our coveralls.

I wanted to go back to my room and lie down. My headache throbbed so badly that I was more nauseous than hungry. I couldn't wait to sit down and rest my feet. I imagined the section of the cafeteria for the West End had tablecloths on the tables, wine glasses, and candles with servers standing by to fulfill their every need.

Housing in the East End depended on your status. Families and couples have rooms while singles sleep in large dormitories crammed with bunk beds and cots. Sometimes people got married just to get a room of their own, or at least get on the waiting list. The Elites still had the antiquated tradition of heterosexual relationships. Violators could even be punished: Code 5A-1526. At least in the East we could love who we love.

Reese, Gibson, and I shared our room with another girl named Remy. The TCC inserted Remy with us to act as a spy because of our parents' involvement in the Revolt. Rude, mean, and stuck up would count as her best qualities.

As if thinking her name conjured her, Remy entered the room, flipping her shiny, long, dark hair over her shoulder. I didn't know her genetic mix, but if I had to guess, she was part Asian, and part Caucasian. Her loud "look at me" voice drawing all eyes towards her as she appeared with her posse all dressed in pink coveralls. Even her aura glowed with the dark pink of an untrustworthy, deceitful person.

My empathic abilities allowed me to see people's auras when I softened my eyes. Everyone had a color surrounding them. Callahan had a sunny, yellow aura because of his playful spirit. Gibson had the vibrant rainbow stripes of a healer. Reese had a red-orange aura, which meant she could survive any circumstance and become self-sufficient.

The black or murky brown auras were the most dangerous. Some dark reds were trouble too. While most auras change intensity, they remain a constant shade, with mood affecting the shade of each layer of aura color. When I caught my reflection, my aura radiated gray, mainly because of my lack of trust in anyone or anything. Auras sometimes changed shades, but in my experience, never changed colors. I trusted people's auras more than their words.

Remy staked out a table in the center of the room. Her shrill, fake laughter sounded like fingernails on a chalkboard. Remy worked in the West End, so she thought she was better than the rest of us. It's too bad the Elites will never see her as one of them, no matter how hard she tried.

"Remy," I muttered under my breath.

"You know better than to use her name in my presence, that westie bunker rat." Gibson adjusted her necklace back and forth until the cross hung under her chin. It was genuine gold, her prized possession, a gift from her Uncle Jagger for her sixteenth birthday. "You know what she did today? She told the Authority I didn't make my bed before work."

"Have to have those hospital corners just right," I teased.

"Do we have to talk about what a nightmare she is to live with? We experience it daily." Reese popped her head up, then back down as she watched a video or something on her tag.

"Why does the TCC care about my bed?" Gibson's forehead creased.

"They don't... they just want to control everything we do." Callahan stood on his tiptoes, searching ahead. "Why isn't this line moving? I'm starving."

"Remy is such a nosy busybody." Reese switched off the video. "You know, I don't want to waste a moment thinking or talking about that bunker rat."

"Shhh! She's coming over here." I gave my friends a warning look, hoping they would keep the peace.

"Did you just shush me?" Reese asked indignantly.

"Forget her, right?" Callahan adjusted his collar. He might not like Remy, but she had friends he wouldn't mind dating.

"Hey, Remy," I said.

Remy and her followers cut into the food line ahead of us.

Gibson clamped her hand over Reese's mouth before she could say anything. She needn't have worried. Remy turned her back without an acknowledgment and conversed with her minions as if we weren't there.

"I'm surprised she doesn't have them throw flower petals before every step," Gibson whispered.

"Hush, she would if she had access to flowers," I said.

Callahan threw back his head and let out a loud laugh. I elbowed him in the side. He groaned. Remy didn't even notice. People like us were invisible to people like her.

"You know, she's out of control. We need to do something about her," Reese said.

"Thunder, I wish she would get married and get out of our room!" Gibson said.

"Who would marry that busybody?" I asked.

"Callahan, do you want to do your sister a favor?"

"Not on your life. I don't love you that much. I'll stay in the dorms forever, thank you very much."

"They gave me two demerit points," Gibson sighed, then shook her head back and forth. "Two! It will take me two Sundays to work off those points."

"Join the club," I said. "Callahan got us both two demerit points today."

"How is it my fault?" Callahan tapped his tray against the railing of the lunch line. A set of drumsticks he had picked up at the bazaar had become his favorite possession. He thumped on everything he could find except drums.

"Simple. If you hadn't come to visit me, I never would have gotten the demerits. Don't forget guys, we have to schedule those two Sunday within the next thirty days, or they will double the demerits. Code 3A-8787."

Callahan rolled his eyes and muttered something under his breath that I didn't catch. The line surged forward. We inched our way to the front of the line to receive our daily allotment of food. A cafeteria employee scooped something on my plate; I didn't ask what it was. Mounds of mush, filling but tasteless.

I tried to be grateful as I watched the colorless mound slide from her scoop to my plate. It could have been worse. At least the government had accessed the Svalbard Global Seed Vault before Attila hit, taking their collection of seeds from the entire world, which allowed us to grow food. The TCC added Vitamin D to our plant-based diet to make up for the lack of sunlight. Sitting at a table, we ate quickly and quietly. I thought of the prisoner's story as I pushed the lumps around; it helped me avoid thinking of what I was eating. Out of the corner of my eye, I saw a fork appear on my plate, snagging a chunk.

"Are you going to finish that?" Callahan asked. His plate was already bare. I'm surprised he didn't lick it clean.

"Nope, it's all yours." I pushed my plate a little closer to him, but not close enough for the cameras to catch.

I pushed out of my chair and said my goodbyes, eager to go to my room. I couldn't stand the crowd any longer. Sometimes it freaked me out how others influenced my moods. I wanted to stop soaking up everyone's emotions like a sponge.

Television screens lined the walls in the corridors, displaying a live feed of the world outside. Originally installed for morale by the old-world government, they thought the screens would give the workers a sense of comfort and make them feel less claustrophobic, inside like looking out a window in a normal office. But now they only show the frozen wasteland our planet had become. On an old TV show called *Game of Thrones* they said, "winter is coming." They knew nothing about winter.

Outside of the bunker, the snow fell in sheets. The wind whipped wickedly, pushing thick piles of snow around the surrounding mountains. The peaks were barely visible in the low light. Snow blanketed the trees with only the tips sticking out above snowbanks. I shivered, imagining how cold it would be outside. I heard in the old-world people used to catch snowflakes on their tongues. I wondered what they tasted like.

The walk from the cafeteria to my shared room was only five minutes long. As I rounded a corner, the Authority stood and watched a girl about ten years old as she painted over graffiti, her punishment for tagging, Code 7A-0410. She would already be in the vault if she were older. She looked up at me with big, brown, sad eyes. She looked exhausted, but nothing I could do would help her. Her sadness hit me like a wave. Graffiti had been showing up with more regularity. Strange symbols and phrases, like the box in my pocket. The Authority funneled me along the corridor past her.

I noticed the TCC had taken down the sign for the fitness center. What a joke, with no weights, and a busted treadmill. The West End had stolen the best equipment years ago, and over time, the rest had broken. The fitness center was more useful when it doubled as an emergency hospital. After the power plant fire in 2145, they had used the built-in curtains to form medical bays. The medical facilities in the shared building normally served the Hollows' needs, but during the fire twenty-seven people died and many more were injured. They had disbanded the fire department years ago; the training lost over time and no one knew what to do or how to put the fire out. The Authority were ill-equipped to do anything besides close the doors and let the fire burn itself out.

I reached building seven and climbed two flights of stairs to room 314. Closing the door, I sighed; I had the place to myself. The tablet next to the door beeped as I entered the room. I punched in my security code, and it lit up, but I muted it. I needed silence, at least for a little while, so I could recharge. The portable device worked anywhere in the room. We used it to watch movies, access the intranet, and correspond with each other. Although, as far as we knew, there were no cameras in our rooms, the TCC monitored everything we did and said with the tablet. The security tags did the same.

I removed my tag and placed it in my storage bin at the end of my bunk bed, then concealed the box in my hiding spot. With a sigh, I climbed the ladder to my bed, relishing my alone time. I closed my eyes for a moment. The next thing I knew, Gibson shook me awake to go to the Stone.

Callahan and Memphis waited for us outside of building four and we walked to the Stone together, passing through three checkpoints. Memphis inherited his father's deep brown complexion and his mother's soft brown eyes. He wore his tightly curled hair so short; I figured he must shave his head daily. With his rangy build, he stood an inch above Callahan. He had a way of observing the world silently, choosing his words carefully before speaking.

His great, great grandfather was obsessed with the state of Tennessee and changed their last name. Since then, everyone in his family had been named for a city in Tennessee.

A dark red aura surrounded him. Besides being self-sufficient, his attributes involved being centered and grounded. Memphis worked with Callahan in maintenance. He always blocked his thoughts so I could never find out much about him. I also got the opinion he didn't like me very much. Never anything he said, but just a feeling I picked up whenever we were around each other. He avoided being alone with me.

I wore my only pair of jeans, a green hoodie, and my beloved Colorado Avalanche hat to keep my hair covered. Going to the Stone became one of the few places we could go out of uniform. My jeans were much-loved, soft and comfortable. I traded a gold stud earring to get them at the bazaar.

Callahan swayed and danced to the music blasting from inside the club while we waited to get through security. His head fell back, and a dreamy expression crossed his face.

"Line's moving," I said, as he didn't notice we were about to leave him behind.

"Who's ready to party?" Callahan threw his head back and screamed as we approached the neon lights.

"Woo-hoo!" yelled Memphis.

Gibson danced forward.

"Let's do this!" screamed Reese.

"Charlie. at least try to pretend you are having fun, right?" Callahan rolled his eyes at my lack of enthusiasm.

I pasted a bright fake smile on my face. He grabbed my shoulders and propelled me ahead.

The Stone used to be a warehouse, but after we consumed all the items stored there, the building fell into disuse. The TCC left it empty until a giant rock broke through the netting and crashed down into the center of the building after a violent earthquake. Preston Crowe petitioned the commission to turn it into a bar, a gathering place, and the TCC approved it. Preston's grandson, Reckson, now runs the place.

You couldn't avoid the massive rock in the center of the room. It was sienna-brown quartz with black striations threaded through. The bar surrounding the stone. Decorative glass bottles crammed onto a makeshift shelf held different colored liquors. Preston left the hole in the ceiling, decorating it with a string of lights he cobbled together. They looked pretty, lit up in the dark.

We dropped into seats at an empty table. A server came to get our drink order. To choose between ale or spirits was a risk. Both tasted awful and the alcohol content varied. I ordered a blue-tailed-dolphin. The server scanned our security tags to take payment for our drinks. In return for our labor, the TCC gave us food, shelter, and a negligible amount of credit.

The music blared, some techno beat. Gibson and Reese went to the dance floor holding hands; they both loved to dance. Between the loud music and the strobe lights, my headache came back hard. Why had I agreed to come out tonight? My friends seemed to be okay with our life, seeing mostly the good. I couldn't see life that way, no matter how hard I tried. I pretended to be happy, but failed. I didn't want to be there. I wanted to go back to our empty room, but to do that would risk making the rest of the Six Pack as irritated and unhappy as I felt staying there.

"Do you want to dance?"

"Not now... maybe later, but thanks."

"Later, then." Callahan and Memphis rose to search for dance partners. It wouldn't be too hard for Callahan to find a partner. As his best friend, girls constantly asked me for information about him. He walked over to a table and sat with some girls we went to Voco. He asked Simone to dance. I didn't even have to read her emotions to sense her excitement. Memphis picked Simone's brother, Asher, as his partner.

The bar filled up fast with people our age. Multiple conversations swirled around me, becoming louder as the liquor flowed. The laughter increased, threatening to overpower the music DJ Dave spun. Their merry mood would change the longer people drank. I hoped to be back in my room by then.

It never bothered me to sit by myself when my friends were busy. I could have searched for someone else to talk to, but for now, I preferred to be alone. If I ever learn how to shield my emotions, things might change. Besides, I hated dancing unless I had too much to drink. I never know what to do with my arms; they flap like a bird getting ready for takeoff, more like a chicken than a majestic eagle.

When the others came back to the table, they found me lost in thought. Callahan touched my shoulder to bring me back to reality. I was thinking about the box and although I had hidden it safely in the room; I wished I had brought it with me. I felt a responsibility to keep it safe. Reckson brought us another round of drinks. A few years older than us, his friendly personality appealed to everyone. He lingered and chatted.

"Reckson, we have a situation," Callie, Reckson's security chief, called to him.

Today, Callie dyed her hair orange to match her homemade eye shadow and lipstick. As usual, Callie wore short skirts with knee-length boots and skin-tight tops. I had seen her break up a brawl single-handedly with a right hook that could drop you to the floor. Scary tough, no one messed with her.

My eyes shadowed Reckson as he approached the entrance to the Stone where three tall young men waited, dressed in khaki pants and button-up shirts. West Enders. Elites never came here. Everyone talked at once.

"Do you know who that is?" Gibson asked.

"Oh, my goodness, I can't believe he's here," Reese said.

"Thunder. I never expected to see him here, not in a million years, right?" Callahan said.

"The Prince is slumming tonight," Memphis added.

"Jumping jeepers," I said. Did my eyes deceive me? The heir apparent, Slade Cutter, just walked into the Stone.

5

Slade Cutter stood slightly taller than the other two men he was with. I had seen the other two before on Hollowpic but I forgot their names. He had a thick white streak that ran down the right side of his hair, making him instantly recognizable. In a room full of earthy people, he seemed different; dignified maybe. Conversations stopped before suddenly exploding with everyone having an opinion on the Elites and the reason for their presence.

"You know that streak has to be artificial." Reese swirled a metal straw around in her drink, threatening to overflow the contents onto the scarred round table. "He dyes it, he must. It can't be real."

"I know, right?" Callahan seemed disinterested in the recent arrivals. Although he sat at our table, he flirted with Simone across the room, maintaining constant eye contact. Simone fluttered her eyelashes while holding his gaze. Memphis and Callahan rose and joined Simone at her table. History told me we wouldn't see them again this evening.

"I like it, it's alluring... if I liked boys, I would be tempted to find out if it's real or not." Gibson licked her lips, then flipped her dark hair back over her shoulder.

I tugged on my hat. "C'mon, you guys know the story... Slade got hurt in a serious accident years ago. The trauma caused the streak. The doctors thought it would eventually grow out, but it never did."

"That could be more TCC misinformation. They never told us what happened. Sounds fishy to me." Reese scrunched up her face in thought.

"Whatever... I know better than to get between you and your conspiracy theories." Something about Slade seemed unique. I couldn't stop staring. I forced myself to look away several times, but my gaze always returned to him.

Slade's father, Joseph Cutter aka the Commissioner, would lose his mind if he knew his son's whereabouts. He was a direct descendant of the President and First Lady who saved us when our people first moved into the Hollows. The Cutter family has controlled the bunker ever since. Our democratic society changed to a monarchy with the Cutter family as the de facto kings. Slade would be next.

Reckson ordered Callie to clear people from one of the better tables. He seated Slade and his friends, setting them up with drinks. I watched Slade as he continuously scanned the gathering, searching for something, or maybe someone. Our eyes locked briefly and a thread of energy, like a jolt of electricity, ran through my body. I quickly broke eye contact. *Wow!*

"*What?*" Gibson asked.

Jumping jeepers, I forgot to shield my thoughts. My felt my face heat; I pressed my palms against them to cover them. "*N . . . Nothing.*" I pointed towards the washroom.

The club was at capacity, so I had to weave my way towards the back of the room skirting around a fight. Two sanitation workers hopped up on booze or synth started swinging on each other as some girl cried and others cheered them on.

I felt relieved when I found the room empty. Inside, with the door closed, the loud music was dulled, though I could feel the rhythmic thuds of the beat. I threw water on my face to cool off. My hat became hot and itchy, so I pulled it off and shook out my hair. Threading my fingers through the strands and itching my scalp. I took a few moments to enjoy the solitude, thoroughly inspecting my hair to ensure the paint still did its job.

What was that crazy jolt of energy from Slade? It felt unfamiliar, unlike anything I had ever felt before. Did our connection mean anything? I couldn't figure out anything hiding in here. I pulled my hat back on, tucked up my hair, and left the room.

I was hardly out of the door before I sensed a surge of anger coming from behind. Before I could turn to find the source, a hand reached out and clamped my mouth, cutting off my voice while an arm grabbed me around the waist, pulling me backward. I tried to scream, but no sound emerged.

In a whisper, my attacker said, "Stop fighting. I won't hurt you."

I didn't recognize the voice. His anger pulsated through his hand and arm where our skin touched. I struck him twice with my elbow connecting with his hard torso. He grunted, then cursed, but didn't let go. He yanked me back into the bathroom, then released me, pushing me forward.

I stumbled but didn't fall. I turned around to face my attacker. Slade Cutter. Stunned, I froze in place; quietly waiting for him to break the silence. It took a moment to realize I held my breath. I slowly exhaled. I felt dizzy and light-headed. My headache raged.

I wrapped my arms around myself, trying to stop trembling, hardly noticing that I rocked slightly from side to side. Slade slid the latch of the door behind him, locking us in the room. He blocked off the only escape route with his body. I scanned the room, looking for another way out. The vent above the sink appeared too small to fit through. Plus, it would be impossible to get there fast enough. He would grab me before I even grasped the vent.

Slade said nothing at first, just stared as if trying to study me. I squirmed under his gaze. His eyes were so brown they look black. I noticed he had black leather wristbands tied around his left wrist. They seemed out of place with his Elite wardrobe of khaki pants and dress shirts. I balled my hands into fists.

"Don't worry, I wouldn't want to fight you. You seem pretty feisty." He raised his hands in surrender. "Nice elbow to the ribs."

Was that a joke? I tried, but couldn't read his thoughts. Strange but not unusual; some people were impossible to read but the thoughts of normal people, or banals, were usually open. We could access their thoughts whenever we wanted.

I met his gaze, determined not to show how much he intimidated me. A word to his parents and anything could happen; I could disappear without a trace. Being the daughter of Zander Edge accounted for enough of a black mark against me. I couldn't get on his bad side. I did not want any trouble.

"Do you have it? Did you bring it?" Slade's voice sounded much deeper than I thought it would.

I raised my shoulders in a silent what.

He had a blue aura. What a relief. Blues were trustworthy; they loved helping people, calm in a crisis. The type of people you run to for support. I felt better for a moment. He had darker skin than most of the Elites who tended to be white or Asian. Maybe because his grandmother was Native American, a Shoshone Chief. It had caused quite a huge scandal when his grandfather, James Cutter, had married a Sub, let alone someone who was Indigenous. Rumors said James did it to rebel against the outdated rule that Elites had to marry the opposite sex as he was gay.

But maybe I imagined it because I knew so much about the history of his family. Really, he looked like any Elite—posh, privileged, and over-dressed, even for a night out.

"Quick, there's no time." He listened at the door like he expected the Authority to burst through at any moment. Who could make him afraid—the most elite of the Elite? He was pretty-much royalty.

"What are you talking about?" I asked. My hands gripped my upper arms so tightly I knew there would be bruises. Instinct told me to keep away from him, like getting too near to an open flame. Immediately, I thought back to the box. Two Elites in one day?

"Don't play games with me. You know what I am here for." He bit off each word carefully, as if they were tiny bites of food.

My brain stopped working. The buzzing of fluorescent lights overhead distracted me from my mushy thoughts. "No, I don't, Prince. You keep asking questions I don't have answers to."

Slade's jaw clenched; a vein throbbed in his neck. Calling him Prince had irritated him. I raised an eyebrow. Everyone called Slade "Prince" since he would be the next ruler of the commission. Why did I taunt him? It wasn't in my nature to provoke people, and this was not the time to make him angrier. He pushed his hair behind his ears, revealing a thin, jagged scar that ran along the side of his hairline from the bottom of his ear to his chin.

"My best friend, Ajax Diaz, told me he dropped a key, a box, in front of you earlier today."

Why didn't I think about that from the start? I felt so stupid. Something about being near him caused my brain to short circuit. I blinked up at him. Could there be a key inside the black box I found? There could be, I never got it opened. "Ajax... so that's his name. Is he one of those Diazs?"

He nodded.

I looked upward. *"Jumping jeepers."* What had I become involved with? Wait, hold on a second. If Slade knew about the message, then what else did he know? How did he know Ajax had asked me to protect it? I saw Ajax get taken away by the Authority. Was this a trap? A test from the TCC.

I couldn't catch my breath. I grasped at the collar of my shirt, trying to move it away from my throat for more air. I backed up until I touched the sink. My mind raced, but I tried not to show any outward signs. Was the Authority on their way to arrest me now? I looked around for an escape, like a desperate animal willing to chew off her foot to avoid the trap.

He spoke slowly and softly, as if to tame a wounded creature. "Hey, hey look at me, directly at me. Breathe. Name five things you can see."

"What?"

"Name five things you can see, four things you can touch—"

"I'm okay. We don't need the . . . panic attack protocol." I shook my head back and forth. I'd become an expert on how to stop one.

A line appeared between his brows. "Listen, I know you don't know me, but you can trust me . . . I know what you are . . . I do not care about all that. I am not here to cause you any trouble. Believe me. I need the key. Just the key." He shoved his disheveled hair from his face, causing his white stripe to fall back into place.

"I don't know what you are talking about," I said. Trust him? Blue aura or not, this was too weird. Protect it, Ajax had said. From whom? From Slade? Trust him? Never, nope, not going to happen. Zero chance. I would never trust an Elite. It didn't matter how good looking he was. Until I knew more, I would keep the secret.

He grabbed my arms gently, pulling me closer, so I had no choice but to gaze straight into his eyes. I felt that jolt of electricity hit me again. Did he feel it too? His closeness didn't feel threatening it actually made me feel safe. How could I feel safe with a total stranger? An Elite stranger. It made no sense. Was I losing my mind?

"I need the key. Do you have it? I promise I won't let anything bad happen to you." Slade acted like a dog with a bone about that key.

"I know who you are, Slade. Who your parents are." I stalled for time, trying to figure things out. He released my arms. Noticing my necklace, his fingers traced my collarbone, straightening it before stepping back.

I took a step back, struggling to create space. I wish I could read his mind. Could I trust him? Was I crazy even thinking about it? What were my options? Suddenly cold, I rubbed my arms with my hands.

"I am not my parents." His neck flushed.

Wonderful, another sore spot. "So?"

"So, I won't hurt you. I won't tell anyone about you. I need that key. Just tell me where it is, and I'll never bother you again. Please, I can't stress the importance. Lives depend on me finding that key."

"I don't have a key," I started. He opened his mouth to argue, but I cut him off. "Listen Ajax . . . tossed a small black box with some . . . symbol on both sides. Is that what you're looking for?"

I should have been happy to get rid of the box. I would be except for the snatches of recollection flooding my memory because of the symbol. It piqued my curiosity. Something about the symbol drove me crazy. It seemed important, but I couldn't pinpoint the reason. It didn't matter what was inside.

Slade let out a sharp breath. He looked as if the weight of the world dropped from his shoulders. "Thank the stars."

"But I, ah, don't have it with me. Did you think I would carry it around?" I tugged on my hat. I needed to go back to my safe, boring life. "I wasn't about to chance getting caught with whatever it is. It could have been contraband. I don't want to become involved in something illegal or illicit."

"Thunder. Where is it?" He strained his words, his teeth clenched again.

"It's safe."

Someone banged on the door. I jumped.

"Charlie?"

"Charlie, are you in there?"

Gibson and Reese called. I had been away too long.

Slade's head whipped towards the door and back at me so quickly he should have whiplash. "I know you have no reason to trust me but tomorrow morning... early... before the assembly at 6 am, meet me at the west gate."

He unlocked the door and pulled me into his arms unexpectedly. I could smell his delightful aftershave. His head tilted, and he lowered his face towards me. Before I knew what happened, his lips touched mine. His lips were softer than words could describe. I surprised myself and kissed him back. He tasted like mint. My hands crept up to rest on his shoulders. Losing myself, I forgot about my friends.

"Oh perfect, that explains everything, doesn't it," Reese exclaimed after she and Gibson burst through the door. "Should we come back later? Close the door, dim the lights?"

I struggled to pull away from Slade, but he held me around the waist in an iron-tight grip. So close, I could feel the beating of his heart against my chest. A rush of heat flooded through me. My face must be beet red. I didn't know where to look. What was I doing? I pushed against his wrists to break his hold.

Slade placed his mouth beside my ear and whispered, "Tomorrow. West gate at 6 a.m. With the key."

I gave him a slight nod. He abruptly released me from his embrace. It hit me he only kissed me to create a diversion, a distraction to throw off my friends. Mortification froze me to the spot.

"Later." Slade turned and left the room without another glance. He didn't acknowledge either Gibson or Reese.

I grabbed my necklace, looking for comfort. I'd been kissed before, but I had never lost myself in a kiss. Where everything around me faded away and nothing else matters.

"He's the opposite of friendly," Reese said.

"Charlie Edge, what are you doing?" Gibson played with her hair in the mirror while frowning. "Why would you ever kiss an Elite, especially that one?"

"You know a guy like him is only looking for one thing from a Sub, from a girl like you. Don't even try to be friends with him," Reese had disapproval written all over her face.

I agreed with them, downplayed the kiss, played it off as an experiment. I begged them not to tell anyone about it, especially Callahan. When we returned to our table, I noticed Slade and his friends had left. I tried to enjoy the rest of the night, but my thoughts kept repeatedly returning to Slade, Ajax, and the mysterious box, wondering why they had made me the center of this weird and dangerous story.

6

I rolled out of bed at 4:00 am Sunday morning before the alarm to a mixed feeling of dread and excitement. Butterflies fluttered in my stomach. My tangled thoughts had kept me awake all night; I twisted and turned, unable to sleep. Gibson's snoring didn't help either.

I took the box out of its hiding place and shoved it under my pillow, but kept reaching to touch it. My fingers traced the imprinting of the strange symbol. What does the symbol mean? Why is it so valuable to Slade? I had so many questions without answers and the thought of spending time with Slade today before the assembly filled me with anticipation and uneasiness. All my instincts told me I should drop the box off and walk away, but I couldn't. It went against all the rules I had for myself, but I just couldn't explain the pull of that symbol.

I slipped out of our room while everyone else slept. Sneaking into the coed bathroom; empty this early in the morning. My nose wrinkled at the smell. A cross between an anti-septic and musty drains. A row of toilet stalls flanked the wall to the left, with the showers in the middle. On the right wall were five stainless steel sinks. The expanse of mirrors above the sinks reflected my image. If I had been electrocuted, my hair could not have looked worse.

Neck high blocks separated the doorless shower stalls. I stripped and stepped into the shower as the water turned on automatically. I flinched as I stepped into the cold water. Braced myself, then just stepped under the hard force of the lukewarm water. Even this early in the day, the water was never hot. The door creaked open. Reaching for the towel, I stepped out, but no one entered the room. The door fell back, and I returned to the shower to rinse out the soap.

I devoted more time to getting ready than I normally would. My face appeared deathly white, so I pinched my cheeks to give them some color. I painted my hair dark brown, then stuffed it into a hat. Putting on my green coveralls, I walked towards the cafeteria wishing I could wear something more glamorous. For the first time, I was heading to the west gate.

Everything felt odd. Typically, we all lingered over breakfast on assembly day. I set my tag on vibrate and turned the ringer to silent, then I messaged Callahan and Gibson that I didn't feel well and would meet them after breakfast. I walked quickly, feeling exposed. At least at this time-of-day the fluorescent lights were dimmed to save energy.

I arrived at the gate early. What am I doing? I thought to myself. I should still be in bed. To kill time, I paced back and forth, tugging at my hat like it was my job. The Authority stared, and I knew I must look as awkward as I felt. Would the guards notice how badly I shook? I checked my tag for the millionth time. It was just after 6:00 am. He was late. I had almost given up when Slade appeared on the other side of the checkpoint.

Relief suffused his features when he saw me standing there. He waved. Gone were the dress clothes from before. He wore jeans, a black sweatshirt, and black boots. The black wristband blended in better with this outfit. I glanced down at my coveralls and scuffed boots, wishing I had on something more glamorous.

The corners of his mouth quirked up, almost to a smile as he approached me. He seemed happy to see me. "Hey, have you been waiting long? I didn't know if you would show up." He didn't pay any attention to the Authority as they ushered him through the gate without having to show ID. Just a "yes sir" "can I help you, sir". He bypassed the body scanner. They didn't even x-ray the backpack he carried. Must be nice to be so privileged.

I gave Slade a crooked smile before glancing away. I didn't know how to act around him. My stomach flip-flopped as it always did in new, unknown situations. I stared at my boots. I couldn't think of a single thing to say. Most times, I felt like I missed out on learning how to relate properly with others. What seemed so natural to people was so hard for me to emulate. There seemed to be a disconnection between my brain and mouth. Nothing comes out of my mouth the same way it sounds in my brain.

"Thanks for coming."

"You didn't give me much of a choice."

Slade tilted his head to the side. "You always have a choice."

"No, maybe you always have a choice. In the East End, you do what they tell you. We don't live in equal worlds." I noticed the guards no longer stared at me.

"You're right, we don't. I wish things were different, but it is what it is." He glanced over at the Authority as if he thought they monitored our exchange. "Did you bring it?"

I shook my head. "No, you said to wait . . . until we spoke. Care to share?" Now I'm rhyming. How embarrassing.

"We can talk later. There are too many eyes and ears surrounding us." He shrugged the backpack onto his shoulders and without waiting walked away; confident I would scurry along behind him. After a moment, I hurried to catch up.

"Where are we going?"

"You'll see." He looked around and threw the hood of his sweatshirt up, slowing to my pace.

His thoughtfulness surprised me. "Just so you know, this isn't a date," I said. Why did I blurt that out? Of course, he doesn't think it's a date. I stumbled mid-stride. Walking and talking at the same time sometimes proved challenging.

"Never thought it was." Slade's mouth quirked up at the corners. "But just a thought. Maybe I should put my arm around you. You know... for the guards." He nodded his head in their direction.

"Um, okay," I swallowed excessively as he wrapped his arm around my shoulder. A tingle swept up the back of my neck and across my shoulders. The heaviness of his arm felt weird.

No one questioned why we were together or what we were doing. He led me up, down, and around the East End corridors, back and forth like a mouse in a maze. Several times I had the feeling of being followed, but every time I turned around, no one was there. It must be just my anxiety playing tricks on me. After endless zigzagging, we arrived at a checkpoint. Not a regular checkpoint, two armed guards stood beside an eight-foot-tall, thick circular iron door built into the sheer rock wall.

"Are you kidding? We . . . can't go in there." I chewed on my lower lip.

He winked. "Do you want to make a bet?" Slade extended his hand to shake mine.

I avoided his outstretched palm. "No. It goes nowhere. The commission sealed it. For our protection. At the start of our confinement. You must know the story. It led to another section of the bunker left incomplete when the asteroid hit."

He poked his tongue in his cheek, looking thoughtful but said nothing.

"At least that's what they always told us."

He smiled at me. A simple grin, but for the first time I saw him smile, really smile. Striking-looking when somber, when smiling there weren't enough words to describe him. Perhaps dazzling . . . stunning. My mouth snapped shut. Caught between fear and excitement, my flight or fight instinct screamed at me to take flight. To run away and never look back.

Slade lowered his hood. As if he could sense my indecision, he grabbed my arm and pulled me towards the door, deciding for me. The Authority snapped to attention as we approached the checkpoint.

"Mr. Cutter, Sir, what can I help you with this morning?" Guard 082099 asked.

I squirmed away from Slade and covered my ears to block out the sound of the guard's voice. It didn't faze him at all. Why was I the only one who couldn't stand their voices?

"Open the door." The timbre of Slade's' voice changed; it became steel, hard, unwavering. A voice demanding instant obedience. The change in his mannerism caught me off guard. Acting more like an Elite than ever. His eyes flickered to the cameras.

"Sorry, Mr. Cutter. No one goes through the door. We have detailed guidelines to follow," Guard 061803 said.

I drew myself up straighter after catching my reflection in his helmet.

"We are under strict orders," Guard 082099 said. "The Far Side is off-limits to everyone without special permission."

He crossed his arms, glaring at the guards. "Do you honestly think 'everyone' applies . . . to me?" His voice dripped with power; each word clipped. He would be used to having his every whim indulged.

"He has the commissioner's permission," I said before I slapped my hand over my mouth. I couldn't believe I just lied to a guard. Where had that come from?

Slade whipped his head around; his brows drew together in a scowl. Did he not expect me to speak? I shrugged.

After a moment of dead silence, the guards glanced at each other, unsure how to proceed. "I'm sorry, Sir, there is no entry beyond this point," Guard 061803 said.

Slade took a step towards the guard. "If you wish to continue to serve, you will recognize my authority." His eyes flicked up at the camera as if he waited for something.

I glanced over my shoulder. It felt like someone was staring at me, but there wasn't anyone there. Guard 061803 placed his hand on the radio then, both guards froze in place momentarily. When they started again, their attitude changed.

"This way, Sir," said Guard 082099. He ushered us to the door while Guard 061803 operated the controls. I expected the thick door to scrape, groan, and creak from years of disuse, but it swung open without a sound, like its hinges had just been oiled. They opened it just wide enough for us to slip through to the other side. I couldn't see much beyond the entrance.

I stood there frozen, afraid to take a step forward. If I went through the door, would I ever return?

"Come with me if you want to live," Slade said.

"What!"

"Nothing, sorry! Just a line from the Terminator movie."

Gotcha, I remembered that movie. "Oh, that was supposed to be funny, right?"

"It's okay. Trust me; I have been through here tons of times."

"Every time you say, 'trust me.' I trust you less."

"Tr... you'll love it, I promise. There is nothing like it anywhere." He extended his right hand, which I grabbed like a lifeline.

"If something bad happens, I'm blaming you,"

"I would expect nothing less." Slade swept out his hand regally.

Together we stepped over the ledge through the door, crossing over to the FarSide. The giant door swung closed behind us, leaving us in pitch-black darkness. The air smelled damp and stuffy. Slade released my hand. I wanted to scream but couldn't force out a sound. Alone in the dark. I couldn't see anything, not even the hand in front of my face.

Would he leave me here? My pulse raced. I couldn't move; my limbs froze. The blood roared in my ears. I couldn't hear, I couldn't see. I had to get out of here. After a moment, I heard a faint rustling. He hadn't left me. I let out the breath I held, trying to calm myself. I heard unzipping. Thunder, I hope he hadn't brought me here for that! More rustling noises. What could he possibly be doing?

"Here, hold this." Slade's fingers brushed mine, causing my heart to beat faster. He handed me a cylindrical object with light coming out of one end.

"What is this?" I asked after I made the mistake of shining the light directly into my eyes. The beam of light made it easier to see my surroundings. As far as I could tell, nothing looked much different on this side of the door except we exchanged the cement floor for a rocky path.

"A flashlight, haven't you ever seen one before? Don't you have these in the East End?" He asked. Our security tags could shine a dim light, but nothing like this. "Here, let me show you how to use it."

His hands gripped mine as he showed me how to flip the switch and adjust the beam of light. His hands were calloused, something I hadn't expected. Not from an Elite.

"Shine the light on the floor so you can see where to step. Come on. The best is yet to come," Slade said. "You've never seen anything like this before."

The best is yet to come. I clung to his words as if they were a life preserver, and I was drowning.

The darkness felt oppressive. I hoped my eyes would adjust. The beam of light glowed like a sliver of hope. It made my surroundings more discernible. I moved my fingers in front of the beam, casting shadows on the rock wall.

"Trust me, Charlie, just follow my lead." Slade's voice held a tinge of excitement.

I wondered if his face mirrored his voice. "Hey, how do you know my name?" I suddenly realized I had never told him my name.

"It wasn't a coincidence that I met you at the Stone last night. I watched the surveillance footage of Ajax getting arrested. It wasn't hard to figure out your identity."

I couldn't see his face, but I could feel his eyes touch my skin.

"I went to the Stone to find you."

"Stalking isn't attractive," I said.

He laughed. "It's not stalking. Your entire life is on camera."

"True."

I would expect Slade could access anything the TCC recorded. In the old world, social networking sites like Facebook, Twitter, and Instagram made it easy for governments to keep track of their people. In this new world, constant surveillance made it simpler.

I stopped walking. "So... you know who I am then. You know about Zander . . . what he did?"

Slade shrugged, "Don't worry; I won't hold it against you. Those were his mistakes, not yours. I'd like to think we are not our parents; I know I am not mine."

"But you used who you are to get through the checkpoint." I fidgeted with the zipper on my uniform while trying to wrap my head around the conflicting information Slade revealed.

"That's different, a means to an end, nothing more." Slade's heavy tone told me to drop the subject. I could sense speaking about his parents annoyed him. "Come on, let's go. We're almost there and we are running out of time before we have to get back for the assembly."

The thin glow from the flashlight did little to illuminate the crooked path we followed. I stumbled once or twice on the loose rocks, just managing not to trip and fall on my face. My unease grew as we continue to walk along the stone path. We were getting further and further from the door. If the flashlight quit working, how would I find my way back in the dark? Slade halted, causing me to run into his back. I reversed.

"Can you hear that?" he asked

The sound of my heavy breathing blocked my ears. "Hear what?" It took a few moments for my ears to register how quiet it had become. The monotonous hum of the machines that kept the bunker operating had disappeared. The lack of sound seemed like heaven for my eardrums.

"This is the best noise I have never heard," I whispered. Touching my ears to ensure nothing blocked them. True silence for the first time ever.

"I ..."

"Shush, let's enjoy the silence," I whispered. We could have communicated without words if he had telepathy.

He put the flashlight under his chin, making a silly face. Despite the darkness, I realized I was enjoying myself. My eyes had adjusted to the darkness.

We continued further along the path. The crunch of our footsteps the only noise besides our breathing. Slade stopped again. "Here's where it gets tricky" He shone his light ahead to show a gap where the path ended and began again. He took off his backpack and threw it across to the other side. It landed with a hard thud.

"We need to jump across; I'll go first and catch you."

I don't know what expression crossed my face, but he burst out laughing.

"Yeah, no. Impossible. Um . . . are you crazy?" I squeaked. "I'm not doing it. No way . . . not happening. That's reckless stupidity. Please let's just go back."

"You're cute when you are all worried." Slade said.

I turned to flee, but he grabbed my arm. I walked closer to the edge to see how far it dropped, shining the light into the gap. The bottom wasn't in sight. I shuddered and backed away, wishing I hadn't looked down.

"Did you bring us here to die?" I asked.

"Obviously."

"I can't tell if you're being sarcastic or not?"

"Look." Slade jumped the gap, landing easily on the other side like a cat on the balls of his feet. "Come on, there's nothing to fear"

"I don't believe you."

"I have been vaulting this since... forever. It's easy." He laughed, then backed away from the ledge to give me room to land, shining the light.

I paused, easy for him maybe. I stood by the edge, debating what to do. Jumping seemed to be a better choice than standing here alone in the dark. The pounding of my heart echoed in my ears. My mouth suddenly lost all moisture as my tongue stuck to the roof. I turned off my flashlight and tucked it into my back pocket.

"Screw it, here goes nothing." Taking a running jump, I leaped a little too early. My feet landed on the ground, but my body tilted

backward off-balance, sliding back towards the drop-off. Before I could even scream, Slade's hand gripped my arms, yanking me back towards safety.

He tripped from the momentum of my weight, and we fell together. I landed on top of him. Laughing, I felt the rush of adrenaline, exhilaration. Our eyes locked, and I suddenly became very awkward, totally aware that I was lying on top of him. I scrambled off him and stood, dusting off my clothes, looking anywhere but at Slade. I had never felt more inarticulate in my life. I fidgeted with my sleeves, pulling them down over my hands.

Slade cleared his throat, breaking the uncomfortable silence. "Ahh, we should go . . . we are almost there. It's just around the corner." He picked up the backpack and set us on the move again.

Exhilaration filled me. I faced my fear and prevailed. Taking too long to pat myself on the back, I scrambled to catch up. A few steps later, I heard the trickling of water.

"Wait here," Slade hurried ahead.

"Not likely." I tried to keep up, but tripped and fell on my knee. The hard-unforgiving rock stung. A rough edge ripped my coveralls. I heard a click and then buzzing before light flooded the room.

The egg-shaped cavern seemed enormous. The lower parts of the rock walls were flat and smooth, while the upper walls had rigid, jagged, and uneven edges. The ceiling arched hundreds of feet above where giant stalactites hung in various sizes. The walls glowed with tiny sparkling crystals, giving it a magical effect.

Rock slabs and wet stone ledges surrounded the pond. A small waterfall deposited water in a pool that fed into another larger pool. It was the most amazing thing I had ever seen. I touched my jaw to see if my mouth hung open.

The stalagmite I tripped over grew upward from the floor. I checked my knee in search of a cut; just scraped, no blood. My coveralls had an uneven rip. I didn't know if I could repair them.

"Are you okay? Are you hurt?"

"No, it's just a scratch, nothing major."

"What do you think?" Slade asked in a quiet voice, running a hand through his hair. His normally confident attitude dipped. For the first time, I discovered a chink in his armor. Was he afraid I wouldn't like his special place? Slade stood back letting me explore.

"It's... enchanting," I struggled to find words to describe its magnificence.

Walking forward, I let my hands touch the rough walls while looking up to admire the stalactites. The humid air in the cavern felt stifling. Unzipping my coveralls, I shrugged my arms out of them, revealing my white t-shirt. I tied the arms together around my waist.

Steam rose above the rippling water. I knelt and dipped in my fingers to test my hypothesis and was thrilled to find the water hot. A crust of minerals skimmed the edges of the water.

"It's a hot spring. The water is naturally hot all the time,"

My nose wrinkled. "What is that smell?"

"Sulfur."

"Sulfur . . . never heard of it."

"You've never heard of sulfur. It's on the periodic table of elements. It's chemistry." He scratched his head. "The smell is not so bad; you get used to the odor."

"The periodic table of... whatever... must be something they teach at Prep because they sure don't teach it at Voco."

"What! It's science. They don't teach you science?" He shook his head.

"Yeah, no."

"Are you hungry?" He unzipped the knapsack and withdrew a few apples and bananas. He pulled out some bread, cheese, and other food I didn't recognize.

"I could eat." I hovered my hand over an apple. "Can I have one?"

"Obviously, that's why I brought them." He picked up a banana and peeled it, then handed me a flask of water to drink and opened one of his own.

I sniffed the apple before taking a bite. My mouth exploded with flavor, a sugary sweetness. It tasted amazing, crisp and juicy; unlike anything I had ever tasted before. The crunch echoed in my ears. Bite after bite, the apple soon disappeared. I reached for another. I had regretted not taking a bite of Callahan's apple since yesterday.

"Eat much?"

"Never had one before. Or most of this stuff."

"Never?" He raised an eyebrow.

I shook my head, too busy eating to answer. The food quickly disappeared. For the first time, my stomach felt full.

Slade tossed his tag on a boulder, then stripped off his shirt.

"What are you doing?" I covered my face with my hands, peeking through my fingers. He was already in the water when I removed my hands from my eyes. "Come on in, you'll love it, trust me." Slade splashed water in my direction.

There he goes with that phrase again. I refused to strip down to my underwear, no matter how much I wanted to go in the water. The TCC standard underwear was less than sexy.

I pulled off my boots and socks and rolled up my pant legs. Sitting on the edge, I dipped my feet into the water. The accompanying warmth felt soothing. I sighed in contentment.

Scanning around the cavern, I realized for the first time in my life no one watched. There were no cameras, no guards. I felt free, unencumbered.

Slade shook his head, then dunked below the waterline. He emerged but stayed immersed except for his head. I couldn't tell if he sat on something or stood. He closed his eyes and let his head roll back, relaxed. "This is my favorite spot. It's where I come to think when I need to be alone."

"It's relaxing, that's for sure." The heat of the cavern caused my skin to glisten. A drop of sweat trailed down my back. I curled my legs up and down, watching the water swell.

"My father brought me here all the time, before the accident. He said it was our special place."

My ears perked up at the mention of his accident. The commission had never released the details to the public.

7

"The accident happened just after my eighth birthday. I bragged about this place to Ajax and Toni. They didn't believe me. They thought I made it up. So, I bluffed my way past the authority just like today. Showing off, I dived headfirst, banging my head off the rock bottom." Slade opened his eyes, lost in thought as he gazed at the far side of the pool. "I'd forgotten about the shallow water. I lost consciousness."

Toni Tango. That name slipped my mind. How could I have overlooked Slade's fiancé? A computer algorithm picked her as the strongest choice for marriage. According to the results, Toni incorporated everything a wife should be: intelligent, sophisticated, and beautiful. I grimaced. I shouldn't be here alone with an engaged man. Especially one I had kissed. I lied to myself that the kiss didn't count because it was just about the box.

Slade traced his fingers along the edge of the pool. The rock at the top was worn smooth from the running water. "I don't remember the accident or the days that followed. I lost four months to a coma." He absently touched the spot on the crown of his head where the blond streak began.

"Wow!" Sorry, that's a lot of time to lose." I tugged on my hat; the balmy heat made my head itchy. This day would be perfect, if only my head would stop throbbing.

"Ajax dragged me out of the water while Toni ran for help. He saved my life . . . he didn't even know how to swim, just jumped in without a second thought. Ajax never thinks first before acting." Slade chuckled at the memory before turning serious. "I owe him my life. That's why I need to get him out of the vault. He saved my life and now I need to save his."

"Jumping jeepers. How do you propose to rescue him?" I shuddered, looking away. "Look I get it; I understand loyalty but be realistic... no one ever comes back from the vault. Not in its entire history!"

"I'll get him out somehow. I know it's a long shot, but I need to try. I have to..." He shoved at the water, causing it to ripple.

His gaze met mine and held. There would be no changing his mind. I believed him; his resolve to help his friend. Not his words. I never trust words. I trust vibes. People can tell you anything, but a vibe told you everything.

"Hey, can you turn around for a minute?"

"Why?"

"Just do it." When he turned, I stripped off my coveralls, then tugged my t-shirt down to mid-thigh, so it looked like a long dress. It was too hot, and I couldn't stand having them on any longer. I tossed my hat and security tag into the pile.

"Can I look now?"

"Yup."

He dunked his head below the surface of the water. Re-emerging, he shook his head, sending drops of water everywhere. He dipped under again. I lost sight of him. His hands grabbed my bare calves. With a quick flip, he pulled me into the water.

I came up for air, sputtering and spitting, completely drenched. My lips tasted like salt. Slade held his sides, laughing as if it was the funniest thing in the world. I splashed him. My hair slapped my face like wet strands of spaghetti. Pushing the sopping mass behind my shoulders, I used my fingers as a comb trying to look presentable, an impossible task. The dark hair paint surrounded me in the water, like the black of an oil spill, but the stream dispersed it.

"You're ..." It looked like Slade was about to say something after his laughter subsided but changed his mind. "How do you like the warm water?"

I had to admit the warmth soothed me; I felt like somebody else. "Wonderful, it feels wonderful. Am I in a dream? I never imagined I'd ever be someplace like this."

"I can verify it's not a dream."

I told myself to relax and enjoy the experience for once, instead of constantly over-thinking. My thoughts were my own worst enemy. I laid my head back and relaxed as the heat encompassed my body. This might be one of the best days of my life. "So, I presume your parents kept the accident details secret because of where it happened."

"Yup, partially. If the truth emerged, everybody would want to try the hot springs. My parents said there wasn't enough security to protect this area . . . but if you ask me, they didn't want to share it." He tossed a rock that pinged off the cave wall.

I tilted my head to the side, considering his words. "Tell me about this place."

"What do you want to know?"

"Anything . . . everything."

"Hmm . . . not much to tell, at least not much I know. The government in the old world tried to expand the bunker way before the asteroid hit, but they ran out of time."

"Everybody knows that much." I flicked water at him. "Tell me something new, something no one else knows. Tell me a secret."

"Um, let me think... engineers found the springs when they dug. After the impact, rock slides sealed the chamber airtight, so the air became breathable. My family used it all the time until my accident. Then they didn't ..." His voice trailed off

I motioned for him to continue. I leaned back, closing my eyes. "The rebels dug it out a little more; they dug tunnels, not sure how far they got or if they tried to escape or…" he shrugged. "I think they stayed here before the Revolt of 2152."

My body tensed and my eyes popped open. Whenever people mentioned rebels or revolt, I automatically think they are talking about me . . . even though they were talking about Zander. Did Zander know about this place? Did he ever come here? Did he bring my mother here? I glanced over at Slade, expecting him to be staring daggers at me.

"So, um… what kind of name is Slade?" I asked. It had always seemed like a weird name to me, and I finally had a chance to ask him.

"It is a family name. Every first-born male in my family is named Joseph James Slade Cutter. My father is Joseph, my grandfather was James, so I am Slade. What about you? You have a boy's name, short for Charlotte?" He asked.

"Nope, my mom was a huge Charlie Chaplin fan."

"Can I ask you a question?" Slade said.

"You can ask, but I might not answer," I said, suddenly uncomfortable.

"Shy and sarcastic, that's a weird mix."

I stuck out my tongue. He forgot to add "mature."

"So, what can you do?"

"Do? What do you mean?" I bunched up my face, confused by his question.

"I mean, what deviant abilities do you have besides telepathy?"

"Why do you think I have more abilities?" I debated how much I should tell him. All my instincts told me I could trust him, but years of keeping things secret stopped me.

"All deviants have at least two abilities. The commission does extensive research on those they find." Slade replied as if it were some kind of established fact.

My heart jumped into my throat. What experiments did they do on deviants? I hunted for more information. "How do you know all this?"

"So, what's your other ability? Snake charmer, unicorn tamer . . . no—ghostbuster, right?" Slade ignored my question. "I know: give me two, no make it three guesses, and if I guess correctly, you owe me …"

"I'm an empath." I blurted out to avoid betting with him. I had nothing worth betting against, anyway.

"An empath, that's different …" He scratched his jaw "What's that like?"

"Painful. I'm controlled by other people's emotions; I never know how I feel because I am too busy being overwhelmed by what others feel. It sucks."

He nodded. "Strange. What about the telepathy? What's it like?"

"Don't you already know? Ajax is a deviant, haven't you ever asked him?"

"Yeah, he's my best friend but we don't talk about stuff like that." His expression closed, and a shadow crossed his face. I could sense his worry about his friend.

I tried to pick the correct words before answering, "Well, it's not like reading minds, it's more like having a conversation without words. We read current or recent thoughts."

"Are all your friends like you?"

"Yeah, no … absolutely not, I'm not talking about my friends." I mimed zipping my lips closed and throwing away the key.

Slade nodded, not pushing me further. Throughout our conversation, he gazed at me intently. He moved closer and touched my hair; it has been drying while we talked. He grabbed a few strands, rubbing them between his fingers before bringing the bulk of it forward to hang beside both sides of my face.

"You can touch my hair but don't mess it up." It would be impossible to make it look worse, but it made him laugh.

"This hair, it's like spun gold… like sunshine. It's a shame you keep it covered. Why?"

"Why? Do you really need to ask? You know why."

"Your father?"

"Yeah. Uncovering my hair would just be a reminder for everyone. I don't need everyone staring at me, wondering if we were alike. Wondering how many deaths I would be responsible for." I shook my head back and forth.

Slade kept staring at me. It made me uncomfortable. "You have his green eyes, too. I haven't seen eyes that color before."

"Jumping jeepers. I'm not like him!" Slade made it sound like he had seen my father in person.

Slade raised his hands in surrender. "Okay, sorry. Do you blame me for what happened to your father? For my grandfather exiling him?" Slade turned away with sudden uneasiness.

"No, no," I answered, forcing a smile. "I blame Zander for everything, for the revolt, for my mother."

"Then why do you think people would blame you for your father's sins." Slade lifted an eyebrow. "You were just a kid when it happened."

I held up two fingers. "Almost two when your grandfather exiled him. His group became the first people expatriated from the bunker. Sent out to die."

"What do you remember?"

"Not much, just some feelings . . . anger, love, confusion. A few vague memories." I struggled to recall more. The symbol popped into my mind. Somewhere buried in the dark corners of my mind were the answers.

"Thunder, it must have been difficult for you, growing up alone. Especially after what happened to your mother and then your father."

"Who said I was alone? My friends are my family. I depend on them, and they depend on me." I moved away from Slade to the other side of the pool, suddenly needing some distance. "What about you? What was it like to grow up with parents?"

"It makes me envy what you have—your friends," he said with a lop-sided grin.

"Yeah right."

"Trust me. No family is ever what it seems from the outside."

I bunched up my face, rejecting his words. Poor spoiled rich boy, what does he possibly have to complain about? I ran my fingers through my hair, trying to separate the strands. It would take forever to untangle. I would never get a comb through it.

"No, you don't understand. My parents are only interested in how I reflect on them. They care about power and nothing else matters. Growing up, I had to have the best grades, the most influential friends, and be perfect no matter the circumstances, no matter ..."

I rubbed my index finger and thumb together.

"What are you doing?"

"I'm playing the world's smallest violin," I scoffed. "Don't expect me to feel sorry for you. You have everything . . . everything you could ever want or need. Apples, bananas. Have you ever had to survive on the stuff we eat—have you even tried an MRE bar? You have the power to go anywhere and do anything. You are the next commissioner, for Attila's sake. Just look what you did with the guards today."

"You don't think there will be consequences." His mouth snapped shut. "There will be."

"Consequences?" I swallowed a gulp. "What consequences? Slade, what kind of trouble..."

He motioned with his hand to forget about it. "Never mind. It doesn't concern..."

"Sure, no problem, I get it." Ouch, in other words: mind my own business.

"No, don't get upset, I didn't mean it like that," he broke off, searching for words. "You say you are an empath so read me, tell me if I'm lying."

"I've been reading you this whole time. I know you aren't lying. Your blue aura tells me you are trustworthy. I wouldn't be here if you weren't."

"Have you read my mind?"

"No, I tried, but I couldn't."

"Is that unusual?"

"A little ... weird! You are a banal, so it shouldn't be so hard."

"Banal. What in the stars is a 'banal'?"

"Someone normal. Someone without psychic abilities. Someone like you."

His mouth twitched. "I've never heard them called 'banals' before. Do you want to try again?" His tone dared me.

"Let's give it a shot."

"What do you need me to do?"

I waded back across the pool and stood before him. "Here, give me your hands, sometimes it makes it easier." At least this time, I was ready for the jolt when we touched.

He put his hands around mine they looked small compared to his.

"Anything…"

"Shh, just be quiet a moment and let me try."

"Bri—who … who are they?" a young-sounding voice spoke.

I twisted my head to see a small boy, maybe four or five years old, holding on to a woman's hand. His white-blond hair shone like mine and there was something about him that reminded me or Reese. They wore colorful clothing, no uniforms. She wore a long dress, her head was wrapped in colorful Kente cloth, a fur covered shawl draped around her shoulders.

As soon as the woman saw us, she turned to flee. Something about her seemed familiar. Clasping the boy's hand, she dragged him along behind her, ignoring his protest and questions. I rushed to the edge of the water and jumped out, calling, "Wait, stop, who are you? Where are you going? His hair—wait, please stop!"

The woman looked over her shoulder, alarmed, but kept going. I turned towards Slade, my eyes pleading with him for help. The rocky floor of the cavern tore at my feet as I struggled to run after them. Turning back, I grabbed for my boots, keeping my eyes on the spot where they had disappeared.

I yanked my coveralls over my wet body. Jamming my wet feet into the boots took monumental effort. Without waiting to tie them, I took off in the direction they disappeared, but it was dark. I only ran a few steps before turning back.

Our security tags beeped with an alert, a reminder the assembly would start soon.

"We need to go. We can't be late for the assembly." Slade had climbed out of the water and was pulling his clothing back on.

I swung back to face him, picking up the flashlight. I turned away again, planning to search for the boy. "No, we can't go. It's impossible. No, no—we have to follow them. The boy has my hair," I gasped, stuttering. Aware my mouth opened, then closed, and the words flowing out were nonsensical.

"We have to go back." Slade took a few steps to catch up. He grabbed my arm, then spun me around, forcing me to stop. "We have to go. If we don't swipe in on time, they will look for us ... they will track us. We have to leave now."

"No, no. I have to find him ... he has my hair ..." I could not explain with words my need to talk to this boy. My head swiveled back and forth between Slade and the place the blond boy disappeared. Was I on the verge of a meltdown?

"We have to go." Slade spoke with steel in his voice. He walked over and started shoving everything back into the backpack haphazardly. "Now."

I puffed out my cheeks before releasing the air, backing away. I couldn't risk the TCC putting a bigger target on my back. Plus, I also couldn't risk him leaving me here with no way to get back.

I looked back at the pool wistfully. Would I ever get to see this place again? Would I ever see the boy again? I almost wished he never brought me here to this refuge.

As if Slade could read my mind, he came up behind me and put his hands on my shoulders and squeezed. "We'll come back, someday. We'll find him, trust me."

I didn't believe him, but it sounded nice to hear. We ran in different circles. Our lives were too different. I gave him a half-hearted smile.

"Turn on your flashlight," he instructed moments before flicking off the switch that plunged us back into darkness.

The trip back to the iron door went faster; we signaled the guards through the intercom to reopen the door. Thanks to the assembly, no one loitered in the corridors to see us emerge. I handed Slade the flashlight.

He covered my hand with his. "I hate to ask, but can we talk about the box now? Do you have it—uhm, it's important that I…"

I almost forgot the actual reason we were here. This wasn't a date or an outing among friends. Just a way for Slade to earn my trust; to get my guard down. If he slapped me across the face, it wouldn't have hurt as much.

"… I was asked to protect it. What if it's from you?" I felt a tightness in my stomach.

"Thunder. How can I change your mind?" He swiped his hand through his hair, agitated. "The key is important, it's time-sensitive. Tell me what I need to do to get you to trust me."

"You don't have to do anything. I'll give it to you. You didn't even need to do all this." I gestured toward the FarSide. "If we didn't get interrupted by my friends last night, I would have told you that. Holy Attila, I wish I could just give it to you now just to get rid of it!"

"Just like that?" He tilted his head to the side, pursing his lips in thought.

"Yeah, just like that. As soon as I give you the box, you'll get rid of me, and I'll get rid of you. I can't wait to start never seeing you again."

He opened his mouth to say something, changed his mind, and closed it again.

"It was a mistake coming here … all this … See you at the assembly." I walked away, tossing the words over my shoulder. I wasn't angry at him, just at myself, because something in the electric jolt I felt yesterday should have been a warning, but I had ignored it. I should have known this would happen. But I'd never felt any kind of a spark with anyone before, so I did not think to protect myself. I had let myself fall for him.

"Don't tell anybody about any of this," he yelled after me.

I kept walking and raised my middle finger.

8

Remy was inside with her minions when I entered our room. "You could knock."

"I live here."

She looked me over. "You look like hell." She flipped her hair over her shoulder, snapped her fingers, and left the room with all the dignity of a queen.

I rushed to exchange wet clothing for dry ones. In my haste, I almost fell trying to strip out of my pants. There wasn't time to paint my hair, so I twisted it into a knot and pulled on a plain black dry hat.

Would my friends still be waiting at the entrance of the cafeteria for me? My tag showed a bunch of missed messages from Gibson and Callahan. My mind scrambled for reasons I could give them for my absence. The truth wasn't an option; it was too dangerous. I didn't want them involved.

I locked the door, then accessed my hiding place, concealed under the wooden frame of my bed. Carving the gap took countless hours, but I needed to have a place to store my special belongings, a place the Authority wouldn't find in one of their random room sweeps.

I grabbed the box, shoving it into the pocket of my coveralls; they were baggy enough that it was unlikely anyone would notice the slight bulge. Grabbing the chain with my mother's ring, I pulled it over my head. I had deliberately left the ring behind this morning as well as the box, in case the meeting with Slade was a trap. I raised the ring to my lips and kissed it, thankful to place it around my neck where it belonged.

The only other thing of value in the hiding spot was Zander's watch. Picking up the watch, I flipped it over. The inscription on the back of his watch read *ab initio*—Latin for "from the beginning." Did those words have any significance? Slamming it back in the hole, I replaced the lid, checking everything remained perfect before leaving.

Sprinting to the cafeteria, I was careful not to bring any attention to myself. I had reconciled myself to entering the assembly hall alone, but my friends lingered outside the door. I sighed in relief; I couldn't believe they had waited. That led to another problem. I still hadn't thought of anything to explain my absence. I kept the door to my mind shut so they couldn't read my thoughts. I didn't like the strange way they looked at me, as if I were an outsider. Was I over thinking things? I sometimes wondered if we would all be friends if the TCC hadn't kept us together. We were all so different.

Gibson stopped pacing as soon as she spotted me. "Where have you been? We were just about to leave without you. Waiting for you will make us late." She pulled herself up to her full height.

"This is not like you, Charlie." A quizzical expression crossed Callahan's face. "You always stick to the same routine, right? Usually, I can set my watch by your rituals. What's going on?"

Reese shook her head and rolled her eyes. "Where did you take off to so early? Sneaking off to meet up with your lover boy."

Her last statement took me by surprise. Did she know where I had been? No, that was impossible. I would have seen her following me. She wasn't invisible.

"Why have you been so secretive lately?" Gibson asked. "It's like I don't even know you anymore."

I don't like secrets; they are like monsters trapped under the bed until daylight came to chase them away. But these weren't my secrets to tell, so I didn't speak. How could I tell them I got sucked into protecting something for an Elite prisoner, and even worse, that I thought an Elite liked me? I knew better than to get involved with them. I shrugged my shoulders. "I've been around here and there." I dropped my eyes to the ground, avoiding looking directly at any of them.

Memphis checked his tag for the time before covering a yawn with his hand. "Guys, we need to go before we are actually late."

"Did you forget to paint your hair?" Reese asked. She tried to grab my hat to check, but I dodged her by stepping backward. Tucking the strand of wet hair that escaped back underneath. I wanted to blurt out everything, but I couldn't. The last warning bell rang for the assembly, saving me from having to lie.

"This isn't over," Gibson warned.

I lifted an eyebrow but remained silent.

THE ASSEMBLY HALL swarmed with activity when we finally made it inside. The enormous oval room had arched doorways and a high coffered ceiling. Thick crown molding connected the ceiling and the walls. Ceramic tiles with geometric shapes covered the floor. Statues and pieces of art jam-packed the edges of the room. An enormous painting of James and Sofia Cutter hung on the wall behind the stage. Paintings hung in every available space. The Government rescued some of the art from the old-world museums before Attila hit.

The room had two levels. People from the east stood on the bottom level while those from the west watched from the balcony surrounding the room on three sides. Rows of lights resembling candles hung in iron sconces lined the railing on the balcony. The head of each of the ruling Elite families sat in ornately carved chairs resembling small thrones. The seven families—Bennett, Chow, Diaz, Morgan, Torres, Turner, and Cutter—governed the Hollows. Each family member had a vote in the Cabinet of Seven, otherwise known as the Commission. The entire West End dressed to the nines while we wore coveralls.

This room contained the remains of Earth's humanity. Unbelievable. 7.5 billion people had lived on Earth before the asteroid struck, but now the entire human population was less than five hundred people. Now, we were troglodytes, true cave animals.

We pushed our way to the center of the crowd. The best place to stand if you didn't intend to pay attention to the speech. The box in my pocket made me anxious. I twisted the ring over and over. It didn't take long for the Commissioner to come out on stage and speak, 11:00am on the dot. Joseph Cutter's voice boomed from the speakers embedded in the walls. Nothing could be more boring than the monthly update on the status of the Hollows. Reports on how much food we had grown, how much water we had used, additional security measures, blah, blah, blah. Rumors from the underground whispers suggested the Commissioner had fallen ill.

I couldn't stop myself from yawning; my eyes watered, either from lack of sleep or boredom. From the glazed eyes to the blank faces, no one surrounding me paid any attention to the speech, either. The other VIPs stood with Joseph, including his wife, Elise, and members of the Security Council. All but one chosen from the West End. As usual, many of the Authority and soldiers were in attendance, surveying the crowds from the stage and standing at each entrance just in case anyone ever thought about starting any trouble.

Elise wore a designer dress of lace over silk that strained at the seams from her pudgy figure. Her short-styled pixie cut made her face appear rounder. What kind of food did she have to get a figure like that? High heels and a handbag completed her outfit along with the jewellery around her neck, ears, and wrists. I was surprised that she didn't have a tiara to go with the rest of her jewels.

My eyes scanned the assembly, looking for Slade, wondering how he would find me. In my anger and embarrassment, we hadn't set a strategy when we parted, just the location. I had let myself believe we were friends; even that we could be more. How could I have been so stupid? I thought of his chosen one, Toni Tango. She was so beautiful, always dressed so lovely, and here I was in baggy coveralls with tangled hair stuffed into a hat. Our worlds were too different. What had I been thinking?

Joseph paused. The crowd clapped. I clapped because it was closer to the end, not because I cared. If I twisted the ring any harder, the chain would break. My head swiveled back and forth, searching for Slade. Where was he? I couldn't stand still, shifting my weight back and forth.

"What is wrong with you?" Callahan put his hand on my shoulder. "Why are you so jumpy?"

"I'm not jumpy." I shook my head and gave him a dismissive wave of my hand. Another lie, I hated lying. We never had a secret between us before this. It felt wrong.

"This is about last night, isn't it?" Gibson asked.

"You know, it's about him," Reese said. They shared a look.

"Him who? Who are they talking about?" Callahan's eyes narrowed.

Heads turned towards us as the resonance of his voice increased. The gathering threw nervous looks and shushed us. Nobody wanted the attention of the Authority.

"No, what?"

"Slade Cutter," Gibson said.

Callahan looked at me as if I had two heads. Rage passed through me like lava from a volcano. I seethed with anger at myself for picking up the stupid box. I had put myself in a situation where I couldn't tell the truth.

My left hand felt red hot. When I turned it over, my palm radiated white light. Jumping jeepers. The light flooded from my hand, cutting a hole in the coffered ceiling. Bits of dust and ceiling floated down, landing everywhere. What was going on?

I closed my hand into a fist, but the white light escaped through my fingers. Callahan captured my hand with both his fists, trying to block the light. The light burned him, but he wouldn't let go. His mind shrieked with pain; he couldn't speak. Gibson stripped off her sweatshirt, throwing it over our joined hands, but the light burned right through, leaving it in two pieces. The smell of burned flesh and wood hung in the air. Reese and Memphis drew closer, blocking us from view.

I couldn't form any words. My jaw went slack. I knew my friends were speaking, but their words made no sense. My heartbeat increased. It rumbled so loud in my ears until it became the only sound I could hear.

Just. Breathe. I repeated this mantra over and over until my breathing and heart rate became normal and I could generate actual thoughts. My hand no longer felt warm. The white light stopped streaming. Only a few moments had passed, but it felt so much longer.

"Callahan let go. I'm so sorry . . . Thunder, I hurt you. Let go. It's okay. I'm okay. Are you okay? What have I done? Oh, my stars," I tried to pull my hand away from Callahan.

He suffered but refused to let go. Typical Callahan.

My hands trembled; my eyes swam in tears while my lower lip wavered. I would not cry, I would not. I hated myself for hurting Callahan. More deep breaths helped. *"Callahan let go. My hands not hot anymore. LET GO."*

He grunted. His eyes squeezed shut; his teeth gritted together. Although I wasn't inflicting any more pain, those few seconds had hurt him terribly.

"Charlie what . . . how did you do that?" Reese rubbed her forehead.

"Charlie . . ." Gibson pulled back the pieces of sweatshirt with care. A sleeve fell to the floor. She stood with the other pieces, not sure what to do with them.

"Careful now," Reese warned. "Everybody's watching."

"No sudden movements. Just keep it natural," Memphis said. He pinched the bridge of his nose, concentrating. Using mind control, he made the people staring at us turn around as if nothing had happened.

Callahan released his grip on my hands. His pain throbbed deep;

it stung, and burned. His hands were red. His skin swollen, blistered, bloody, and raw. Gibson reached for his hands with hers. Violet light flashed as she healed him. Callahan threw back his head, biting his lip as the healing wave passed through his body. The healing had been excruciating, but not as painful as living with the burns would have been.

Slowly, I opened my fist, staring at the spot where the white light radiated; my hand seemed unchanged. I touched my palm, tracing the familiar lines. The heart, head, life, and fate lines looked the same as before. I dug my fingernails into my hand, relishing the pain, trying to find a spot that should feel different after such an experience. I peeked at my friend's faces. They wouldn't meet my eyes, looking down and away from me. They had protected me, but now disbelief and confusion radiated from them. I felt sick, jamming my hands into my pocket as I tried to reorient myself.

Memphis continued using his mind control to keep everyone fixated on the speech. He didn't do it for me, I had no illusions of that. He had absolute loyalty to Callahan. We stood awkwardly, trying to pretend everything remained the same, that white light hadn't spontaneously shot out of the palm of my hand. I touched Callahan's shoulder, and he flinched.

"I'm okay ..." He gulped deep breaths of air. *"Gibson fixed me. How did you do that?"*

"Yeah, how long have you been keeping that a secret?" Gibson asked, looking at me like an outsider again.

Reese stepped closer. "What in Attila was that?" She shook her head in disgust.

"I don't know what happened. I didn't even know I could do that." There were no words to explain myself. I kept my hands in my pocket to keep them out of sight.

Gibson paused for a moment. Her face went paled and then she fainted. All signs of a vision. What had she seen? Callahan reached to catch her before she hit the floor. Reese let out a roar, attracting eyes to us, as she moved to grab the unconscious Gibson. Together, they kept her propped up, looking like she stood on her feet.

I backed into the crowd while they were all preoccupied with Gibson. My heart felt sore from the damage I had caused. I couldn't hurt them anymore. Busy scanning the faces of everyone around me, I jerked when Slade touched my arm.

"Hey, did you bring the box?" Slade whispered beside my ear; dressed as a soldier, he pulled the brim of his cap down low over his eyes, to hide his recognizable white streak. No wonder I hadn't been able to find him. He was doing his best to blend in.

"Yeah," I reached inside the pocket of my jeans, but my fingers trembled so badly I had trouble hanging onto the box. It would have tumbled to the ground if Slade hadn't caught it.

"Hey, what's the matter? You're shaking. Did something happen?"

My lips moved, but no sound came out. The tears that threatened before streamed down my cheeks. Uncontrollable, silent sobs racked my body.

Slade threw his arms around me, pulling me close. His hand rubbed up and down my spine, stroking my back while I continued to ugly cry all over his uniform. I needed to stop crying before we drew more attention. Memphis would be too far away for his mind control to work. I struggled to pull away. I could feel his heart thumping against my chest. I caught a movement from the corner of my eye.

"Ahem. Am I interrupting something?" Callahan cleared his throat. He crossed his arms over his chest. "What... the... hell, Charlie!"

I twisted out of Slade's embrace. How could I explain this? More lies. I closed my eyes. I couldn't bear to meet Callahan's gaze. Why did he have to follow me? He should have stayed with Gibson.

"Hey, buddy. Wanna take your hands off my friend," Callahan threatened, taking a step closer. *"Gibson needs to talk to you right away."*

Memphis appeared behind him. He pinched the bridge of his nose, concentrating, making the crowd oblivious to the conversation.

Slade raised his arms. "I don't want any trouble."

"He's not bothering me ..."

"Really? Then why are you crying?"

"I'm not crying." I wiped the tears from my eyes with my fingers,

denying the obvious. I had trouble getting past my embarrassment. First not controlling my powers and second the embrace with Slade. Did Callahan recognize him?

Callahan snorted. "Who's he?"

"He's . . . never mind. I'll explain everything later. Just give me a minute."

Slade stood there, silently watching our exchange. He should have disappeared when he had the chance. He gripped the box tightly in his hand. Why was he still here?

I tossed a look at Callahan, begging him to trust me.

"You should go before we draw the attention of the Authority," I said to Slade. "I won't tell them anything. I promise."

"I know, I'm not worried." He shoved the box into his pants pocket. Grabbing my hand, he stroked it with his thumb. "Thank you for ... the key."

I stared at the spot where his hand touched mine. Raising my gaze to meet his, our eyes locked. I couldn't meet his eyes without feeling heat rush to my cheeks. Would I ever see him again? So many questions ran through my mind. There were so many things I wanted to know; I needed to know. Things I might never understand. What was the importance of the key? What did the symbol mean? How would he free Ajax? What would happen to him if he couldn't.

"Charlie, we need to go. NOW," the pitch of Callahan's voice increased with every word. "Gibson needs us."

I pulled my hand away from Slade. "You need to go . . . It was nice meeting you." Jumping jeepers, could I get any lamer? Conversation wasn't something I was good at, but that might be the dumbest thing I ever said. Get a grip, Charlie.

He kissed me quickly on the cheek. His face turned so close to mine when he whispered in my ear. "Someday I'll explain everything to you."

I couldn't think of anything to say. I touched the spot where his lips touched my cheek.

Callahan's frustration built as I conversed with Slade. He stepped in and grabbed Slade by the collar, throwing him down on the ground. Slade had been unprepared for the attack. He quickly got up, attempting to leave, but Callahan wouldn't let him go. He grabbed Slade's arm, twisting him around before throwing the first punch.

"Stop it, Callahan. This is crazy. Stop it. Please."

Slade threw the next punch with such force Callahan stumbled backward. They exchanged punches while I stood by helplessly. How could I stop the fight? They battled evenly. I heard grunts and moans. It shocked me that Slade could fight, being an Elite.

Memphis lost his control on the crowd. They parted to give the fighters more space. Their mood whirled like a current, delighted by this change of pace. The cheering became so loud Joseph stopped his speech, snapping his fingers for the Authority to intervene. They moved forward, displacing people. It would only be seconds before they reached us.

I tugged at the chain around my neck. *"Memphis, do something."*

He stood there frozen. His eyes narrowed, his lips curled as his anger played out on his face. *"It's too late."* He disappeared into the mass of people.

Out of options, I jumped on Callahan's back, desperate to stop the fight before the Authority arrived, or someone got hurt.

"Get off me."

"Callahan, stop this! You need to get out of here ..."

The Authority grabbed me from Callahan's back like I weighed nothing and tossed me in the air. I was on a collision course with one of the colossal statues at the edge of the room. I put my arms around my head and braced for impact, but it never came. I looked upward, stunned by what I saw.

9

___

Slade's face twisted into a grimace. The cords of his neck extended to the point of bursting. His outstretched hands lowered my body to the floor, creating a gentle landing instead of the violent one I expected.

"Charlie, are you okay?" he asked.

I swallowed to moisten my dry mouth while I rested on the tiled floor, stunned. My mind couldn't wrap around the fact that he had just used his powers in front of the entire assembly to save me. That he had powers stunned me. Why had he done something so reckless? I gave a quick look at the statue behind me, noting the sharp edges and solid frame. I shuddered, thinking of what those edges might have done to my head.

"Charlie, are you hurt? Thunder—answer me." Slade rushed to my side, dropping to his knees. His eyes scanned me for injuries.

All the eyeballs in the room turned our way. I sensed them touching my skin; it was too much. I couldn't handle all the attention. I traced the geometric pattern on the tile, avoiding the feelings of disbelief, curiosity, and fear flooding the room. Whenever the Authority appeared, fear became the common emotion people projected.

Rising to his feet, Slade extended a hand to pull me up, but I refused to take it, standing on my own. I couldn't even look at him. The surrounding people were deathly silent; their mood swirled like a fast-flowing river as they waited to see what would happen next. Their fear and anxiety hung heavy in the air, swirling my emotions until I felt the urge to vomit but swallowed it back. It was overloading my senses to the point that I couldn't think or move.

The Authority knocked Callahan to his knees, twisting his right arm at an unusual angle behind his back. They held his jaw in a vise-like grip to keep him immobile. My heart dropped to my stomach. I rocked back and forth on my feet, like a boat in the ocean. The Authority also froze, waiting for their next command. It felt eerie, how they could remain motionless and then move in an instant when ordered.

"Bring them forward," Joseph Cutter commanded, his voice gravelly.

The crowd buzzed, a drone of low speaking voices. Outbursts at the assemblies were infrequent, and this was pure entertainment. They couldn't help themselves. Joseph hushed them by holding up one finger in front of his lips. They quieted but followed the events with glee.

The Authority yanked Callahan to his feet. Then they escorted the three of us to the front of the room where they pushed us down to our knees in front of Joseph with the stage in front of us and the crowd to our back. I ended up between them, unable to push through the emotions that overpowered me. My heartbeat raced so fast it caused pains in my chest. I felt dizzy. My legs felt like they couldn't support my legs, my knees wouldn't bend properly. Everything was moving too quickly for my mind to process the information. I struggled against the guard who had gripped my arm, but he smacked me hard across the top of my head.

The scuffle had knocked Slade's cap off his head. We must be a sight, Slade with his white streak, Callahan with his spikes, and me with my uniquely blond hair.

Joseph's eyes flickered over his son. Outwardly he showed no emotions, but inwardly fear and anger radiated from every pore.

What would happen now? The questions wouldn't stop running through my mind. They went around and around on a loop, driving me crazy. I braced myself against the multitude of emotions I felt. They overpowered me to the point that I couldn't even string a sentence or thought together.

"What do we have here?" Joseph walked back and forth on the stage, taking his time. His suit was immaculately pressed. A wide, symmetrical triangular Windsor knot perfectly secured at his throat. He shoved his hand through his short, clipped salt-and-pepper hair.

My eyes popped open to meet his when I felt his gaze. He stared intently; I felt powerless to look away. His big brown eyes were hard as granite, his expression closed. I closed my eyes to avoid looking at his face and those of the Security Council. Could this be a dream? I had never wanted to flee from a situation more in my entire life.

"Security tags," Joseph ordered.

The Authority took our security tags, then handed them to Joseph. Without looking, he scanned them through the computer system set up to the left of the podium.

Callahan's information appeared first, then mine. Every single piece of information the TCC had gathered on us flashed on the big screens hanging on either side of the stage. Information such as my work record, pictures of me from the orphanage, from Voco, our known friends, and family history.

Everyone in the assembly gasped when they displayed a picture of Zander Edge, the vile rebel leader exiled for the Revolt of 2152. My hair shone just like his. My desire to stay hidden in the background had ended forever. When the computer presented Slade's photo, an ear-splitting roar arose from the assembly.

Joseph emitted a multitude of emotions over his son: rage, frustration, embarrassment. They flickered through him like a candle in the breeze. His thoughts danced wildly. They flit through his mind faster than I could read them. He wondered why his father hadn't exiled the children of the Rebels with their parents. One act of leniency would cost him his son. When he thought of Zander, he burned with hate. Why hadn't they kept a better eye on us.

The smirk on Elise Cutter's face had disappeared once the Authority identified Slade. Her body froze momentarily before she took a step or two backward.; soundlessly, her mouth opened and closed in a way that would be comical in a different situation. For the first time, Elise didn't present calm, cool, and collected. She looked rattled and bewildered. Her cobalt-blue eyes flashed and her unadulterated rage hit me like a slap in the face. She clacked her high heels impatiently.

The weight of this discovery staggered Joseph. He straightened the sleeves of his suit jacket, smoothing the wool material, pulling imaginary lint from the sleeves as he fought to regain control. He warred within himself on how to proceed; practically screaming his thoughts until they drowned out mine.

"I'll have silence in this room, or you will all be on half-rations for two weeks."

Joseph's words had the desired effect on them. He had bought himself some time. His exaggerated look of anger covered up a vulnerable concern about how he could protect his son. Slade was wrong; his father did care for him, but we all knew the rules. Enforcement of Code 1A-9966 was absolute for the detection of deviants. Even if Joseph wanted to, he couldn't bend the rules for his only son. No one could.

Crazy thoughts ran through Joseph's head. One of them grabbed my interest: *"Not even the zappers, could take care of this."* I had never heard the term zappers before. What were they?

I turned my head as much as I dared to peek at Slade and Callahan. Slade looked relaxed with closed eyes; his head lowered. There were no signs of an increased heart rate, no shortness of breath. A sheen of sweat appeared on Callahan's forehead, his hands clenched tightly together. What did I get him into?

A guard snapped his fingers in front of my face, bringing my attention back to the front of the room.

"Search them," Joseph Cutter said. The guards immediately complied.

The guards patted me down forcefully, checking my empty pockets. When they tried to take the ring from around my neck, I raised my hand to protect it. The guard snapped his baton roughly against my fingers. They pulled the chain from around my neck, ripping out strands of hair. I glanced sideways to see Callahan and Slade receiving the same treatment.

The Authority dumped all the items they gathered from their search on the podium in front of Joseph. He took his time examining the limited items one by one. I wondered if I would ever get my mother's ring back. They confiscated Callahan's headphones, some guitar picks, and a tube of his custom-made hair gel. Slade still had the two flashlights and the black box. Thunder, they had the box.

"Jumping jeepers. There are at least twenty-five ways this could have gone better, like I'm actually counting them in my head right now."

"Prince, anything you can do to help here would be appreciated." Callahan fiddled with the zipper on his coveralls.

"Says the guy that threw the first punch and got us into this mess. Just stay calm. Don't let your mind get ahead of you." Slade's eyes remained shut. He must be meditating. How else could he hide his physical reaction?

"Easy for you to say. I don't have your family connections, right? Prince. I'm not an Elite,"

"Quit calling me that. It's not my name. I'm Slade Cutter."

"Right, you are somebody. Got it. Good for you."

"Stop it, both of you. This isn't helping." I shifted my weight back and forth as I struggled to bring some relief to my knees, but the hard-stone steps would not provide any.

Joseph picked up the black box gingerly, as if he were afraid to touch it. The crowd hummed as they became agitated. They wanted action; they wanted to see someone exiled. Bloodthirsty because of their monotonous underground existence, they craved the excitement. And now an Elite was on stage, the son of the Commissioner. Of course, they wondered what punishment would be applied in this case. If rules were broken, they needed to see the punishments enforced.

Gibson, Reese, and Memphis had shoved their way to the front of the hall to stand behind us as we faced Joseph on the stage. Their emotions ran the gauntlet from fear to sadness to anger and then back to fear. This was my fault. I thought they must hate me.

Remy had also crept closer to the front with her minions. A strange expression crossed her face. Was it concern? She needn't pretend to care; more likely, it was curiosity. She often talked about the Elites and the Cutters in particular, and now I was kneeling beside her idol.

"Don't worry, big brother. I'll come after you."

"Don't you dare, Gibson . . . don't you dare? I would rather think of you safe, here. I love you, little sis."

"Don't talk to me like this is the end."

Is this what appeared to Gibson in her vision? Did she know this would happen? I remained silent. I noticed Gibson made no offer to free me. Even if it were an impossible, it still would have been nice to hear. I focused on remaining calm like Slade; it was all that chaos in my head that triggered the light in the first place. Despite my fears, I had to keep the white light hidden.

Joseph turned the box repeatedly in his hand, looking for an opening, the same as I had done the night before. What secrets did the box hold? He traced the symbol with his index finger. He thought, *"not again"* before Elise drew his attention. Sick of waiting for Joseph to do something, Elise moved closer to the edge of the stage.

Elise scrutinized my bone-white hair before her gaze rested on her son. Her honeyed voice bristled with anger. "Slade, what do you have to say for yourself. How long have you hidden the fact you are nothing but a subordinate mutant?" Her mouth twisted when she spat out the word "mutant."

Elise assessed her son as if he were a bug or a rodent that needed eradication. Slade didn't respond. He didn't even open his eyes to look at her. What was he doing?

"Elise." Joseph's voice was low but menacing.

"How could you do this to us? To your father, to me?" Elise glared at Joseph but continued, ignoring his warning. She crossed her arms, clasping her fingers so tightly around her upper arms her knuckles turned white. "*Look at me when I am talking to you!*"

I don't know how I expected Elise to act, but this wasn't it. I hoped Slade did not read her thoughts. Elise didn't seem concerned about him at all. Her anxiety revolved around having a deviant son and how it would reflect on her. If they would lose control of the commission and the Authority with this black mark against them.

Slade finally opened his eyes. They blazed with fire, but he remained defiantly silent. Elise examined him as if he were a total stranger.

"*Slade, don't listen to her. She's just worried. She doesn't mean it.*" I tried to comfort him.

"*Of course she does.*"

Elise's lips pressed together in a straight line. She paced back and forth. "When I think of all the sacrifices we made for you."

"*Your mother is acting like you chose to be a deviant!*" I said.

"*She hates deviants with a passion.*"

"*She can't possibly hate her only son.*"

"*You are born a deviant, right? There is no choice. I wish ... I would give my powers away in a heartbeat.*" Callahan shook his head in disbelief.

"Enough," Joseph roared at Elise. This time she bristled but obeyed. Years of marriage taught her how far she could push him before he would push back.

One of his aides handed him a note. He skimmed it through the first time and then slowly reread it. He dropped the note on the podium, still clutching the box in his hand.

General Logan Campbell approached the commissioner. "Sir, the Code 1A-9966 is explicit on what has to happen in this situation. Your son has shown his deviance. He has to—"

Joseph waved his hand to silence the General. "I know the code; you don't have to explain it to me. My family wrote the code. Which one of you had this box in your possession?"

"It's mine, Sir." Slade spoke up.

Something about the box scared Joseph. He held it cautiously, as if just holding it could cause harm. Joseph leaned towards his face. "Slade, you know the punishment for deviance, Code 1A-9966. What I need to know is this: what are you doing standing with the offspring of rebels and holding onto a box with the insignia of the Revolt of 2152?"

10

I sucked in a breath and coughed.

Slade remained still. *"Don't react."*

"Thunder! Charlie, did you know about the box?" Callahan asked.

"Yeah, but I didn't know it belonged to the rebels!"

"Holy Attila, what have you got me involved with?" Callahan drummed his fingers against his coveralls. I reached for his hand, but a guard whacked me with his baton. I struggled to prevent myself from falling forward. *"They will exile us, won't they?"*

"No never," said Gibson loudly. I looked back and saw a guard push her as she lunged towards the stage.

"Thunder, you know they will! Because of this Elite? Charlie, how could you? How could you get my brother—all of us—involved in this!"

I bit the inside of my cheek hard and kept biting; the pain kept me focused. *"Slade, for Attila's sake! What could you, of all people, be doing with rebel material?"*

"Calm down, all of you!" Slade transmitted. *"Just be quiet for one minute and let me think!"*

Joseph waited for a response of any kind from Slade. His hand moved to massage the back of his neck. "Slade, not only have you committed the crime of deviancy, but treason. Possession of rebel propaganda is treason. Do you have anything you would like to tell me? Anything to . . . explain this situation."

General Logan stood again, but Joseph glared at him. "Sit down, General."

Slade lifted his shoulder in a half shrug.

"I'll give you one last chance to answer." Joseph's voice was strained, betraying his mounting frustration. He couldn't look weak, not in front of everyone. "Do you think I enjoy asking you, of all people, these questions?"

"No, but I think you love having the power to get them answered." The corner of Slade's lip curled into a sneer.

Why did he provoke his father? What good would it do?

"Watch your mouth!" Joseph said.

It took all my willpower to keep a serene look on my face. My mind raced thinking about the rebels. What rebels? When they exiled Zander and his followers, the revolt ceased. Did I miss hearing whispers of the beginning of another revolt?

"Jumping jeepers, Slade! They will never believe I'm innocent in this ... because of Zander. Thunder!" As if my fingers had a mind of their own, they fidgeted with the zipper on my coveralls. I forced myself to still my hands and drop them to the sides.

Callahan scanned the room, searching for an escape route. *"We have to get out of here, right?"*

There were no places we could go to hide, not in this mousetrap. It would be suicide to run. The Authority would fire on us if we moved.

My mind could only process one singular thought. It echoed over and over on replay. The symbol. Did I remember the symbol from all my time in the archives? I hadn't seen it in any computer files, but it was clear they had wiped all the information on the revolt from the servers. It's why I spent so much time in the archives, looking for any traces left behind they would give me clues about my family.

Now all the surrounding sounds seemed distorted, as if I were underwater; the noises of the crowd behind me, the questions of

Joseph, it all felt indistinct, far away. Nothing made any sense. My brain flashed back to the digital footage of the first exile. I watched it repeatedly in the archives; I knew each moment by heart.

In the video, The Authority unshackled Zander and the rest of the rebels, removing their restraints. They herded them towards the tunnel leading to the surface. Two guards in decontamination suits and respirators drove the group forward, nudging them inch by inch at the point of a gun barrel. They forced them through the three-foot-thick door, outside into the cold, frozen abyss.

Some people cried, while others comforted them. Some looked back, wondering if there would be a reprieve. One by one, the rebels squared their shoulders, walking out the door with nothing but the clothes on their backs.

Zander had been the last to leave. An absent look crossed his face. He seemed no more upset than if he stood in line at the cafeteria. He turned at the last moment and winked at the camera, blowing a kiss to the crowd watching, some in person and the rest on the intranet. His mouth moved to form words, but "I" became the only word heard before the camera faded to black.

Is that what would happen to us? Would I die in the frozen wilderness? No one cared I wasn't a rebel. Would anyone care about my innocence? I doubted it.

"Charlie," Callahan said.

Callahan's voice inside my head snapped me back to reality. I couldn't afford to get stuck in my brain. My friends' thoughts blended with the others. Too much mental noise-blocked them. The flowing emotions, both mine and theirs, sapped all my mental strength.

"Charlie, are you listening to me?"

"Yeah, sorry. Drifted off for a moment."

"Kinda got a lot going on here. It would be helpful if you paid attention."

Joseph still wasn't having any luck extracting answers from his son. Slade had told the truth earlier when he described his relationship with his parents.

Another question invaded my mind; it took over like a bad weed. Why would Slade become involved with the rebels when his family oversaw the Hollows? Why wouldn't he wait until he became commissioner to enact any changes he wanted, especially if the rumors were true about his father dying? Joseph's aura had changed recently from a brilliant yellow to a lemon-yellow aura signifying a fear of loss. Loss of health or the fear of losing control over his destiny? I didn't know which.

Slade just stared up at his father. A wisp of a smile crossed his face.

I pleaded, *"Say something, do something! They will help you. Beg for mercy if you have to."*

"You understand nothing. If I hadn't revealed my powers, it would be different. They could have made something up. Protecting me now would cause them to lose face. That is their only concern. My father will do his duty no matter the cost. If he didn't, my mother would force him."

"Really?"

"Really."

Callahan broke in *"I hate to break up this stimulating conversation but what are we going to do? Any brilliant ideas? Huh?"*

General Campbell tried to get Joseph's attention. He cleared his throat several times. Then pressed on. "Excuse me. Sir. Sorry to interrupt. We caught your son red-handed using telekinesis... plus possession of rebel propaganda. An obvious violation of the Code 1A-9966. I don't know why you are hesitating, worrying about the box, and dredging up..."

A distasteful look crossed Joseph's face as he broke off his questioning. He fixed the General with a hard stare until he backed up a step or two.

General Campbell's face burned red from his collar to the roots of his hair. His thoughts projected loudly. He couldn't understand why the commissioner delayed in sentencing us. The code outlined the consequences of violating a rule. There were also one or two thoughts concerning his place in the succession of the Hollows.

"I've got a plan," Slade said.

"Well, let me hear it, Prince, because things are looking pretty bleak," Callahan said.

"I dare you: Call me that one more time."

Joseph waved off the General. He motioned for Blaze to join the conversation.

Blaze had an orange-yellow aura because she had a scientific mind. With a genius level IQ as well as serious computer and mechanical skills at seventeen, she became the youngest Secretary in commission history, joining the security council. Who knew playing video games could lead to a job in government?

Callahan and I shared a look. I didn't have to use my telepathy to know what he thought.

Blaze Ahuja had become one of only a few people from the East End to hold a power position. A tiny girl with a wide mouth and forehead, she shaved her hair on one side of her head, letting it hang long on the other side cut in layers. She dressed in a three-piece suit with her shirt buttoned up to the top; a red tie accented her red wire-framed glasses. Draped around her neck hung a set of white headphones.

Blaze pulled an earbud out of her ear as she approached Joseph, leaving the other one hanging loosely. She avoided eye contact with us. Joseph passed her the box, dropping it into her outstretched hand like it emitted contagions. He rubbed the ends of his fingers with his thumb as if trying to erase any remaining traces of the box. "Figure out how to open this."

"Yes, sir!" Blaze rotated the box in her hand, searching for a way in. A line appeared between her eyes as she puzzled it out. "If you will excuse me, sir, I need to take this to my lab."

Joseph nodded. Blaze reached the north door to the assembly room when Joseph called out. "Be quick about it."

She dipped her head in compliance and scurried out the door without looking back, two of her underlings at her heels.

Joseph picked up a tablet from the podium, using his fingers to scroll. Without looking, he said, "Do any of you have anything to say for yourselves before your sentencing?"

My mouth opened, then closed. There were many things I could say, but nothing that would help. This wasn't the old world where people were innocent before proven guilty. Due process only happened in "Law and Order" reruns. There would be no trial. No presentation of evidence. No words spoken to prove guilt or innocence. I would be guilty by proximity.

Joseph paced while he studied the tablet. The silent crowd waited to hear what our punishments would be. If it were not for the constant whirling of the overhead fans circulating the air, there would be complete silence. Would they be overjoyed or outraged? It would give them something to debate for weeks.

"Charlie Edge." Joseph spoke my name as if it were a vulgar word. "Daughter of Zander and Amy Edge, both deceased."

My heartbeat faster. This was the moment I had avoided for years.

Joseph looked from me to the tablet to the gigantic screen, as if something didn't add up. All the images of me were as a brunette, but the person in front of him stood blond.

"You look exactly like your father."

Not a question, but a statement. Did I need to answer? My voice squeaked. "Y... yes." Squirming under his scrutiny, I wished with all my heart to not be the center of attention.

"Hmm, maybe we should have kept a closer eye on you. Maybe we have been too complacent with security procedures. Did you forget we spared your life in the first exile? But I will deal with that later." Joseph pinned the Secretary of Defense with his stare before snapping his gaze to Callahan. "Callahan Malone, son of Mercury and Ava exiled in the 2152 Revolt, brother of Gibson. Is your twin sister involved?"

Callahan met his gaze without a hint of fear, raising his chin higher. He refused to blink until Joseph broke contact. "No sir, it does not involve her. I'm not..."

Joseph motioned for Callahan to be quiet. He drew himself up to his full height, squaring his shoulders. He stepped in front of his son. "Slade, my son. You don't know how much it pains me to do this. Slade Cutter, Callahan Malone, I have found you both guilty of

Possession of Treasonous Propaganda and Assault in the First Degree. Charlie Edge, you—."

"Wait—." Slade rose from his knees. A guard rapped the butt end of his gun off the back of Slade's skull. He winced, twisting his head to the side, his eyes rolled in pain.

"Jumping jeepers. What the... you can't do that. *Slade, are you okay? Talk to me.*"

"*Yeah.*" Slade rubbed the spot where the guard made contact. "Father, the girl . . . has nothing to do with this. Check the digital feed if you don't believe me. You can do what you want with me, . . . but . . . she's innocent. I don't even know how she became involved. This was a fight between me and him. The box was mine." He jerked his chin in Callahan's direction.

"I've already checked the feed." Joseph held up the tablet.

"Why were you even on the main level?" Elise asked. "Your place is up here with us."

"Elise please, this is official government business."

Elise stiffened but backed off.

Why would Slade stick his neck out to save me? Someone he barely knew. It made no sense.

Callahan said, "He's right, Sir . . . just caught in the wrong place at the wrong time."

"*CALLAHAN, WHAT ARE YOU DOING? Don't drag yourself any further into this!*" I felt loss for words. Sometimes the struggle to find the exact words was inconvenient, but right now, it felt downright frustrating.

"*If he can win your freedom. Let him try. I can't do anything to save myself from the consequences of an assault charge, but let him try. We agree with each other. Don't we?*" Callahan said.

Slade agreed. "*I promised I wouldn't let anything happen to you and I won't.*"

"*No! This isn't fair, it isn't fair . . .*" Tears leaked from my eyes. Big fat drops trailed down my face, running under my chin. I wiped them away with the back of my hand. This wasn't real—it couldn't be happening. A nightmare. I just needed to wake up from this frightful dream and everything would be the same again.

"Father, the box is mine. Neither of them had anything to do with it. And the girl, she just tried to break up the fight," Slade continued. "There is no crime in trying to enforce a rule from the code. You should reward her, not punish her."

Joseph paused, tilting his head in consideration. "What caused the fight? Wait... never mind, don't answer. The reason doesn't matter. The charge is the same. Assault in the First Degree as per Code 4A-8771."

I felt powerless. I wanted to say something, do something, but what could I do?

"Father, could I speak with you alone for a moment?" Slade asked.

"I'll give you one minute but not a second longer." Joseph motioned to the Authority to allow Slade to follow him. He stiffened with each step as he limped across the stage with his son by his side. Their footsteps resonated in the silent Assembly Hall. They passed through the double doors off the back of the stage and disappeared.

I let out a breath, blowing the hair out of my face. I felt so exposed without my hair paint and hat. I became so angry at myself for ever touching that stupid box. If I had just left it lying in the dirt, none of this would be happening. I placed my best friend in danger. The rest of my friends hated me. Lowering my chin to my chest, I closed my eyes, afraid to face my future—a future without my best friend.

"Charlie, at least I got to eat an apple before—"

"Before I ruined your life..." Our eyes met.

"You didn't . . . ruin my life, right? It's my fault. I did something stupid. I let my temper get away from me."

The tears began again. I hated crying; it made me feel weak.

"Charlie, don't cry. Please don't cry. You're my best friend, please don't cry."

"I'm so sorry . . ."

"Screws fall out all the time . . ."

"What!"

"Screws fall out all the time. The world is an imperfect place."

I smiled despite myself. He quoted a line from *The Breakfast Club*, my favorite movie. I countered with *"Did you know without trigonometry, there'd be no engineering?"*

"Without lamps, there'd be no light."

"Could you describe the ruckus, Sir?"

It felt good to be back to normal with Callahan, if only for a few moments. My face felt tight as the tears dried on my cheeks. The crowd became restless again. Hungry for excitement after a long week at their soul-sucking jobs.

Joseph ripped open the door, flinging it back to bounce against the wall as he re-entered the room. Only the door jamb kept the knob from going through the wall. His face heated to until it was beet red, skin-tight against his features. He gazed straight ahead, jaw set. I had heard the term "steam coming out of his ears" before, but this was the first time I could ever picture it. What did Slade say to Joseph to produce such a visceral reaction? Slade rejoined us in front of the stage. The Authority pushed him down with more force than necessary; they wouldn't have dared an hour ago.

Joseph regained control of his emotions. His face masked his internal torment. He looked tired and worn. I was positive the rumors of his sickness were true. The underground whispers implied he suffered from Parkinson's disease. The tremor in his hand and slow movements seemed to agree with the diagnosis.

"By the power of the commission, Slade Cutter and..." Joseph paused and glanced back over his shoulder to remember Callahan's name. "Callahan Malone. You are both guilty of Assault Code 4A-8771, Deviancy Code 1A-9966 I banish you both from the Hollows. You will spend the rest of your days locked in the vault."

"Noooooo," Gibson's voice rang out. Callahan's sentence ripped through her like a wicked thunderstorm. I knew her heart shattered because so had mine. Joseph's words splintered inside me, like a thousand shards of broken glass. I whipped my head around to see Memphis and Reese restraining Gibson. Her anguish was visible.

Joseph continued. "Slade, I will know why you were in the possession of rebel propaganda. Mark my words. As of this moment, you are no longer my son. Remove them both from my sight." He motioned to the Authority.

The crowd erupted, causing a sensory overload to my system with countless opinions on the matter. The Authority yanked us to our feet, almost ripping Callahan's arm out of his socket. Slade jumped up before being prodded. They snapped a thick silver bracelet around Slade's right wrist, then Callahan's. I could no longer hear their thoughts. We exchanged surprised glances.

Elise, who had been silently gritting her teeth on the sidelines, spoke in a scathing tone. "What about the girl? Shouldn't she face punishment too? She's his daughter." Elise had a dark green aura. A dangerous sign. Greens were jealous people, full of resentment; refusing to accept responsibility for their actions.

Elise pointed her finger at me, flinging her hatred. I felt as if a million tiny forks stabbed me all at once. Why did she hate me so much? Her behavior confused me. As far as Elise knew I had only broken up a fight, she had no clue Slade had been in the crowd to meet with me.

"Elise, I've made my decision, but not to worry. We will monitor her closely for now," Joseph said. "She can always join them in the vault at a later date."

Elise clenched her jaw until her teeth almost broke, unhappy with her husband's decision. She pivoted and stomped away. Flinging the north doors against the wall as she exited.

"Charlie Edge, you are free to leave." Joseph said. "However, you will need to work fifteen Sundays in the next six months to work off your community service."

My stomach churned. What could I do? How could I make this better? All my life, I always tried to make everything perfect. I tried to solve problems before they started so I could avoid situations like this. I felt sick, drained of all emotion.

Automatically, I reached for my mother's ring before I remembered they confiscated it. I felt lost without the familiar sensation of it hanging around my neck. I have a vague memory of Samantha, draping it over my head. Telling me my parents loved me and I should never lose the ring.

In all the excitement, Blaze quietly re-entered the room and positioned herself next to Joseph. "Commissioner, the box is empty." Blaze showed the empty open box to Joseph and the room.

Slade whipped his head around to look at me. His eyes, that usually held so much warmth and affection, instead gazed upon me with disbelief and suspicion. His face gave his feelings away: he thought I was a traitor.

The Authority escorted Slade and Callahan away before I could say anything.

Joseph roared, "Silence! Clear the hall. Meeting adjourned."

11

What? The key had been there when I left my room. Did Slade somehow take it? No, he couldn't have; the look on his face seemed genuine. Still lost in thought, an Authority member, number 090905, grabbed my upper arm. "Mrs. Cutter would like to have a word with you." I winced at the sound of his voice. Not a request, but a demand. He gripped my arm tightly, like a part in a vise.

The guard spun me around towards the exit. Most of the crowd had dispersed, but Gibson, Reese, and Memphis remained. A multitude of emotions flowed through them. Gibson's eyes were red and swollen from the tears streaming down her face. Reese's arm surrounded Gibson, providing comfort. Memphis has a stony expression on his face. I couldn't meet their eyes.

"I'm so sorry!" The guards wrenched me away before I could say anything more. I felt numb, not scared, only numb.

Just before we left the room, Remy walked up to me. She threw her arms around my shoulders and hugged me tight. I was so stunned I didn't even hug her back. The guard pulled me away and four Authority members escorted me through a maze of corridors to an unfamiliar section of the Hollows. Was I still in the East End? I couldn't be sure. We entered a long hallway with a door every six feet. A guard unlocked one and pushed me into a small white room. The fluorescent light overhead blinked several times until the room lit up. The air uncirculated: still, stuffy, and hot.

I flinched when the door closed behind me with a click, rushing to it, turning the doorknob to find it locked. I hated being locked in. The room was vacant except for two black metal chairs placed on either side of a scarred wooden table with skinny, spindly legs. A thin monitor hung on the back wall, broadcasting the news. I shut it off to avoid the replay from the assembly. I had lived it. I didn't need to see it. For once, I got some silence; I needed to be able to think, to clear my head.

A large mirror sat in a recessed section of the wall beside the door. Was it two-way glass? Was someone watching me from the other side? Act normal, I told myself sternly, but what was normal in this situation? I regarded my reflection. My hair had become a chaotic mess; most of the strands had escaped the loose knot in the scuffle when I lost my hat. I felt naked from the loss, exposed, without the hat to conceal my identity.

Removing the elastic from my hair, I placed it around my wrist for future use. I shook out my hair. Using my fingers, I combed through the mass of knots. My knees knocked while I performed this routine task. Acting like a vain girl with no additional thoughts running through her head other than the way she looked. But it wasn't that. I'd spent so much energy hiding my hair and now that it was exposed, I at least wanted it tidy. Turning away from the mirror, I left it down. It seemed pointless to hide my hair any longer. The commission wouldn't forget about me again. I would be lucky if I didn't have a twenty-four-hour guard for the rest of my life I tucked the hat in my back pocket.

Being trapped in a room alone with my thoughts was a living nightmare. Nothing could be worse. Strangers interrogating me would be easier to deal with than the self-doubting flagellation I gave myself. My mind spun, pushed and pulled a million different ways. What was I going to do? I couldn't imagine my life without Callahan.

He had been with me almost every single moment of my life, other than work.

I knew I had to do something. But what? No way could I just abandon him to the vault, but how could I rescue him? I didn't even know the hidden location or how I would even begin to attempt such a thing. I couldn't even leave the East End without the proper clearance. Was it foolish or crazy to think I could rescue him by myself? Maybe just hopeless.

The mystery of the empty box puzzled me. Where did the key go? It had been inside when I handed him the box. I had checked before I left my room. It took all night for me to find the hidden mechanism that opened the trick box. You had to slide, unlock, lift, and press in a specific order. Inside the box sat a flash drive in a velvet-lined compartment. What could be on the drive to make it so valuable? I hoped the contents were worth all the trouble it caused.

I picked up the tablet on the wall beside the door, hoping to play a video game to distract myself, but I couldn't get it to work. I repelled technology like a vampire that couldn't stand the sunlight. It had been hours and I was still locked in the room; there was nothing else to do. I tried pacing, but the cramped room had no space. There were two hundred ninety-five small beige tiles on the ceiling and seventy-nine larger white tiles with black swirls on the floor. A spider spun a web up in the corner, trying to entice a bug. I took a seat across from the door, waiting for it to open. Out of boredom, I fell asleep on the table, using my arm as a pillow.

Elise Cutter burst into the room flanked by two of the Authority, startling me. My heart pounded from the violent awakening; my mind foggy, until everything came rushing back. I wiped the back of my hand across my mouth, hoping I hadn't drooled. My other arm had fallen sound asleep; the painful tingling of pins and needles as blood rushed back to the nerve was enough to clear my mind.

Elise's arms were full of files and papers, which she dropped onto the table. So many paper folders looked out of place in this digital age. She took a seat across the table, staring at me for so long it made me squirm. I checked the time: only 2:10 pm. It felt like I had been in there for days.

"Charlie Elisabeth Edge."

"Y . . . yes, madam."

Elise pinned me with her eyes until I looked away. Her gaze lingered on my hair for a long time. I felt like a bug she would like to crush beneath the heel of her red stiletto pumps. She shuffled papers around, picking them up from one pile then stacking them in another methodically, stopping to straighten each page as she transferred them. Elise was in no rush. She dawdled, taking all the time in the world. After our initial engagement, she acted as if I wasn't in the room. Was this some type of psychological torture? She sat on the metal chair as if it were a throne, tapping her red painted fingernails against the rough wooden table.

"I..."

"Yes," she said without glancing up, writing notes on a piece of paper.

I swallowed the words of my prepared statement before they emerged. Nothing sounded right in my head.

My right leg shook back and forth, the result of too much nervous energy. I placed my hand to my knee to stop the trembling. I was too frightened to read Elise's mind. I jerked when she spoke.

"I think this is yours." Elise held the chain with my mother's ring wrapped around her wrist, the ring suspended in the air.

I dug my fingers into my arm to resist grabbing it from her. She dangled the ring from the chain before shoving it across the table. I gathered it tenderly in the palm of my hand before squeezing down tight on it.

Elise closed the file folder and set down the pen. A misaligned file folder drove me crazy. I stopped myself from pushing it back into place. "Do you remember your parents?" Elise asked. The honey missing from her voice at the assembly returned. I could imagine her as an old-fashioned southern woman of the 21st century saying, "Bless your heart," as she plotted to kill you. She was the spider in the corner waiting for me to fly into her web.

She stood briefly, picking up the tablet next to the door before re-seating herself. She brought up my profile, casting it onto the monitor behind her. Why couldn't I get the tablet to work? She made it look so easy. Just like the assembly, my history displayed on the monitor. There were a ton of documents, considering my life had been uneventful. Some documents had redactions. I thought it could probably be information relating to Zander.

Elise slipped two photos from the file folder and positioned them on the table. Photos of my parents. They looked young, maybe my age. My fingers itched to grasp the photo of my mother. I checked with Elise, who indicated her acceptance. Printed photos were a rarity. I pulled the photo closer, tracing my fingers over my mother's face as if I could touch her. "I don't remember my mother; she died two months after my birth." Why was she questioning me on things she already knew?

A picture flashed on the monitor of my mother holding me in her arms in a medical clinic bed, a sweet smile on her face. I wished I had a copy. Why weren't these photos in the archives with the others?

"And your father?" she prodded. "It says here you were two at the time of his exile."

"Um, I vaguely remember Zander, not sure if . . . if they are actual memories, more like flashes; hazy images." Gazing at the photo of Zander, it would be impossible not to see the resemblance. The hair, the eyes, the cheekbones, were the same as mine. I was a mirror copy of my father.

"Painting your hair, what a splendid idea. It kept you off our radar. In hindsight, the Commission should have exiled all of you with your parents. I told Joseph his father's leniency would come back to haunt him. We won't make the same mistake again. Expect to be monitored closely." Elise threaded her fingers together. She was a master at making threats without raising her voice.

"But I've done nothing wrong." My voice came out indistinct, barely audible. I rubbed my temples. My head ached.

"Did you say something? Speak up."

"I—."

Elise interrupted. "I searched back through your history. There don't appear to be any images of you as a blond. I visited you at the clinic the day you were born. You had a head full of dark hair then. Did you know I knew your parents?"

"N… no." I tucked my hair behind my ears self-consciously.

"Your mother, and I were best friends in Prep. In fact, I… even sort of dated your father for a time."

Elise dating Zander. The image made me want to vomit. "My mother didn't go to Prep. She went to Voco, she's from the East."

"No, she's not. She is from the West End," Elise said. She clicked a button and another photo appeared on the screen. My mother at about fourteen years of age with four other girls posing in front of the Prep sign. A young Elise Cutter appeared to be one of the girls. I studied the photo, checking for evidence it could be a fake. It looked authentic, but I was no expert.

"Why are you showing me this?" I scooted back on the metal chair as far as I could go, the legs screeched on the tiles; trying to escape the lies Elise told me.

Elise displayed more photos. Photos of my mother with Elise and the same group of girls. There were also photos of my mother with an older couple in a luxuriously decorated room. I raised an eyebrow. "Who are they?"

"Your grandparents, Hugh, and Laura-Jane Clark. They weren't part of the commission, but Hugh served on the Security Council in the West End for years and years. Their apartment was my second home when I was a teenager. I practically lived there."

"What, no. That's not true." I scratched my head "My grandparents are all from the East End. My mother's parents were Sasha and James Morgan. Zander's parents were Violet and Stephen Edge. That's the information in the archives. Isn't it?"

"No." Elise licked her lips, relishing the moment. "Well, yes and no. Your father's parents were Stephen and Violet. Both deceased before you were born; killed in the power plant fire that claimed twenty-seven lives, including Sasha and James."

I nodded in agreement.

"But your mother's parents were Hugh and Laura-Jane Clark. Hugh paid the Kings to have the records changed after your mother died."

"Why? I don't understand. If my grandparents were alive, why didn't they come for me when my mother died or when they exiled Zander? Why was I raised in the orphanage when I had a family?" I felt so confused. What I thought I knew as the truth had become a lie. Why had my grandparents abandoned me?

Elise sighed; she tapped her finger against her bottom lip. "It's a lengthy story... where to start."

"The beginning," I muttered as I crossed my arms and wiggled around, trying to get comfortable. My butt was numb against the unpadded, hard chair.

"Pardon? I didn't catch what you said."

"Nothing."

Elise rose and walked around the table in slow, measured steps, her four-inch heels clicked on the tiled floor. I shuddered as the clicks slowed, then stopped when she paused behind me. I had never heard the odd sound of footsteps made in heels before. Although I had seen them worn at the assemblies, I didn't know anyone who owned a pair. Life underground did not suit those kinds of shoes and I could not imagine walking in them. I wondered how badly they contorted your feet. How was she able to walk upright with straight posture? How badly did they crush her toes? The life of an elite where you didn't have to walk very far or stand for long. When the clicking restarted, I realized I had been holding my breath the entire time.

"It's almost a funny story." Elise re-emerged on my left, where I could see her. Her smile curled her lips but did not reach her eyes. "I'm the reason Zander and Amy met."

I didn't interrupt, remaining expressionless. Elise would take pleasure in keeping the details from me if she knew how much I wanted answers.

"I wanted to have some fun, so I thought a trip to the stone would amuse me. It would be something different to break up the monotony. Elites weren't permitted to go at that time, but I blackmailed Preston Crowe into letting me in."

Elise coughed several times, then ambled over to the door. She opened it, asked for water, then waited for delivery. A guard entered, placing a full glass pitcher of water and two glass tumblers on the table: pouring a glass for both of us.

She took a sip before continuing. "I met your father there a time or two. It was an exciting time sneaking into the club and flirting with the East End boys. Your dad and I hit it off, making out more than once. He certainly knew how to kiss."

Eww! Way too much information.

"Zander had ambition. I think he believed dating me would give him an advantage. Not that I would have ever helped him. Silly boy, he was just a plaything to me. Back then, I had recently become engaged to marry Joseph; the algorithm picked me. I dragged Amy out with me." She paused for a sip of water. Her lipstick made a little smudge on the glass. She picked up the jug and added a drop of the water to my glass, then filled her own.

"She didn't even have any interest in going, but I talked her into it. I could always talk her into anything. The moment we walked into the Stone and your parents locked eyes, everyone around them ceased to exist." She drifted off, looking in the mirror to fix a stray lock of hair. "Amy started slipping over to the East End every moment she could. She called off her engagement to marry Logan Campbell, forgot about him altogether."

Logan Campbell—as in, General Campbell? Joseph Cutter's enforcer and confidant? In another lifetime, he could have been my father, or Elise could have been my mother. Unthinkable.

"They were mad about each other. She said they were fated to be together. Whatever that meant. Then your mother did the something silly and got pregnant. I don't know how she could have been so stupid." Elise shook her head at the thought. "Hugh and Laura-Jane lost their minds when Amy told them about her pregnancy with Zander's child. They gave her an ultimatum: abortion and marriage to Logan, or they would cut her off and banish her to the East End."

Wait. I did the math: my mother wasn't pregnant with me then. "Do I have a sibling?" The words were out before I could stop them.

"No."

For a moment, disappointment flowed through me. I shook it off; I couldn't mourn a sibling that didn't exist. Everything she told me seemed wrong. Could she be stringing me along with a bunch of lies?

"Amy, as you know, chose your father. Claimed to be in love. Whatever that means. She left the comfort of the West End. Hugh and Laura-Jane cut her off as they warned, but it didn't matter. I never saw her happier than living in squalor with Zander. They didn't even have their own place. Barbaric." Elise shuddered at the thought. She twisted her mouth at the word love as if it were offensive. "Silly girl, she only talked about 'baby this' and 'baby that.' Sickening behavior. And worse: boring."

She inhaled deeply. The material of her dress rustled as she adjusted her sleeve, then looked in the mirror. "It wasn't good for my image consorting with someone from the East. Joseph certainly didn't approve. Then, she miscarried. She cried all the time, carrying on like it was the end of the world. Even more boring. I couldn't stand her constant sobbing, so I ended our friendship."

Wow, Elise deserted her best friend in her time of need. What a piece of work. I actually felt bad for Slade growing up with Elise as a mother.

"I heard they got married as soon as she turned eighteen. The underground whispers spread rumors she had trouble getting pregnant. It didn't happen again until after she turned twenty-three, with you." Elise sat down, crossing her legs. She inclined her head in my direction. "You know the rest of the story, don't you Charlie."

"Yeah, I do. Long-story-short, my mother became pregnant with me, but a complication developed after my birth. The commission wouldn't give her the surgery she needed because of Zander, and she died two months later. Zander blamed the commission then started the rebellion and eventually the Revolt of 2152."

Elise narrowed her eyes. "Is that what you think?"

"Yeah, it's what they have always told me." My hands gripped the edge of the table. "Is it the truth?"

Elise shrugged her shoulders.

"Is it the truth?" I repeated, surprised by my bravery.

Elise only raised an eyebrow. A knowing smile crossed her lips.

I could tell from her expression she wasn't going to tell me anything further. I tried another tactic. "None of that explains why my grandparents deserted me."

"I think Laura-Jane wanted to see you when you were born, but Hugh wouldn't let her. After the revolt, after everything . . . Hugh wanted to distance himself from the scandal, protect his position on the council. He paid the Kings to have your birth records changed to shield himself. Sasha and James Morgan were already dead, and people eventually forgot Hugh and Laura-Jane had a daughter. I would have done the same. In fact, I helped him." Elise smirked.

Imagining Elise conversing with Jagger Malone was intriguing. Thinking about it too much could make my head explode.

"Are . . . are they still alive?" I asked, though I shouldn't care about people that abandoned me.

"Hugh died of a heart attack a few years ago, but Laura-Jane is still alive. She's the head of the Beautification Committee. We had lunch together just last week."

The beautification committee? Wow, only in the West End. I had a grandmother. A living family member, even if she wanted nothing to do with me. I didn't know how I felt about that. "Could I—."

A loud knock on the door made me jump. Elise's mouth set in a hard line. She looked annoyed but stood up and unlocked the door, letting two men enter. I took the time to drink some water. My mouth seemed dry, even though Elise did most of the talking.

I slid my gaze to study them; both men appeared to be in their early thirties. One of them wore a gray suit with a navy-blue tie. He had a wide forehead with a hooked nose, clean-shaven, his hair clipped short. The other one wore white, baggy scrubs. He had golden brown skin with a long narrow face and big beautiful brown eyes. His long shaggy curly hair hung to his shoulders and his beard was braided. It looked almost comical how different they appeared. The man with the shaggy beard had a thick silver bracelet on his right wrist, the same as the ones they had put on Slade and Callahan.

"Well, since we are all caught up on history, the interrogation begins."

At the word "interrogation" an image of torture flitted through my mind and—*pfoom!*—water spewed out of my mouth all over the table.

12

"I thought you would never get here. What took you so long?" Elise shut the door behind the two men with a resounding click. I grabbed a napkin the guards had brought earlier when they delivered the water and dabbed at the mess.

"Sorry, madam, it took—," the man in the suit began.

"Save it. I'm not interested in your excuses. Your response time is unacceptable." She flicked her wrist, motioning for the men to move into the corner. She straightened her blouse, adjusted her sleeves, then shifted the pearls hanging around her neck before reseating herself. She picked up a file and thumbed through it. I noted this was part of her routine, making people wait. I glanced up at her face; her brow furrowed as she studied her paperwork. The men stood awkwardly, waiting for Elise to tell them what to do.

"How long have you known my son?"

"I don't . . . know him." I gripped the edge of the table until my fingers turn white. "I just tried to break up the fight. Just like he said. Just like your son said."

"You are lying. Do you want to know how I know you are lying?" Elise displayed more pictures on the screen. "This is how I know you are lying."

There were photos of Slade holding me when I cried and kissing me on the cheek at the assembly. Photos of us walking around this morning in the corridors and photos of us at the gate by the FarSide. Did the cameras ever miss anything?

"Ugh!"

I scanned the photos, looking for a specific picture. There didn't appear to be any images of the box transfer. That could help. If I ended up in the vault, I wouldn't be of any use rescuing Callahan and Slade. I knew rescuing them would be a long shot, but I vowed to try. I just needed some help and a plan. I felt entirely out of my element. I didn't have any hero qualities; a glance at my blond hair reminded me of my visibility. I couldn't hear over the pounding of my heart. How could I explain away these pictures?

"I—"

"The photos tell a different story?" Elise smirked and stood again, clicking her heel against the floor. Her angry eyes radiated a ferocious, unbending intellect.

"I can explain." The words popped out of my mouth before I can stop them or figure out a reasonable explanation.

I took a chance and read her mind. Outside, she appeared cool and collected, but inside her thoughts raged. Her son lowered to deviant status. It terrified her how the Council of Seven would perceive her in the future. She debated which of the seven families she could count on to support her. She wasn't about to let everything she worked so hard for, go down the drain because of her son. I never had a mother, but shouldn't she feel alarmed or distressed about the fate of her son?

"Be quiet. I'm talking now. These pictures prove Slade lied about knowing you." Elise said. "I showed them to my husband as proof that you are not an innocent bystander, but someone well acquainted with our son. I told him you must be as guilty as Slade, but he wouldn't listen to me. He ordered me to leave you alone."

She circled the table to stand directly behind me, leaning over my shoulder, whispering right into my ear. "What does Slade hold over

Joseph to make him protect you?" She twisted the diamond encrusted wedding ring on her finger absently.

Was I supposed to answer these questions or stay silent?

Her eyes flashed. "Why would my son protect you? Are you in love with him?"

Where had that question come from? I played with the zipper of my coveralls, wishing I could disappear. "No. I barely know him."

"Your blush gives you away."

"It's not what you think. I just met him yesterday, only yesterday."

"Achoo!" The man in the white baggy clothing sneezed. They were so quiet standing in the corner I almost forgot they were in the room.

Elise snapped her attention to the man in the suit. "Titus, we should start the interrogation now. This would be over by now if you didn't spend so much time getting here."

Stop, go, fast, slow. Her speeds were giving me whiplash.

"My apologies, Madam," Titus said. "The Authority delayed me in the vault and Simon—."

"Titus, you should know how to deal with a deviant by now. If you can't do your job properly, then I will find someone who will."

He had my full attention. So, the guy with the braided beard—Simon—was also a deviant? Maybe he could help me. Did he see Callahan and Slade in the vault? Were they okay? Did he know how to get there? I needed his help. How could I convince him to help me?

"Yes, madam."

Titus made Simon raise his right hand, then used a device to remove the silver bracelet with a click. Titus warned him what would happen if he misbehaved. Simon rubbed the spot on his wrist where the bracelet had been. He walked over and immediately placed his hands on my temples. I jerked back instinctively to avoid being touched.

Simon paused; a sympathetic look crossed his face. "I'm terribly sorry. I should have asked permission before I touched your face. May I touch you?" There was a kindness in his eyes. His aura projected sky blue. Blues were truthful, serene, and excellent communicators.

Titus, on the other hand, had a gray aura like mine, which meant he didn't trust anyone or anything.

I blinked my assent. He placed a hand against each temple. I threaded my fingers together to stop my hands from shaking. I felt sick to my stomach.

"Is she a deviant, Simon?" Elise asked, clacking her heel against the floor.

"It takes more than a few minutes, madam," Titus told Elise. "A mind is a tricky place, and it is not always easy to extract information immediately."

Simon ignored the question but continued to touch my head. I put up a barrier so he couldn't read my thoughts, but he broke it down. No one had ever shattered my barrier before; it felt like a violation. He combed through all my memories as if he could download the images from my head. This wasn't telepathy, this was something else. He extracted information.

"Can you hear me?" he asked.

"Y . . . yes."

"I am so sorry for the intrusion into your thoughts. My name is Simon. You don't have to worry; I won't tell them anything. The TCC has enough of us under their control. Just bear with me and follow my lead."

"Um... Thank you." Was there a proper response to someone sifting through your brain? Filtering through your life? Flipping through my memories like pages in a book.

"How did you break down my barrier?"

"I'm a zapper."

"What is a zapper?"

"A zapper is..."

"Simon, are you getting anywhere?" Titus asked.

"Almost there," Simon replied.

"Ugh, this is ridiculous." Elise threw up her arms in exasperation. "Titus. I thought I told you to bring me the best zapper we had. I would hate to see how bad the others are if he is your best."

"Are you part of the rebels? Do you know anything about their plans?"

"No, no, I don't. I promise. Today is the first I have heard about the rebels. Well, since Zander's crew... years ago."

Simon continued to touch his hands to my temples. I wanted to pull away from him.

"How well did you know Slade Cutter? Never mind your memories will tell me."

I didn't know what to make of him. Just because he hadn't yet revealed my deviant status didn't mean he wouldn't. *"What's going to happen?"*

Simon quickly related his heartbreaking story. It was like a download, quicker than conversation. Discovered as a child, the commission forced him to work against other deviants. The silver bracelets "restrainers" can control abilities; when deviants wear them, we are unable to access their powers. He lived a life of solitude in the vault with other deviants like him.

He described the vault in such detail I could picture it: a sterilized, spotlessly clean environment. White alloy lining the walls and ceiling, synthetic access panels on the floors and walls. Steel plating beside metal grates. Halogen lights on eighteen hours a day. Endless rows of cells, each with a bed with a thin mattress, a sink, and a toilet. Red lasers crossing the compartment opening keep the prisoners in their cells.

"Did you see anyone new in the vault? Two men, one with spiked hair and an angular face, the other with a white streak and a thin white scar on his jaw. Both young; my age."

"I saw the boy with the white streak. I would know Slade Cutter anywhere. I didn't see the other boy."

We locked eyes. I promised to keep his secrets, and he promised to keep mine. He dropped his hands to his sides.

"What did you learn, Simon?" Titus asked. He played with the restrainer, fastening, then unfastening it until the clasp threatened to break.

"Yes, Simon, do tell us what you've learned." Elise perched on the edge of the table, swinging a leg back and forth.

"Madam, the girl is not a deviant. Charlie is no threat. She met your son at the Stone last night. They had a flirtation... a fling, for lack of a better word. She chased after him, trying to pursue the relationship. He wasn't interested in her and tried to let her down easy. The other boy got jealous and threw the first punch. Stupid teenage stuff." He rubbed his wrist, waving toward the monitor. "Just look at the photos. There's your proof."

"You aren't painting me in the best light. Callahan would never throw a punch because of jealousy. He is like my brother."

"Better, she thinks you are a gold-digger than a rebel."

"Thank you... I guess. Do you... know where my friend Callahan could be? They sentenced him to the vault, just like Slade. Where else would they take him?" The rescue would be problematic if they weren't together. Extra complicated.

A shadow crossed his face. *"There is another place they could have taken him, but you better pray he isn't there."*

"Where?"

"The Nest, if he's there you must—."

"Is she a rebel?" Elise asked.

"No, madam."

She raised an eyebrow as if she doubted him. "Are you sure?"

"Quite sure, madam."

A vein pulsated in her neck. "Fine, you are dismissed. Thank you for nothing."

"My apologies, madam," Titus said. "Sometimes—."

"Hold your tongue, Titus." Elise snapped her head up as if remembering something. "Instruct Simon to zap her so she doesn't remember this conversation."

Why didn't she just give the order to Simon herself? My eyes widened at the term "zap." Um, no thanks, that doesn't sound good. I would rather avoid being zapped.

"Simon, please proceed, you heard Mrs. Cutter."

"Madam, is that necessary? She knows nothing; she has learned nothing. There is no point in damaging her brain with an unnecessary procedure."

Titus paled, jerking his head up. He gave Simon a warning look. "Simon, hush, you know better than to speak to Mrs. Cutter directly. It is not your place to question her."

Elise tilted her head as if to ponder his request. "Proceed."

Simon touched his fingers to my temples again, his mouth turned down at the corners. *I'm so sorry. I have no choice.* His hands shook, vibrating against my forehead.

What were they going to do to me? I blinked up at him to tell him I understood.

"Never mind. Simon. Leave it for now. Maybe knowing about zappers would be good for the Subs. Teach them what we have the power to do if we want."

He dropped his hands to his sides, as if they burned hot. Relief flooded his body. He moved away from me.

"Titus, if you would take Simon back to his home, we can all get back to our lives and forget this entire misuse of time." She re-stacked the files she had extracted, collecting them one by one.

Titus approached Simon, placing the silver bracelet back on his wrist, severing the link between us. Titus gave two quick knocks, and the guards opened the door. Simon wiggled his fingers goodbye as he exited the room. Alone with Elise, again. Wonderful.

"So, you had a moment with my son and now what. What was your plan? I'll bet you wish you never met him now that you know he's a mutant."

I should say something, but what, she didn't want to hear my side of the story. People like Elise only talk, they never listen. They don't place any value on anyone's opinion but their own.

"Did you think you were the first girl from the East End to attempt to entrap my son? What did you think would happen? Do you think you would fall in love, move to the West End, and live 'the good life'? Is that what you hoped? Someone like you could never be with somebody like my son." Her voice picked up volume as she talked.

"I just liked him." Simon's story seemed the most logical choice to keep following.

"Have you ever been inside the West End?" She punched something into the tablet and a log appeared on the screen. "No, there are no records. Well. Good. Today's your lucky day."

ELISE GAVE two quick raps on the door and motioned for me to follow her. The Authority fell into line behind us. We walked in silence until we reached the West End checkpoint. The guards waved us through, although they scanned me with a security wand and patted me down. Elise barked at them to hurry.

Crossing into the West End was as different as crossing into a strange alternative world. Bright, vivid shades adorned the freshly painted walls. Paving stones lined the floor. Everything shone shiny and fresh. My eyes scanned the area, taking in the dissimilarity between the East and West ends. I loved the color. How wonderful it must be to live here. A form appeared before me, something I had only seen in books until now. Unable to move, I stood still while the enormous creature approached me. Another creature appeared behind him, and I could only watch.

The dogs came up to me, sniffing my legs, brushing up against me. For a moment I stood frozen, unable to decide whether to run, double back through the gate or just scream. The bigger dog growled, baring his teeth while the smaller dog sneezed on me.

Elise whistled, and the canines returned to her side. Elise bent to pat the big dog on the head. "Sit Bruno." Bruno sat.

Bruno, a German Shepard, stood tall with black and white markings on his thick fur, an arched forehead, and an extended square-cut muzzle. His ears were huge and stood erect but pulled back during movement. His powerful jaws looked like they could snap me in two. A spiked collar encircled his neck.

A smaller tan dog, a pug, with a fine fawn coat, appeared at his side. The dog had a wrinkly, short-muzzled face, with a curled tail. His eyes were dark brown; the saddest eyes I had ever seen. Etched on his collar was the name "Brutus." Brutus wore a sweatshirt with a hood—better dressed than half the East End. Since the bigger dog hadn't attacked me, I slowly bent to pet the smaller dog, but Elise scooped it up before I could reach him. The timbre of her voice changed as she spoke to the dog, whispering ridiculous made-up words.

My friends would never believe there were dogs in the West End. I couldn't wait to tell Callahan. Then my heart ached with the memory that I could not. My stomach clenched with worry at the thought of him. Without him, I felt like I was dying by degree.

Elise moved down the hall carrying the dog. "Bruno, come." She didn't give me any instructions, but I followed behind her and Bruno just the same. The guards trailed behind us.

We strolled past several stores displaying fashion, shoes, and jewelry. It looked like new things, not all worn out like what we would sell at the bazaar. The bazaar in the East End couldn't begin to rival these shops. A man dressed in multi hues with a black top hat played a black baby-grand piano, providing background music for shoppers. Music to shop by, only in the West End. What surprised me the most were the cut flowers everywhere, roses, lilies, sunflowers, and others I didn't have names for. We didn't have food to eat and they were growing flowers.

A bake shop window displayed scrumptious treats; loaves of bread lined the window. The air tasted delicious as the aroma wafted out the door, causing my stomach to grumble. Was the purpose of this excursion? Did she just want to rub the things we didn't have in my face?

Elise picked up the pace. We entered Building 14, climbing the stairs to apartment 3B according to the sign on the door. Elise raised her tag to open the door when the beautiful Toni Tango beat her to it. Toni appeared to be on her way out. She was a tiny girl with radiant brown skin: the word "beautiful" was not sufficient to describe her. With full lips, expressive dark eyes, lashes too thick to be real, she was immaculately dressed, with impeccable hair and makeup. As close to perfect as a woman could look.

"Toni, what a pleasant surprise. I didn't expect you to be here." Elise hugged Toni, air-kissing both her cheeks.

"Have you heard any news on Slade?" Toni asked. If the news about her intended upset her, she hid it well. Her eyes were clear. She looked at me strangely, but didn't question why we were entering the apartment. "Any chance of a pardon or release?"

"Hush dear, that's not for you to worry about. We will find you another quality match. Don't you worry your pretty little head about it."

Toni visibly brightened with her words. Elise gave her another quick hug and waved her on her way. We stepped into the room.

I winced as a voice rang out. "Good afternoon Master Cutter. How was your day? Is there anything I can do for you?" An artificial intelligent (AI) cartoon character lit up on all the monitors in the room, ready to serve Slade's needs.

"What are you waiting for? Come in," Elise commanded. "Take a good look around."

The massive room was amazing. Beautiful pieces of art hung on the walls. Was that the original Mona Lisa? The room had a sprawling sectional sofa and armchairs; a glass desk stood off to the side with several computer monitors hooked up. Photographs on the mantle above the fireplace showed the Cutter family in better times. The center photo displayed Slade, Ajax, and Toni with their arms around each other; smiles as wide as this room. A gray and orange cat slept, cuddled up in a soft slate-colored blanket. Perfectly content to while away the day sleeping on the comfortable sofa. It stirred, raising its head to look in their direction, stretched, then settled back into the blanket.

The old-fashioned parquet floor blended brown and tans together; area rugs scattered throughout. A table that seated twelve people looked like it was constructed out of genuine wood; I ran my hands across the table, unable to resist touching it.

Embarrassed, I glimpsed over my shoulder to see if Elise watched me. No. She was too busy ordering the guards to feed the dogs from silver bowls on the floor etched with their names.

There were three doors at the back of the room I opted to explore. One door opened into a bathroom with a stone and glass shower with a marble vanity. The word luxurious was not even capable of describing it. I knew my mouth hung open. Slade could shower in privacy. I couldn't even imagine it; it must be heaven. I'll bet he even had hot water.

The other two doors opened into enormous bedrooms, the wide beds could sleep three or four people comfortably. I wondered how many people lived here.

After I finished my tour, Elise said, "This is Slade's apartment. This is what you cost my son. This is where he would have brought his wife, where he would have raised his children, my grandchildren. You cost my son his future." Her voice started as a whisper but ended in a yell. Her thoughts didn't match her words.

My mouth opened and closed without words escaping. This is where Slade lived. By himself. One person had all this space. In the East End, twenty or thirty people would have been happy to share this space.

Elise inched closer until we were standing nose to nose. "I don't know why Joseph didn't send you to the vault. He will not tell me what Slade threatened him with. Know this, I will find out the truth. When I do, I will have you exiled if it's the last thing I ever do. Just like your father. Until then, you will spend every day here in the Hollows in misery. I'll make sure of it. You embarrassed me, you cost me my son. I will do everything in my power to ruin your life and the lives of everyone you care about. You're playing my game now and I am unbeatable."

I wrapped my arms around my torso, aware I had just made a powerful enemy. Tears threatened, but I blinked them back.

Elise opened the door to the room and spoke to the Authority. "Escort her back to her quarters."

13

I could hear the sobs as soon as I entered the building, the raw primal sounds of a breaking heart. If I had a time machine, I would go back to when I picked up the box and leave it on the ground. I climbed the stairs slower than normal, putting off the uncomfortable discussion I knew I had to have with my friends. My shaky hand gripped the doorknob; I hesitated a moment, bracing myself before pulling the door open.

Gibson and Reese lay entangled on the bed, their arms wrapped around each other. Reese consoled Gibson as she cried. Gibson used Reese's shoulder as a pillow. Reese looked up and met my gaze with fire in her eyes.

"Would you look at that? Charlie Edge back from the edge of oblivion. Untouched. Saved from damnation by the heroic men in her life." Reese bared her teeth snarling, "You know, everyone is entitled to act foolishly once in a while, but you misuse the privilege."

Gibson lifted her head. Her eyes were red-rimmed and puffy. She wiped at the tears on her face with the sleeve of her shirt. "What happened today? I still don't understand how things went so wrong so fast."

Stuffed up from sobbing, Gibson sounded like she had a cold.

Without warning, she jumped off the bed, flying at me in a rage. She grabbed my shirt by the collar, shoving me hard against the steel door. I shrieked as my back slammed against the doorknob. It didn't hurt as much as when Gibson looked at me as if I were a stranger. She pulled back, her fist ready to hit me before Reese intervened, placing herself between us. I put up my hands, surrendering to the venom of Gibson's attack.

"No, G don't," Reese said. "You can't get an assault charge too."

"At least then I could see my brother," Gibson said.

For a moment, I had hoped that Reese decided to defend me, but she didn't. I'd prepared for their anger, practicing what I would say. How I would explain the compounding of events that had left us all heartbroken and bewildered.

Tears welled up as her sadness overcame my emotions. I blinked several times before speaking. "I... I'm so sorry; so sorry. I..." The words fell away. I couldn't meet her eyes. I was drowning in their sea of tears.

"Don't. I don't need to hear your pathetic excuses," Gibson transmitted.

Gibson sobbed again; Reese pulled her into an embrace, stroking her lower back, softly mumbling sympathetic words. The fight had gone out of her; she stayed stiff for a moment before melting into Reese.

"I'm so sorry... if I knew... if someone... if anyone had told me what would happen... I would have done things, differently. You know that, right?"

"Save it. Look what your *obsession* with Slade Cutter has gotten us. Look at what happened to Callahan. Are you happy now? Is this what you wanted? Huh? DOES THIS MAKE YOU HAPPY?" Reese's voice chilled with every word she spoke.

A sizable lump had formed in my throat. I croaked, "How can you think this is what I wanted? Don't you think I feel bad enough? Don't you think my heart is breaking? This isn't my fault, Reese. I never asked Callahan to get involved. I never intended for him to get caught up with any of this."

Gibson's head jerked up. She moved out of Reese's embraced towards me. "Caught up with what? What exactly are you 'caught up' with, Charlie?" Reese watched Gibson like a hawk. "Is it just Slade or is something else going on? Did you have something to do with the rebel box?"

I ducked my head and gave it a slight shake. "It doesn't matter, not anymore." Thousands of "if only" scenarios ran through my brain. At what point could I have changed things to prevent this outcome? It felt like a game of dominos where one tile fell over and toppled them all.

"It matters, Charlie, it matters more than anything else." Gibson collapsed back on the bed, shoulders slumped, rocking back and forth. She grabbed a pillow, wrapping her arms around it; she stared straight forward, her eyes blank and haunted.

Reese moved towards Gibson to be close but seemed unsure of what to do.

"My brother's gone; I'll never see him again."

I covered my face with my hands, pushing my hair behind my ears. I shuffled my feet in place, my back still against the cold steel door.

"It's my fault too. I could have stopped it, but I didn't." Gibson grasped the pillow tighter.

"How?"

"G, don't even say something so silly. You know it's not your fault," Reese said. Her face made it plain that she blamed me.

"I had a vision this morning at the assembly, remember. That's why I sent Callahan to get you, Charlie. In my vision, I saw you with Slade kneeling before the stage, but Callahan wasn't there. I shouldn't have sent him to warn you. Arggg. What good is having these stupid visions if they don't come early enough to change anything?" Gibson threw the pillow across the room. When it didn't have the desired effect, she stood up and started pacing in the limited space.

"G, we know who's to blame—and it's not you." Reese jerked her head in my direction. Reese could hold a grudge. She once went six months without speaking to me when I wore one of her t-shirts.

"Callahan is my best friend. His loss hurts me just as much as it hurts you. I love him too. Don't you get it?" Couldn't they see I grieved too?

"I know... I know you do. I just—"

"You know, I didn't realize until today, but you look just like Zander, especially with your hair uncovered," Reese interrupted.

I shuffled my feet. "I know. Don't remind me."

"How many deaths are you going to be responsible for?"

"It was a mistake coming here." I reached for the doorknob.

"Go, then. Leave. See if I care," Gibson said.

I spun around, grasped for the doorknob. It was too much; I had to get out of the room. I found the latch and ripped open the door, slamming it shut behind me. Taking the stairs two at a time, I burst through the doors of our building into the hallway, bending over at the waist, fighting for breath. I stopped and looked around, wondering how I got here. Not to this location, but at this point in my life. Wrenching my head up, I searched for somewhere to throw up, and found a garbage can close by. I gripped the edges tightly as I emptied the contents of my stomach. When I came up for air, I jumped; a figure stood over me.

"Are you okay?" Memphis asked. He stood, shoulders slumped, his hands crammed into the pockets of his coveralls. He had lost most of his anger since we last saw each other.

I shook my head and walked over to the water fountain to wash out my mouth. The 7:00 pm dinner horn sounded. My world had changed, but the schedule of the bunker persisted. It felt like a week had passed since yesterday. A member of the Authority watched us with interest. I tried to slouch down and become invisible.

"Are you going to eat?"

"I can't eat. I'm hollow inside." The throbbing in my head returned, stronger than ever.

"Yeah, me neither. Do you want to do something, maybe go for a walk?"

We fell into step, strolling in silence, both of us lost in our own thoughts, circling the corridors with no destination in mind. We avoided talking about Callahan. We had never really been alone before. Although we were part of the same friend group, we weren't close.

Just ahead of us, Remy and her friends flirted with a young soldier. "Woah, Blondie, you look awful. Have you looked in the mirror recently?" Remy called out as we passed. Her friends broke out laughing.

"You do that plenty enough for both of us," I shot back.

She snapped back her head, surprised, then gave a tiny smile.

Rounding the corner, we walked into a stop and frisk. Two members of the Authority blocked off the hallway, checking identification tags, something they did regularly. They noticed us so we couldn't back up and go another way without drawing suspicion. A guard patted me down and let me go. The other guard checked Memphis with extra enthusiasm, giving him a shove into the rock wall face first. They hit him in the back, the ribs, and the back of the knees with a baton.

We hadn't been doing anything besides walking. I balled my hands into fists. Enough was enough. Something snapped, and before I could stop myself, I screamed, "Leave him alone." The force of my voice threw the guards back about five feet, slamming them against the wall. They dropped to the floor like a ton of bricks and didn't move.

I stood there bewildered, unable to budge. Memphis stood pressed flat against the wall; we exchanged a look. He rubbed his eyes, skeptical of what he had seen.

An alarm sounded and lights flashed. I glanced up, looking for the cameras that captured everything. Soon more of the Authority would pour into the hallways. I looked both ways, trying to figure out which way to go. My knees wobbled like jelly while my feet stood frozen in place.

Memphis recovered quicker than I did. Placing both hands in front of his chest, he gripped and pulled at the air. The air shifted, swirling, becoming white and hazy. He dragged at the edges, creating an opening. The hole became transparent. I could see beyond our location to somewhere else. Like seeing two places at once.

"Quick, give me your hand," Memphis said. "I don't know how long I can hold it open."

A quick look at the guards let me know they had stirred and would soon be back on their feet. I placed my hand in his and we dove through the opening, alighting on a hard cement floor. My left shoulder absorbed most of the impact. The breath whooshed from my body. The opening immediately shrunk until it disappeared.

We lay there for a moment, recovering. I propped myself up on one elbow to see where we had landed. The compact room had shelving on two sides stocked with supplies. Mops, brooms, and dustpans hung on one wall with a door on the remaining wall. The air held a tinge of bleach or antiseptic.

"Are we in a closet?" I asked.

"Is that your takeaway after everything that just happened?" Memphis cracked up. He laughed long and hard until he grasped his side in pain. "We are so screwed."

I tried to fight the laughter, but it burst free with loud, involuntary howls. You can only be strong for so long then you break. I could laugh or cry. My entire life I had done the peaceful thing, chosen the easy road. I kept my head down and stayed inside the lines, but I see now I wasn't really living, just surviving.

Memphis hurried over to a gray device and turned a few dials until the box hummed. "It will block the trackers in our tags."

"Good to know." I didn't know such a thing was possible, but tech wasn't my thing.

Once I recovered my breath, I sat upright. Rotating my left arm, I flexed my shoulder, rubbing at the soreness, trying to massage away the pain. "What are we going to do?"

Memphis shrugged his shoulders. "Umm, good question. I don't know, but I have a couple ideas." A gash bridged his nose. He wiped at it and his hand came away bloody. His face had a few scratches and his left eye puffed out. It would soon close from the swelling.

Memphis gingerly touched his side where the guards hit him, wincing when he felt a sore area. "I think they broke my ribs."

"Can I look?" I asked, gesturing towards his face. The guard had done a number on him. He nodded. I place my hand next to his eye socket and gently touched all around his eye. The blood vessels had burst under the skin. He winced. "Your nose is broken. They definitely left a mark."

"It's fine. I've been through the same thing lots of times." Memphis shook me off and moved away before I could check his ribs. I expected him to be pulsating with fear or rage, but he didn't project any emotions.

"How do you know how to do that, whatever it was?" I asked. My mind pushed away all the trouble we were in, refusing to think about it. Our old lives were over.

"I'm not talking about this with you, it's private and irrelevant. Plus, I could ask you the same question." He stood up, dusting off his jeans, extending a hand to pull me up.

I reached up to grab his hand. "I have absolutely no idea. It has never happened before. Light is shooting out of my hand, and I can throw people with my voice. Two things I could never imagine even saying, let alone doing, yesterday. I'm an open book, Memphis, no secrets."

I rummaged through the supplies, trying to distract myself from the horror show my life had become. All-purpose cleaners, disinfectants, cleaning clothes, toilet paper, and various other boxes stocked the shelves; nothing worth pilfering. "Memphis, I know we are still in the Hollows, but where exactly are we?"

He remained stubbornly silent.

"Come on Memphis, I don't understand why you won't share with me. You made an immense hole in the air and pulled us through space to this... closet. It's obviously not a secret anymore." I needed answers and I would annoy him until I got them.

He raised his shoulders in a silent "so?"

"Jumping jeepers... What was that? How long have you been able to do that? Who knows you can do that? And where exactly are we?" I counted off the questions on my fingers.

He closed his lips and blew his cheeks full of air. "First teleporting, second five, third a couple people and fourth, we are in a maintenance closet in the basement of my residence. This is where I go when I am in trouble. Sometimes I come down here when I need to be alone. It's difficult to get a moment to yourself when you sleep in a dorm with fifty other people."

"You come down here to hide in a closet?"

"Not the closet..." He walked over and pulled a shelf away from the wall. Behind the shelf, a large metal grate stood about three feet square. Unclipping it from its bracket, he pulled the cover off to display a galvanized steel tunnel. He duck-walked into the opening. He said something, but the staccato percussive thump of each step drowned out his muffled voice.

My curiosity piqued. I followed him into the tunnel, choosing to crawl on my hands and knees. It only went about five feet before it opened into another tiny room. Memphis doubled back, pulling the shelf back into place and restoring the cover over the grate.

Drawings covered the walls, black and white portraits of people and imaginary characters. One image sparked a memory, but the thought fluttered past too fast to grab. I spotted a caricature of myself and traced the lines of my face; it seemed so lifelike. He used to draw when we were at Voco, but I didn't know he had kept up with it.

In the corner lay a thin mattress with a ratty blanket, an old laptop, and some tattered comic books. I sauntered over to see what other treasures I could find. Dropping to my knees, I noticed a tiny shabby brown teddy bear, missing one eye and an ear, stuffing emptied from various holes. I remembered the bear from the orphanage. Memphis wouldn't go anywhere without the bear when we were little.

I reached to pick up the bear; I think he named it Kenny, but the look he shot me made me change my mind. "I can't believe you still have the bear."

His head jerked up, then he snorted and said, "Yeah, I tried to throw it away, but I couldn't. It's one of the few things I have left..." His voice trailed off.

"So, do you live here? Don't they miss you in the dormitory?" I thumbed through the comics; it gave me something to do besides look at Memphis.

"I just stay here sometimes. Not too often or they would notice."

"How did you find this place?"

He hesitated. "By accident, I spilled some cleaning solutions over by the grate. I had to open the grill up to clean and crawled through to find this little niche. It's not even in the plans for this complex. I checked. It's a forgotten space."

"Nice! You have your own untraceable apartment." I shoved my hair back over my shoulder. It constantly got in my face without my hat, annoying me.

"I guess, sort of. I wish I could stay here all the time."

"How did you learn how to teleport? Do you teleport in and out?" Talking with Memphis was frustrating. It felt like pulling teeth to get any answers.

"It's crazy, but I remember the first time I opened a portal. At Voco. Mrs. Pearson kicked me out of class into the hallway. I punched at the air when suddenly the air shifted, and I ended up back at the orphanage. Scared the crap out of me. It took me a while to figure out how to use it properly. Never pulled anyone through with me before. I wasn't even sure it would work."

"You didn't know you could take someone through the portal... and you pulled me through it with you. Are you crazy? You could have killed me." My voice came out at a higher pitch than I wanted.

"Relax, you're fine. It worked, didn't it? They didn't arrest us."

The Authority would be searching for us by now. They would find us soon. I sobered at the thought. I dropped the comic back in the pile and a photo fluttered out. Reaching to pick it up, I gave it a quick look before studying it further.

"Why do you have this photo? Do you know the woman in the photo?" I asked, tripping over my words.

"My mom. It's my parents and me as a baby."

"That's impossible."

"What's impossible?"

"I saw this woman this morning. She had a young boy with her. The boy had blond hair like mine. But they exiled your mother with all the others, with Zander. She's dead." When Memphis did not reply, I added, "Isn't she?"

I watched the emotion play out on his face. "No, she's still alive."

14

———————

I slumped back against the wall, grabbing my head with my hands before it exploded Questions flooded my mind and I needed answers. "How Memphis... how can she be alive? I don't understand?"

Memphis wavered, tilting his head from side to side as if weighing his choices. "My mother didn't die. She's alive. Some people from the first exile survived."

"I don't believe you." I studied his face, waiting for something, some hint he was lying. My abilities told me he wasn't. Thunder! I pulled at the collar of my shirt to loosen it; there wasn't enough air in this tiny room. "Zander?" I held my breath, waiting for his answer. If the answer was yes, I honestly didn't know how I felt. Did I want the person responsible for my mother's death to be alive or dead?

Memphis frowned, then tilted his head from side to side, weighing his options. He hesitated before giving a slight nod.

"I can't believe it . . . I saw the exile footage. I saw them. I saw Zander . . . the recording shows them walking into the abyss with nothing but their clothing." I lost my train of thought, unable to absorb any more information. Could Zander still be alive? It wasn't possible.

I sent Memphis a pleading look, asking him to fill in the missing blanks, but he remained obstinately silent.

I felt like someone had punched me in the stomach. "Please Memphis, tell me what you know. I can't take much more. The blows keep coming and coming. The past forty-eight hours have changed… everything. Everything I once believed to be true is a lie."

"So, what you are telling me is you have been having a couple of rough days. Boohoo. Who hasn't? This isn't about you. You are not the center of the world. How do you think Callahan feels right now or Gibson?"

"Forget you, Memphis. You knew about Zander, and you didn't tell me. How long have you known my father was alive? How long have you been in contact with your mother?" I advanced on him. I felt the anger surge through my body. I wish I had something to hit. "What about Gibson, Callahan, and Reese's parents?"

Memphis shook his head, then turned to walk away from me, but I grabbed his arm, catching him unawares. I spun him back around.

"I can't believe you. I know you don't like me but… jumping jeepers, don't you think I deserved to know?" I dropped the photo like a hot potato.

He grabbed for the photo before it hit the floor, straightening the image tenderly. He picked up the comic and tucked it back between the pages. "I wanted to tell you, but I couldn't. I had orders. He didn't want you to know."

"Who? Who didn't want me to know?"

He tried to turn away, but he couldn't avoid me in this tiny, concealed room.

"Your father."

"Zander? You've talked to Zander?"

"The General… your father didn't want you to know yet, he wanted to keep you out of it."

"You call Zander the General? Keep me out of what? You are talking but not telling me anything…" I went quiet, trying to collect myself and he didn't interrupt. "That's it, isn't it?"

He raised his hands in a soundless what.

I wheeled on him, and he stepped back, hitting the wall. "That's why... you never let me read your thoughts."

"No, I just don't want people inside my head. Everything here is just so crowded, there's no space and I just need to have my brain to myself, without a conversation in my head." Memphis rubbed the side of his nose, a clear tell he was lying.

"I'm calling malarkey."

Memphis looked to defend himself, but I raised a hand to stop him.

"Never mind, it doesn't matter, not now, anyways. We have bigger problems."

"I know."

"We can't hide here forever. The Authority will find us soon. Once the TCC reviews the feed, they can identify our faces. What are we going to do Memphis?"

"I'm not sure; I've been trying to contact the General all day for my orders."

"Are you working for the rebels?"

He nodded.

"Memphis . . ."

"What?"

"Nothing." I moved away from him, stumbling over his scratched and dented laptop. An idea crossed my mind. "Does this laptop work?"

"Yeah. Why?"

"Can you get on the network?"

"Don't let the way this laptop looks fool you. It's completely rebuilt." He picked it up and flipped it on. It only took a second to boot-up. He propped the laptop up on a shelf so I could see the screen.

"That's not a standard-issue laptop. Where did you get it?"

"I work for maintenance, remember? They send stuff like this down to the reclaim area all the time. This one just never got there." He typed furiously until he logged onto the internal network. "What are you thinking?"

"We need to get a message to Blaze. If she can remove our faces from the security feed, we might be safe for a bit."

"Yeah, no. She'll never do it, she's not one of us anymore, remember."

"I remember, but she used to be. She grew up with us. Part of the Six Pack. It's worth a shot. Can you do it, or not? Contact her tag without being traced."

"Maybe, probably, but she abandoned us the first chance she got. She's the flipping Secretary of Communications. She won't help."

"She didn't abandon us; she had no choice. She tested off the charts with her computer skills. No one could code like her." Blaze had broken into the intranet enough times the TCC finally let her design the new system to keep out other hackers like her. It surprised us when they recruited her instead of sending her to the vault or exiling her. They must have really needed someone with her skills.

"I can."

I waved my hand in a dismissive gesture when he protested. "They conscripted her, but can you blame her? I've seen the West End. If I were her, I wouldn't come back to the East End either."

Since I discovered the luxury of the West End, I could understand why she had never been back. Who could give up living in lavishness? Not to mention, the power her job gave her, Secretary of Communications. I'm sure it became addicting. Still, I just couldn't understand how she could walk away from us and never look back. We were friends—family—yet she never came back for a visit. Once, Blaze walked down a hallway where I worked. When she saw me, she put her headphones in her ears and didn't even acknowledge me. It stung.

"She won't help us. She stands on stage during the assembly as if she's royalty. You saw her today; she wouldn't even look at us when they sentenced Callahan. I tried to catch her attention, but she looked through me as if I were a total stranger." Memphis' fatigued voice was filled with resignation. He stopped typing. "Are you sure about this? She could turn us in."

"We don't have a choice, but if you've got another suggestion, I'm all ears."

"This could be a colossal mistake. We can't trust her. If she turns us in, this is on you."

"It wouldn't be the first time I've made a mistake. Not even the first mistake today. But give me another option and I'll listen. She's kept our secret this far. She knows we are deviants, and she has never told."

"Only because she's a deviant, too! We keep her secret, she keeps ours." Memphis said. "Otherwise, it's mutually assured destruction."

Blaze had telepathic abilities, but it wasn't her real gift. She could use technology psychically as a technopath. She communicated with machines better than people. Her eyes went weird when she connected to a computer. Numbers, letters, and binary code flashed behind her eyes. She remembered everything she ever read or heard.

Memphis paused with his hands over the computer keys for an eternity. Then he typed:

```
Blaze
Please Help
In a Jam
Need security footage erased
- MT & CE
```

We watched the screen, waiting for a response. The cursor blinked forever. I felt my hopes slip away. If she could erase the digital feed, we could have a slim chance to rescue Callahan and Slade. If the rebels survived outside this long, so could we. For the first time, I felt hopeful about saving them. I had been assembling a plan in the back of my mind, but something still seemed to be missing.

Almost an hour later, the screen blipped with two words. I had to look twice to believe it.

```
Done!
- Blaze
```

Memphis and I exchanged a look of relief. A half-smile crossed his face.

The laptop buzzed again. Blaze's face appeared on the screen with her trademarked red glasses balanced on her nose. "Hey guys, in trouble again I see," she said casually. She acted as it had only been a few days since we last spoke instead of years.

She had an earbud in one ear, while the other dangled loosely. Music played, but she had turned the volume too low for me to over-hear the song. She used to have unconventional music tastes every-thing from pop to country to rock to jazz. She must have listened to everything in the archives.

I felt lost for words. What did you say to an old friend who turned into a stranger? I know at times people think I am being rude when I take so long to respond, but sometimes, I just need time to figure out what to say.

Memphis jumped in. "Hey stranger? How are things? I'm shocked you still remember your old pals back in the East. Now that you are big time."

"Memphis be nice," I reprimanded him. Why would he be so mean to her after she had just done us a huge favor? "So, did you do it? Did you erase the footage?"

"Duh, what do you think 'done' means?"
I ignored the insult. "Thank you. It means a lot that you are helping us. Will you get into any trouble?" I should have thought it through before I asked her for help. I had already gotten Callahan in trouble; I wouldn't want to put anyone else in harm's ways.

"No, I'm golden. I erased it from the system before you even asked."

I raised my eyebrow in a silent why.
"I was there this morning, Charlie. They arrested Callahan, and I just had to sit there helpless... nothing I could do. I wouldn't let the commission take you guys too if I could do anything to stop it." Her glasses kept sliding down her nose, causing her to push them back up continuously.

"Wow, you're my hero Blaze." Memphis mocked. "Should have been simple work for someone with a genius-level IQ."

"Cut it out."

"Well, yes Memphis, elementary work for me but it would be hard for someone of your aptitude."

"Why? Why did you erase the footage?" I interrupted. "Was it for..."

Blaze ran her tongue over her front teeth. "I always watch out for you guys whenever I can."

"Really?" I did a double-take.

"I've also disabled the trackers on your tags."

"I already looked after that." Memphis added.

I turned back to the screen. "Thank you, Blaze."

"Yeah, you could say I've been acting as a protector; watching after you, erasing any troubling behavior, not that you guys needed much help. You play by the rules."

Memphis made a disbelieving noise in his throat. I hoped the same look didn't appear on my face. I thought she had left us behind when they drafted her. Off to better and more important things. Maybe we had been too hard on her for leaving.

"Did you see my interrogation with Elise?"

"Yes, I've erased levitating apples and footage of you complaining about your demerit points ... what else." She tapped her fingers across her lips. "I have scrambled the feed and mikes in your room so you can talk freely. They don't watch you now as much since they don't think you are deviants.... they think you are harmless Subs."

"Then you know about the captured deviants and how the TCC is using them? You know about Simon and the horrible conditions within the vault?"

"What are you talking about? What deviants?" Memphis questioned. He tugged at my arm, forcing me to split my attention.

"You are not the only one who has secrets, Memphis. How do you like being left in the dark?"

His face fell.

"I'll fill you in later."

"You'd better," he warned.

"They use captured deviants in various ways. Simon isn't the only one." Blaze hunched her shoulders, head down, typing furiously.

"And you can't help him?" I hated thinking about all the people the TCC were exploiting. "Can't help any of them?"

"Charlie, I'm just one person. I don't run the place. I do all I can do, but even I have my limits." Blaze adopted a challenging tone.

I felt her flicker of irritation. I don't know why I expected more from Blaze when I had never stuck my neck out for anything. She had done more for us than I had ever done for anyone. "Blaze, my bad, I'm sorry. You've done a lot for us today, and I shouldn't have made you feel you weren't doing enough."

Memphis mumbled, "Yeah, thanks."

"Don't mention it. You guys are still my friends... my family." I sensed she wanted to say more, but it felt like something held her back.

"I hope you mean that Blaze, because I will need your help with something else." I quickly filled her in on what I needed her to do.

"Okay, I'll get it done and message you later." Blaze looked over her shoulder; a commotion behind her caught her attention. "I have to go." She hung up and her face disappeared from the screen.

"So, are you going to tell me what they are doing to the deviants?" Memphis asked.

I divulged all the information I had learned from Simon, the restrainers, and anything else I could remember.

"Ahh, that's rough. I would rather be dead than have the TCC control me." Memphis jammed his hands in his front pockets, clearly agitated and maybe a little scared. "Why would you ask Blaze to do that for you? I don't understand what you are planning."

"I'll let you know everything soon, but first can you open a portal to anywhere?"

"Sorry, what?"

"Can you teleport anywhere?"

"I usually only portal to places I have been to before; places that aren't heavily guarded, places I can pop up in without people noticing."

"Like the closet, this room, or..."

"Yeah, but... I need to picture it to go there. Or I can follow the trail of another person who can teleport, like my mother. Why?"

"Ok good. I think we can work with that. I have an idea. I've decided I am... going to rescue Callahan and Slade, and I need your help."

"Are you crazy?"

I quickly filled him in on my plan. "What do you think?"

"I think it is the most insane thing I have ever heard. Yet it makes total sense.

"We've got nothing left to lose."

MEMPHIS USED a portal to get us back to my room with no one seeing us. Even though Blaze had wiped the digital feed, we didn't want to cross paths with the Authority. The guards would remember me and my distinguishable hair when they regained consciousness. Blaze had only bought us time.

Gibson fell from the surprise, banging her head hard on the wooden frame of the bunk beds before hitting the floor. I guess I wasn't the only one who didn't know Memphis could teleport.

"Oh, my stars..." Reese said, too shocked to grab Gibson before she fell.

I put two fingers under her chin and closed Reese's mouth. She shot me a dirty look.

Memphis picked Gibson up from the floor and laid her on the bed. He examined the back of her head. Luckily, she wasn't bleeding

"Who bashed up your face?" Reese asked.

"What happened?" Gibson's eyes fluttered open and closed before they opened wide. She pushed herself up on her elbows. Memphis plopped down beside her, folding his tall frame under the top bunk. "How did you get... here?"

"A portal," Memphis answered.

"Memphis is full of... surprises, but I think he can help us." I felt a bit wobbly coming out of the portal.

"What happened to your face." Gibson brushed his face with her fingers. Memphis winced. Violet light poured from her fingertips, healing all the marks.

Memphis pointed to his injured rib area. Gibson ran her hands over his side with the violet light. Afterward, Memphis stretched, testing out the repair.

"Huh? Help us do what?" Reese said. "You are not making any sense."

"I have a plan to rescue Callahan and Slade." A dead silence followed my statement.

"You are kidding, aren't you!" Gibson pointed towards the cameras. *"Watch what you are saying?"*

"Don't worry. it's been taken care of." I said.

"Hey, stop it!" Reese said. She could always sense when we spoke telepathically.

"How?" Gibson asked.

Reese motioned what with her hands.

"Blaze has disabled or scrambled the feed or something like that. You know I repel technology, so I don't know the correct terminology."

"Blaze?" Reese questioned.

"Yeah, Blaze is um . . . helping us." I waited for the questions about Blaze to follow but they didn't. I guess they could only absorb so much at once.

"You're crazy. You won't be happy until we are all locked in the vault with Callahan and your stupid boyfriend. What do you know about rescuing anybody? You are afraid of your own shadow." Reese burst out.

"It's not like that. I swear,"

"And where would we be going after we rescued Callahan?" Gibson argued. Her eyes were red-rimmed. Black circles smudged underneath from all the tears she had cried.

Reese said, "It's not like we have anywhere to escape to. We live in an enclosed underground bunker. Or did you forget that piece of information?"

15

———

"Are you sure you want to do this? I don't know what will happen. I can't promise anything. My plan may not work." I leaned forward, running both hands through my hair. I noticed one of my hats lying on my bed and tugged it over my head. I immediately felt better, more in control, more like myself. Somehow, the hat gave me a sense of comfort like a security blanket.

"Let's not and say we did. Your idea is dangerous and stupid." Reese's arms were crossed over her chest like a barrier to the idea.

"So, how do we get my brother back?" Gibson had turned into a ball of nervous energy, bouncing on her toes as if she had just gotten a new purpose in life.

"Reese is correct. It will be dangerous. We may all end up incarcerated or exiled. I need your help, but you have to make this decision on your own. I have enough guilt to carry already." I wiped my sweaty hands on my pant leg.

"We only have to worry about the vault. If we got exiled that would be a good thing because we would all be out of here, with the rebels." Memphis looked to be pleased with that prospect.

The image of Zander getting exiled popped up into my memories, but I blocked out the visual.

"Don't do it, Gibson. You need to think this through. If this goes bad, we are all screwed. I can't lose you." A pleading look crossed Reese's face as she worried her teeth against her lips.

"Complain all you want, Reese. Just stay out of the way while we rescue Callahan," Memphis said.

"Easy for you to say, Memphis; you are already in trouble. All you and Charlie are doing is avoiding the obvious before you are both arrested. Gibson and I are clean.

"You don't understand, Reese. It doesn't matter what happens to me if I lose my brother. He's my twin, the most important person in my life." Gibson wrapped her arms around her torso in a self-hug. "I can't explain it. He's like a part of me; my other half. I find it hard to breathe when he's not around. If there is even an infinitesimal chance we can save him, I'm willing to take it. Guys, just tell me what to do."

Reese reacted as though Gibson had slapped her across the face. She sat down on the bunk bed, drawing her legs up towards her torso. I knew Gibson well enough to know that Reese shouldn't take everything Gibson said literally; it was her grief talking. Gibson loved her just as much as Callahan. Love wasn't quantifiable.

Gibson met my eyes in a mutual understanding. I knew I could depend on her. I hoped I was worthy of her trust. I felt nervous. My stomach tumbled. I had never come up with a plan before, let alone been in charge. What if it didn't work?

"I'm getting Callahan back, no matter what I have to do. I won't leave him to rot in the vault." A fire glowed in Memphis' eyes. "He doesn't deserve that."

"Nobody does," I said.

Gibson gave him a quick smile of thanks.

"Have you had any more visions, G?" I asked.

"Nada since the one I had before the fight. I wish I could control them; I wish I could tell you this plan of yours will work, but I can't." Gibson played with the gold cross around her neck. She closed her eyes, mumbling a prayer.

"When are you going to get around to telling us the plan, Charlie, or are you going to keep it all to yourself?" Reese gritted her teeth.

"Okay." All the ways that my plan could go wrong ran through my brain. I rubbed my hands together nervously. "I have a plan."

"Duh, I think we are already way past that part. Just waiting for the details." Gibson dropped back down on the bed beside Reese.

"Sorry, but as soon as I say the words, it makes what we are doing real." My next words exploded in a whoosh as I prepared for the reaction. "Gibson, you are not going to like my plan because it involves going to your uncle, Jagger, for help."

"Absolutely not. You know I have nothing to do with Jagger! I doubt he would even want to help me." Gibson extended her hand towards Reese, who rebuffed it. "I haven't spoken to him since he threatened Callahan for not becoming a King."

"You can't ask her to do that, Charlie," Reese said. "You know she detests him and his degenerate group of thieves and cutthroats."

"They aren't pirates, Reese," Memphis said.

"He takes advantage of people when they are most vulnerable. When they need help the most. He uses their fears against them," Gibson said. "It took me a long time to open my eyes and see him for what he is."

"I know and I hate to ask G, but we need his help, and I can't figure out any other way. There isn't anyone else who can get us what we need." I sagged back until my head rested against the wall. Reese hadn't exaggerated about how bad the Kings were, but we would have to risk dealing with them. There wasn't another choice.

"The underground whispers say he has access to special security tags. Tags to open the doors to the vault. To get the prisoners out, we need one." Memphis moved the empty bed away from the wall, pulling a marker from my storage bin. He started drawing. "Part one."

"I'll talk to him if I have to, for Callahan. What's part two?" Gibson asked.

"Part two involves Blaze getting us the location of the vault," Memphis said.

"Okay, genius. Say we find out the location of the vault. How do you propose we get inside?" Reese asked. "It's only the most guarded area in the Hollows."

"It's not," I said. Typical stubborn Reese. I knew she would be the hardest to convince. Her hostility filled the tiny room with negative energy. I checked my watch: it was just after 8:00 pm. How could it still be Sunday?

"It's not what?"

"It's not heavily guarded. I received information about the vault today through Blaze and Simon." I found myself moving my arms more than normal, expending my nervous energy. "Long story short, it's heavily secured but not heavily guarded. We access the vault, open the cells and release the prisoners, but to do that we will need the special security tag."

"Oh, is that all? That's easy and *so* obvious. No problem at all," Reese quipped.

"Who is Simon?" Gibson narrowed her eyes and sent Reese a withering look.

"Not now, Gibson. We don't have time to lose." I wanted to wave away their questions about Simon. It would take too long to explain, but she stepped in front of me, demanding answers. I quickly filled them in on my interrogation, the West End, reconnecting with Blaze and the warning Elise had given me. I had never talked that much at a time before my throat was dry.

"Well, you've had quite a day." Reese tucked her legs underneath her.

"So, how do we get in?" A shadow crossed Gibson's' face. "I wish we had some way to contact Callahan, to tell him we are coming. That we haven't forgotten him. I'm furious we don't have long-distance twin telepathy."

"Memphis will portal us to the vault, but first you need to pack up your stuff... just the essentials. Especially anything warm. We won't be coming back here. We need to get out of here as quickly as we can. When the guards can give my description, the Authority will come for Memphis and me." I grabbed a bag and started jamming in the basics, a change of clothes, a hairbrush, and anything else I could carry in one bag.

"What are you drawing, Picasso?" Reese drummed her fingers against the bed frame.

"Memphis, can you portal four people at once?" Gibson flipped open the lid of her storage bin and started pulling things out, throwing them on the bed.

Memphis shrugged his shoulder. "I think so."

"You THINK so?" Reese's voice rose in pitch. She hadn't moved an inch since she sat down, obstinately refusing to do anything. "I think we need a little more assurance than 'I think so.'"

"Look, I could portal with Charlie today, so I am reasonably sure I can do it again. We just need to connect, holding hands or.... I think it will work." He continued drawing. The likeness of the vault became clearer with each stroke of the marker.

"Well, as long as you are reasonably sure." Reese frowned at the back of Memphis' head. If looks could kill, he would be dead.

"Cut it out, Reese!" I had never heard Gibson raise her voice against her girlfriend. "If you aren't ready to help, then leave. Or at least stop being so negative."

I pressed my lips together. "Yeah, Reese, don't feel you have to come with us. You can stay here all by yourself. Maybe you'll like your next roommates more. At least you'll still have Remy."

Reese mimed zipping her lips and throwing away the key. She grabbed a bag and moved towards her storage bin, finally packing her stuff.

At the thought of Remy, I shuffled over to her bed. She made it to bunker specifications, prison corners. Most mornings, she used a ruler to make sure the comforter measured exactly six inches from the floor. Her pajamas were tucked under her pillow. I pulled the sheets from the bed and rolled everything in a ball. A goodbye gift.

Gibson stood ready, but even though Reese was packing, she still wasn't ready to commit to the risky battle plan we were formulating. "Okay, so we teleport into the vault and release the prisoners," she said. "Then what? Where do we go? Where do we hide? And are we really—going to free all the prisoners? Some of them might deserve to be there. This is crazy!"

"Yeah, all the prisoners. Nobody deserves to live like that. Memphis has been in contact with the rebels, we'll go to them. We'll go to Zander." I stopped packing, covering my mouth with my hand. I glanced up, and they looked at me as if I told a vulgar joke and they waited for the punch line.

"Your father, Zander?" Gibson asked,

"Isn't he dead?" Reese asked. "Yeah, Memphis informed me a few hours ago that Zander is still alive." I turned my face away, back to the packing, rolling my t-shirts to fit more in the bag.

Memphis cleared his throat and they looked towards them. "Yeah, I've seen Zander. And my mom too. I've been working with the rebels. I've been to their camp. I'll teleport us there as soon as we get Callahan."

"I still can't imagine it. I won't until I see him for myself," I said.

"My parents, Reese's mother?" Gibson held her hand over her heart, holding her breath as she waited for an answer. She looked at Memphis before turning to me.

I shook my head. Reese stood motionless, then her shoulders slumped. I felt the sadness wash through them. I wanted to cry, and a headache started at the base of my skull.

"Stop it, you're freaking me out." Reese put her hands over her ears. "I don't want to hear anymore."

The TCC didn't exile Reese's father in the Revolt of 2152, just her mother. They couldn't find any evidence of his involvement. Almost a year after the exile, they arrested and convicted him for drunk and disorderly as well as damaging commission property. That's how Reese ended up in the orphanage with us. He had a heart attack and died a few years later.

"I feel like I woke up in another world this morning," Gibson said.

"Sorry... I couldn't tell you earlier. They swore me to secrecy." Memphis gripped the marker tighter. "Zander told me if I said anything, I wouldn't be able to see my mother. I couldn't risk losing her again."

"Why didn't you just stay there with them? With your mom. Why did you come back?"

"Zander said he needed me here. You can't imagine how hard it has been keeping it from you guys, to be on guard all the time."

Reese snorted. "It feels like you've both been keeping a lot from us, keeping secrets. It's quite an information imbalance."

"Don't be like that, Reese. Everybody has secrets. I'm sure I don't know everything about you. We need to focus on freeing Callahan." Although I had come clean about a lot, I still had secrets I hadn't told them yet.

"So, your father is alive, but you hate him. You are risking our lives trusting a traitor?" Reese said.

Memphis paused his drawing. "He not a traitor. I know him and trust him. Things will be much better living with the rebels, you'll see."

"I never said I trusted Zander. I don't even know the man, but we don't have many options. We can't stay here. We can't leave without help, without having somewhere to go. Do you have any suggestions, Reese, cause I'm listening?"

Reese crossed her arms across her chest.

"Just say what you want to say. Just get it all out in the open. Let it all out, Reese. You know it's easier to shoot down everyone else's ideas than to come up with your own," I said.

"And how long have you known about your mother?" Reese made a face and finally turned back to her packing.

"I wish my mother was alive." Gibson struggled to fill her bag, shoving the contents down to make room for more. I wondered how she could have so much stuff, but then remembered that she spent all her money for stuff to trade at the bazaar.

"Since my fifteenth birthday," said Memphis. "She appeared in front of me one day. Now we meet twice a week at least."

"It must have been nice for you to see her again. I would have done anything for the same chance," Gibson said.

"Me too," Reese echoed, then she found another thing to be annoyed about. "And what have you been drawing all this time? All this is going on and you are standing there, doodling?"

Memphis brushed off her comment. He tucked the marker into

his pocket, and we looked at his sketch. "What do you think? This is as close as I can get to the image you described of the vault. I need a strong image of where we are going to get us there."

"From what I remember, it's pretty close," I said.

"Give me your bags, we need to get going," said Memphis.

I tossed my bag to him, and he gathered the rest. He assured me he had enough stuff stored in his closet, so he didn't have to go back to the main dormitory to pack. That would have been too risky. He opened a portal to leave. "I'll be right back."

"I don't think I will ever get used to seeing that." Gibson blinked up in disbelief.

"Me either," I said.

"Does it hurt in the portal?" Gibson asked.asked.

I took a second to ponder her question. "No, it felt like walking through a spider's web."

"Where's he taking the bags?" Reese asked.

"Someplace safe. Are these questions going to end eventually, Reese?" I asked.

Reese wheeled on me. "Well, excuse me, for wanting just a little information. You are asking me to have faith in you and this plan, so I want to know everything. I have a right to know everything. We have about one percent chance of pulling this off."

"I'm not great at math, but I think one percent is still better than zero. If we stay here, it's only a matter of time until they catch me and Memphis. We are all in trouble. Elise Cutter has promised to ruin my life and the lives of everyone I know. We have zero percent chance of surviving here. Zero." I had to push all my negative thoughts away. Push them down and bury them. I couldn't have any doubts. So many pieces had to work in sequence for the plan to work. I made a wish on my mother's ring and kissed it.

Only this morning everything seemed normal, and now we planned to leave this room and the only home we have ever known. I had never been so scared in my life. If this plan failed, things could get so much worse. If Zander and the other rebels turned us away, we could starve or freeze to death.

I accessed the hiding place concealed under the wooden frame of my bed, seizing Zander's watch. If Jagger and the Kings wouldn't help Gibson, it would be the only thing I had that I could bargain with. The only valuable item I owned.

"More secrets, Charlie?" Reese raised her eyebrows.

"We can use the watch to trade for the special security tag if we have to," I explained.

I had never seen Reese and Gibson act this way with each other. They were usually so loving, so in sync with each other, but today their fluctuating emotions were exploding, causing my mood to be out of whack.

Memphis opened a portal back into our room. This time no one jumped; how quickly we adjusted to something new.

My tag vibrated. Blaze messaged:

`We have a problem.`

I messaged back:

`Call me.`

The tablet by the door buzzed. I grabbed it so fast I almost ripped it from the wall.

Blaze's face filled the screen. "It's secure. We can talk without being recorded." Her eyes lit up when she spotted her old friends. "Gibson, I'm so sorry about what happened to Callahan."

"Did you do it? Were you able to get the location?" There was no time for small talk. The teachers in school used to tell me I could only think about one thing at a time. They called me a "myopic thinker." They weren't wrong.

"Yeah, I did. That was the simple part, but it's not the problem."

"Then what is it?" I asked.

"Okay so, um . . . protocols changed today because of Slade's arrest. The Authority used to just monitor the vault through security feeds and do a head count twice a day. I planned to loop the security feed they watched so they wouldn't notice the rescue attempt."

"Still not seeing the problem," I said.

"That won't work now because of what happened today. They installed soldiers inside the vault twenty-four hours a day. General

Campbell's aides, not Authority members. I don't know how we can get inside without them setting off the alarms."

"Jumping Jeepers."

"That's it, time to call off this stupid rescue," Reese said.

"Shut it," Gibson said.

"Are you talking to me," Reese asked with wounded eyes.

"Is there someone else in this room that needs to shut it? If you are not part of the solution, you are part of the problem," Gibson said. A pained expression crossed her face. She turned her back on Reese.

"Is there some way we could get to the guards, some way we could drug them or knock them out or something?" Memphis asked. "Blaze, did you get the schematics? The more information we have, the safer it will be for all of us."

"What about a stun gun? Could we get one of those and laser them?" I asked.

"A stun gun? Holy Attila, where can we get a stun gun?" Reese asked. "Be realistic."

"One sec," Blaze said.

The tablet beeped, displaying a few images of the vault. Memphis pulled the tablet from my grasp and scrolled through the photos. Simon had described it perfectly. Like the image Memphis had drawn on the wall. All our tags beeped at once with the same images.

"They grow a flower in the foot plant for the Elites. It's called morning glory. It's beautiful with stunning indigo and pink flowers first thing in the morning," Gibson said.

"And how do beautiful flowers help us?" I motioned for her to hurry with the story and noted that I had sounded just like Reese. We needed to get moving, to get out of this room. I kept having visions of the Authority busting through the door.

"The seeds cause sleepiness, nausea, stomach cramps, and vivid hallucinations. Enough seeds will knock you out." She placed her hands on her hips. "Does that make it worth talking about?"

"That could work. It won't kill people, will it?" I asked. My hands clamped tightly together, knuckles white. "I'm not like Zander. I won't have blood on my hands."

"Even if it's the soldiers or the Authority?" Memphis said.

"Even then."

"It won't kill them. Just incapacitate them briefly. Make them really sick."

"That only solves one problem; we still need to get close enough to the guards to administer the drugs," Gibson said.

"Short of being invisible, I don't know how we can pull this off," Blaze said. "The guards will have enough time to sound the alarm and they'll trap you."

"I can do it," Reese said.

"Do what?" Memphis asked.

"How?" Gibson said.

The air around Reese shimmered, glistened, and shifted. One minute she stood there and the next minute she disappeared before our very eyes. Could she teleport too? I felt a shift of air before something pinched the end of my nose. Slowly, I raised my hands, hoping to sense movement.

"Boo!" Reese's disembodied voice reverberated around the room.

16

"Thunder . . ." The air changed around me. I moved back slightly to increase my personal space. Even though I still couldn't see Reese, I knew she remained close. I could smell the lavender shampoo she made.

The door creaked open. Remy, who was just entering the room, jumped, stopped with a look of shock on her face, then backed out quickly, slamming the door behind her. What had she seen?

"Thunder! Why didn't anyone lock the door." Memphis asked before he slid over and locked it.

"Jumping jeepers. That bunker rat will be on her way to squeal on us faster than you can say 'Attila'."

Reese reappeared just as quick as she disappeared. It took a second or two for it to sink in. "I can explain."

"Pot, kettle, black." I shook my head and almost laughed.

"What's one more surprise in a day full of them?" Memphis gave a half-shrug.

Gibson's mouth opened, but her body didn't move as she stared wide-eyed at Reese. She raised a trembling hand to touch her, then pulled her hand back just as quick, acting as if it burned her. Her hands carved through her hair, holding it back and then releasing it.

All the comments Reese made about my secrets when she had secrets of her own. She had some nerve. Secrets were like monsters trapped in the closet. They go on a rampage when you open the door and let them out.

Somebody had left the door open today because all of our secrets poured out and muddied the truth. What a close-knit group of friends we were; all of us keeping secrets from the others. I had a sobering thought. Maybe we weren't friends, maybe we were a bunch of kids stuck together because of the sins of our parents.

"You followed me this morning, didn't you?" I asked. "In the bathroom, in the hallways. That was you, wasn't it?"

Reese dropped her eyes to the floor.

"I thought I was going crazy thinking someone was following me." I shook my head. I should have trusted my instincts.

"Charlie, you were right about what you said about everybody having secrets." Memphis echoed my thoughts. He propped the tablet on the top bunk so we could still see Blaze on the screen. He put a reassuring arm around Gibson's shoulders, pulling her into a hug and whispering soft words in her ear, trying to soothe her. What do you say to someone who has had shock after shock?

"This is absolutely crazy, maybe disturbing, but definitely crazy. You guys are one dysfunctional group . . . portals, invisibility. What else can you do? Turn people to ice, maybe." Blaze pushed her glasses higher on the bridge of her nose, her lip lifted in a smirk.

"That's our next trick." Memphis spoke over Gibson's shoulder. "Blaze, maybe you should see if you can do anything else besides your cyberpathy—."

"Blaze doesn't need powers, she has her big brain and photographic memory." I grimaced. The pain from the headache rebounded. Every time the pain left it came back stronger than ever. I didn't know if I wanted them to retreat or if that short-term comfort meant the returning headache would be even more agonizing.

"You know it." Blaze pretended to dust dirt off her shoulder.

Gibson wiped her eyes, then stiffened her shoulders; her expression hardened. She drew in a steadying breath. *"No more tears. No more."*

" . . . you know I can explain." Reese drew her lower lip between her teeth nervously while pulling at the hem of her yellow sweater. I always thought she looked good in yellow.

Gibson threw up a hand. "Save it. I'm not interested in anything you have to say. I don't even know who you are, not anymore. Just leave me alone." Her eyes flashed fire.

Anger radiated from her fiercely, making me angry, too. I just couldn't believe Gibson didn't know. They were like two halves of a whole.

"Gibson, please!" Her bottom lip quivered; her shoulders dropped in resignation.

Whatever reason Reese had for keeping her invisibility secret must be important. I hoped so, because it may have cost her the relationship she had with Gibson.

Gibson stormed past her, then spun back around. "No, forget that Reese, I tell you everything. EVERYTHING. I didn't think we had any secrets from each other. I just don't understand."

An alarm sounded. A red light flashed in the room behind Blaze, drawing her attention. "Uh oh. Get out of there now, go. Get out."

"Why, what's going on?" I shifted closer to the tablet, hoping to see what she could.

"The guards you assaulted are awake. The TCC dispatched the Authority to arrest you and Memphis. They will be there any second. Go." Blaze ended the chat. Her image disappeared from the screen.

A knock reverberated from the door, quickly followed by more thumps, harder with each strike. "Open the door in the name of the Authority." Before they could use the key, Memphis twisted the metal lock, slowing them down.

"Just a minute, the door is stuck," I called out. My friends stared at me like I was crazy. I shrugged my shoulders; it seemed worth a try.

Memphis used his telekinesis to push the lines of this drawing together, so the image became unreadable. Gibson grabbed the comforter from Remy's bed and wiped at it, further blurring the image. Memphis then made the familiar motions of creating a portal until the air churned white.

"The law requires you to appear forthwith," a guard stated.

"Hurry, Gibson, Reese help me push the bed against the door." We grabbed the frame and lugged the bed. The metal legs screeched against the floor. We piled books and anything we could find on the bed, hoping to slow the Authority down.

Memphis stretched the portal until it became big enough to walk through. "Grasp my hand." I clutched his hand and reached for Gibson. It took Gibson a few precious seconds for her to grab my hand and stretch her arm out for Reese. We stepped through the opening.

I FELT BETTER PREPARED for the effects of the portal this time, having been through it twice before. Gibson and Reese ended up in a pile of arms and legs. They quickly disentangled themselves.

"Can you imagine the look on their faces when they busted through the door finding an empty room?" Memphis chortled. A silly smile spread across his face. "I would give anything to see that."

"Jumping jeepers…" My heart thumped wildly. I briefly wondered if I could have summoned the ability to throw them back with my voice again.

"I can't say I liked it much." Reese busied herself assessing everything. We weren't on an episode of Star Trek pixelating into a million pieces. "Could you have found a better place to take us, Memphis?"

"Always complaining. Where would you like to go, Princess? The beach?" Memphis ambled over and locked the door, pulling down a thin white blind over the window to hide us from prying eyes. Dust flew from the blind, causing him to cough.

"Are we in a closet? It smells like antiseptic in here." Gibson checked to see if the gold cross still hung from her neck.

Memphis and I exchanged a look. *Not again.*

Gibson busied herself checking the inventory on the shelves. "Are we really doing this?"

"Thunder, I guess we are in it now. What's next?" Reese played with the string of her hoodie, pulling it open and closed. She kept glancing over at Gibson, hoping for a hint of forgiveness, some sign her icy veneer would thaw. It would be a long wait if I read Gibson correctly.

"Oh, this is where you brought our bags." Gibson noticed the bags piled up in the corner. She pushed her hair behind her ears just to do something with her hands. "What do we do now?"

"I don't know," Memphis said. "Why are you asking me? I'm not in charge."

Their eyes turned to me. "Now we continue with the plan. What other choice do we have? My life here is over. Yours too. We either rescue Callahan and the prisoners or end up stuck in the vault with them. Don't you think?" I judged the look on their faces to see if they were still on board with the rescue attempt.

"We have to," Gibson said.

"Life will be better with the rebels than here, trust me," Memphis said.

"You can't be serious. How do we expect to win? The TCC has all the advantages: they have the weapons, they have the cameras, and they have the Authority There is no way we can win. No way. We need to throw themselves on their mercy." Reese folded her arms..

"Never. It's riskier to do nothing. Either way, we may as well be dead." I ran my finger across the cold metal shelf.

"True," Gibson said.

"I, for one, am happy to get out of here. I've been waiting forever," Memphis said. Strangely, I had been feeling waves of happiness flow through him since we teleported away from the guards.

"So, I think we need to split up. Gibson and I will go to meet with the Kings. Memphis, you and Reese can sneak into the food plant and get some leaves from the morning glory plant." I felt weird making the plans, telling people what to do, but it also felt oddly right somehow. Memphis and Gibson nodded in agreement.

"Wait, hold up. Who put you in charge, Charlie? Why do you get to make the plans? You're not the boss of me. We need to stay together. I'm not leaving Gibson." Reese put her hand on my shoulder, and I stared her down until she removed it.

"That's funny because in my head you just said, 'Brilliant plan, Charlie. Thank you.'" With the events of the day, I felt more confident than ever before.

Reese waved her finger in my face. "We wouldn't even need a plan if it weren't for you. You seem to have conveniently forgotten that. Who do you think you are?"

I glared at her, but I would die before admitting she was right. "Maybe I'm special. Tell me who you think I am, Reese. I dare you." I was the reason our lives were in shambles. The catalyst. They should all run from me as if their hair were on fire.

"This isn't helping Reese. What's done is done. We all agreed to help with Charlie's plan earlier, but if you don't want to, don't help. I don't care. Just quit your whining and moaning," Gibson said.

Reese glowered at me. "You've changed, Charlie. I can't put my finger on it, but you have changed."

"I just realized something..." All the negative vibes Reese pushed at me made me doubt myself, but I had to be strong. I rubbed my forehead, hoping to scrub away the pain of my headache. Ignoring her, I said, "Gibson, how many leaves do you think we will need from the plant. What do you call it morning—?"

"Glory, it's called the morning glory plant. It is not the leaves we need, it's the seeds. I don't know how many seeds we'll need. How would I know? Do I look like a botanist to you?" Gibson seemed edgy, almost vibrating; she started opening and closing boxes on the shelf as if trying to burn off her extra energy.

"Okay... okay." I grabbed my security tag and sent a message to Blaze:

```
Find out how many morning glory seeds we
need to knock out two guards.
```

I got a reply immediately:

```
On it.
```

"Gibson, how easy will it be for Memphis and Reese to get into the food plant and get it? Is it accessible?" I asked.

"It's easy enough. It's not in the restricted part of the food plant. If Memphis can get there, Reese knows where to get it."

"You can try talking to me instead of around me. I'm in the room, you know," Reese said.

"Is it dangerous to touch?" I asked. I knew nothing about plants. I didn't have access to the food plant. I spent most of my time welding in the water plant, power plant, or corridors. I kept checking for Blaze's response, as if watching my tag would bring the information faster.

"No, it doesn't work quite like that. It's just the seeds that are poisonous if ingested in substantial quantities. The leaves won't hurt you." Gibson rubbed at her eyes. "The Elites use the seeds to get high."

"I've been in the food plant, it's part of my regular route. I can find the plant if Gibson describes it. I can go by myself. I don't need Reese," Memphis said. "Maybe, I'll slip a few extras for myself."

"No, you'll need Reese. You can keep the gateway open while she gets the seeds. Once you open the portal. The alarms will sound, and they'll see you on the cameras. You won't be fast enough by yourself. Maybe we can get Blaze to put the video on a loop."

"Why can't I go with Gibson, and you go with Memphis?" Reese asked. "Why do you get to decide who goes where?"

"Because Gibson has to go to her uncle. You know the food plant and I can't teleport," I explained.

Reese gave me a sulky look.

"Do you have something to say?" I asked.

"Yes, I do, but I'm keeping it to myself," Reese said.

"And because I don't want to be anywhere near you right now," Gibson said. *"Are you telepathic?"*

Reese didn't acknowledge she heard the question Gibson posed. Maybe she wasn't a telepath. Slade said we each had at least two abilities. I briefly questioned what her other ability would be. I had four new abilities. It might be wonderful if I could ever learn to control one of them.

"You aren't the only one upset, Reese, but being a brat isn't going to help anyone," Memphis said. "What about if I hold the portal open from this side and she slips through when she's invisible. Then no one will see us. It might not set off the alarms."

"Oh wow! Can you? That's an outstanding idea. Those are the kinds of suggestions we need."

My tag beeped with the response from Blaze:

```
You need over 400 seeds or 10 grams per
person. Grind and soak the seeds in purified
water for half an hour. Then strain the strain
the seeds and put them in a drink. It will
cause slumber, diarrhea, and hallucinations.
It should keep them temporarily incapacitated
for 6-10 hours
Good Luck
```

Memphis peeped over my shoulder to read the message. I quickly relayed the information to the others. "Do you need me to write this down?"

Memphis pointed to his head. "Got it. My memory is like a steel trap."

I raised an eyebrow. He used his tag to take a photo of the message.

Memphis' head popped up as if he were just struck by lightning. "Reese go invisible again."

"No, why?"

"Just do it."

As before, the air around Reese altered and fluctuated until she disappeared.

"Touch my arm," Memphis said. A second later, he vanished. "Awesome. Works just like my portal: it's transferable. Connected, we can take on each other's abilities. You can let go now, Reese."

They both reappeared. I wondered if it would be the same for my empathic abilities.

"Awesome. Now we can get Blaze to run interference for Gibson and me on our trip to see the Kings." My body felt calm compared to my tangled mind. "Although once Reese releases you, you'll be visible while you hold the portal open. Are you good with that?"

"Yeah, plus, it's fun to do," Memphis said.

"The only thing that matters is that Callahan is in custody, and we have to get him back," Gibson said. "No more talking. We need to get going. Charlie, what can we do about your hair? They might check for a girl wearing a hat."

"Nice catch." I whipped off my hat, placing it on a shelf, then picked it back up. I hurried over to my bag, tucking it inside. I had thrown my hair painting gear into the side pocket earlier today in case I needed it. I squeezed some paste out into a small mixing bowl, swirling it around with a brush.

When the consistency became smooth, I brushed the strands with the paint, starting at my roots and moving to the ends. It felt cold and wet and smelled like ammonia. Gibson grabbed the brush from my hand, then painted the back of my head. After completely covering the blonde, I combed the color through so it would be even. Hopefully, it wouldn't take long to dry. I thanked Gibson.

"Reese and I are ready. Message me after your discussion with Jagger and the Kings. We can decide where to meet," Memphis said.

"Okay yeah, sounds good Memphis." Now we were about to begin, I felt so scared. I tried to put on a brave face and tell them I believed in our plan. But what if I made a mistake, what if the worst happened? "And Memphis... please be careful."

"You too, both of you. I'll see you after," Memphis said. Memphis and Gibson hugged goodbye. I settled for a wave. Reese and Gibson stood there awkwardly. Watching their estrangement was painful. Gibson finally broke down and gave Reese a half-hug, telling her to stay safe.

"Reese, if you die before I learn the reason, I will kill you," Gibson's voice cracked.. She might want to kill Reese, but she wouldn't let anyone else.

"I should have told you a long time ago," Reese said.

As soon as Memphis opened the gateway, they latched hands and disappeared. I forgot to wish them good luck.

Gibson checked her tag for the time. "Jagger should be at the bazaar; he spends most of his time there."

"That's what I thought. Hey, how does my hair look?" I reached up to touch my hair to test the paint. It always dried fast.

Gibson inspected my hair. "I think it will pass, but maybe you should put it in a ponytail." Gibson grabbed a makeup pencil out of her bag, adding wide strokes around my eyes. I never wore makeup.

I took the elastic from my wrist, tossing my hair up into a messy bun. "Better"

"Yeah, you'll pass for a brunette." She put her hand on the doorknob, then hesitated. "Do you think we can do this, Charlie? Can we pull this off?"

"I do." The butterflies fluttered in my stomach. I hope my voice didn't shake.

She smiled and took a deep breath. "Okay, then. Let's go."

"Gibson, there's just one more thing I haven't told you or the others."

She raised an eyebrow in a silent what.

"Callahan is not in the vault. I don't know where he is."

Gibson clenched her jaw. Rage pulsed through her like a heartbeat.

17

Gibson wouldn't speak to me as we walked to the bazaar. I didn't mind since my thoughts spun out of control, planning and re-planning each aspect of the rescue. Blaze became our eye in the sky, letting us know which corridors to use or avoid. I tried to control my nerves, but I had my head on a swivel, scanning for anything out of the ordinary. It would be hard not to draw the Authority's notice.

In the corridors, the TV screens displayed my image. They could have picked a better photo. I gave myself a mental shake for my vanity. I had bigger things to worry about. Words scrolled along the bottom of the screen, outlining our crimes against the commission. The TCC offered a reward for information leading to our capture. Wonderful, there wasn't a person in the Hollows that wouldn't sell us out for any price. We needed to get out of the bunker as quickly as possible.

No matter which way we went, we couldn't get to the bazaar without passing through a checkpoint. We picked the busiest one, hoping to blend in with the crowd. When I swiped my security tag, my heart pounded so loudly I was positive the guards could hear the beat. Blaze had created new clean usernames for our temporary use, but she cautioned they may not last. Blaze changed my name to Elisabeth Clarke. The Authority didn't even give me a second glance, just waved me on my way.

Before we rounded the last corner to the entrance, Gibson paused. She surveyed the corridor uneasily, then sagged against the wall, bending her leg and placing her foot against the rock.

"So, let me get this straight. We are actually rescuing your boyfriend and you think if you rescue him, he can lead us to Callahan because even Blaze, with her supercomputer skills, doesn't know where he is. Do I know everything now?" She rubbed at her eyes as if they were itchy.

"Yes, to both. Memphis and I spoke at length with Blaze, and we all agreed this is our only shot at finding him." My hands sweated profusely, so I wiped them on my pant legs. "Callahan is not in the vault. Simon and Blaze both confirmed that. If he's not there, then there are only two options."

"Don't even say it." Gibson worked her bottom lip between her teeth. "Why didn't they keep them both together? It would be so much easier."

Gibson thought if you didn't speak about unpleasant things they couldn't happen. I had already deduced if Callahan wasn't at the vault, there were only two other options. Either they exiled him, or they took him to wherever the Authority lived. They wouldn't have exiled him without a show. The TCC loved the pageantry of an exile, so that left one choice.

"I don't know. Blaze can't find him anywhere and with her access. She tried tracing his tag, but no luck. Who knows if he even has it anymore?"

Gibson rubbed her forehead, giving me a skeptical look. "This is insane."

"I know... trust me, I know. I think we need to rescue Slade first and go from there. If what I think is true... then he's our only chance to find Callahan."

Her head pulled back as her shoulder pushed forward. She twisted her hair around her index finger.

"Today Slade took me to a secret place. A wondrous place. A pond with hot water." I shut my eyes and let myself envision the hot springs. "Slade knows everything about how the Hollows operate. He'll know where to find him. Trust me, he knows all kinds of secrets."

She let out a lengthy breath. "Okay, as long as this isn't just a trick to rescue your stupid boyfriend."

"Huh, he's not my boyfriend." I fidgeted with the zipper on my sweatshirt.

Gibson's lips curled up in a tiny smile. She winked at me. "Okay if you say so." She pushed off from the wall and we rounded the corner.

"Miss Gibson." A voice called out. Mammoth, who had been handling security at the door, approached Gibson. "Miss Gibson, it is you. This is a surprise, what brings you to the bazaar today. Are you here to see Mr. Malone?"

Mammoth got his name from his size. He stood like a wall of solid muscle. A real gentle giant, at six-foot seven-inches tall. Tattoos covered every inch of his sculpted arms and neck. His upper arm displayed a red and black armband with a black skull. All the Kings wore them.

"Hey, Mammoth! How are you? I haven't seen you in . . . forever. Is Uncle Jagger in his office?" Gibson's demeanor softened when she spoke to him.

"He sure is, Honey, and the boss will be so excited to see you. Yes, he will. He mentioned just the other day he hadn't seen you and your brother in a long while. Yes, sir, he will be absolutely delighted. Especially after what happened to poor Callahan today. That boy never deserved what happened to him. The boss thinks so too." He smiled, revealing two missing front teeth. Mammoth didn't terrify me, unlike the other Kings.

Mammoth opened the door to the bazaar like a true gentleman. Another group of people tried to squeeze ahead of us through the door, but Mammoth scowled fiercely, waving his hand at them to wait. They backed up in a flash. Noise poured out the entrance as soon as he opened the door.

"Thanks, Mammoth. So good seeing you again."

"You too, Miss Gibson, don't be a stranger now. Maybe you can sing for us again some time like you did when you were younger. You sure do have a nice voice."

"Thank you. Maybe, I'll do that someday soon. I'll let you know."

Mammoth smiled and waved. "I'll call back and let them know you are on your way." He picked up a black makeshift radio from a table beside the door and spoke into it.

Gibson had a beautiful voice, clear and powerful. She used to sing all the time using an old karaoke machine Jagger scavenged from somewhere. In the old world, she would have been a rock star, but here they don't appreciate the ability to sing.

Entering the bazaar felt like stepping into another world, a colorful scene. Crammed with people, stallholders lined the rows selling distinct types of merchandise. Sunday had always been the busiest day. It was after 9 pm and the bazaar would be busy until closing time at 11. There wasn't an empty place between the stalls without people or stock to sell. The air smelled of spices, candles, and sweat, giving the market a unique fragrance.

Gibson and I weaved through the crowd, pushing through the thick mass of people, zig-zagging our way to the back of the building where Jagger had his office. All the vendors were busy upselling, each trying harder than the other to unload their goods. Brash voices haggled for the best price.

The Authority didn't patrol within the bazaar; it was the only area with that exemption. There weren't any cameras here either. Somehow, the Kings ruled this tiny section like their own kingdom. Two members of the Kings stood guarding bright red French doors. The small windowpanes painted black for privacy. They opened the door as soon as they recognized Gibson.

Jagger glanced up from his tablet as we strolled in. He stood, straightening the lapels of his suit. Wisps of gray threaded through his full head of hair. Not the biggest man, but something about him oozed danger. Something about his eyes suggested he wouldn't hesitate to "end you" if you got in his way.

Clutter filled his office. There were piles of books everywhere. Manila folders stacked haphazardly on his desk as looking as if they could topple over at any second. Floor-to-ceiling walnut bookshelves covered the walls, marked and scratched from years of use. A small jade Buddha rested among the many knick-knacks scattered among the books. A burning cigarette was smoking in a glass ashtray. Cigarettes were a rare item.

"Gibson, this is a surprise. I didn't expect to see you today kid, especially after what happened to your brother this morning. I have been..." He rose from his desk, enclosing Gibson in a hug, kissing her on both cheeks. He squeezed her upper arm affectionately before releasing her.

"Hello, Uncle Jagger. Thank you for seeing us. You remember my friend, Charlie."

"Hi." I stuck out my hand clumsily for him to shake. My hand felt small when he enclosed it with both of his, squeezing it tight.

Jagger had a murky brown aura. It usually signified control issues, being afraid to share yourself with others, being afraid to let go, being afraid of losing personal power. I didn't want to spend much time in his presence.

"I know who she is. Welcome, Charlie. Please have a seat. What brings you to my neck of the woods?"

I snorted at his choice of idioms. None of us had ever seen a tree except on a screen.

I plopped down in an oversized reading chair, checking out the titles of the books on his shelves. *To Kill a Mockingbird*, *1984*, *Lord of the Rings*, *Great Gatsby*, *Pride and Prejudice*, and *The Book Thief* were just a few of the titles in his collection. Some of these books weren't even available at the archives. A framed painting hung on the only wall without shelves depicting dogs playing poker. It was the funniest thing I had ever seen; I bit back a laugh.

"Do you like my collection?" Jagger asked.

"I do. Your anthology rivals the archives. Where did you get them all?" I must look like a wide-eyed fool admiring his books.

"Uncle Jagger, I um... hate to ask, but we need your help." Gibson sat on the edge of his desk, her words rushing out. "We have a plan to rescue my brother."

"A plan, well now. Let's hear this glorious plan. You know I'm always here for you." Jagger took his time seating himself, crossing his legs at the ankles. He snuffed out the burning cigarette.

Gibson sighed. "Great, because—."

"I hate to say this, but I don't think it's possible to get Callahan back. I've been working with my contacts all day trying to secure his release, but no dice. No matter what I offer, and I can offer a lot of things, kiddo, they keep coming back with a 'no'."

I dove in avoiding the simple pleasantries. My myopic personality rose again. "The underground whispers say you have access to security tags that override the doors to the vault. Is it true?" I looked him in the eye. This wasn't the time to show fear.

"There could be some truth to the rumor, but say I do... have something like that. What's in it for me. I am a man of business after all." He crossed his arms, leaned back on his chair, clicking a pen open and closed.

"We're family. Callahan is your nephew. And you want something in return for helping us. Really?" Gibson pulled at her ears as if she couldn't believe what she heard.

"I have a reputation to uphold. I can't give away something and get nothing in return. Even for family. If that ever got out, it would be bad for business. Plus, I have expenses to cover. My sources don't give me information for free."

"Oh, for the love of..." Gibson pounded her forehead with her fist.

"Don't worry, I came prepared to pay." I stood up and reached into my pocket, pulling out Zander's watch, setting it on the desk. "This is the last remaining thing I have of his. It's a collector's item. I know people paid a lot of money for his things before."

Jagger's eyes lit up when he laid eyes on the watch. "May I?"

"Help yourself."

"Does it still work?"

"Yeah, you just need to wind it up every day with the little knob on the side. It never loses a second."

"I can't believe you still have this." He floated it over with a wave of his hand and examined it. The gold and silver links glinted off the fluorescent lights. There were diamonds inserted where the numbers should have been on the dial. Jewelers constructed the bezel from solid gold.

"Samantha kept it for me until I could look after it myself." I rubbed my temples, trying to ease my pounding head.

"Oh, my dearest Samantha, I remember her. I had forgotten all about her until now." He made a tsking sound with his tongue, shaking his head at the thought of her. "What a messed-up crazy woman. A staunch believer in the cause. A fanatic follower of Zander."

"Fanatic?" I shared a look with Gibson.

"What do you mean by 'fanatic,' Uncle Jagger? Samantha practically raised us at the orphanage. She wasn't a fanatic. She treated us wonderfully." A puzzled look crossed her face. She hooked her feet around the chair legs, almost toppling it over. "If you were so concerned about her, why did you allow her to be near us?"

"Believe me, I tried. I only had allegations that she wasn't as innocent as she seemed, no proof, and with my reputation…" Jagger put his feet on the desk and tilted his chair back. "Don't worry, Gibson, I always had my people watching all of you. If you were in any danger from her, they would have put a stop to it."

Why would Jagger care about my safety? "Samantha cared about me—."

"Samantha belonged to a fraction called the Sisters of Freedom. The sisters believed Zander Edge walked on water. They claimed he could do miraculous things. Things ordinary people couldn't do. They prayed to your father like he was a God instead of a mortal man."

I read about the Sisters of Freedom in the archives. Crazy things. They worshiped Zander, taking vows of chastity and obedience in service to him. It was the strangest thing I had ever heard. It made me feel squeamish just talking about it.

"Did you ever see Zander do anything extraordinary?" I wondered if he could be a deviant. If he could do the things I could do.

Jagger gave a half shrug. "No, I don't think so. He was nothing more than an ordinary man as far as I knew. But you must under-stand... Zander had charisma. A true leader, he had a way of making every person who joined his rebellion feel they were exceptionally special, that the rebellion couldn't operate without them. He made each person feel they were integral to his plan. Zander gave his people a purpose, a vision of an original life. He let the rebels feel heard and sometimes that's all people need in a place like this."

No one had ever described Zander in a positive way. They always told the story of the revolt. When he and his group breached security and occupied the food plant for forty-one days. Fifty-three innocent people starved to death during the siege. Mostly the old and young. The Authority stormed the food plant as soon as they could break through the barriers the rebels erected. Thirty-seven people died in the fight.

"Sounds like a genuine hero. Too bad he got my parents killed, along with all the other deaths he triggered." Gibson's voice registered her irritation. "You should tell him when you meet him."

"Gibson, I'm not saying Zander is a wonderful guy. I'm . . . just saying . . ." I broke off. Just mentioning Zander's name drove me crazy.

"My brother Mercury loved Zander ... loved him more than me." A frown crossed Jagger's face at the thought. "Wait ... 'meet him'? Then you know your father is still alive?"

"You know Zander is still alive?" My muscles quivered as I fought to stay on my feet. "Is there anybody who doesn't know? It would have been nice to be let in on the secret."

"And how do you feel about that?"

"Like I don't want to talk about it. Why do you care? People either loved or hated Zander, but he's still a perfect stranger to me." I bit the inside of my cheek so hard I drew blood. The metallic taste soured in my mouth My irritation built and I looked down at the palm of my hand, hoping light wouldn't spontaneously begin. "Can we just get down to business?"

"Are you sure you want to part with this?" Jagger rubbed his thumb over the face of the watch before flipping it over to look at the inscription "Do you know what the inscription says?"

"Yeah, if the price is right, and yes, I know what it says."

"Uncle Jagger, Charlie wouldn't have brought the watch here if she wasn't willing to trade but I can't believe she has to." Gibson glared at her uncle; her nostrils flared.

"Gibson, it's complicated. I can't ever look weak, otherwise, my life and the lives of the people I care about could be in jeopardy."

"Callahan's life is in danger. What part of that don't you understand?" Gibson snapped, baring her teeth. "You have some crazy definition of family."

"Look I'm perfectly willing to trade the stupid watch straight up for a clean security tag to access the doors to the vault. Quid pro quo."

"Do you want to bounce something off me? Tell me about your plan to rescue my nephew? Maybe I can help."

"Not particularly," I said.

"No. We don't need your kind of help. I know what that brings. The fewer people who know, the better." Gibson jammed her hand in her front pockets.

"Are you worried you'll implicate me?" Jagger asked.

"No, I'm worried you will mess things up somehow."

"Suit yourself... you don't have to get ugly about it." Jagger threw up his hands.

"Do we have a deal?" I asked.

"Charlie, I'll tell you what I'll do. A trade: the watch for a security tag and one more thing."

I raised my hands in a silent what.

"I need you to release, Ed Meyers, from the vault—"

"We were planning on releasing everyone."

"Then kill him."

I exchanged a long look with Gibson. Acting as if I considered his request. I had no plans to kill anyone, but he didn't need to know. "Done."

Jagger's mouth twisted at my quick agreement, but he said nothing. He moved the painting of dogs playing poker, revealing a small metal safe. He entered numbers into the electronic keypad and a beep sounded. The door swung open. Jagger took out a thin security tag, tossing it at me. "The code is 042902. One catch... you can only use the tag once for the computer and once for the door, in that order. Screw up with the sequence and you'll trigger a lock down."

"Lock down sequence?" Gibson asked.

"Got it." I tucked the tag inside the top of my boot out of sight. I couldn't leave the room without asking him a question. "Hey, the Buddha on your shelf, where did it come from?"

"The scavengers supply me with most of the things in the bazaar. Why do you like it?" He floated the statue from the shelf to his desk so I could have a better look.

"Scavengers?" Gibson raised an eyebrow.

Jagger paused, tilting his head to the side, considering his words. "After the TCC began exiling people instead of imprisoning them, those that survived found their way to Zander. Because they weren't part of his original rebellion, they had to earn their keep, so he gave them the worst jobs. Jobs like scavenging, braving the freezing elements in the old world to search for useful things."

"And what do you supply them with?" I asked.

"Several things, things they can't get outside. Some plant and herbs, but mostly information. Information is more powerful than anything else in the Hollows."

I slapped my hand against my forehead. Duh, that made so much sense. No wonder the kings never ran out of inventory when all the other vendors sold reused, reclaimed products.

"Is it true? Are my parent's dead?" Gibson worried her lip between her teeth. Her eyes searched his, seeking the truth. Hoping Memphis's information proved wrong.

"Oh, honey," he glanced up sharply. "I wish I could tell you they were still alive; I'm so sorry, but no. Neither of them adapted to the inhospitable environment. They both died within a week of being exiled. Many from the group died in the first week."

"Okay." Gibson's shoulders shrunk down at the news.

Her sadness washed over me. I wasn't aware she still had hope. I felt bad I still had a parent when she didn't. I didn't even want to see Zander again.

Jagger picked up the watch and admired it. He used a key to open the locked drawer in his desk. He pulled out a black case and used another key to open it. A single item lay nestled on a pillow of purple velvet, a watch. He pulled out the watch and handed it to me. It looked exactly like Zander's watch. I flipped it over and saw the same inscription: "Ab initio"

My head popped up. The watches were identical. Why?

18

———————

I had so many questions I wanted to ask Jagger. Was he part of the original rebellion? Why did he have the same watch as Zander? Did the inscription mean anything? When was the last time he had seen Zander? How often did he see the scavengers? The questions kept swirling in my mind, but we didn't have time to get the answers. Not that Jagger would provide them without a price. We needed to be on time to meet the others at the rendezvous point.

Jagger let us out through a concealed rear entrance to the bazaar, giving us directions to avoid the checkpoints. I had a feeling he knew more hidden secrets. He bid us goodbye and good luck. If the security tag worked at the vault, it would be worth losing the watch.

Gibson and I navigated our way through the corridors to the service area. This area of the complex featured three vast horizontal passages that led deep into the mine for access and drainage. The arched passageway constructed entirely of cement floors, ceilings, and walls. loomed over us. Bundles of cable and wires ran down the ceiling, fastened together on thick iron beams. The air tasted stale, cool, and musty.

We arrived before Memphis and Reese, disappearing into a blind spot to hide. I brushed aside a spider web but left the spider alive.

The spider had found the perfect place in the dim light. Only every third light had a bulb in the fixture, a cutback they began years ago to extend resources.

I wondered if Memphis and Reese retrieved the seeds and prepared them. The plan would be a bust without them. I had been unable to reach them through my tag since we split up.

Gibson stiffened. She began counting under her breath. I didn't blame her. Places like this would bring back the nightmares of her kidnapping. I didn't know how to bridge the gulf I could feel between us. "Hey Gibson, I realize... you are in pain, that you are hurting over Callahan... but you are not alone. I just wanted to say, I know how you feel."

"Of course, you do Charlie, you are an empath you feel exactly what I feel." Gibson dipped her head to the floor. "Look, I know... you are sorry, but sorry fixes nothing. I know whatever happened to Callahan isn't... I know you would never do anything to hurt him. Not intentionally."

"I messed up, but I didn't mean for this to happen. This wasn't what I wanted. Not any of it. I just tried to return something, and it snowballed into this horrible mess." In all that had happened, I forgot the key had gone missing from the box. I still didn't understand what had happened to it. How had it disappeared?

"I appreciate you didn't mean for this to happen, but I feel like I can't breathe since Callahan left. I am so worried about him. What if I never see him again?" She adjusted the collar of her sweatshirt as if it choked her. "I wish I could tell Callahan we are coming to get him."

"You can't think like that. We'll find him. We won't stop until we do. Callahan is smart. He'll hang on until we get to him. He's a survivor." All those talks of the TCC experimenting on prisoners kept coming back to haunt me. I envisioned terrifying situations. If the Authority had him, who knew what kind of evil torture they could be performing.

I thought about what Gibson said. Closing my eyes, I cleared my mind, inhaling a couple deep breaths, centering myself. *"Callahan, hang on, we are coming for you."* I repeated it over and over, pausing in between to listen for a response. Trying another tactic, I projected my thoughts from my body. *"Callahan, hang on, we are coming for you."*

When I turned away to give up, I heard, *"Hurry."*

I opened my eyes. Did it happen or was it a hopeful fantasy? Should I tell Gibson? Nah, I couldn't prove it so best to say nothing.

"I hope you are right."

"Of course, I'm right, I'm always right." I tried to lighten the mood with a joke. "Any visions?"

"No."

I broached another tough topic. "You seemed disappointed back there with Jagger... about your parents not being alive."

"Yeah, no. I don't know." Gibson gave a half-shrug, slumping back against the wall. "I know Memphis didn't lie about my parents being dead, but I thought... if others were still alive, maybe they could be too. Silly to even think it could be true."

"It's not silly to have hope," I said. I lived on hope. It seemed easier keeping the fear at bay while we were in motion , but once I stopped it all came rushing back and I struggled to step forward.

"It is when you live here." She jammed her hands in her front pockets. "If we can pull this off and get Callahan back, I might be okay, we all might be. But even then, what will our new life going to look like?"

"I don't know. I honestly don't." We could just be jumping from one terrible situation to another. I had to believe it would be better with the rebels. From what Memphis told me. it didn't sound so bad.

"Just tell me it will all work out okay. I just need to hear you say the words."

"It's all going to work out perfectly. We will get Callahan back, find the rebels, and everything will be fine." We both knew I was lying. I reached over and grabbed her hand. giving it a reassuring squeeze.

"Do you hear something?"

Gibson cocked her head, listening attentively. "No."

"There it is again." The slight scratchy, squeaky disturbance increased in volume. I flashed the feeble light from my security tag in the direction of the sound. A mass of whiskered animals with brown fur, long tails, and beady black eyes ducked back into the shadows away from the light.

Gibson screamed, then covered her mouth. Standing on her tiptoes trying to get a foothold to climb the wall. "Do something, burn them with your light."

"No, they aren't hurting anything, just trying to survive like us." I shone the light away from the creatures. Back in the darkness, the rats flowed past us in a frenzied eruption. A furious stampede of tiny feet. They hissed and chattered. The mass became a trickle until they disappeared.

Gibson shivered. "I don't know why you like those nasty creatures."

"I don't particularly like them I just don't see the need to kill them. They are just trying to survive like us."

A horn blared. A half-hour warning the lights were going out for the night. I glanced at my security tag to confirm the time, 11:30 pm. At least we were on schedule.

"At least I won't miss all the horns, telling us when to eat, sleep, and work," Gibson said.

"True that."

I winced at the pain in my head. What was with this crazy headache? It kept coming and going. My subconscious tugged at me, telling me I missed something.

"Is the headache back, Charlie?"

I nodded as I rubbed my hands against my temples.

"You should have gone to medical when you had the chance. How long has it been since you've slept?" Gibson asked. She clutched something small in her hand. It looked like Callahan's key chain.

My stomach gave a loud growl, reminding me it had been hours since I had eaten. Gibson dug her hand into her pocket and pulled out an MRE, handing it to me. She always stashed away food in her pockets, constantly hungry. Plus, her kidnapping made her want to always have food close. I thanked her, biting into it; it helped to soothe my hunger pains but did nothing for the headache.

"Are you worried about seeing your father again?" Gibson asked.

"Yeah, that's an understatement, I've been trying not to think about it. It's so confusing." I covered my mouth while I chewed.

"How?" Gibson rolled her shoulders, letting her head sway from side to side.

"On the one hand, I'm still so angry at him for what happened to my mother, but on the other hand..."

"He's still your father."

"Yeah, he's still my father. Is it wrong for me to be happy he's alive when I've spent my entire life hating him for what happened to my mother?"

"I never understood why you hated him so much."

"Really? You don't understand. I've told you why a million times. Because he's the reason my mother is dead. Because he started the Revolt of 2152. And you know how that turned out. How many deaths he caused?" I swallowed down my frustration.

Talking about this always caused my blood to come to a boil. This would never even happen now because of the rule changes after the revolt. If the commission even suspected someone of something, they arrested them, without proof, without a trial, without justice. 'Innocent before proven guilty' didn't exist.

"I've heard it different," Gibson said.

"Different how?" I pushed the hair back out of my eyes as it kept falling out of the loose ponytail I wore. I missed my hat, trapping it all in one location.

Gibson raised a shoulder and let it fall.

"Different how?" I repeated. "C'mon Gibson, you can't toss that at me and not tell me what you have heard."

"Umm, so, okay... don't shoot the messenger, but the underground whispers say when your mother got sick, Zander begged the TCC to do the surgery. He promised he would do anything they asked him to do. Someone high up denied the surgery."

"What. My grandfather had a role on the Security Council. Elise and my mother were friends. They wouldn't have let her die."

"They were friends?"

"Yeah, best friends, Elise gave me a whole story…"

"Well…"

"Just spit it out, Gibson."

"Umm, I heard…"

The air swirled around us. We backed up, away from the opening portal. Memphis and Reese walked out. The tension in the room increased with Gibson and Reese together again.

Memphis beamed. Such a cheerful thief. "What's up, ladies? Look who's back from a successful break and enter." It seemed unusual, but he hadn't been unpleasant since the start of this whole escapade.

"Any problems? Were you able to boil down the seeds to make the elixir?"

Memphis dusted off his shoulder, congratulating himself. "Easy, peasy Charlie, but maybe next time start with a 'hi Memphis, happy to see you again'."

"Sorry, that's a given. Small talk is unnecessary." Exchanging fake and meaningless pleasantries took time we didn't have.

"Yes, Charlie, even simpletons like us can boil water." Reese rolled her eyes. She had lost none of her surly nature in our time apart. She pulled two vials out of her pocket. The clear fluid inside the vial seemed a little cloudy. I crossed my fingers this plan would work. It had to.

I nudged Reese with my elbow as she ventured past. "That's all you had to say?"

"Hey, watch it," Reese said.

"Sorry, not sorry." I checked my security tag for the time, almost midnight. I sucked in a deep breath and released it slowly. The nervousness blasting from them gave me doubts. "Gibson, Reese, are you sure you want to go through with this? The TCC has nothing substantial on you yet, but this is a crime, a punishable offense."

"They have already committed punishable crimes if you haven't been paying attention," Memphis said, the corner of his mouth quirked up.

"Well unlike us, they haven't got caught yet, have they?"

"Thanks for giving us the heads up. Not that it would stop me, but at least we have all the facts. I am absolutely, a hundred percent on board." Gibson wrung her hands together nervously.

"There is no turning back now. We would just be guilty by association, anyway. You said Elise Cutter promised to ruin our pathetic lives. Why would we stay?" Reese absently rolled the vials in her palm, then one dropped.

Without a thought, I widened my hand, stretching the tips of my fingers as far as they could reach. The vial froze just before it hit the ground, rose a few inches, then floated on air into my outstretched grasp. It surprised me as much as anyone to feel the smooth glass vial in the palm of my hand.

"Telekinesis," Reese said. "Is there anything you can't do?"

"I honestly don't know." I handed her back the vial with a shaky hand. Yesterday, I had empathic and telepathic abilities. Today, I didn't understand how to describe the other things I had done. Did they have names? "Next time, don't drop it."

Reese inserted the vials into a syringe.

The alarm on my tag beeped. Time to go. It buzzed again. It was Blaze:

`Ready on my end.`

I messaged back:

`All good here. See you soon.`

Memphis opened a portal while Reese disappeared. It didn't even phase me anymore when they used their abilities.

Memphis said, "Reese and I discovered—"

"When you are on the other side you can't see the portal. Memphis had to stick out his hand for me to find him again. All he could see were the seeds floating in the air," Reese said.

I would never get used to hearing her talk without seeing her in person. Reese must have tucked the syringes away because they disappeared. The air hummed, I felt it shift as she stepped past me through the portal.

Gibson hushed us.

The vault looked much like we expected it to. Two soldiers rested at a round black metal table near the control panel under the exit sign. The console looked complex with flashing buttons and levers. In the center of the dashboard a monitor played the TCC news channel softly. One soldier had his feet up, his chair pushed back on two legs. The other soldier had his head down on the table, lying on his arm. He might have been asleep.

The soldier, with his head on the table, sat up abruptly, grabbing his left arm. "Ow. Something stung me." He rubbed his hand against the sore spot.

"What could sting you in here? Ouch, something bit me," the other soldier said. He stood, waved at the invisible bug, then toppled over backward, tumbling onto the floor. The first guard's head dropped back on his arm with a thud.

Reese reappeared. Gibson and I stepped through the portal. Memphis followed closely behind. As soon as he released his power, the portal closed.

"You know, that went better than I expected." Reese removed the empty vial from the syringe, tossing it in the trash can.

"The shot worked so fast, outstanding." Memphis rubbed his palms together.

"Blaze made the right call." Gibson marched over to each of the guards, pulling back the collar of their uniforms that covered their necks. She placed her pointer and middle fingers on the side of their windpipes just below the angle of the jawbone, shifting her fingers until she could easily feel the pulse of their beating hearts.

Blaze had researched the morning glory plant further, suggesting we would have better results injecting the elixir straight into the soldier's bloodstream. I just hoped we hadn't given them too much.

"Alive?" I asked.

"Only sleeping, but who knows for how long," Gibson said.

I peeked up at the cameras. No alarms yet, Blaze would have the feed on a loop. "Keep monitoring them while I try to open the cells."

The vault had been larger than I envisioned, vast; the cells stretched as far as I could see. Inside, most of the prisoners stood looking through the barrier of lasers that kept them within. They were all dressed in white baggy tracksuits, men, women, and young teens alike. Familiar expressions crossed their faces, surprise, fear, shock. Some of them cowered at the back of their cells.

The familiar sensation of being controlled by the feelings of others engulfed me. It seemed almost too much to take.

Simon waved from the third cell on the left. He didn't appear surprised to see me. No sign of Slade, but he could be in the cells down the hall further. Bending over, I grabbed the security tag we had bartered from Jagger out of the top of my boot.

Memphis tapped my shoulder. "I'll get Blaze." He blinked out of the room.

"Do you know how to open the cells or has this been a colossal misuse of time?" Reese said.

"Give it a rest, Reese," Gibson said.

Ignoring her, I walked over to the intimidating control panel, studying the maze of buttons and switches of assorted colors and sizes. What if I hit the wrong buttons? I pulled up the instructions on my tag that Blaze had sent earlier, getting to work.

"What happens if you push the wrong button?" Reese asked.

"Bite your tongue." I already felt out of my depth trying to figure this out without her second guessing over my shoulder. I had double checked Jagger's instructions with Blaze.

Memphis popped back into the room with Blaze. She seemed so small standing next to him. "I'm back."

"Hey, fancy meeting all of you here." Blaze's attempt at humor fell flat, but she laughed at her joke as if it were the funniest thing she had ever heard. She embraced Gibson, then Reese, then yelled across the room, "Did you do what I said? In the precise order?"

"Yes. Blaze. I... can... read. Here goes nothing." I swiped the security card that Jagger gave me, inserting the override code written on the back, 042902. I pushed the black, gold, and red buttons in the correct sequence and pushed up a large white lever. A loud snap and a whirl reverberated, then the lasers withdrew, releasing the prisoners. They stepped out of their cells. The door would be the next problem. "Memphis 042902 is the override code for the door. Lock it down."

There was only one entrance to the room. An enormous, tightly fashioned steel door with a complex lock. Memphis punched in the code. Several massive metal cylinders extended from the door into the surrounding frame. The locking mechanism engaged, and the pressure system sealed the door shut. Sealing us inside.

The interior of the room had become congested and boisterous as the prisoners left their cells. They milled around; exchanging greetings with each other.

I jumped up on a chair, scanning the crowd for Slade. Ajax emerged from a cell, yawning. I jumped down, placing myself in his path. "Have you seen Slade?"

"Thunder, are you stupid or stupid? You're messing everything up, what in the stars... are you doing." Ajax seethed with resentment, arms straight, hands locked into fists.

The aura around Ajax glowed bright red, suggesting he was competitive, passionate, strong-willed, and full of energy. Bright Red wasn't bad as far as aura colors went, but dark reds were.

His wave of anger felt like a slap in the face. I didn't know what reaction I expected from him, but it certainly wasn't anger. "Oh no, you have insulted me. What will I do? I'll be mentally and emotionally scarred for years. I think the words you are looking for are 'Thank You'." Last time I rescued him. I pushed past him without waiting for a response.

Gibson searched the opposite side of the room with Reese, hoping to find her brother. It was a challenge to navigate through the room with everyone thanking me and asking what we do next. Memphis tried to quiet the prisoners as they became rowdy.

Simon stopped to hug me. There were tears in his eyes as he thanked me. "My vision promised this would happen. I knew you would save us."

Slade appeared from a cell near the back of the room. I took in the sight of him. He stretched his arms over his head and bent backward, shaking out his cramped muscles. He rubbed at his eyes as if he had just awakened. He did a double-take when he noticed me. He blinked, looking puzzled to see me. "You have to be joking! What are you doing here?"

Gibson caught up with us. She grabbed Slade's wrist to get his attention. "Where is my brother?"

"I don't know where he is; they separated us. I haven't seen him, not since the fight," Slade replied, shrugging his shoulders.

19

———————

There must have been almost seventy prisoners in the cells, so many more than I expected. The oldest, maybe sixty, while the youngest might have been thirteen. Once the initial excitement of their release subsided, they quieted, then stood in clusters of five and ten. They seemed to be waiting for something.

"A rescue. Are you kidding me?" Slade asked. "Did you come here for... me?"

"Don't flatter yourself. I'm here for Callahan." I hoped I pulled off that lie. Selfishly, I wanted to save them both. "I need your help to find him."

"You shouldn't be here. What were you thinking? Are you trying to get yourself killed? Zander won't like this." Slade's nostrils flared. He rubbed at his left wrist where his leather wrist band previously rested.

I stood there like an idiot. What was with these Elites? Couldn't they just stay, thank you, and keep quiet? I felt disappointed because he didn't even seem happy to see me. Well, forget him. I wanted to walk away, but I couldn't worry about my hurt feelings. We needed to find Callahan and escape, and we couldn't do that without his inside knowledge.

Gibson clutched at my elbow, spinning me around to face her. "I thought you said he would know where to find Callahan. How are we going to find him? How?" Her voice traveled to the verge of panic. Her shoulders drooped in resignation.

"The one thing we are not doing is giving up. Don't worry, we will figure something out. We won't quit looking until we find him." I hoped I sounded more confident than I felt.

"Why would you tell her that?" Slade jerked his thumb towards Gibson. "Who is she, anyway?"

"I'm Gibson, twin sister to Callahan. You know the guy you punched in the face earlier today." Gibson shot Slade hostile looks. "You also met me last night when you kissed Charlie."

"I'm sorry. I thought... after this morning, I thought you were privy to everything in the Hollows. Thunder, how do you not know where he is?" I pulled my lip between my teeth.

"Think Slade. Is there a place they would take him? Is there any place other than the vault they send people? Could they have exiled him?" Gibson asked.

He touched his chin absently, "He could be at the Nest... that's where the Authority are kept, but I don't know; they rarely take deviants there."

"I told you, they wouldn't have exiled him, not yet. The commission always makes a big commotion about the exiles, televising it. There hasn't been enough time. The protocols are too rigid. They won't break them for any reason." I grabbed my left arm with my right hand and squeezed, digging in my nails, past desperate. "Am I right, Slade?"

"Unless they don't know he's a deviant," I said. "Simon mentioned the Nest to me earlier today, but I didn't know what he meant."

Gibson and I exchanged a hopeful look. "Do you know the location?"

"I've been there."

Ajax bounded up from behind Slade, interrupting our conversation.

"You should get some sleep, bud. You look horrible." Ajax's lips curled in a smile, then he winked at Slade.

"I look better than you." Slade forked his fingers through his hair.

"Not even possible," Ajax said.

They clasped hands, bumped shoulders then hugged briefly, slapping each other on the backs; thrilled to see one another. I could sense they had a bond. Were they friends or something more?

Slade ambled towards the rows of metal lockers. He pulled the items out one by one, dropping them on the floor until he discovered his leather wristbands, which he slipped back into place.

Mesmerized, I drew back when Memphis snapped his fingers and tapped me on the shoulder. "We need to get these people out of here. I'll take them to Salvation's Keep, the principal rebel camp. Blaze says the loop isn't working anymore. She says…"

As if hearing his words, an alarm blared. An ear-splitting screech, rotating between varying volumes and pitches. Red lights flashed, whirling fast. The central lights in the room went out and the auxiliary lights switched on, bathing us in muted rosy glow.

"Yeah. But… you can't teleport seventy people at once, can you?" I yelled over the raised voices that had increased because of the darkness. We planned for Memphis to portal the prisoners to safety, but there were a lot more people than we expected. He wouldn't be able to get them all out before the Authority arrived.

"No, I can't, but… wait a minute… I have an idea." Memphis jumped up on a chair and whistled loud and long. "Hey, listen up. If any of you can teleport, come to the back of the room."

It took a moment before a woman with long gray hair walked to the back. Slowly, others trickled towards Memphis until about fourteen people surrounded him in a semi-circle. Memphis gave them instructions on how to follow his trail. They fanned out into the crowd, linking hands with others. Within seconds, they all flickered out of the room until there were only a few of us left. At least that part of our plan had almost gone according to schedule.

I tried to navigate past Slade, but he blocked me and touched my arm. The warmth of his hand sent a shiver down my spine.

"Don't touch me." I took a step away from him. He inched closer, making me feel strange. "You are very close."

"Am I making you uncomfortable?" He shuffled back.

I nodded.

He shoved his hair back away from his face, then blew out a lengthy breath. "Sorry, I'm sorry. I didn't mean to be so harsh earlier. I just can not believe you are here. It's . . . what did you do with the key? I thought about it a lot and look... I'm not mad you took it. You still have it, don't you?"

"Thunder, you never let up. I don't have your stupid key." I spat the words as I walked away from him.

Reese and Blaze worked at the control panel near the front of the room. Blaze frantically typed into the computer connected to the control panel. Buttons flashed and flickered with a life of their own. Symbols flashed behind her eyes. How long would she be able to access the network before the TCC revoked her privileges? I strode to the front of the room, Slade, Ajax, and Gibson trailed behind.

We gathered around a table with rod-iron legs located beside the control panel. I knelt a knee on a chair. The soldier at the table. appeared to be sound asleep, but I could see his chest rise and fall so he was still alive.

"Can you do anything about the alarm?" I asked Blaze, covering my ears with my hands to muffle the noise.

"What do you think I'm working on? My resume?" Blaze said.

With a few more taps on the keyboard, the squawking finally stopped. An instant later, the red light faded away. It drove my eyes crazy. Blaze put her headphones back in her ears so she could focus.

I introduced Gibson, Blaze, and Reese to Slade and Ajax. I'd forgotten they hadn't all met. They exchanged greetings but seemed uneasy with each other. Trust didn't exist easily between Subs and Elites.

"Any luck in the search for Callahan?" I peered over Blaze's shoulder, trying to make sense of the code on the blue screen.

"There isn't a digital trail to follow to the Nest," Slade said.

I voided the sentence from my memory, choosing not to hear it.

"Nothing yet," Blaze answered as her fingers danced on the keyboard. She had plugged her personal laptop into the control panel. "I'm checking all security feeds plus I am running an algorithm using his name and appearance but no hits."

"Aren't the files encrypted?" I asked, proud of myself for remembering one computer type word.

"Yes, but who do you think wrote the encryption code? Me. I left a backdoor in case the TCC ever denied me access." Blaze explained, as she tossed everything from a drawer onto the floor "Also, I need everyone to throw their security tags in this drawer. I'm going to destroy them."

I removed my tag; it had been part of my wardrobe since I remembered. It seemed strange to throw it away.

Blaze scanned the tags through the computer, deleting the contents. She asked, "Who can manipulate metal? I need these bent until they are unrecognizable." Slade volunteered, twisting the metal tags until they became a lump stuck to the bottom of the drawer.

Outside the door to the vault, we heard voices, then a loud bang as the Authority hammered a battering ram against the door. The ram thumped like a rhythmic pulse. Blaze tapped into a security feed, allowing us to see the guards attempting to open the door with a battering ram. A soldier had a computer hooked up, trying to hack past the new codes Blaze had put on the door.

"We need to move." Blazes' eyes moved from side to side rapidly. Sometimes she seemed more computer than a human. "I estimate we have three minutes and forty seconds before they breach the door if the Authority follows its usual procedures."

"How do you know the time to the second?" I asked.

"I just do. The Authority constantly runs scenarios of all the potential threat assessments that could theoretically happen within the bunker. There isn't a circumstance they haven't run a drill on since—" Blaze said.

"The Revolt of 2152." I finished her sentence, too nervous not to interrupt.

The red light on the overhead camera popped back on, emphasizing her point. I waved my middle finger in defiance.

"Real mature, Charlie." Reese rolled her eyes.

I stuck my tongue out at her, doubling down on the immaturity.

"Hey, I'm trying to talk to you." Slade tapped me on the shoulder. "I asked you a question. Where's my key?"

"I asked you one first. Where's my brother?" Gibson stomped her foot, trying to get his attention. It wouldn't be long before she kicked him.

"I already told you everything I know, weren't you listening," Slade said. "Maybe you should clean out your ears."

Gibson glared at Slade, placing her hands on her hips.

"Reese, will you please tie up the soldiers in case they wake up?" I spun away from them.

"Why me?" Reese asked.

"I'll help." Gibson replied mostly to diffuse Reese. "Anything to get us out of here faster."

They found some zip ties in a metal locker and tied the soldier's hands and legs together. They seemed to be sound asleep. I was concerned we had given them too much elixir and they might never wake up. I didn't want to be responsible for their deaths. Gibson checked their pulses again.

Reese came up behind Gibson, whispered something into her ear. They both walked into a cell. That might be bad.

"Who are you, anyway? At what point did you think this would be a wonderful idea?" Ajax tilted his head in my direction. Agitated, he opened and closed his fist. "I didn't see you doing anything to help me the other day. Where was the rescue then? Huh."

Ajax looked as if he wanted to throttle me, but Slade intercepted. Irritation flowed up inside me. My brows collided together in a scowl. I could look after myself.

"Did anyone ever tell you you're a...?" I broke off to find the correct word, idiot, ass, jerk, ungrateful.

"Bud, cool it. You're talking to the General's daughter... Charlie Edge," Slade warned.

"Come again? Isn't she supposed to be blond?"

Slade bit back a laugh at the incredulous expression on his friend's face. "You knew he had a daughter, Ajax. This is her."

"Why would I help you? I don't even know you." I curled my lips in icy contempt. I shoved my fingers through my dark painted hair. "You're the whole reason I'm in this mess. Asking me to protect the stupid box."

"Whatever, Princess. You can blame me all you want, but I didn't pick up the box. You did." Ajax winked at me. "You could have left it for someone else to find but you didn't."

He wasn't wrong. I let my curiosity get the best of me. I was the catalyst in this catastrophe, no matter how much I wanted to believe otherwise. I let it drop, too exhausted to nag back at him. I didn't owe Ajax any explanations.

A familiar hum and a rush of air proceeded Memphis into the room. He bent over at the waist and rested his hands on his knees, fighting to breathe.

"Are you okay?" I asked. All this teleporting around had taken a toll on him.

He waved me away. Once he could speak, he eked out a "Yeah."

"All good? Did you get them to safety?" I made further introductions.

"Sure thing, they are all at Salvations Keep." Memphis wet his lips "Massive problem, I ah... had to tell my mother what we were doing. She'll tell your father and he won't be happy at all. He wasn't at the Keep, he's at the Frozen Fortress, or he probably would have followed me here. My mother has gone to get him."

"Zander worried... he hasn't worried about me for my entire life. I doubt he cares," I said. Salvation Keep, the Frozen Fortress. They felt like names straight out of a movie or video game. My imagination envisioned fortresses or castles.

"You've been to Salvation Keep?" Ajax rubbed his hands together. "Oh man, I've always wanted to go there. Have you been outside yet?"

"Did the General give you any instructions for us? For me and Ajax?" Slade rocked back and forth on his heels.

"As if." Memphis narrowed his eyes. He looked at me to see if they were lying. I shook my head, determining they told the truth. "You work for the General?"

"Yeah," Ajax said.

"We both do." Slade waved his hand between Ajax and himself.

"Is there anybody here who's not working for Zander?" I rubbed the back of my neck. I felt left out.

"Prove it then. What's your code name?" Memphis asked as he edged closer to them.

Slade folded his arms across his chest. "My code name is Polar number 032666."

"Code name Phoenix 062164." Ajax grabbed an empty chair from the table, spun it around and straddled it. He placed his hands on the top of the chair.

Gibson and Reese emerged from the cell holding hands. They both had red-rimmed eyes. It appeared Gibson had accepted whatever reason Reese gave her for keeping her invisibility secret. My curiosity peaked, but the explanation would have to wait until later.

"Code name Spartan 092687," Memphis said.

"Code name Olympus 081593." Blaze briefly glanced up from typing lines of code Was she cracking encryptions or creating a computer virus? I really did not understand what the words and symbols meant.

"Thanks for verifying," Memphis said.

"Wait. What. You too, Blaze?" I spun so fast to face Blaze, I thought I got whiplash. "Gibson, Reese: what about you guys? Are you part of the rebels?"

"Nope."

"Not me." Reese's arm curled around Gibson's waist, tugging her closer.

"Nobody calls us rebels anymore," Ajax said. "We are the Salvation Resistance."

"Cool name. You printing t-shirts with that slogan?" I asked.

"Gees, Charlie, sometimes you need to make your sarcasm a little clearer, you know. I'm not sure if the Elites picked it up," Reese said.

"Make fun of the name all you want. I didn't pick it, the General did," Ajax said. A muscle in his jaw twitched. "If it's good enough for him, it's good enough for you. We are humanity's last salvation, last chance."

"Oh, okay, sure, sure," I said.

"Olympus, so that's who you are. It's so good to meet the famous Olympus. I've talked to you a few times before. Like this morning... thank you for blocking our tracking signals," Slade said. He stuck out his hand for Blaze to shake. She looked at his outstretched hand but didn't accept it. She never shook hands because of the germs.

"Jumping jeepers, you blocked our tags this morning, Blaze?"

"Yes, silly. How do you think the Authority didn't notice you were out of bounds this morning?" Blaze looked up and her fingers found the keys without looking.

"I put in a call to Olympus earlier today. Otherwise, your alarm would have sounded as soon as we crossed over to the FarSide." Slade moved closer. "My dad put that into protocol after my accident. There are other ways around it for me, but not for you."

"I just thought..." I didn't know what I thought. I knew they tracked us, but I just never really thought about it when we were at the hot springs.

"You've met me a hundred times before, Slade. We have sat at the same table at countless West Side functions." Blaze put her glasses on top of her head. "Besides, I promised Zander I would always keep Charlie safe."

"I've met you as Blaze, but never as Olympus," Slade said. "Your exploits are legendary. We've been working towards the same goal for years. You are part of the Sisters of Freedom, aren't you?"

"If you are all part of this rebel alliance, how come you all don't know each other," I asked. I would not touch the comment about the Sisters of Freedom with a ten-foot pole. How could Blaze be one of them?

"It's on a need-to-know basis," Slade said. "I didn't even know Ajax had become part of the rebellion until I received the message to retrieve the key he had dropped."

"Glad to know we are both fighting for the same side, bud," Ajax chuckled. His eyebrows elevated. "It was rough not being able to share that part of my life with you."

"Same, same." Slade graced Ajax with a smile and a slap on the back.

Another piece to the puzzle. I believed Slade had gone to Ajax's aid because of their friendship, not because of the rebel alliance. I refused to call it the Salvation Resistance. At least now I know why Blaze provided overwatch.

"Zander keeps three to four people to a group in small cell structures. We only know the identities of the people within our cells. It's safer this way in case one of us gets arrested. Then we could only give away the names we know. It protects the network. It's totally logical." Blaze said. Behind her eyes, I could see long strings of code. She stopped typing and pressed the enter button. All the monitors showed a countdown.

"What are you listening to?" Slade tried to pull the ear bud from her ear to listen.

"If you pull out my headphones, I will pull out your internal organs one by one." Blaze looked upward, pushing the glasses back up her nose.

"Whatever?" Slade let his hand fall away.
"Back to my brother. Slade, how do we get Callahan from the Nest?" Gibson jumped on the empty silence.

Slade tilted his head to the side. "If he's at the Nest, he won't be the same. If they have processed him... the man you knew won't exist anymore."

"Maybe they have exiled him without the ceremony?" I asked. Did we miss something when we were puzzling this out? He could already be safe with the rebels.

"Actually, they haven't exiled anyone in a few years. They only imprison them now." Slade answered.

I could hear the blood pounding in my ears. My tongue felt so thick I thought I would choke. I had given everyone hope we could find and rescue Callahan. I lost consciousness and then everything went black.

I woke up lying on the floor with my head cushioned in Slade's arms. Everything seemed foggy. "What happened?" We held eye contact slightly longer than normal.

"You fainted." Slade looked concerned. "Right into my arms. You know if you needed my attention that bad you didn't have to go to such extremes, trust me."

I inclined my head to get a better look. Gibson had also fainted. Reese tended to her as she had done so many times before. Reese must have broken her fall.

I thumped my fist against my forehead, then chastised myself. The headache had finally disappeared, and I didn't want to bring it back. I remembered. "I saw Callahan."

"He's alive," Gibson said at the same time. "I knew it. I would have felt if he was gone."

Rising to my feet, I quickly embraced Gibson. We jumped up and down, shouting in excitement; hands waving in the air. The others looked at us like we had lost our minds. "He's alive, he's alive."

"Does somebody want to fill in the only non-telepath in the room?" Reese asked.

"Where is he? I'll go get him," Memphis said. Re-energized suddenly, his body vibrated with the need to move.

Gibson shared her thoughts with the details of the vision and I interjected with others.

In the vision, I saw Callahan seated on a bench in a steel cage with other young people, two guys, and a girl. A long dark tunnel with torchlight illuminated the blackness. There were members of the Authority scattered everywhere. Some of them worked out, lifting iron, running on treadmills. Others practiced mixed martial arts on a blue gym mat.

"I was afraid of that. He's at the Nest with the Authority," Slade said. "If they have started the process... there is a point of no return. Especially since..."

"What process?" Memphis asked. "Oh, my stars, I can't believe this."

"Then we have to hurry." I didn't have any idea what he meant by 'the process', but I had to find out. "Especially since what?"

"Since when are you clairvoyant?" Reese scratched her head. "Can anyone time travel? Any vampires? Do unicorns exist?"

"Since today. I guess." I shrugged. I couldn't explain it any more than any of my other new abilities. It simply made me happy to know Callahan was alive.

"It's emotion, Charlie," Blaze said. "You are an Alpha like your father. Emotion or need triggers your abilities."

"What... in ... thunder... is an Alpha," I didn't know what that meant, but if it meant I would become like Zander; I didn't want it.

"An Alpha? Like a werewolf?" Ajax asked.

"You have all the psychic abilities of the Alpha Mind State, just like your father does. Your white-blond hair is a sign." Blaze stood up, then planted her hand against the dashboard as if communicating with the machine.

"I'm sorry, run that by me again." I wanted to cover my ears, afraid to hear more, but I resisted. I couldn't hide from anything anymore. I wouldn't.

"How do you know this, Olympus? I mean, Blaze?" Slade said. "The Alpha part, not the breach part."

"I think, I actually heard something about this." Ajax tipped the chair back on two legs. It took all my willpower not to kick the chair legs out from under him.

"So do I, now that I think about it," Reese said. "The underground whispers said he used mind control to get others to do what he wanted. Are you like Memphis? Is that what you have been doing with us, Charlie?"

"What, no way!" How could she even think I would do that?

Memphis puckered his lips, then blew, getting everyone's attention. "Guys, guys, none of this... matters... now. If you haven't noticed, the Authority is about to invade us."

"Listen to Memphis. We need to rescue my brother. I'm ready to go." Gibson held out her hand towards Memphis.

"Shouldn't we have some kind of plan, you know... figure out what to do before jumping into the middle of the Authority's lair," Slade said.

"Especially since they own all the weapons in the Hollows." Ajax had found candy somewhere. He tossed it in the air, catching it with his mouth.

"I teleport easiest to the places I've visited before. I've never been there." His brows knitted in a frown. "Not with six of you, at least. I don't think I have enough power to make two trips. What if I can't do it?"

"Don't bail on us now, Memphis. If your positions were reversed, Callahan would do anything to get you back," Gibson said.

"Sure, you can. You have to." I awkwardly touched his arm. Trying to reassure him, which is not something I usually undertook. "You can do this. I have faith in you."

"I'll figure something out." Memphis pressed each finger together from pinkie to thumb, then repeated the process.

"What if we reduce the number of people? It would help, wouldn't it?"

"It would," Memphis confirmed

"Then can you take Blaze, Ajax, Gibson, and Reese to . . ." I snapped my fingers, trying to think of the word.

"Salvation Keep . . ." Ajax offered up the missing words. He rubbed his hands together. "Astounding. Let's go already. Tell me what to do. How does this teleporting work?"

"First, we need to move the soldiers out of the way, otherwise they'll be in the line of fire when the Authority bursts through the door. They shouldn't die for being in the wrong place at the wrong time."

The banging and voices outside the door became louder. I observed the digital feed out of the corner of my eye; the guards were still battering the door. More guards had gathered. The commission must have called them all to duty. Locking the Hollows down. A thought crossed my mind. Could it work? I needed to think it through.

"One minute until breach," Blaze said. She monitored the data on her tablet. She had one headphone in her ear, the other one dangled. The music sounded like... Justin Bieber.

"We don't have time." Ajax kicked his foot against the wall. I spun on him. "I'm telling you, we are not killing anyone. We don't kill people. Not today. Not ever." I briefly wondered about the man Jagger asked me to kill and what had happened to him.

Memphis nodded. Everyone but Ajax helped to move them into one of the empty cells, placing them on the bed.

"I'll help rescue Callahan. I feel responsible. It is partly my fault he got arrested," Slade said.

"Partly." Gibson raised an eyebrow. "I'm going. You can't stop me. He's my brother."

"No, you aren't. You only have telepathic and clairvoyant abilities. You can't protect yourself if we get in a fight. Neither can Blaze or Reese."

"I'm not squandering my time rescuing someone I don't know," Ajax said. "Get me out of here."

"Exactly what I thought," I replied.
"Okay, sorry I'm not an Alpha like you," Reese placed her hands on her hips.

"I don't care what you say, it doesn't mean jack squat. He's my brother and I'm going," Gibson said. "And Reese can do more than turn invisible."

"And it's called apportation, not invisibility, thank you very much."

"Okay... we don't have time to argue," I said.
"Why does your boyfriend get to go?" Reese asked.
"We really need to wrap this up," Blaze said.

"I'll take you to the Nest. I'll help find your friend on one condition," Slade said.

"What's the condition?" I tried not to react.

"The only thing I have been asking of you since we met. The key." He shoved his hand through his hair.

"I told you. I don't have it," I said.

"But I do," Blaze said.

20

The hammering at the door ceased. I could hear the hiss of a welding torch as the Authority tried another tactic. A sound I knew better than others. I checked the camera feed to see how many additional guards had arrived. There were twice as many as before.

Blaze systematically thumbed through the folders piled indiscriminately on the table, absorbing the information. "Charlie, I really can't believe you didn't figure it out. It seemed only logical."

"Yeah, no." It made total sense as soon as Blaze said it, but I had been too busy with other things to spend much effort figuring it out. I rubbed the back of my neck to remove a kink and ease my aching head.

"You have the key, are you positive?" Slade flopped back onto a chair as if someone had removed the weight of the world from his shoulders. The cast iron legs screeched as his weight shifted the chair on the cement floor. He pressed his hands against his eyes and rubbed them. "Ah, thank the stars. You have it, Blaze."

"What are we waiting for?" Gibson grabbed her hair with her fists, ready to pull out every strand.

"We can talk about this later. If you haven't noticed, we aren't in the proper place for a chat," Reese said.

Blaze straightened her tie, adjusting it until it lay just the way she liked it, perfectly aligned. She dug out the key from the inside suit pocket of her single-breasted jacket, quickly flashing it at Slade before tucking it back inside the silk-lined pocket, refastening the top and middle buttons.

Ajax reached over and slapped Slade on the back. "Told you it would all work out, bud. All that worry for nothing."

"What is it, anyway?" I placed my hands on my hips. "Why is it so valuable?"

"Beats me. I'm a soldier, I don't question my orders." Ajax smacked his hand on the top of the chair. "I picked it up from a dead drop. Don't even know who left it."

"Me either. The General said it was a life-or-death matter. I had instructions to speak with Ajax, find out what he did with the box, and then retrieve it. I intercepted Ajax before the Authority transferred him to the vault," Slade said. "I'm just happy the commission doesn't have it."

"True that," Ajax said. They bumped fists.

All eyes turned towards Blaze. "Don't look at me, I don't know what it is. Don't worry though, I'll hand the flash drive to Zander personally." Blaze pulled on her earlobe. A clear tell she lied. I didn't call her out. The box wasn't my priority. I noticed she had stacked all the file folders in one pile in alphabetical order.

"Helloooooo," Gibson said. "Do we really need to talk about this right now when the computer is counting down the end of our lives?"

"We are multitasking," Blaze said.

"Sure, you will, so you can take all the credit." Slade shook his head, muttering something under his breath.

"You bet." Blaze winked at Slade.

"Why the worry, Slade? It looks like you have found another way to get into Zander's good graces." Reese nodded her head in my direction.

"We can discuss it later; we need to leave now." Blaze whipped around towards Memphis.

"That's what I've been saying," Gibson said.

Memphis made a noise in his throat and swallowed hard. "I'll take Charlie, Blaze, Reese, and Gibson. They can fend for themselves." He pointed at the Elites.

I raised a finger. "Wait, a minute." Blaze said my powers worked with need. Well, I needed them to work now. I gripped and pulled at the air as Memphis had done. Nothing happened. I tried again, then again. I shook out my hands, trying to calm myself. I let myself succumb to my emotions; give in to the desperation.

"Charlie, quit wasting time. We don't have time for you to learn how to teleport." Reese clicked her fingernails against the table.

"Relax and feel the air; become one with it," Memphis advised. "You've teleported before with me; you know how the air feels. You should be able to see the threads of air."

"Charlie," Gibson's eyes widened to large saucers. "Callahan is depending on us."

"Twenty seconds," Blaze said. The computer screens did a superb job keeping us apprised of the time without Blaze's verbal commentary.

"I can give us more time." Slade raised both hands over his head to his left. The ground shook. As he lowered his arms, concrete blocks shook loose, piling in front of the door. Dirt swirled in the air then rained down, covering us with debris. He pushed the tables, chairs and everything not nailed down towards the door in a heap. It sounded as if the roof caved in.

Ajax jumped into help as soon as he noticed what Slade was doing.

I covered my ears against the roar until it ended. "Memphis, please take Blaze, Reese, Ajax and go. Take them to Salvation Keep." I wiped my sweaty hands on my pants. "And Memphis, don't come back here. Meet us at your place."

"I'm sorry, I don't take orders. I barely take suggestions," Reese said.

"Reese, please go. I need to know you are safe. Please . . . please do this for me." Gibson pleaded with her eyes. She embraced Reese and spoke into her ear. Whatever she said worked. They hugged, then kissed goodbye. Reese gave her hand to Memphis.

Memphis nodded. His eyes met mine and held. "Good luck." He linked with the others, then quickly departed.

I tried to focus. To block everything out and concentrate.

"Are you sure you can do this?" Slade asked.

"Of course, she can." Gibson leaned closer before she whispered, "You can do this right?"

"If I can't, then at least we won't have far to go when they arrest us. We could have our choice of cells." My joke bombed. I could feel their eyes. "Don't look at me, you are making me nervous."

I swallowed to moisten my dry mouth. I gripped the air again. I felt the pressure the air created against my hands. I pressed and dragged against it until a tiny white hazy spot appeared briefly. I repeated the process, but this time it became easier to make the tiny hole. I yanked on the edges until the chasm became larger and larger. Huge enough to step through. "Gimme your hand."

"Don't you dare let go," Gibson warned as she reached for my extended hand.

Slade gripped her other hand tightly. "Here goes nothing."

WE TELEPORTED BACK to the closet. I tilted my head back, raising my arms above my shoulders. I punched my fist in the air in triumph and did a happy dance. These extra powers were invigorating. I felt wonderful.

"Did you see what I did?" I had never felt so alive before. For the first time in my life, I believed I could do anything. I felt wonderful, invincible. I have never been good at anything before. I was an average welder, an average student, an average friend, an average person, never anything special. It felt good.

Slade raised me in the air by the waist and swung me around until I became dizzy. *"You did amazing. You saved us. I could kiss you."* A smile dangled on the corner of his mouth, simply dazzling.

Our eyes met. I couldn't look away from the hypnotic pull.

"Ahem..." Gibson cleared her throat. *"Calm down, Dynamite. We still have more work to do."*

Slade set me on the floor. He ran his knuckle down my forearm. I shivered, moving a step away from him. Did we have a connection, or had I made it all up in my head?

"Do you hear something?" I asked.

Heavy footsteps sounded outside the closet. The doorknob rattled. We all held our breath, hoping the Authority wouldn't check the closet. Voices murmured outside the door and the guards moved on.

"Close, too close." Gibson closed her eyes briefly. She set her lips in a grim line. Missing her brother had taken a toll on her. Her sadness tugged at my emotions like they were the bait and I the fish.

"I guess we should always expect trouble," I said.

Slade took in his surroundings and asked. *"Are we in a closet?"*

I couldn't help it: I burst out laughing, covering my mouth with both hands.

"What?" he said. *"Did I say something funny?"*

"No, nothing. You wouldn't get it." I placed my hand over my mouth to muffle my giggle. How could I explain the same thing happening three times in one day?

"Also, where am I?"

The hair tingled along the back of my neck. I could feel the air vibrate an instant before Memphis appeared. I seemed more attuned to how the air moved now that I had created a portal on my own.

Memphis looked visibly relieved to see us. He graced us with a lopsided smile before sagging back against the shelf. *"Nice work, now what?"* He extended both arms and stretched.

"Now we get my brother back." Gibson shook her hair out of a ponytail, smoothed back the strands, then put it back up again. She

bounced on her toes, almost vibrating from her need to get to her brother. *"Let's go already."*

"*Everything good on your end, Memphis? Any problems?*" I asked. Slade stared at me; I could feel his eyes touching my skin. He immediately turned away when I noticed.

"*Nada.*" Memphis yawned and rubbed at his eyes. He looked depleted and drained. We were all exhausted. "*Well, maybe one. Your father...*"

"*He's not a problem.*" I waved my hand at him to let it go.

"*We still have an enormous problem with the Nest. All the Authority does is train, work out, patrol, sleep. We are no match for them.*" Slade moved his arms casually, but I could tell was used to having people listen while he spoke. "*There is always a large concentration of guards at the Nest at any given time. You won't be able to repeat the same thing you did at the vault; we need an alternative plan.*"

"*We couldn't use the same plan even if we wanted to, we are out of seeds.*" Gibson rubbed dirt from her chin.

"*We don't have any weapons to fight them.*" Memphis screwed up his face in thought.

"*We have our abilities.*" Slade rifled through the supplies on the shelf. "*Is there anything we can use in this room for a weapon? What about bleach? Were any of you good at chemistry?*"

"*What in all the stars is 'chemistry'?*" Memphis asked.

"*Science,*" Slade threw his hand up in the air, cursing under his breath. "*Why didn't they teach you science?*"

"*We don't need to hurt anybody. I've got a better plan. What if we tricked them into leaving?*" I suggested. "*We create a distraction, some kind of diversion.*"

"*A distraction?*" Memphis said.

"*Like what,*" Gibson said.

"*What are you thinking?*" Slade asked.

"*You saw how many guards showed up when we locked them out of the vault. If we teleport to random places, the TCC will have to send out more guards,*" I said.

"Right, so we blink in and out all over the Hollows? Smart," Memphis said.

"So, like... all of us or...?" Gibson asked. *"You and Memphis are the only two that can teleport."*

"How about two groups of two? So, we cover more ground... make the Authority chase us all around the bunker," I said.

"I'm going with Memphis," Gibson said. Black circles lined her eyes. She looked like she could drop any moment. *"You've only teleported once. Do you honestly think you can do it a bunch of times in a row? Not trying to be snarky, just worried."*

"She's right: you'll have to teleport multiple times quickly. Are you up to it, Charlie?" Slade asked. He edged closer, placed his hand on my shoulder and squeezed. *"What if you can't do it..."*

I shrugged off his hand.

"She can. The first time is always the hardest. Then it becomes easier every time you do it." Memphis shrugged it off. *"Although doing it multiple times is tiring."*

"Who said you were coming with me, Slade?" I twirled my hair and tucked it behind my ear. My heart skipped a little. He wanted to partner with me. Why couldn't I stop these stupid useless thoughts? I had more important things to think about.

"Well, I'm not taking him; I still don't know him or trust him. He's your problem." Memphis' eyes flickered past Slade as if he didn't exist. He wouldn't even use his name.

"Wow, after all we've been through, Memphis." Slade pressed his hands against his chest, acting like he had a broken heart. *"I'm so hurt, just when I thought we were getting closer."*

"I can do it, I'll be fine." I pulled at my collar, wincing at their doubt. *"I just need a minute."*

Slade blinked a couple of times. *"This won't be a popular opinion, but I think we need to wait until morning to launch our next offensive."*

"What, no way," Memphis said. *"The longer we wait... the more danger Callahan is in. You said it yourself, Slade."*

"*Excuse you, Mr. Elite. Who put you in charge?*" Gibson stiffened at Slade's comment. "*We are going now. I don't want to leave my brother for another second. Who knows what he's going through?*"

"*Shh! Wait. Just listen to him.*" I threw up a hand.

"*Are you really taking his side against me?*" Gibson slammed her fist down on the shelf so hard the boxes jumped.

"*You are both right, but we need to work the problem, not tear each other down. I'm not taking his side, I'm just listening. He knows things we don't.*" I turned towards Slade. "*Why? What do you know? Explain your reasoning.*"

"*It's after lights out now. That means the bulk of the guards are back in the Nest, refueling and recharging. If we wait until morning, most of the Authority will be on patrol, with only a few remaining back; those untrained. Then we teleport around the bunker. Drawing as many guards as far away from the Nest as possible. The commission won't have any choice, but to empty the Nest. Then we free Callahan.*"

"*That sounds sensible.*" Memphis' muscles jumped under his skin. He rubbed at his sunken eyes. He tried to cover a yawn. He looked ready to drop. Teleporting wasn't as easy as he pretended. He needed rest; we all did. "*Maybe too obvious. I still don't know if I can trust you.*"

"*What? No way. We can't wait. Callahan is depending on us,*" Gibson said. She kept wringing her hands like she didn't know what else to do with them.

"*And for another thing: you are all exhausted. Just look at all of you with your bloodshot eyes and... we need to sleep,*" Slade said.

"*But what about the process thing you mentioned earlier?*" I reached for my mother's ring, clutching it for comfort. "*Won't he be in more danger the longer we wait?*"

"*If they haven't started the process yet, they won't until the morning. The bunker powers down to minimal use this time of day. They need full power to complete the transformation. If they have already processed him, then there is nothing anyone can do for him now.*" Slade explained.

"*I agree with Slade. This isn't just about what we want to do... it's about what is best for all of us in the long run. I think we need to get some sleep. It's after midnight and I know I've been awake since four am.*"

"I don't know… I don't know if we can trust what Slade is saying. What if he is trying to trick us? What if something happens to Callahan while we are waiting?"

"He is not lying. I'm an empath. I can tell. Trust me, I know exactly what I'm doing… mostly."

*"I could use some food,"*Memphis admitted reluctantly. *"I'm going to talk to Blaze. See if she confirms his story about the Nest."*

Gibson looked at her watch. She pressed her lips together; a pained look crossed her face. She shoved against the rack of supplies and kicked at the rolls of toilet paper, sending them flying. *"Fine, we wait. But this better not be a mistake."*

"I will take the first watch while you sleep. I already had a nap in the vault," Slade offered.

"Then we wait." Memphis moved within an inch of Slade's face so he could look him in the eyes. *"And if you are lying to me, so help me, I will end you."*

21

———

Slade talked me into teleporting to his apartment so he could change his clothing and collect his belongings, including Cuddles, his cat. I showered and changed out of my coveralls into my one good outfit. I took the time to wash the paint out of my hair. I vowed I would never hide its color again.

Slade changed into jeans and a sweatshirt and got rid of the highly visible baggy white tracksuit the prisoners wore in the vault. Guards paced outside his door, but they didn't post anyone inside. We tiptoed around his home, gathering items. I tripped over an area rug, almost knocking over a vase, but Slade caught it before it smashed on the floor. We returned to the supply closet, with Cuddles in her special container, as quickly as we arrived.

Memphis dug some MREs out of his stash. They weren't much, but they were better than nothing. I was beyond hungry, having missed lunch and dinner. I almost missed the hot mounds of mush they served us in the cafeteria. We inhaled them as if we hadn't eaten in weeks.

There wasn't enough space in the supply closet for the four of us to spread out to sleep. Gibson and Memphis moved into his secret space to find some legroom. They volunteered me to stay with Slade since Memphis and Gibson still didn't trust him, saying he was my responsibility. Gibson took Cuddles with her. She fell in love with the bundle of fur at first sight.

Now, Slade sat crossed legged across from the closet door to keep watch. I burrowed in the opposite corner of the room, on the floor, wedged between two shelves. I rested my head against the soft toilet paper rolls. I pretended to sleep while watching Slade out of the slits of my eyes. My eyes closed until he became little more than a shadow. I nodded off a few times but kept waking up. Nightmares kept invading my dreams.

Every time I wrenched my eyes open; I became conscious of Slade's eyes on my face, but he looked away as soon as I peeked up. I wiped around my mouth just in case I drooled. I kneaded the muscles at the back of my neck. They were so tight they threatened to break.

"Can't sleep?" Slade asked.

"No, I'm too tired to sleep, if that makes any sense." My eyes watered from suppressing a yawn. I swiped at the hair in my eyes. Yesterday's early alarm seemed like days ago now. So much had happened.

"I get it. I have too much adrenaline flowing through my body to sleep. Do you want to talk about it?"

"Talk about what?"

"Whatever you are thinking about."

"Mmm." He made me nervous; I didn't know what to say. I thought about several topics we could discuss but discarded them, deciding that silence was better than fumbling for words like a fool. I fidgeted with the zipper on my hoodie.

"Earlier... thanks for having my back," he said.

He carved at a small piece of wood with a knife, blowing a puff of air to remove the shavings. His head kept darting up to stare at the door. He tilted his head, listening for footsteps in the corridor. At this time of night, only the Authority had permission to roam the halls.

"I didn't. I just... did what I thought was best for Callahan." I drew my knees up tight against my chest and wrapped my arms around my legs.

"He's important to you, this Callahan?" he asked.

The remnants of the florescent lighting trickled through the door. He dropped his head, hiding his expression. He gave his attention to the wood in the palm of his hand.

"He is. He's the most important person in my life. I love him."

"Oh, sorry... I didn't know he was your boyfriend."

"He's not my boyfriend, he's my best friend. My family. He and the rest of my friends." His head tipped up and our eyes locked; I couldn't look away. *"When I'm with Callahan, I'm a stronger person, a better person. When I'm with him, I like who I become. I like who I see in the reflection of his eyes. He thinks I can do anything, be anyone. When we are together, I believe it too. His confidence strengthens me."*

"So, not your boyfriend."

"What? No, I just said that. I don't think of him that way. He's like my brother. Why?" I chewed on a fingernail, a bad habit leftover from childhood, before I realized and pulled my hand away from my mouth. *"Is it important, somehow?"*

"I just wondered why he was so quick to punch me for the kiss on your cheek, yesterday. Is he in love with you, maybe?" His head tilted to the side, listening intently.

"Huh, no." I laughed at the thought of Callahan as my boyfriend. *"Callahan would never think about me that way."* I covered my mouth to smother the sounds as there wasn't any point in speaking telepathically if they caught us laughing. *"Sorry about the punch. He never thinks before he acts. What happened to Gibson upset him and then... things snowballed. He's just overprotective of me. He's the only person who knows me. He knows I'm strange. He gets me."*

"Excellent, then it had nothing to do with the other kiss."

"Jumping jeepers, what kiss? I didn't kiss you." That lie spun easily off my tongue.

"Your lips, my lips, I call that a kiss."

"Oh, that... kiss." He meant the kiss in the bathroom, not the kiss on the cheek. I was happy for the darkness in the room since I could feel my face heat. I used my hand as a fan , then covered my cheeks with my palms. *"He doesn't know about the other kiss... unless Gibson or*

Reese told him, but they would have no reason to. Besides, you just did it for a distraction, didn't you?"

He shrugged his shoulders. His hand slipped, and he stabbed his palm with the knife. *"Ow."* He placed his palm against his mouth. Drops of blood stained the wood he held.

"Are you bleeding?" I maneuvered closer and knelt beside him, reaching for his hand. *"Here, let me see."*

"No, leave it." Slade scrunched his hand up, pulling it closer to his body. He tried to pull his hand away, but I wouldn't let him. He grimaced and swallowed hard.

Uncurling his finger, I pried open his hand. There was a deep gash where the knife had slashed. I ripped open a package of toilet paper and wrapped it around his hand to slow the bleeding. Then I had another idea. I unwrapped his hand then held my hand over the top of his as I had seen Gibson do a million times. I tried, but the violet healing light wouldn't flow from my hands. I tried again, but my attempts to heal him failed.

"Um... what are you trying to do?" Slade looked at me as if I had lost my mind.

"I thought I would try to heal you. Test these so-called Alpha powers, but I couldn't. It wouldn't work. Sorry." I re-wrapped his hand then applied pressure until the bleeding stopped. I rummaged through the boxes until I found a box of uniforms, tearing a strip off a shirt. I removed the toilet paper, replacing it with the strip of cloth. I wrapped the rag around his hand then tied it off, using my teeth to pull the edges tight. *"There, that should prevent infection."*

He flexed his hand. *"Thank you. You missed your calling. Trust me: you should work in medical."*

"Cause I'm a natural doctor." I laughed, taking in my motley lopsided handiwork. *"It's too late now."*

"I guess it is." Slade patted the ground beside him, suggesting I should sit. Two pairs of eyes on the door were better than one.

"Where did you get the knife? If you can call it that." The knife was old and worn, the extended blade had become rusty. Duct tape held the warped and broken black plastic handle together.

"From the shelf over there. They must use it to open the boxes of supplies." He showed me the block of wood he was chiseling. *"I don't think whittling is my thing."*

"What is it? Is it supposed to look like that?"

"I think... so?"

"Is that a question or a statement?"

He laughed and his leg bumped against mine. *"I guess I'm hopeless. I was trying to carve a dog."*

"A dog? Hmm... you sure?" I flipped it over, looking for some sign it could be a dog, but there was no tail or perky ears. *"Yeah, I think you have a future in wood carving. I am sure there is an enormous market for it. Maybe you could sell them at the bazaar. Put up a booth every weekend. I'm sure they'll be a big hit. You could carve cats, dogs, maybe get fancy and carve an elephant..."*

He flicked his finger against my shoulder. *"Yeah, no. I was carving it for you, as a thank you. I'm sorry for blowing up your life."*

"And you thought a wooden dog . . . would fix everything?" His thoughtfulness surprised me. I picked a piece of hair from the back of my head and twirled it around. *"This is real life; you don't get to restart things when you make a mistake. The stars know I've made enough of them lately."*

"No, it wouldn't fix anything... but it's a start." He shrugged and dropped the block of wood in my lap. *"I've got nothing else to offer."*

"Thank you, I guess." I twisted and turned the block of wood, trying to figure out how he had imagined the dog to look. Totally absorbed, I couldn't figure it out.

"What did you mean earlier when you mentioned Callahan knows about your strangeness?"

"Yeah, I'm not normal. I'm weird. I wondered how long it would take until you noticed."

He laughed. *"Define normal. Everyone seems normal until you get to know them."*

"My brain never idles—it bounces all over the place. I blurt out words when people are talking because I get so excited to have something to

contribute to the conversation. I spend so much time in my head I don't know how to communicate with other people."

He reached for the dog, but I wouldn't let it go. His hand touched mine longer than he needed.

"*It's hard to describe, but... no one who meets me ever likes me. At least, for the first time. I need to grow on people before that happens...*" I worried my tongue between my teeth. "*I'm used to it now. I'm different. It doesn't bother me anymore.*"

"*Why do you think being different is wrong? There is no such thing as normal. There is no right or wrong way to exist.*"

"*I don't know. Maybe it's how other people always make me feel. My empathic nature twists the way I perceive myself. It makes me feel inferior.*"

"*Well, trust me. I like that you are different.*" A corner of his mouth lifted in the hint of a smile.

"*You do, why?*" I bunched up my face. "*Why are you smiling? Is this funny to you?*"

"*No, it's not funny. I just think you are wrong about how people perceive you. To me, you come across as smart, brave, pretty...*"

I didn't hear anything else after pretty. I dropped my head, unaccustomed to flattery. It made me uncomfortable. "*If it makes a difference, you aren't who I thought you were either.*"

"*Yeah, who would that be?*"

"*An entitled brat,*" I transmitted. "*Someone who never had to work for anything and got everything handed to him.*"

He rolled his eyes and made a funny face. "*Sounds about right—that's how everyone thinks of me. But... can I tell you something? But it has to stay between you and me.*" He edged closer to me.

He took my hand, opened my palm, and placed his against mine; palm to palm, fingers to fingers; he intertwined my fingers with his.

"*You can...*" I licked my lips. His touch made the butterflies in my stomach flutter. "*You can trust me.*"

"*My mother hates me; she has hated me my entire life and I don't know why. In public, she seems like the perfect mother, but behind closed doors, she would just hand me off to the nannies.*"

"Nannies?"

"Yeah, does Elise look like someone who would change a diaper or wipe a snotty nose.'

"No, I guess not."

"Family dinners were full of constant criticism, humiliation, guilt-tripping, and manipulation. She mastered the art of passive-aggressive behavior. Dinner conversation became a treat. 'Excellent job Slade, you've done so well for someone with your limited intelligence' or 'If only you were as handsome as your father.'"

I blinked up at him. His sadness dragged on my emotions. *"Sounds rough. Elise sounds like an indifferent woman. I didn't know she treated you badly. I'm sorry."* I drew closer. I lay my free hand on his forearm, feeling the heat radiate from his skin.

"That's not even the half of it. She has no personal boundaries. She controlled everything in my life, from my friends, to how I dressed, to how often I had to trim my hair." He broke off, eyes focused straight ahead. His voice heavy with shame. The muscles in his jaw bunched. He grabbed at his hair. *"She hated this white streak in my hair with a passion. She wanted to cut it out all the time, but my father overruled her."*

"What about Joseph, your father? Why didn't he step in and help you?"

"Too busy, too indifferent, too afraid of my mother..." He twisted his mouth and turned his head away. *"I'm not sure. Sometimes it seemed like he cared, but not enough to do anything. He listened too little and cared even less."*

"You almost make me happy I grew up in the orphanage," I teased, trying to lighten the mood. I needed to change the subject before his sadness made me cry.

"I told you before I envied your life, and you didn't believe me." He released my hand and pulled away.

"I'm sorry, I have..." I winced. *"I don't have faith in words, only emotions and actions."*

He drew in a breath, then exhaled slowly, almost nervously. *"No, I'm sorry. I hope you don't think I'm a complainer. I know you have your own childhood trauma to deal with."*

I gave him a half-shrug. *"I try not to think about it."*

"I know the General cares about you. I overheard him talking about you once."

"Hmm, I don't believe that. If Zander loved me so much, he should have retrieved me from the bunker earlier. But he didn't, which proves he doesn't care." I shoved the thought away. I lived without Zander practically my whole life. I didn't need his love.

"Can I show you something?" Slade stood then picked up the laptop from the shelf where Memphis placed it earlier. He punched the keys until a digital video played. He plugged in a set of headphones and handed me one ear bud, keeping the other. *"Lean in closer."*

I leaned in until our foreheads almost touched. The familiar scene of the first exile appeared on the screen. The video blasted in my ear before Slade turned the volume low. I peeked at the door, convinced the sound would draw the guards.

"Oh, I've seen this. I've watched the exile recording... like a million times." I gave him a flippant wave.

"Trust me, wait until the end."

I watched the footage until Zander turned and winked at the camera. I saw him blow a kiss. I waited for the screen to go black when he started to speak, but it didn't.

"I thank you. You have given me exactly what I wanted. Out." He turned his back to the camera and walked out with his head held high.

I exhaled noisily through pursed lips. *"How did you get this footage? What does it mean? Why would he be happy to get out? "*

He made a sound in his throat. *"I never asked him, but he must have known we could survive outside. Somehow."*

"If he knew, why wouldn't he have taken me with him?" I fought back the threatening tears. I told myself it didn't matter, it wasn't important.

"The Commission wouldn't let him. They wouldn't release any of the kids, you know that. They didn't hold the children responsible for the sins of their parents."

"Sure, I get that, but..." I worked my bottom lip through my teeth. *"He has a network in the Hollows, people to do his bidding. You are one of them. So..."*

"So, why didn't he come for you?"

My tears silently streamed down my cheeks. I wiped them away. He didn't want me. Nobody did. It didn't matter. I told myself I wouldn't ever forgive him for my mother's death.

"I don't know the reason. I wish I did, but he must have done it to protect you. The General is an honorable man. I've only met him twice, but he is inspiring. He's why I joined the Resistance."

"So inspiring he became responsible for almost a hundred deaths."

"And how many innocent people do you think the Commission has executed, imprisoned, or exiled?"

I consented. The world wasn't black, and white, it was grey. Innocent people had died on both sides of this rebellion.

"Do you want to hear something funny?" I asked.

"Sure."

"Your mother interrogated me today."

"She did? Really, I'm surprised."

"Yes, but that's not—never mind. Did you know your mom introduced my parents to each other? At least according to her."

"I wouldn't believe a word she told you. And it's 'mother.'"

"What?"

"It's 'mother,' not 'mom.' She wouldn't let me call her 'mom.'"

I scrunched up my face. *"Believe me, I didn't want to either, but she had proof. Photos of them together when they were younger. My mother was an Elite. Your mother told me she dated Zander first."*

"Eww. Not an image I ever wanted to have."

"I know the feeling." I inched backwards.

"Oh, I also ah... went to your apartment today. Met your fiancé."

"Huh. My what? My apartment?"

"Your... Toni."

"Oh Toni, she's not my..." Slade's eyebrows pulled together. His eyes swept heavenward. *"I'm so grateful Toni looked after Cuddles for me. If*

something had happened to my baby.... I don't know what I would do. I couldn't handle it. I missed my furball."

This was another side to Slade I had never seen before. I had never seen someone so compassionate about a pet before. But then I had never seen a pet, besides in movies and television shows, until today.

"You are lucky you have Toni to look after Cuddles. She must love you a lot." I flicked my gaze away, afraid of his response. I liked him and I didn't want to pretend I didn't anymore. Life was too short to play games. I turned my head to look at him. *"She seems like she would make the perfect wife of the next commissioner."*

"Why don't you just ask me what you want to know." His eyes sparkled, and a smile surfaced on his lips.

"What, no, I don't..." I squirmed. My mouth opened, then closed.

He bumped his shoulder against mine. *"Toni is one of my best friends. I care about her very much, but I wouldn't marry her."*

"Does she know?"

"She does. She doesn't want to marry me either. Or any other man."

"Oh... I see." My eyes widened as understanding crossed my face. *"Oh, so yeah. That's good."* I wasn't looking at him, but I could feel his smile.

"Yeah, we are just friends. The algorithm picked us as a perfect match, but computers can make mistakes. Besides, I'm interested in someone else," Slade said.

"Well, I'm sure if you make it out of this... situation unharmed you can find somebody." The butterflies in my stomach tumbled around like crazy.

"That's not what I meant, and you know it." Slade placed his arm around my shoulder, pulling me closer.

"Oh, what did..."

He leaned in closer, so close our foreheads touched. The air shifted around us. Warm fingers under my chin tilted my head upward. He held my face in his hand and rubbed his thumb across my cheek. I clasped his hand.

"Trust me, I'm pretty sure I met you for a reason."

His face seemed inches from mine, so close I could feel his warm breath against my skin. I traced my fingertips over his scar along his hairline. I wet my lips with my tongue. He moved even closer. His lips almost touched mine when a sound alerted me. I jumped away from him a moment before Gibson and Memphis slid open the grate to take their watch.

22

———————

I got little sleep before the 5:00 am Monday morning wake-up call when the bunker came to life for the day.

"Do you have everything you need?" I asked Memphis.

"I think so. I didn't know I would transport a cat today. I didn't even know they still existed; I thought they were extinct." Memphis eyed the cat as if it were a lion.

Memphis intended to teleport our belongings to Salvations Keep. We weren't planning on returning, ever. He bent over and picked up the plush cat carrier where Cuddles fought against the closure; she traveled reluctantly, but in style. Memphis had our most valued possessions in bags wrapped over his shoulders and back.

"I have never seen anything as cute as this in my life." The tiny creature completely captivated Gibson. A cooped-up Cuddles acted less than pleased.

"I know! Isn't she the sweetest? Her fur is the softest thing I have ever felt," Slade said. Was he attempting to get on Gibson's good side? From the look she flashed, it wouldn't be easy to win her over.

"Thank you for doing this. I can't go there, not yet."

"You'll have to meet your father sometime." Memphis paused, sucking in his bottom lip. *"We should ask him for help. He has people, weapons. He has experience in these types of situations."*

"Maybe you should listen to Memphis. The General has loyal people installed everywhere," Slade said.

"No way. I'm not arguing with you, I'm just telling you we don't need his kind of help." I shook my head. We could do this without him; we had come this far by ourselves. We could finish it, although controlling my unknown powers still made me nervous. *"His help involves people dying. Do you honestly want to put Callahan's fate in his hands?"*

"I don't. The man is responsible for my parents dying. I won't trust him with my brother's life."

"It's Gibson's call, her decision." I didn't want to discuss it further. Teleporting drained my system more than any of my other powers. I needed to save my energy for the day ahead.

"You know it will happen sooner rather than later. I am surprised the General hasn't come looking for us already."

"Later works for me."

"Whatever. I'll be back in a few." He opened a portal and disappeared.

We plotted out the best points to teleport to within the Hollows while we waited for him to return. We considered places that would maximize the effect and draw out as many guards as possible. I worried I wouldn't have enough energy to teleport so many times in a row.

The air sizzled as Memphis stepped back into the room alone. I don't know what I would have done if he had returned with Zander. I knew I couldn't avoid him forever, but I would for as long as I could.

"I hope we made the right decision in waiting." Memphis nodded in Slade's direction. He still would not refer to him by name.

"I thought Blaze confirmed—," I said.

"She did. I'm just worried. We can only hope they haven't processed him already; whatever that means," Memphis said

Gibson's face sported the same haunted look. She would never be the same if something happened to her brother.

"Did you think I lied about the Nest; why would I?" Slade asked. A muscle in his cheek ticked. *"I'm a deviant. I am one of you."*

"You are an Elite. You're not one of us. You never will be," Gibson quipped.

"Excellent. Project Distraction is a go." I ignored everything else. Their warring emotions dragged on me, making me irritable. I glanced at my watch. *"It is 5:55 am. Breakfast is over and the bunker is operating at full strength. Quit your bickering and get ready to move."*

SLADE and I teleported into the corridor outside the iron door to the FarSide. The surprised guards didn't have time to draw their weapons before we quickly teleported somewhere else. I didn't have to fake the fear that allowed me the ability to open portals quickly.

We repeated the process six more times. Like Memphis said, the more you did something, the easier it became. On our last jump, we landed as deep in the Hollows as we could get, on the tunnel road to the blast doors near the ninety-degree sideways hairpin curve.

Slade assured us we were close to the Nest. As expected, the Authority had virtually no presence in the area. They let the cameras do the patrolling.

When we arrived, a track of auxiliary blue lighting ran in the center of the wall flickered, triggered by motion. I blinked as my eyes adjusted. A cave salamander scurried away with a cricket in its jaws. Blind from birth, its other senses were heightened.

Slade threw back his head and laughed.

"What," I sagged back against the rough rock wall. Here and there water dripped, giving the stagnant air a moldy scent. I wrapped my arms around my torso to ward off the clammy coldness. "Why are you laughing?"

"That was the most entertainment I have had in years, true fun. Did you see the guards in the cafeteria? The tall one fell on his butt trying to draw his weapon from the holster. Exceptional. I wish I could teleport." His face lit up as he spoke. Exhilaration radiated from every pore.

"I have to admit it was... exciting. Just the way everyone reacted. Did you see..."

The click of a camera whirling from side to side interrupted our stories. I flattened my back against the wall. Creeping forward, I felt around for something to cover the camera, finding a wooden box that contained several cans of cleaning solution. Emptying the box as quietly as possible, I searched for a stool or a ladder to climb up on. Nothing was available, so I had to consider another plan. I splayed my hand wide open and stretched out my arm. My fingers tingled; the camera vibrated momentarily. I wiped my sweaty hands on my pants. Trying again, I managed to maneuver the camera, pushing it upward so it would only view the ceiling. Hopefully, the TCC would think the camera malfunctioned. If they didn't, we wouldn't be here long, anyway.

Slade found a metal control panel and pushed the breaker on, flooding the tunnel with white florescent light. The panels hissed and sizzled before they lit up, as if they were fighting against the years of dirt covering them. The hissing echoed in the tunnel, making that tiny sound twice as loud and last three times as long. They only used this area of the Hollows for occasional maintenance. It certainly didn't live up to the cleanliness standards of the rest of the bunker.

The air hummed; Memphis and Gibson burst into the room, dragging a member of the Authority with them. "Jumping Jeepers, Memphis! I said to create a distraction, not this."

"I swear it was an accident." Memphis quickly tied up the guard with zip ties from his back pocket and forced him to his knees, so his spine touched the wall.

"Memphis didn't have a choice. The guard stood too close. We had to drag him with us, or he would have died when the portal closed on him," Gibson added.

I slapped the palm of my hand against my forehead. Why didn't I know that was a possibility? What if my inexperience had caused somebody harm or worse? I couldn't live with myself if I had hurt someone by accident, let alone on purpose.

Memphis dropped to one knee. He placed his fingers under the edges of the guard's helmet, then felt around for a clasp or snap. When it didn't work, he tried to yank it from his head. "I've always wanted to see under the hood."

"No stop. You will kill him without the helmet. He needs it to live. It's the control center," Slade warned.

"Come again?" I said.

"Wait, isn't he human?" Gibson asked. Her eyes narrowed to slits.

Memphis reached for the guard's left arm. He applied pressure until the guard reacted to the pain. "He feels pain."

"The body is human... but the brain is not. It's augmented, computerized."

"How?" I asked.

"I'm not a doctor, so I don't know the specifics, but the body is basically human. Sometimes they augment arms and legs with bionic features because of injuries or amputations and... they replaced the brain with a computer. Giving the commission complete control of them."

"That can't be right, can it?" Gibson bunched up her face in horror.

Memphis grabbed the guard's helmet and ripped it from his head. Underneath the mask, his face was a mishmash of human and machine. Two different sized android red eyes peered back. A large round sensor sat in the center of what used to be his forehead. They had replaced the ears with round speakers to absorb sound. The nose and mouth remained human. The guard rocked her head against the wall in distress. The airline to his nose disconnected when Memphis removed his helmet.

"Your he is a she," I said. The curved skull, smoother ridge along the brow, round eye sockets, and pointed chin made it clear. When the helmet wrenched off, her long hair tumbled out.

"Put her helmet back on, she can't breathe." Slade knocked all of us out of our frozen funk. We had just been staring at the guard's android face in a human skull, unable to move or think. Slade charged in, clutching the helmet. He snapped it back in place on the guard's face. She stopped rocking against the wall and sagged; able to breathe.

"Thunder, I ah…" I couldn't think of any words to describe the horrific image of the woman turned robot. Monsters don't sleep under your bed; they sleep inside your head. This image would stay with me forever.

"That's not right. How could they do that to a person?" Gibson placed her hand over her mouth, looking like she would retch.

"What's with the Darth Vader hookup?" I asked.

"Yeah, why can't she breathe like us?" Memphis asked. "She has a nose."

"From what I understand, they removed the part of the brain that controls breathing. They carry cylinders of air in their equipment." He leaned down and patted her equipment until he found the air cylinder. "Her tank is full; she should be good for a while."

Memphis adjusted his sweatshirt sleeve over his hand. His fingers tightened against the cuff. His mouth moved but no sound emerged.

"Is this what they will do to my brother? Oh, my stars, what if it's too late? What if…" Gibson's eyes widened to twice their size. She turned away, unable to look at the guard for another second. Her eyes darted wildly as she searched for something to retch into. Unable to find anything, she emptied the contents of her stomach in the corner behind us.

"We have to go *now*. Every moment we wait is another moment Callahan is at risk of being transformed into this atrocity." Memphis pointed at the guard. He bent his foot to kick her.

"Don't kick her. Do you think she did that to herself?" I asked.

"No, no, no, no. This can't be happening!" Gibson shuddered, clutching at her empty stomach.

"I don't understand how you knew what the TCC was doing to these helpless people, and you did nothing about it. You did nothing to stop them. What kind of person are you, Slade?" Memphis asked.

"How do you sleep at night?" Gibson wiped at her mouth with the back of her hand. "Those are people. What gives you permission to turn people into that."

Slade clenched his jaw tight, his hand balled into a fist. "Why do you think I joined the Salvation Resistance? To enact changes. To stop the barbaric practices of the Commission. I'm not in charge of anything. I've got just as much sway with the commissioner as the rest of you do: none."

Footsteps reverberated in the corridor as the Authority approached.

"Jumping jeepers, she must have a tracker embedded in her gear. I was afraid of that," Slade said.

"You didn't think to tell us earlier?" Memphis asked.
"It would have been useful information to have *ten minutes ago*." Gibson said.

"I thought we would have left by now, but you had to do your science experiment, didn't you?" Slade said.

"Slade, how do we get to the Nest?"

"I'm not exactly sure." Slade couldn't meet my eyes.

"I thought you said you knew where we were going. Did you lie to me?" I trusted him. We create this entire plan around his words. My abilities had told me he was telling the truth.

"I didn't lie. You asked me if I knew the location, and I told you I'd been there. I have been there... but when I was just a kid, four, maybe five. I have seen the schematics of The Hollows; I know we are close."

"Close? Are you kidding me? I knew we couldn't trust you. I knew it." Memphis' eyes blazed with fury. "We have five guards trying to kill us. What are we supposed to do?"

"Actually, it's more like eight," Slade said.

"Oh, sorry I wasn't specific enough for you."

"Accuracy is important," Slade retorted.

The Authority positioned themselves behind an old shed, rifles up, waiting to pounce. A guard yelled, "Come out with your hands up. You have two seconds to comply."

Without thinking, I tugged at the air, pushing and pulling.

"Charlie, we can't teleport without a clear destination. We should go to Salvation's Keep. Get reinforcements. I'm sure the General can help," Memphis explained.

"Over my dead body," I said.

"No, we can't abandon Callahan, not now that we know they will turn him into..." Gibson resisted looking at the bound guard on the floor, who was awake and alert, taking in her surroundings. "We can't let them hurt my brother."

"Why are you so stubborn?" Memphis rolled his eyes while gritting his teeth. "Do you need five minutes to get over yourself?"

"No, I've been thinking, and it makes sense to me. Instead of jumping to a place, I think I can teleport to a person. I think I can do it."

"How sure are you?" Gibson asked.

"About seventy-five percent or maybe fifty... well, as sure as I am about anything else I've attempted lately. My powers work with need. I need Callahan. I think I can teleport to him. I've also got part of an image from the vision we shared earlier today."

"That's crazy. I've been teleporting forever, and I wouldn't even attempt something so risky. If you don't have a clear destination in mind, you could get lost in space forever."

"She can do it. She got us this far, didn't she?" Slade said. "If you don't want to come, go someplace else. You have the ability."

"It's worth the risk," Gibson said. She would say anything, risk anything to get to her brother.

The captain counted down. We were out of time. I opened the portal and extended my hand. Gibson connected first, then Slade, and finally Memphis. We stepped through the portal. Shots pinged off the wall behind us.

～

WE STEPPED INTO AN UNLIT ROOM. It had the same dank smell and darkness of the tunnels with a major hint of body odor. Like my vision, only torchlight illuminated the blackness. Unlike my vision, no one used the exercise machines or practiced their skills. Twenty or more dead members of the Authority littered the floor.

The steel cage ahead stood empty. The door twisted at an impossible angle. Outside the cage Callahan stood with Jagger Malone and another man I recognized—Zander Edge, my father. Both Jagger and Zander dressed in camouflage, knives tucked in various places with automatic weapons and several handguns tucked into their waistband.

Gibson shrieked and ran straight into Callahan's arms, careful to leap over several lifeless bodies in her haste. He picked her up and spun her around. Her feet dangled in the air. Callahan let out whoops of joy. I glared at Memphis.

Memphis scratched his head. "Sorry, I warned you that I reported what we were doing to the General, but I didn't know he would be here, or do this. They must have fired first. He wouldn't have done this without provocation."

"I agree with Memphis. The General is an exemplary man, you'll see," Slade said.

They both walked to the other side of the room. I wanted to follow, but I felt like someone encased my feet in cement. What would I even say to this stranger I shared blood with?

After he pried himself away from his sister, Callahan and Memphis embraced, slapping each other on the back. Callahan avoided Slade's outstretched hand and bounded over to me, picking me up and squeezing me tight. "It's so good to see you. Let me see your funny face." He ran his fingers down my face like he always did.

I reached up to touch his poor, battered face. His eye was black and bruised. Callahan winced when I gingerly touched the affected area. A red partially healed cut, span across the bridge of his nose. When he turned his head, I noticed another bruise on his chin.

"You'll never believe what I've been through," he said. "If you think this is bad, you should see the other guy."

He meant it as a joke, but I could see right through him. I hugged him back tightly. "I never thought I would see you again. I missed you so much."

Gibson appeared over Callahan's shoulder, hesitant to let him out of her sight. Slade and Memphis were deep in conversation with Zander. I kept track of Zander out of the corner of my eye. He didn't even acknowledge my presence.

"It's only been a day, silly girl." Callahan set me back on my feet and gave me a kiss on the top of my head. "Thank you for sending the message. It helped."

"Jumping jeepers, it actually worked! I wasn't sure." Callahan was saying and doing all the right things, but there was something off with him. I could sense it.

Callahan smiled, then grabbed me by the hand, dragging me towards Zander and the others. I wanted to drag my feet, but with everybody watching, I went with the flow.

Zander Edge was busy giving orders. I cringed when I realized I sounded just like him when I did the same. Zander ordered Memphis and Slade to check for weapons and see if there was anything of value on the deceased guards. He asked Gibson and Callahan to gather some supplies from the Authority's stock room. He asked Jagger to check the door and prevent it from opening.

It was strange how he spoke to each group differently. He went from giving order to asking politely. Everyone disbursed to accomplish their tasks. I would rather do something than talk to Zander.

Jagger used his powers to fuse the door closed. The metal screech threatened to make my ears bleed.

Zander waited for me to approach. I squared my shoulders, trying to look unaffected by his presence, even though my insides flipped around like crazy, making me want to vomit. I wasn't prepared to see him, not emotionally.

"Come closer, Sunshine. Let me look at you." Zander grasped both my arms, pulling me into an awkward, one-sided embrace. "When Memphis told me your plan, I thought my men and I could help. Nice work on the distraction, by the way. You have good instincts."

I stared at him bullishly. Unsure what to say or do. I moistened my lips. My mouth had suddenly gone dry.

His fingers touched my chin and moved my head from side to side, appraising me as if I were a prized heifer. "You are one hundred percent my flesh and blood."

"Why did you do this? Why did you kill all these innocent people?" I asked.

He seemed surprised by my question. He gazed at me condescendingly through half-lidded eyes. "These half-breeds aren't even human anymore. The TCC already killed them. They can't even think for themselves. They are killers. Trained assassins."

Callahan shuddered. A shadow passed behind his eyes. "This could have been me, right?"

"But it wasn't." Gibson reached out and squeezed his arm "We wouldn't let it happen to you."

"Jumping jeepers. They were innocent until the TCC violated them, changing them into monsters. They didn't deserve this," I said.

"Sunshine. They are better off dead than living like this. We did them a favor, put them out of their misery; we've eliminated the TCC's control over them." Zander's green eyes radiated a fierce, uncompromising intelligence.

Zander looked the same as he did in the tapes I watched over and over. Well, except for the crow's feet around the eyes. His skin was darker, weathered, and looked leathery, but otherwise he looked the same. I couldn't read his emotions. He didn't project an aura, either. Everything I had ever read on Zander said he was proficient at projecting superficial charm and charisma. If that was true, I certainly wasn't feeling any warm and fuzzy feelings towards him.

"They fired first. We had to defend ourselves... to rescue my nephew," Jagger interrupted. The only one brave enough to disturb our conversation. "We had casualties too."

For the first time, I noticed some of the dead dressed differently than the Authority. "Your people?"

"Two men and a woman from my team, a man from Jagger's."

"Yeah, Ed Meyers. Your group released him from the vault with all the other detainees. Did you see him earlier?" Jagger asked.

"Nope. Never saw him. It was a crazy time," I said. That was a not-so-subtle reminder from Jagger that I had broken our deal. What would I have to do to appease him?

"Charlie, this was a no-win situation for anyone. We achieved our target. Can we debate this later? Someplace safer." Slade returned and fluffed the hair at the back of my neck in plain view of everyone before Memphis called him to help with something else.

Jagger asked to speak with Zander privately. They walked to the furthest point in the room. Was he planning to tell Zander I reneged on my deal? The twins drifted back with several containers of supplies.

Callahan eyed the fallen guards. "I didn't want anyone to die… because of me." Callahan's voice broke. He hung his head.

"It's not your fault," I said.

"You are worth a million dead guards to me," Gibson whispered to Callahan. She clung to his side, afraid to let him wander too far away. She had already healed all his wounds. Her happiness radiated from her in waves, making me instantly feel better.

"What happened there?" I asked. Taking in the bent iron bars of the jail cell that stood twisted beyond repair.

"Oh… kinda, just happened when Jagger removed the silver cuff that took away my powers. I let out some of my frustration and kind of destroyed it." Callahan's voice resonated higher than normal. He lowered his head, turning partially away. Whatever had happened to him had shaken him to the core. I could sense how tormented he was, even if he tried to put on a brave face. I couldn't wait to talk to him in private.

"Impressive. What happened to all the others in the cage with you?" I asked. "I saw at least a half-dozen other people in my vision."

"At least," Gibson said.

"Zander sent them ahead to someplace with a weird name. Wait, did you say you are having visions now? When did that start?"

"Yeah, I have so much I need to tell you," I said. The others returned before I could ask Callahan more questions.

"General, we have secured all the weapons. Should we leave for the keep?" Memphis asked. He had looped five or six automatic weapons around his body. He stuck pistols in the top of his pants.

Slade kept his eyes trained on the only exit. His arms strained under the weight of a case of ammunition.

"Yes, yes. We have spent more time here than I expected." Zander's smile didn't reach his eyes.

Jagger tapped Zander on the shoulder. "Time to go,"

"I couldn't have done it without you, brother. Thanks for everything. Dad would be proud of us working together." Zander hugged Jagger briefly. Jagger squirmed a little, then hugged him back.

"Brother?" I exchanged surprised looks with Callahan and Gibson.

23

———————

"How are you... brothers?" Caught off guard, I took a few steps backward, wobbling on my feet.

"What is even happening?" Callahan gulped, closing his mouth. He ran his fingers through his spikes, but they popped back up. Even imprisoned, his hair was never out of place. He still wore the same clothing as yesterday.

"Uncle Jagger, why didn't you tell us Charlie was our cousin?" Gibson stood with her arms across her chest. "It would have been nice to know we had more family."

"Same," I said. Mercury and Jagger were brothers, but where did Zander fit in?

"Half-brother, to be correct. We only share a father." Zander acted indifferently. "Can we discuss this later, back at the keep where it is safe."

"My mother was Stephen Edge's first wife. She died giving birth to Mercury and me. Twins run in the family, as you know." Jagger's hard eyes softened when he mentioned his brother. "Our maternal grandparents raised us. Mercury and I took their last name, Malone."

"News to me. There is no mention in the archives. I have read everything there is to read on our family history," I said.

"I paid to have the records changed after they exiled Zander and Mercury to keep attention off of me," Jagger said. "I needed to destroy all traces linking me to Zander."

"I'm surprised you didn't get exiled with Mercury. You are identical twins. Could the Authority even tell you apart?" I asked.

Jagger raised an eyebrow but didn't answer my question. Always with the secrets.

"The watch..." I muttered under my breath. Jagger and Zander had the same watch with the same inscription. Did Mercury have one? The pieces were coming together, but there were some major ones missing.

"What watch?" Slade inched over until he was standing close enough to touch. He sat the heavy boxes down, then slipped his hand into mine, our fingers intertwined.

"Doesn't matter... I'll fill you in later," I whispered.

"I thought it was impossible to alter the records in the archives." Gibson held her hands together behind her back and sort of rocked back and forth from heel to toe.

I knew it wasn't impossible as my grandparents had done it. It would only take a technopath like Blaze to pull it off.

"I know my way around. I know a guy who knows a guy who knows a girl." Jagger and Zander shared a look.

"You forget you are talking to the man who runs the underground whispers, Gibson." Callahan yanked me away from Slade. He swallowed me in a hug, pulling me so tight I couldn't breathe, and lifting me off my feet. "I knew there was a reason I felt like you were family."

"Are we good? Are there any more questions or can we leave now?" Frustration crinkled Zander's eyebrows.

Gibson joined in the bear hug. I embraced them both, soaking in our shared happiness. Although they had always felt like family, I couldn't put into words how much it meant knowing we shared blood. I drew in a lengthy breath that quavered as we broke up the hug.

Jagger started to speak, but Zander cut him off. Jagger wasn't used to someone giving him orders, and he didn't seem to appreciate it.

"Memphis, take Slade back to the Keep. The rest of us will follow in a moment. This is a family matter," Zander ordered as he paced with his hands on his weapon.

"Yes, General! Right away, Sir." Memphis saluted Zander. He muttered under his breath, "I thought I was family considering you are dating my mother."

Was it weird our parents were dating? I would have to revisit that later.

"Memphis, did you say something?" Zander's expression closed. His hands clamped tightly together, he leaned forward.

"Nothing, sir." Memphis bobbed his head, chewing on his bottom lip.

Zander stared at Memphis, edging closer. Memphis blinked twice before looking away. Zander said nothing. The look on his face did all the talking.

Memphis opened a portal and Slade mouthed "see you later" before disappearing into it with him.

I turned towards to my cousins. "I love you both. Cousins. I like the sound of the word."

"Don't get all weepy on us. I know how you get." Callahan squeezed my shoulder. His eyes sparkled briefly before a cloud passed.

"You know she will." Gibson made a face that reminded me of Elise's pug, Brutus. I brushed at my eyes, sniffing. Trying to resist the tears of happiness leaking out.

"Enough of this, you have all the time in the world to catch up later. We need to go before more guards arrive." Zander slammed his hand on the weight rack. Several of the weights tumbled off the rack, hitting the floor with a deafening bang.

A guard popped up off the floor. Wounded, blood seeped from his right side forming pool formed around his position. His arm swung up as he fired his weapon wildly two or three times. A shot rang out, echoing in the vast room. The moment played out in slow motion. He rolled behind one of the exercise bikes, looking for cover.

Automatically, I ducked at the sound, dropping against the hard rock floor, my body surging with adrenaline. Jagger rounded the corner and took out the guard with two shots to the heart. I scanned my friends, looking for any sign of injury.

I felt Gibson's shock of pain as if I experienced it first-hand. The shot propelled her backward; blood tricked then poured, soaking her light grey sweatshirt. I told myself to move, but my legs wouldn't obey, like I was sinking in quicksand.

Callahan dropped to his knees, picked up his sister, cradling her in his arms. His words rushed out, "Gibson! Wake up, G! Open your eyes. What do I do? What do I do? Help me somebody, please *help me*." His eyes were wide and wild when he looked up.

"Put pressure against the wound," Jagger ordered, gun raised, looking around for another shooter. "I'll be there in a second."

"I can't believe those boys missed checking the guard. There will be consequences for disobeying a direct order." Zander stood with his hands on his hips, shaking his head.

Callahan ripped off his shirt, balled it up and placed his hands against Gibson's side, trying to stop the flow of blood. There was so much of it. How could someone lose so much blood and still live?

More shots rang out. I flattened myself down behind a rack of weights until I realized Zander and Jagger were making sure the rest of the guards were dead. I raced over to Callahan, falling to my knees beside him. "How can I help? Tell me what to do?"

Gibson opened her mouth. Blood poured out. "Tttt... tell Reese I...." her eyes fluttered shut.

"Don't close your eyes. Please don't close your eyes," I pleaded.

"You can tell Reese when you see her, right?"

Gibson's eyes opened a slit. *"I forgive her..."*

"I don't know, I don't know what to do!" Callahan's fear shone in his eyes. He tapped Gibson's face gently with trembling fingers, trying to wake her. Her eyes flickered open. She mumbled her brother's name before her eyes rolled back in her head.

"I know this hurts, G, but you have to stay awake. Stay with us. Open your eyes. Please, Gibson. Please open your eyes!" I pleaded.

"Keep pressure on the wound, Callahan, or she will bleed out." Jagger holstered his weapon, swinging his rifle behind his back. He knelt and put two fingers against Gibson's pulse. Jagger tilted her head back slightly by lifting her chin. He put his ear next to her open mouth, listening, "She's not breathing. Place her head to the floor we need to do CPR."

Callahan lowered her, as gently as possible. Jagger put one hand on top of the other. He pushed hard and fast against her chest, using his body weight to compress her chest an inch or so. He repeated it six or seven times until Gibson inhaled. Her eyes flickered, but she didn't open them. Jagger stopped the compressions. "She's breathing again."

"Here, let me try something." I pulled Gibson's shirt up, pushing Callahan's hand aside so I could see the wound. It was small with jagged edges. It started bleeding profusely as soon as Callahan removed the pressure.

"Check her back to see if the bullet came out the other side," Jagger ordered. "Zander, stop messing around and get over here."

Zander snooped around opening drawers' lockers and cabinets. He pulled everything out and threw the contents on the floor. Ransacking the room.

Callahan and I rolled Gibson on her side. There was no exit wound, the bullet was still inside. Gently, we pushed her on her back. I held my hand out, palm side down over the wound, trying to heal her. As hard as I tried, the violet light refused to come. I took a deep breath and tried again.

"What are you doing? You aren't a healer, Charlie!" Callahan yelled.

"She is failing. Move over." Zander stooped and pushed me to the side, out of the way. The violet healing light radiated from his palm. Gibson made a sound in the back of her throat before she stopped breathing again. "It's too late... too much damage to her internal organs. I can't save her. She's already gone. I'm sorry."

"Maybe you should have tried to heal her earlier instead of going around shooting people who are already dead." The words flew out of my mouth before I could bite them back. I was angry he had pushed me aside without a thought. With a quivering hand, I wiped at the tears that had been leaking out of my eyes and continued to fall for Gibson.

Callahan let out a primal scream. His agony was unmistakable. He banged his fist against the unforgiving concrete floor, crying out, then gathered Gibson in his arms; he lowered his head against his sisters. "No, no, noooo.... she can't be dead! She can't be! Wake up Gibson, wake up." He rocked back and forth, openly sobbing. There were no words I could say to take away his pain, heal his broken heart. Kneeling behind him I wrapped my arms around his neck leaning against his back. We wept together.

The name Salvations Keep made me envision a medieval castle built from square stone blocks with turrets and a drawbridge. At first glance, the rebel base wasn't even close. One sizable building constructed from logs with a thatched roof stood surrounded by hundreds of smaller identical buildings. Gaps in the logs were filled with mud, clay, and straw. Ice and snow covered the roofs of the houses, like something out of a movie

It took me a moment to realize that I had left the bunker, that I was outside. I pinched myself to make sure it was real. Snowflakes whirled as they drifted softly to the ground. I stuck out my tongue, trying to catch one. I took in a deep breath of fresh air and coughed; it was so frosty it threatened to freeze my lungs, but I took another. I delighted in the fog created when I exhaled. Rubbing at my arms to fend off the cold, I realized that none of my clothing was warm enough for this but it didn't matter. I twirled around until a wet flake hit my tongue. For the first time in my life, I was free, totally free. Happy. Then I remembered Gibson was dead. The moment forever tainted by her loss.

The survivors built the town in the dip of a mountain, shielded on four sides from the wind and other elements. The imposing mountain stood before us, a craggy, deep blue and grey. I took a moment to appreciate the exceptionally majestic picture. Snow draped over the surrounding majestic peaks; the mountain tops swept upward until they reached the clouds. The apex disappeared in the mist. Short, stocky pine trees popped up all over in clumps or singles. The first trees I had ever seen.

The rebels had erected some buildings against or into the rock walls. A fire burned in an enormous fire pit surrounded by multi-colored stones outside the largest building. The air smelled wonderful, of what I learned was burnt wood. Firewood was piled up high all along the outside of the building. It was noisy and crowded.

Most of the people had bulky coats or furs draped around their shoulders. Curious citizens peeked out drawn curtains to get a look at the latest arrivals. Some people wore black masks covering their mouth and nose, hooking behind their ears. Two plastic spinnable buttons placed on either side of the nose made them look like a respirator. Some of the prisoners rescued from the vault still wore the white track suits and had blankets wrapped around their shoulders.

Spontaneous clapping began when people noticed Zander. The respect in their eyes for him was unsettling, almost fanatical. Silence ensued once people noticed Callahan carrying Gibson. People bowed their heads in reverence as we passed. It was weird that no one stared at my blond hair here.

Callahan refused to leave Gibson behind at the Nest or let anyone else touch her, insisting on carrying her without aid. Zander directed us into the gigantic building. The sign outside the door said, "Salvation Lodge." Then he instructed his men to clear the room and keep everyone out.

Inside, the ceiling was high, the wooden beams and logs exposed, the thatch visible. Many tables and chairs filled the room. Jugs, trays, ladles, and bowls stacked along a long table, ready to serve the next meal. The carvings on the wooden furniture seemed simple yet intricate. In the center of each table, the symbol from the box was displayed. I wondered if Blaze had given Zander the box. Maybe here I would finally get some answers.

My fingers traced the pattern. Each side of the room had a door leading somewhere. A fire roared in the center of the room, the smoke vented out a stone chimney. Something was roasting on grates being tended to by an older woman wearing a long, flowing dress. She was the only person who did not to leave the room. She didn't give us a second look.

Near the back of the room stood a round table with seven chairs set up on a stage. Ornately carved, each chair had high backs with puffy cushions in colorful fabrics on the seats. Behind the stage stood an upright piano, several guitars, and a couple of other instruments I didn't have names for.

Callahan laid Gibson's body gently on a long wooden table surrounded by matching chairs. He pushed her hair off her face and straightened her clothes. Zander gave orders to someone on a radio. The mood was solemn inside the room. I needed to focus on something—anything besides the loss of my friend and cousin. No matter how numb I felt, I knew Callahan felt worse. Grief radiated from his every pore.

Jagger broke the silence. "I need to get back to the Hollows before anyone realizes I'm missing. My people will worry if I'm gone longer than expected."

"Why do you go back there when you can leave anytime? When you could live free here," I asked.

"That would be for me to know and you to find out," Jagger said, he touched the tip of my nose with his finger. His answer vague, like always. He acted like he had all the secrets in the world, but he wouldn't share them without a price.

"We can lay her to rest beside her parents." Zander massaged the back of his neck. "We have a person here who will say some prayers for her."

"Don't talk about her like you know her." I bit my lip and glanced away before I said something I would regret.

"I'll be back for the service." Jagger tapped Callahan on the shoulder. "Callahan, at least you have the comfort of knowing your sister is reunited with your parents."

Callahan nodded. He wiped at his red and swollen eyes.

"I will have my soldiers gather some rocks and we can entomb her in the morning." Zander's voice held no emotion.

Jagger shook hands with Zander leaving via the door. How would he get back to the bunker? Could he teleport?

"Bury her?" Callahan pulled up a chair beside his sister and held her hand. Kissing the back of it.

"They cremate bodies in The Hollows," I said.

"I don't want to think about her cold... laying in the ground." Callahan's voice broke. He put his hand through his hair, then rested his forehead against the table.

"I know, but the ground is too hard and frozen to bury people here. We don't have the technology to cremate people properly, so we surround them with rocks and leave a marker. Our graveyard is larger than I would like it to be." Zander gave a humorless laugh. "I can show you where we buried your parents. It's a peaceful place. It will please you."

There was a commotion at the door. Slade, Memphis, Reese, and Ajax were stuck outside in the gathering, trying to get in. It hit me that Reese still didn't know about Gibson. Rushing over to the door, I threw it wide open, much to the surprise of the men guarding it. Frosty air poured in. "Let them enter."

"The General said no entry, so no one enters." The guard pulled his weapon from his holster and pointed it at them. The other guard leveled her shotgun. My friends raised their hands and stepped back.

"Slade, use your telekinesis to take the gun," Ajax said.

"Think! These are the General's soldiers. We are on the same side as them. They are our allies, not our enemies. Besides, why don't you hotshot?" Slade said as he pushed Ajax good naturedly. *"Can you please go be stupid somewhere far away from me?"*

"Whatever. At least we are living the good life now," Ajax said as he shoved Slade back. *"Free and clear of the Commission and their stupid rules."*

Their joking ceased as soon as they noticed my tear-stained face.

"What's wrong, Charlie?" Reese intuitively knew something was wrong. "Whose blood...?"

I looked down at my shirt, surprised to notice the blood splattered all over. Gibson's blood. I opened my mouth, but nothing emerged. I shook my head, refusing to meet any of their eyes.

"It's bad, whatever it is. How bad is it? Is it Callahan? He was fine when I left." Memphis' expression tightened. He jumped up, trying to see behind me since I blocked most of the door.

"Maude, George—they can enter," Zanders' voice boomed behind me. The guards instantly obeyed, lowering their weapons as they moved out of the way.

Reese and Memphis pushed past me, barging into the hall. I couldn't turn around. I felt Reese's panic turn into grief the moment she realized something had happened to Gibson. I heard Memphis ask Zander how this could have happened. Zander filled the newcomers in on what had transpired. Ajax excused himself and left the room, not wanting to intrude.

Reese screamed and sobbed. She begged Callahan to help Gibson. He tried to hug her, but she pummeled him with her fists. Callahan put up his hands to protect himself. Zander grabbed her arms, restraining her, then lowered her onto a chair beside Gibson. Reese pulled herself into a tight ball, refusing to look at anyone. She rocked back and forth. She reached out and stroked Gibson's hair and touched her face.

"Are you okay, Callahan?" As soon as it came out of my mouth, I knew the words were wrong. The light that normally shone around him had dimmed. I felt something different about him even before Gibson died. "I'm sorry, that was a stupid question. You are not alright. How could you be?"

Callahan wiped his lip where Reese had punched him. A tiny bit of blood smeared on his hand. His lip started to swell.

"Can I do anything for you, get anything for you. Just ask, buddy. I'm here for you, whatever I can do," Memphis said.

"N . . . no... but thank you."

Reese popped her head up. Her eyes swam with tears. "I'm sorry Callahan. I didn't—."

Callahan waved her apology away. "Don't worry about it."

Their sadness piled on top of my own. It was too much, I couldn't absorb it all. I hung my head and cried. Slade hauled me into his arms. "It's okay. I got you. It's okay. Everything is okay. Hear my heartbeat, just focus on me."

I rested my head over his heart, comforted by the rhythmic beat and sobbed. Slade rubbed his hand up, and down my spine, whispering soft soothing words. My tears soaked through his sweatshirt, but he didn't complain.

I left Slade's embrace, hoping to help Reese and Callahan any way I could. I squeezed his hand. "Thank you."

"Anytime." He ran his thumb over mine before releasing my hand.

THE DOOR to the room at the back of the building swung open. The woman from the caves, Memphis's mother, appeared. She seemed surprised to see the room full of new people. Memphis waved her over. She kissed her son on the cheek. Memphis introduced her to everyone as Bristol. He quickly summarized what had happened.

"Call me Bri. You poor, poor babies. You have been through so much. Well, you are welcome here, and you are safe. Make yourself at home. I will have quarters prepared for you and I'll take you to them later. It's been a busy time making room for all the recent arrivals. You missed breakfast but I will try to find you something to fill your bellies."

My stomach growled as soon as Bristol mentioned food.

Bristol's smile seemed friendly and trusting. She had a light green aura suggestive of love, healing, and innocence. Zander came up behind Bristol and slipped his arms around her waist. "Bri, have you met my daughter, Charlie? She has finally come to join us."

I tried not to react to his statement. He had some nerve acting like he had been waiting forever for me when I only found out he was alive a day ago. It was awkward to see Zander embracing anyone, especially Memphis's mother.

"We've met before, haven't we, Charlie?" Bristol's voice sounded like sunshine. "Your father has been talking about this day forever. He has been so excited to see you again."

"I'm sorry. I didn't know who you were. Your hair is so different from the pictures in the archives. I didn't recognize you as Memphis's mother. And it shocked me to see anybody else at the hot springs."

"We can access the hot springs on the mountainside of the village, there is a tunnel running deep to different destinations. Our people come and go from there all the time," Zander explained.

The door to the back room opened again and the boy with white-blond hair skipped across the room over to where we stood. He held a tiny blue metal toy car in his fist. Dressed in jeans, a hoodie and running shoes, the boy seemed at ease in the room.

"It's the boy from the hot springs," Slade whispered beside my ear. "Now is your chance to get the answers to all your questions."

The boy stopped and stared, tilting his head as if trying to remember where he had seen me before. "Daddy, I saw that girl before." He put his finger in his mouth and clung tightly to Zander's leg.

Who was this boy?

24

———

Just after 10 am, Bristol fed us a late breakfast of hash browns, pancakes with syrup, and toast. The tastes were all new: sweet, crunchy, and so delicious. I ate meat, what they called "bacon," for the first time in my life. It felt weird in my mouth. I thought about the poor pig that had given its life but pushed it aside. Callahan and Reese refused to eat. Refused to leave Gibson's side. Zander had a private talk with Memphis and Slade just before breakfast was ready. I don't know what he said to them, but they both had red faces when they returned and didn't speak during the meal. I felt guilty for eating with such gusto, but I was beyond starving, and this new food was too tempting.

After breakfast, Zander led me out the door at the back of the hall to one of the larger houses next to the lodge. His quarters. The snow had stopped falling as I stepped onto a carpet of white, marveling at the impressions my feet made as I walked.

Pegs on the wall just inside the front door held coats, scarves, and toques. A large sitting area was populated with chairs, tables, and benches. One table held a partially done jigsaw puzzle of at least a thousand pieces. A throw carpet of red, blue, and green made the area homey. An oval oak table stood surrounded by ten or twelve mismatched chairs. Shelves with plates and cups decorated the walls of the eating area. In the corner stood a desk piled high with books. There didn't appear to be any tech in the room.

Another stone fireplace held a banked fire that Zander stoked. Over the fireplace hung a painting of the symbol, the rebel symbol. A bookcase had strange statues, colorful bowls, trinkets, and ornaments instead of books. Treasures from the old world. Framed paintings took up most of the wall space. They differed from the ones in the bunker, newer maybe. A hallway to the left had several closed doors. An old restored wooden trunk caught my eye.

Zander noticed my interest in the trunk. He gave me a half-hearted smile. "Bri likes to restore old furniture, things the scavengers find from the old world. She chose everything in here except Amy's paintings."

"Which paintings are my mother's?" I peeked over the paintings, wondering if I could tell just by looking which were hers. He pointed to several landscapes. A portrait of Zander, at a younger age, was suspended from the ceiling. How did I miss that the first time? I wish I had her talent, but I couldn't draw a straight line with a ruler. "I didn't know she was an artist, but then I didn't get a chance to know her."

"I paid Jagger a small ransom to have her paintings smuggled out after our exile."

I edged closer to view her artistry. I knew nothing about art, but I thought they were beautiful. Zander let me take my time inspecting them. My whole life I had wanted to get the answers to my questions. Now that I had the opportunity, I dragged my feet, worried the responses would be worse than what I had imagined.

"Amy also painted the symbol over the fireplace." Zander waved his hand towards the symbol. His eyes followed mine to the painting. "She designed the pattern. Do you remember it hanging in our old quarters?"

"No. Why would my mother design the pattern for the rebel symbol?" I asked.

"Umm, well . . . it didn't start that way. She created it. For us, for our family. After she died, I started using it as my personal symbol on all my communications and it grew from there."

"Our family?" I rubbed the back of my neck, massaging out the kinks.

"The symbol is the Chinese symbol for ZAC: Zander, Amy, and Charlie. She believed in symbology. She thought it would be something to have a symbol of our own. We knew we would name you Charlie no matter which gender you were born. She worked tirelessly to get it done before you arrived. You were just two months old when she died." Zander moved his arms about casually as he talked.

I closed my eyes and tried to remember the symbol hanging in our old quarters. That must be the reason it tugged at my memories. My subconscious must know it, even if I couldn't recall.

"Amy was the creative type, always doodling or drawing on the tablet or any scrap of paper. I had Jagger search for supplies every time he sent his scavengers out on a supply run. She was unlike anyone I had ever met before." Zander's eyes animated; his entire demeanor lit up when he spoke about my mother. "She was light in the darkness. Instead of walking, she danced. Instead of talking, she sang. I don't think I ever saw her without paint in her hair or on her hands. She always had a smile on her face. She was my sun, moon, and stars. I think about her every day."

I ate up his words as if I were starving. I welcomed any information on my mother. "I wish I could have met her."

"So do I, Sunshine, so do I. Your mother loved you more than anything." He scrubbed a hand over his face, sighing heavily. "I'm sorry you never got to know her. You would have loved her, of course. She left the earth way too soon."

"Because of you. I know my mother died because of you." I loosened my collar, searching for my mother's ring. Grasping the chain but dropping it before pulling the ring into the open. Not wanting him to see I still had it. I wished I could read his thoughts, but he had shut me out.

"Come again?" Zander's eyebrows drew together, perplexed by my accusation.

"You're the reason she is dead. She needed life-saving surgery the TCC wouldn't give her because of you. Because of your stupid rebellion." The words flew out. I had been holding them back for years and couldn't bite my tongue any longer.

"Sunshine, you don't have a single clue what you are talking about. I did everything I could to save her, *every single thing I could!* I pulled in every favor, made promises. You don't know how hard I tried... I did... I have never loved anyone as much as your mother. I never will. Who are you to judge me? You weren't there. You don't know what happened." He put his hands on his hips, glaring at me. He drew in several deep breaths before continuing. "Listen, Sunshine: I have been giving you a pass on your snarky attitude but that will not last much longer."

"Jumping jeepers, I don't care..."

The blond hair boy inched open the door and peered around the heavy structure. He dropped to all fours then rolled behind an overstuffed chair. Crawling on his belly, he snaked his way closer. He tried to be silent, but he touched a chair, causing a scraping noise. He was a welcome interruption, unaware of the tension in the room.

"Good try, Bowie, but you will have to be much quieter if you expect to go hunting in the valley with me next weekend," Zander said. "Come here and meet your sister, Charlie. Use your telepathy to talk to her."

Bowie jumped out of his hiding place and ran straight into his father's outstretched arms. "Daddy, you promised me I could go with you. My brothers and sisters get to go. I wanna go too." Bowie stuck out his lower lip.

"Are you kidding me? Brothers and sisters. There's more than just Bowie?" I stepped back, hitting the edge of a chair. I sat down.

"Did you expect me to spend the rest of my life alone? I have eight children, including you. Zeppelin is fifteen, Zappa is thirteen, Segar is twelve, Frampton is nine, Lennon and Santana the twins are eight.

Last, but not least, is four-year-old Bowie here. Five boys and three girls.”

“I thought nothing, considering until recently I thought you were dead.” I gave him a half-shrug.

“Hi, Charlie. I’m almost five.” Bowie held up five fingers. *“I seen you before at the hot springs. I member.”*

“Hey Bowie, it’s nice to see you again. I remember you too.” I waved at him awkwardly. Kids made me nervous.

“Bowie, you just turned four.” Zander tickled Bowie under the arm, making him squeal and squirm.

“Is Bristol their mother? How many of them are blond like us? Alphas? Can I meet the rest of them?” I asked.

“But I’ll soon be five.” Bowie persisted.

Zander plopped down in an unattractive brownish wooden rocking chair with Bowie on his lap. The chair wasn’t anything special, marked and scraped from years of use. Zander started rocking back and forth, gliding on the curved rockers.

“No, Bri couldn’t have any more children after Memphis. It’s an extensive story, but most of them have different mothers. I would love for you to meet all your siblings. I’ve told them all about you. They are in school now, but they will be back later this afternoon.”

“What could you possibly know about me to tell them? You haven’t seen me for like... fifteen years. You started this brand-new life and left me behind like I was nothing.” I clenched my jaw so tightly my teeth threatened to break.

A colorful photo album on the wooden side table caught my eye. Flipping through the photos, I recognized Bristol at several ages. This was the Bristol from the archive photos, her hair in dreadlocks. Her short new hair-do changed her looks dramatically. At least I had an explanation for why I didn’t recognize her right away.

“That’s not true. You know I had no choice; the TCC wouldn’t let us take our children. I installed Samantha at the orphanage to ensure your health and safety. She’ll tell you herself.” Zander lifted his chin, jutting out his jaw.

“She’s here?” I hadn’t let myself hope she had survived.

"Yes, she lives at the Frozen Fortress, but she will visit soon. After the TCC exiled her, I had others looking out for you. I have people all over the Hollows, even in the highest levels of government. People like your friend, Blaze. You were never alone."

"I was always alone." I wanted to stomp my foot like a child, but I refrained. I promised myself I wouldn't get emotional and cry, so I stuffed down my feelings.

"Bowie, will you run over and see your mother in the greenhouse? I need to talk to your sister alone. You can spend more time with her later." Zander set Bowie on the ground and patted him on the butt.

Bowie pouted and squirmed, but finally left after being promised an extra dessert at dinner. Clearly, Bowie had our father wrapped around his fingers.

"Sunshine, I think you need to learn the truth about your mother." He stood, putting his hands on his hips.

"I know the truth. The TCC wouldn't give my mother the operation she needed after I was born because you oversaw the rebels. They wanted to punish you. So, she died because of you." Anger thrummed through my veins, like a fire about to ignite. I monitored my hand for any changes.

Zander drew in a lengthy breath. "It's not that simple. There is a lot more to the story you don't know."

"Like, what? How do I know I can believe you?" I stood up, unable to sit any longer. Pacing around the house, picking up the items in the bookcase, careful to place them back in the same position. I didn't know what half the objects did. Almost dropping a small orb, I accidentally flipped it over. When it righted, snow fell from the top down onto the small farmhouse inside the globe.

"I'm your father. I've had nothing but the best intentions for you." Zander leaned his weight on a chair, drumming his fingers on the top. "If you don't trust me, trust yourself. You are an empath. A natural lie detector. Use your abilities to determine if I am lying."

"How do you know I am an empath?" I asked.

"I told you I know everything about you."

"Okay then, let's hear it. Let me hear your side of the story." I waved my hand for him to continue. I sat back down, closed my eyes, then opened them to a half slit. I still couldn't read his aura, but he told the truth of that much I was certain. The trouble was when people believed what there were telling was the truth it messed with my abilities.

"Your mother had a damaged heart. She was born with a congenital heart defect. Amy needed a trunk... trun... truncus arteriosus repair. I think that's what they called it. Surgeons fixed the defect at birth, but she needed to have several more operations as she grew older. She had the last one at sixteen. The doctors warned her children weren't in her future. Pregnancy would cause too much stress on her heart."

All this new information was hard to process. I placed my hand over my heart wondering if I the heart defect was hereditary. There was too much nervous energy running through my body. I needed to do something with my hands. I ran them through my hair, pulling it up into a ponytail, and released it again.

"The first time Amy was pregnant, she lost the baby. I thought we had dodged a bullet. She promised me she would have her tubes tied, but she didn't. I think it was the only time she ever lied to me. I wouldn't risk losing her to have a child. She was my everything." A single drop of grief welled up from the corner of his eye, but he brushed it away. He stood and paced back and forth.

It took a lot of willpower not to stop Zander's story to ask my questions, but hopefully there would be time later to ask them if he didn't answer them all.

"I underestimated how much she wanted a child of her own. She didn't even tell me about you until she couldn't hide her pregnancy any longer. I missed all the signs, too busy trying to get ahead and build us a better life. By the time I discovered what she had done, the damage to her heart was too extensive. The TCC offered to do the surgery but there was a risk to the baby, to you, so she wouldn't hear of it, wouldn't even listen to the doctor's advice or mine." He ran his hands across his face. His love for Amy was clear in his remorse.

I almost fell over. Had my birth killed my mother?

"Right after you were born, Amy promised to have her heart fixed... have the operation. The doctors thought they had a slight chance to repair the damage, but the TCC wouldn't allow the surgery. They said it was too risky, that they could put the resources to better use. But I knew the actual reason."

"Yeah, you. You're the reason." I rubbed my arms. Even though it was warm inside the room. I felt cold from the inside out.

"Yes, it was because of me but not for the reasons you think. It wasn't about the rebellion. The rebels were nothing then, just a group of people that liked to whine. They never did anything about anything. My family and the rebels have been intertwined for generations. My father encouraged me to join, so I felt obligated to continue the family tradition, but the rebels were no threat. Not then." Zander pushed his white hair away from his face. He wore his hair longer than most men his age.

"You haven't changed my mind so far. I want the truth. That's all I want from you," I said.

"Patience, child. I'm not done my story yet." Zanders' eyes flashed with irritation. "The TCC proclaimed I was the mythical leader of the rebels, but I wasn't. Not then. I was out of my mind with worry while trying to look after a newborn by myself while Amy's health declined. But then I discovered the actual reason. Elise Cutter."

"Elise was Amy's friend..."

"Where did you hear that? Elise has no friends. She's a self-involved narcissist. Not interested in anything not involving her." Zander snorted. His face twisted into a hateful expression.

"Elise interrogated me this afternoon, told me about her friendship with Amy. Showed me pictures. Said she dated you first but was happy for Amy when she fell in love with you." It felt weird calling her Amy, but mom or mother didn't sound right either.

"What did you tell her?" Zander asked.

"Nothing. What could I tell her when I don't know anything?"

"Good, good. That's part of the reason I kept you out of everything." Zander shifted his weight from one foot to the other. "Elise never told the truth a day in her life. I dated Elise first. Back then, I was a bit of a player…"

"Eww! Spare me the details of your love life." I covered my ears with my hands.

"I wasn't planning on sharing them," Zander said. "Quit interrupting or we will never finish this story."

I mimed zipping my lip shut.

"When I saw your mother, her smile took my breath away and, to make a long story short, I never had eyes for anyone else. Elise didn't take it too well when I told her I couldn't see her anymore. We were never serious. We both dated other people at the same time we dated each other. Even though she would marry Joseph Cutter, she wanted to keep seeing each other in secret. I wouldn't do that to Amy."

"Was she in love with you?" I asked.

"I doubt Elise has ever loved anybody but herself." His mouth twisted, the muscles in his face tightened. "Elise pretended to be happy about our marriage, but she was slyly using subterfuge to sabotage our relationship. I told Amy she was toxic, to distance herself from Elise, but Amy thought there was good in everyone. She couldn't see it at first. Couldn't see how destructive her friend was."

He was telling the truth. Every fiber in my body told me his story was real.

"Elise poisoned Amy's relationship with her parents, telling lies and twisting half-truths until her parents disowned her. Not that Hugh and Laura-Jane needed much help. They hated me on sight. Elise tried to tell Amy lies about me, but your mother didn't believe her. When Amy started to distance herself, things took a turn for the worse."

"Worse how? What else could she do to the two of you?" I jumped. There was a loud banging outside, followed by a bunch of chatter. The sounds here differed from the bunker and would take some time to get used to. Even the smells were unfamiliar, the usual smell of antiseptic replaced with polish and burning wood.

"She had my job switched from maintenance to sanitation. She had us moved from one quarter to another. She even had us living separately for a time before we got married. She lied to our friends, turning them all against us." Zander smoldered. He squeezed his eyes shut as if to stop the past from replaying in his memories.

"The worst thing was Elise didn't even care about me. She just wanted to punish me for saying no. It was all a game to her. She's diabolical. She influenced the TCC to deny the surgery because she could. She killed my Darling Amy for no reason and there was nothing I could do to stop it. Nothing."

All my life, I blamed Zander for my mother's death, holding on to anger and hatred like a lifeline. I was unsure how to move forward. I tried to process everything I had just learned and compare it to the old information. "I'm sorry, I didn't know. No one told me."

"Hush, Sunshine, it's not your fault. Only a few people knew of our situation. How badly Elise treated us."

"It's my fault she's dead. If she didn't get pregnant with me, she never would have—."

"No, don't let me ever hear you say that again. Ever! She wanted you more than anything else in the world."

"But you never did, did you?" I was dying to hear him say I didn't need to try so hard to be perfect. That I was enough just the way I was, no matter how strange or awkward. That he loved me.

25

"How can you think I didn't want you? You are my daughter, my firstborn. I love you!" Zanders' eyes almost bugged out of his head followed by rapid blinking. He seemed appalled by my suggestion.

"Don't look at me like that."

"Like what?"

"Like I matter to you. You left me alone for fifteen years. You could have sent someone to get me, but you didn't. I didn't know you were alive, but you knew I was." All the emotions of the past fifteen years threatened to breakthrough. I repeated 'Don't cry' as a mantra in my head.

"Truthfully, I never meant for you to stay in the bunker as long as you did. It was always my intention to bring you to me earlier, but things happened... preventing me from coming to you." Zander scrubbed his hand across his face.

"And those things were more important than me?"

"No, of course not." Zander's head popped up. He paused as if to gather his thoughts. "At first it wasn't safe to get you. We barely survived.... I knew the TCC had been faking the jaunts for years."

"I'm sorry, run it by me again. How? Why would the TCC lie to us?" I wasn't oblivious to the fact they lied to us all the time, but what would they achieve by faking the jaunt. It didn't make sense.

"Jagger and Mercury broke down the footage of all the jaunts. They determined the scenery never changed, only the individual. They edited it somehow. Those outside views displayed on the screens are just rerun footage. It's not nearly as frozen as it appears. The planet has thawed a lot in the past one hundred and eighteen years."

"I've only been outside for a few minutes, but it's freezing, stormy." When we came through the portal from the Nest, I immediately felt the change in the temperature. It had shocked my body to feel the first waves of cold. The wind felt like a slap in the face.

"Yes, here in the mountains it is cold, but in the valley, the temperatures are much warmer in the spring and summer. It's beautiful. There are lush green grasses, trees, and shrubbery. Plenty of animals and fresh water. We have a camp down there—The Solar Stronghold—with another one further up the mountain called 'The Frozen Fortress.' But this was the original camp. We don't need to live underground anymore."

"Where do you get the names? From comic books?"

"Could you listen for two minutes without a cynical comment?"

I paused. "I gave it some thought, but I'm afraid it's not possible."

Zander stared at me, unimpressed with my sarcasm. "Just give me two minutes. That's all I'm asking. Two minutes. If you don't like what you hear, then we never have to cross paths again. You can avoid me forever."

I motioned for him to continue his story. I moved over to the table holding the jigsaw puzzle. The box lying next to it showed lions lying in green grass with a blue sky and a yellow sun. I picked up a few pieces, trying to place them. Zander pulled up a chair beside me.

"I petitioned to test the outside air several times independently, but the TCC always turned me down. It became my obsession to get outside. My brothers worried I put my sorrow over losing Amy into this new fixation. Looking back, they were partially right. It took me a long time to admit this to myself... but I had a hard time looking at you, Charlie, because every time I did, I thought about your mother. But it doesn't mean I didn't love you."

"You just didn't want to spend any time with me. You started a rebellion instead of looking after me." My hands worked to find the correct position to place the puzzle pieces.

"I did it for you. Searching for a way out so we could have a better life together."

"And how did that turn out for you? Because it didn't work out very well for me." Why couldn't I stop the snarky comments? This wasn't me.

"It wasn't all fun and games for me either. I became a leader within the rebels, pushing for changes, mobilizing them into a fighting force. We were the second generation with powers, and I taught them how to use them to their fullest potential. The Commission didn't know what I could do as an Alpha. Even I didn't know at first." Zander continued with his explanation, determined to ignore my comments.

I almost had the pieces of the lion put together. I searched for the last piece of the mane.

"I heard rumors the Elites were designing a building on the surface with plans to leave those of us from the east behind. They planned to use us as slave labor. Jagger, Mercury, and I started mapping out the Hollows, determining the weak points until we finally found a way out."

"Through the hot springs?" I asked.

"That is one way but there are others. We built here at Salvations' Keep first. Erected the principle building and some smaller ones. We planned to leave the Hollows as soon as we could. But the TCC got wind of our project somehow. They arrested my brother, Mercury, and some of my other men. Took them as hostages to ensure our good behavior. I knew I had to get them back." Zanders' hand gripped the edge of the table until his knuckles went white. "That's when I knew the TCC would never let us go. I knew Elise would seize every opportunity to punish Mercury, to hurt me."

"So, you invaded the food plant, holding it hostage. Did you know how many people would die in the process? Did you even think about them?" I closed my eyes, trying to block out the images my mind witnessed. The archives had photos of all those who died during the siege. I studied all their faces until I knew their names by heart.

"People do destructive things when they are trying to survive, necessary things. I'm sorry they died, but if the TCC would have just let my people go, none of that would have happened. It's on them as much as me. They say I'm a demon and maybe I am, but I am the demon they created. An Alpha demon." Zander folded his hands over his face and blew out a noisy breath. "All I know is I did what I had to do for my people."

I moistened my lips. My mouth had gone dry. "How did you keep the TCC out of the food plant for forty-one days?" I concentrated on placing one piece at a time. Working on the puzzle was oddly calming.

Zander shrugged. "For starters, we blocked off all the exits. Twisted the doors, dropped all the furniture in front. Kept people using their powers on the doors. We also had seventeen hostages, four Elites including Alessandra Torres, the CEO of the food plant . Everyone else busied themselves working on the keep. My demands were simple. First, release Mercury and my men from the vault. Second, let all those who wanted to leave the Hollows... leave. Two simple concessions could have prevented all the deaths. The blood is on the TCC hands, not mine."

"I don't even know what to do with that."

"There were two minor battles; we won the first but the TCC eventually broke through our blockade regardless of the hostages. I fought for my life. Near the end of the battle, Logan Campbell brought Mercury to the food plant with a gun to his head and a zapper. I had no choice but to surrender."

"Your brothers' life must have meant a lot to you considering fifty-three people starved to death and thirty-seven people died in the fight."

"Sunshine, how many people did the TCC turn into mutant robots? How many of our people do they still control with the restrainers? Are you so programmed you don't even realize what is happening right underneath your nose?" Zander gave lengthy explanations for some questions, with quick or no explanation for others. "What were you willing to do to get your friends back. Would you have killed someone if you had to?"

"It's not about the TCC. I'm not defending them. Two wrongs don't make a right. Just because they are monsters doesn't mean you get to be one too."

"How do you destroy a monster without becoming one; it's impossible." Zander clapped his hands on his hips, arms crooked. "I did what I had to do, and I would do it again."

I couldn't talk about the revolt any longer. "What is a zapper? I've heard the term a few times recently." Joseph said the same word yesterday at the Assembly. Simon did too. Was it only yesterday? It felt like the past few days had all blended into one.

"Zappers can read minds and erase memories from people. If you have enough zappers, they can erase memories from multiple people at the same time. They are the only people that can perform a thorough analysis of someone's brain."

"Then I guess Memphis is a zapper. We just called it mind control. He covered for me at the assembly when I couldn't control the light radiating from my hand."

"The TCC uses them at assemblies all the time. It would surprise you to learn what the TCC has gotten people to forget. But Memphis isn't a zapper. He controls or changes thoughts but he doesn't erase them. It's similar, but different. They are no threat to you as an Alpha."

"What are these Alpha powers I keep hearing about? What other powers do you have? What other powers will I develop?"

"All the powers of the Alpha mind. The common ones, telekinesis, telepathy, clairvoyance. Some uncommon ones like electrokinesis, which is generating and controlling lightning and electricity. Energy manipulation, levitation, the sky is the limit. Oh, there is a quick one I can show you." He walked over, putting his right hand out palm first. "Give me your hand."

I did as he instructed, touching his hand with mine. I felt a blip of a power surge. "What was that?"

"I gifted you with the power of transference. You can copy anyone's powers now. They can gift it, or you can take it. It gives you an advantage while you wait for the rest of your powers to arrive."

I pushed my hair back behind my ears. It might be the first gift he had ever given me. I wondered if transference worked the same as joining hands together, as Memphis and Reese had done earlier.

"One of my favorite powers is putting people to sleep with a thought."

That would have been a useful power to have a couple of days ago. Why hadn't Zander done that when he attacked the Nest? "Do all your people have powers?"

"The people here at the Solar Stronghold do. The people at the frozen fortress don't, but most of them have been with me from the beginning. You know—."

I massaged my temples; my headache raged again. Closing my eyes, I sagged my head back against the chair.

"Do you have a headache?"

I nodded.

"Use your powers."

"What?"

"Use your powers." He walked over and lifted a book off his desk. "Use telekinesis to take this book."

"Why?"

"You'll see. Just trust me."

I opened my hand, stretching the tips of my fingers as far as they could reach; the book floated across the room to my outstretched hand. "What was the point?" I set the book down on the table beside me.

"How is your headache?"

My body stiffened. The headache had disappeared. "Totally gone."

"When the headaches start, you need to use your abilities, any ability except telepathy. It is the only way to get rid of them. You're an Alpha coming into your powers, but you won't be at your full strength until you are twenty-one. That's when I planned to come to you. Then they arrested Slade and Ajax… and added you to the most wanted list, so I needed to move up the timeline."

"Thank you for the tip." My head jerked upward as I replayed his sentence. "You were planning on leaving me there for four more years. Why?"

"You were safer there than out here."

"Safer maybe, but not free. It seems safe here. Did you want me or just my powers?"

"There are still many dangers here." Zander sat across from me, playfully swatting my knee.

"What dangers?"

"That's a story for another day. Let me just say we are not the only people to survive. There are other groups out there, and none of them are friendly. Plus, you can't be in power for as long as I have without making enemies." Zander looked away, refusing to answer my question. What was the big secret? I grabbed for my mother's ring for comfort without thinking, drawing it out into the open.

Zanders' eyes lit up when he saw the ring. He edged closer to me, trying to get a better look. "You have your mother's ring. I thought they lost it."

"Samantha saved it for me."

"Can… can I see it?".

"Maybe."

"What do you mean, 'maybe'? That was a yes or no question."

Pulling the chain over my head, I felt reluctant to let Zander touch it. When I placed it in his palm, I noticed the watch back in place on Zander's wrist. He walked over to a lamp, switched it on, and examined the ring.

"Did Jagger give you back your watch?"

"Umm."

I repeated my question several times. The ring absorbed Zander as he remembered the past.

"Hello? Anybody there?"

"What did you say?"

"The watch, did Jagger give it back to you."

"Back?" Zander tilted his head to the side, pursing his lips. "Umm, no, this is my brother Mercury's watch. Mercury and I were close. Closer than the twins ever were. Which angered Jagger. I can't believe Jagger has my watch and never told me? Thunder…"

"Three identical watches?"

"Stephen, my father, gave all three of his sons watches when we joined the rebels. My ancestors smuggled them into the bunker, hoping they would translate to currency. They were jewelers in the old world. My grandfather inscribed them with the "ab initio" inscription because our family were among the first rebels in the bunker, and he was proud. How do you know Jagger has my watch?"

"Samantha gave it to me. I needed to trade Jagger the watch for a security card for the vault; to break out Slade and the others."

Zander scoffed but said nothing else. He handed me back the ring. I quickly placed it around my neck and tucked it away. Zander gripped his chin with his hand, perplexed.

"Can you turn your emotions down a bit, you are overloading my senses?" For the first time, I felt emotions flowing from him. Usually, he emoted nothing.

"Can't you turn off your empathy?"

"No, I wish." Was it possible? It would be wonderful to feel only my feelings. Not feeling overwhelmed by those of everyone else.

He reached for my hands. His were rough and calloused from years of hard work. "I will let you read my thoughts. *Can you hear me*?"

"*Yes.*"

"*Shut the door to your mind, block me out.*"

I did what he said, blocking his thoughts.

"Read my emotions."

He emoted sorrow, anger, frustration, and a sliver of fear.

"I want you to push against my emotions the same way you pushed against my thoughts. Try it."

I tried, but I could still sense his feelings. Trying again, then again, failing every time.

"You're overthinking it. Calm your mind and push my emotions away."

I glared up at him, inhaled a deep breath, and tried once again. This time I pressed against his emotions with all my mental energy. At first, I felt a resistance but eventually, I pushed his emotions far enough away. I slammed the door shut, erecting a mental dam. I couldn't sense him anymore.

"Very good, you've got it. It takes a bit of practice, but you'll figure it out."

I felt lighter than ever, lighter than air. "Thank you... I have been wanting to shut that door for years." I gave him a tiny smile.

"I have to warn you not to shut your own emotions off. After your mother died, I had to turn off mine. I couldn't handle them. It turns out I left them off for too long, losing part of my humanity."

I ran my tongue over my teeth. "I can shut my own emotions off. Why would I?"

"Sometimes it's necessary, like when I lost Amy." He shrugged it away. "Do you want another suggestion?"

"Sure, why not? Give me fifteen years of parenting advice in one day."

Zander winced. "Only close off your emotions when you're in a crowd. Don't do it when you are with your friends or your boyfriend, otherwise, you won't know how they are feeling. Trust me. I know from experience."

"Boyfriend?"

"Don't think I haven't picked up on your closeness with Slade Cutter. I've seen you looking at each other when nobody's watching. You are fated. Just like Amy and I."

I put my hands up to my cheeks. "It's not... he's' not..."

Zander laughed at my embarrassment. "Slade is a decent man. He has a good heart, he's nothing like his mother. You could do worse."

I jumped up from the chair, placing my hands over my ears, turning my back on Zander. "Na-na-na-na-na. We aren't having this conversation."

"Come back and sit down. I promise not to tease you anymore."

I wasn't comfortable with his banter. We were still strangers. Once again, I searched through the items on the bookshelf to avoid our conversation. There was a picture I hadn't noticed before, tucked behind a figurine of a unicorn. I pulled it closer to have a better look. A photo of Zander, Jagger, and Mercury when they were much younger, in their early teenage years. It still seemed strange to find out they were brothers.

"Why did Mercury and the others die if the air is safe to breathe?" I turned and held up the photo of the brothers.

"Fifteen years ago, the air wasn't as good as it is now. The dust was tremendously thick. When we first went outside, we were only out for brief periods, so we didn't feel the full effects. The air still has dust particles. For now, when you go outside, wear a respirator. We call them rebreathers. Take it off for short periods to build up your tolerance. Drink a lot of water and rest. It will take time to adjust."

I nodded. It still hadn't sunk in that we were free of the bunker. No more horns, no TCC, no Authority, no security tags. Reluctantly I asked, "Will some of us ... die?"

"You should be fine, but it doesn't mean you shouldn't take precautions. So many of my people died in the first week, including Mercury. I wish I knew then what I knew now."

"I'm sorry about your brother. It must have been tough to lose him after everything you did to free him."

Zander nodded. "It was devastating. All the survivors became sick for a time, including me. We had the lodge partially built, so we had some place to stay even though it was cramped. After years, our physiology adapted, allowing us to stay out longer and explore this great big, beautiful world. I lost everything, so I built a new everything."

"Does the TCC know about this place?" Should I worry about an attack?

"Not to my knowledge. They haven't located this place, or the Frozen Fortress, yet. We stayed hidden from them for years. They believed the air would kill us without them getting their hands dirty." Zander scoffed. "They found out about us a little year ago, that we were still alive ... that I was still alive ... when we built the Solar Stronghold, the solar farm generates all our power here now. The TCC sends out drones to spy on us. My men have taken down a few of them."

"Didn't you mention earlier the TCC was already outside, building a new community?" I felt nave at how long the TCC had kept us in the dark. I should have questioned more instead of just going along with anything they said.

"They built a city of their own on the other side of the mountain, the Silver Settlement. They started a few years ago and my scouts tell me they will complete it within the year. They use our captured people to do the heavy lifting. My information tells me they are installing a special dome to keep out people with powers when it's finished. Elise—."

"I'm sorry if I placed you and your people in their cross hairs."

"Don't worry your pretty blond head about it. You didn't. We had been planning for the day they found us for years. Once they move above ground, they will come for us. It's just a matter of time."

"Then what?" I was afraid to hear the answer.

"Then we pay them back."

"Pay them back? For what?"

"For creating us and then turning against us. The flash drive Blaze gave me has all the information we need to—."

"What do you mean? Creating who? Do you mean deviants like us? The radiation created us."

"No, the TCC did. They used my grandparents' and parents' generation as guinea pigs, running experiments on them. Haven't you ever noticed almost all the deviants are from the East?"

"Deviants don't exactly advertise who they are."

"There are so many of us now; they are afraid. It's why they created the restrainers to harness our powers. You can't even believe the things they did to your Uncle Jagger. Twin experiments where they did unmentionable things to him while leaving Mercury as a control subject....and please don't use the term deviant again. We are gifted or legends but never deviants" Zander's mouth twisted when he said the word.

26

After our conversation, Zander walked me to the house I would share with Reese and Blaze. I was relieved to find out he didn't expect me to stay with his family. I felt more comfortable staying with my friends.

The stroll allowed me to see more of my new home. Equally spaced rows of identical houses stood on streets with names and numbers. To differentiate the homes, cute wooden signs decorated the different colored front doors. Some porches had pine branches wrapped around the spindles. Everyone saluted Zander as we passed, while he nodded. He pointed out the school, medical clinic, and a few of the major buildings.

Reese and Blaze weren't home when we arrived, so Zander left me to explore on my own. My new home was a small version of Zander's. There was a sparsely furnished common area with an unlit fireplace. The smell of freshly cut wood permeated the house. Whether it came from the woodpile or the walls, I couldn't tell.

I opened the door to two of the bedrooms before I discovered my bag from the bunker laying on a bed. Some well-read books sat piled high on a desk with a stool. In the corner, a large, comfortable chair took up space. My entire life I wanted a room to myself, but I never expected to get one. I could handle living here forever.

There was a brown dresser and someone had placed my clothing within the drawers along with other clothing that didn't belong to me. A red and blue quilt covered the bed with matching pillowcases. On the wall was a painting of a mountain. I was certain my mom had painted it.

My first thought was to send a message to Callahan and Gibson, then it hit me: Gibson was dead. It felt like a punch in the stomach every time I thought about her. I wondered how they communicated here. Since Slade destroyed our tags in the bunker, we couldn't send messages to each other anymore.

I tossed the bag on the floor, kicked off my boots, lay down on the bed, falling asleep fully dressed before my head hit the pillow.

THE HOUSE WAS STILL empty when I awoke a few hours later. After showering, changing my clothes, brushing my teeth and hair, I set out to find my friends. Zander had supplied me with appropriate clothing for the weather and a rebreather, so I bundled up warmly. I memorized my house number and street: 14 Rose Drive.

I threw a few snowballs, watching them impact and split apart when they hit a target, though most fell short. Then I made a few snow angels. I tried to make some designs in the fresh snow using my boots. I felt like I was the only one in the world to have walked here. I supposed Neil Armstrong must have felt the same way when he walked on the moon.

Walking on ice took some getting used to. There were a few spots where I ended up falling on my butt. I got some funny looks from people, but it was worth it to play in the snow. I took a few wrong turns before finally finding the lodge. Since I didn't know where anyone else lived, I thought I would start looking there.

Slade waved me over as soon as I entered. Our eyes met and held as I approached. His smile made me feel warm on the inside. Slade occupied a seat at a table with Ajax and, much to my surprise, Callahan and Memphis sat with them. Reese and Blaze were nowhere in sight. Gibson's body had been removed.

The warm feeling left as soon as I saw Callahan. He looked up as I passed. His eyes were red-rimmed and swollen from his tears. I squeezed his shoulders. Sleepless, even his spikes seemed to droop. I felt so guilty for leaving him alone in his grief while I slept.

"How are you doing, cousin? So sorry for disappearing. Is there anything I can do for you?" The word cousin felt weird coming off my tongue.

"I feel numb. I just want to be numb. I don't want to feel anything. I still can't believe my sister …" Callahan's voice broke as his eyes filled up with fresh tears. He held his precious drumsticks in his tightly clenched fist. Memphis must have retrieved some of his stuff.

I worried my lips between my teeth, wishing I could think of something to say.

Workers busily prepped for the evening meal, setting the tables. The air smelled heavenly, a cross between fresh bread and herbs. My mouth watered thinking about our next meal. Anything tasted better than the mounds of mush from the cafeteria.

There was a group of men in the corner drinking something from mugs. Did they have alcohol here? They spoke in hushed tones but kept glancing over at our group with strange looks on their faces. Were we the subject of their conversation?

"Where did they take Gibson? Where is Reese?"

"Zander's men moved Gibson to a cold cellar until they can bury her . . . body tomorrow." Memphis said. "Blaze is working on something for Zander. Something to do with the information on the flash drive we brought him."

I had forgotten the flash drive in all that had happened. It didn't seem important anymore.I sat beside Callahan, wrapping my arms around him. He tucked his head into my shoulder. "I know. I know… there are no words I could ever say to express how sorry I am. I feel like it's all my fault. I tried to get Gibson to stay behind, but—."

"She never listened, right?" Callahan snorted, rubbing at his eyes.

"It's not your fault. I know that. I was there. Whatever you do, don't listen to Reese. She is a mess, saying crazy things. She's in a bad place."

"They gave Reese a sedative. She wouldn't calm down, so they took her to the clinic. My mom has someone staying with her now. She is busy trying to find places for all the newcomers," Memphis said.

"You'll be okay. I'll help you through this, Callahan. We all will." I rubbed my hand up and down his arm.

"Promise." Callahan sat upright and looked me in the eye.

I nodded. I stuck out my little finger so he could intertwine his finger with mine. Our silly tradition seemed comforting.

"This is on us, Slade and me. We missed checking a prisoner." Memphis shook his head, giving Slade a dirty look. "He was on Slade's side of the room. I should have checked them myself. Then this wouldn't have happened."

"Hey…"

"I checked all the guards on my side of the room, Memphis. Maybe you missed one of yours." Slade's posture stiffened; his muscles tensed visibly. "Don't be a jerk to me, because then I have to be a jerk to you. And I'm way better at being a jerk than you are. Elites practice it."

"Amen. What's your problem with us, man? Jealousy?" Ajax asked Memphis.

"Jealous of you, hardly. I just hate all Elites on sight," Memphis said.

Callahan slammed his hands down on the table so hard the dishes rattled and jumped. "Stop arguing. This isn't doing anyone any good. It won't bring her back, nothing will. What's done is done. It doesn't matter who's fault it is, right?"

"Why can't we all just get along? We live here now. There is no West or East End here. At least I haven't seen one. We need to leave those prejudices in the past." I placed my hands on my hips.

"Everyone follows the General and his rules here," Memphis said.

"Ajax and I just want to be like everyone else, no special favors," Slade said.

"Yeah, what he said." Ajax jerked his thumb towards Slade. It was obvious Ajax would go along with anything Slade suggested.

"Don't judge us on the past, judge us on the present." Slade crossed his arms.

"I'm sure it will take a little getting used to. Give them a break, for now Memphis. They have been a big help so far," Callahan said.

"I'll try, but no promises." Memphis set his mouth in a hard line.

"Don't look now, but what's with the group in the corner? They don't look so happy." I subtly inclined my head in their direction, trying to ease the tension and change the subject.

"Who? Nestor and his cronies?" Memphis turned to look.

"Don't you recognize him, it's Nestor Gyn. They exiled him when we were nine or ten. For... I can't remember, can you?"

"Must have been a major crime," Slade said. "Murder, assault, rape, theft, or drugs."

"I think he killed his wife," Callahan said.

"Are you sure?" Ajax said.

"Not a hundred percent," Callahan replied, "but pretty sure."

"Don't worry about them, they're scavengers, harmless loud-mouths. They get the worst jobs and accommodations. They shouldn't even be here, but they just made a delivery. They live at the Frozen Fortress." Memphis waved away the thought of them being a threat.

"How do I not get that job?" Ajax chewed on his lower lip.

"Scavenger jobs are harder now since they have looted all the surrounding towns for supplies. They have completely ransacked Colorado Springs. They go further and further, all the time, searching for anything of use. These days they go to the remains of Salt Lake City, Minneapolis, and Kansas City in search of supplies."

The thought of cities I had only heard about in stories and movies made me sit up and take notice. I hoped I got to explore the world, even the destroyed parts.

"So basically, they are just waiting to see if they get to move up in status with today's recent arrivals," Slade said.

"I'm sure we'll get better jobs. With our skills." Ajax inhaled through his nostrils and exhaled loudly. He nervously looked to the others to confirm his statement.

I sucked in my lips to avoid laughing. Ajax had it plush and comfortable his whole life. Life here wouldn't be as easy. I still didn't know his reasoning in joining the rebels. "I guess we will all have to earn our keep somehow."

"Ah, look, daddy's baby girl giving orders. You know you'll get the best available job," Ajax said.

Slade elbowed him in the side. "Hey"

"Ouch, that hurt. What did you do that for?" Ajax rubbed at his ribs.

"If you are trying to be a smart ass, you have to be smart. Otherwise, you are just an ass," I said.

"Ajax, I can't believe what you said. Are you always this stupid or are you making a special effort today?" Slade asked.

"What did I ever do to you to make you hate me so much?" I didn't know what Ajax's problem was with me. Something about him let me believe in annoyance at first sight.

"I don't hate you. I'm just not excited about your existence," Ajax said.

"In order to insult me, I must value your opinion. I don't. Nice try, though. I don't have the energy to pretend to like you today," I said.

Slade watched our interchange without comment. His lips pinched together, then he placed one arm behind his back, gripping one wrist with the other.

"Speaking of daddy's little girl, how did the talk with your father go? Everything good?" Callahan bumped his shoulder against mine.

"That's a loaded question. I don't even know how to answer. Things are friendly, friendlier, friendly... ish, I'm still processing everything he said. My head is spinning from everything. I don't even know where to start." I explained some of the things Zander told me.

Confused looks crossed their faces when I brought up the TCC creating deviants.

"So, the TCC created deviants by experimenting on our great-grandparents." Callahan's mouth fell open, his upper lip curled back. A quizzical expression crossed his face. "What was the point?"

"Zander wouldn't tell me much about the experiments. Just that they happened. Do you know anything, Slade?" I asked.

Slade turned away, running his hands through his hair. "Yeah... I overheard my parents talking about the experiments almost a year ago. My mother berated my father for all the trouble deviants caused, cursing my great-grandfather for his experiments. She was angry the testing wasn't adequate to catch mutants, as she calls deviants. The commission tried to fix their mistake by eliminating all deviants, all of us. When I went looking for answers, I found most of the files redacted or missing."

"So, Zander was right," I said. There was so much we didn't know.

"Why didn't you tell us?" Callahan asked.

"I haven't had time to relate everything from my entire life." Slade stood from the table, fists clenched at his sides. The muscles at the back of his neck tightened.

"I knew about the experiments too." Memphis' nostrils flared. "What they did to our people makes me sick."

"From what I could piece together, their goal was to adapt human bodies so we could survive outdoors. With the bunkers resources dwindling, if they could improve our body's physiology, especially our respiratory system, then it would have been possible to live amid the polluted air. At first, the TCC tried physical and mental experiments, too horrifying to discuss, on adult patients—" Slade dropped his gaze to the floor.

"Disgusting. It sounds medieval. But it doesn't surprise me in the least, not after learning what they do to the Authority." Callahan made a choking noise in his throat. He looked as if he had seen a ghost.

"I am ashamed to admit my great-grandfather spearheaded the research and development. He made it mandatory. All newborn babies in the East End had to take part in the experiments. They made it sound like the babies would get an extra vaccine to protect them, but they were getting an experimental dose of different chemical concoctions. Scientists inserted viruses into the host cell DNA. Whatever was in those serums mutated their DNA and caused the subsequent generations to be born with psychic powers." Slade exhaled, then sat back down.

"Imagine the suffering they went through," I said. I had never met Zander's parents, but they must have been terrified when their children's powers appeared.

"The subs are expendable in the TCC's eyes." Memphis shook his head in a slow, back-and-forth sweep of disgust.

"Then why are Slade and I deviants? We are from the West End? Our families are on the commission. They wouldn't experiment on our parents. Would they?" Ajax tapped his foot against the table.

"I've given it a lot of thought and I have a theory," Slade said.

"Different concoctions could explain why we all have unique powers," I said.

"Couldn't the radiation have changed our DNA as well?" Callahan asked.

"Possibly... honestly, all this stuff is way beyond my understanding. I'm not a scientist by any means," Slade said.

"You try to mess with Mother Nature, and she bites you back hard." Memphis stretched both arms out and yawned.. "I for one appreciate my powers. Maybe I owe the TCC a thank you."

"Still doesn't explain why—?" Ajax said.

"Would you let me finish? They must have exposed one of our ancestors with the serum somehow. It's the only thing to makes sense. Both of our grandmothers volunteered at the clinic when they were young, so maybe they got infected. Stuck with a needle or something. It doesn't matter now does it."

"Nothing like that will happen again, not here anyway," Memphis said.

Callahan narrowed his eyes. "Charlie, something is different about you. Why aren't you affected by all these emotions?"

I winked at him. "Because I know how to control them now."

AT THE EVENING MEAL, Zander gave a speech welcoming all the newcomers. He apologized for not having enough space to house everyone arriving from the vault and the Nest. Some people would have to relocate to the solar stronghold and Frozen Fortress in the morning. I looked for Simon, but I didn't see him amongst the others.

I met the rest of my siblings after we ate. They were all blond like me, future Alphas. It was an awkward meeting for all of us. We were the same but different, in personality, in race, and skin colors. They seemed to be close to each other. I stumbled around trying to say the appropriate things. My inexperience with kids left me feeling uncomfortable. Even though Zeppelin and Zappa were only a few years younger than me, we had nothing in common. I felt relief when they left to do their homework.

Slade asked me to take a walk. Callahan and Memphis went back to their house to turn in for the night. I didn't bother to ask where Ajax wandered off to because I didn't care. Reese would spend the night at the clinic. Blaze's whereabouts were still unknown. If there was a computer somewhere, that's where I would find her.

IT WAS DARK AND FOGGY. Slade tried to take my hand in his, but our gloves were too thick. We walked side by side, chatting about our expectations of our new life. It was snowing again, big fat fluffy flakes. I lifted my face so I could feel them touch my cheeks.

"Until recently, I never thought we would get outside in our lifetime. I still don't know if my parents have been outside, or anything about their new settlement." Slade pulled down his rebreather. He kept blowing out his breath to see the mist it created in the cold air.

"I still want to pinch myself to believe it."

"The air is so cold it hurts. Hey!"

When he wasn't looking, I lobbed a few snowballs squarely into his chest.

He blinked a moment. "Oh, okay, if that's the way you want to play, you're on."

The air became thick with snowballs as we pelted them back and forth. They burst open on impact, tumbling to pieces on the ground. I tucked my head low into my coat. I discovered getting hit with snowballs wasn't as fun as throwing them. I stumbled over a small tree, then ducked behind a house for cover. This new warm, heavy clothing made me slow and awkward. Slade walked out into the open, exposed. An easy target. I bombarded him with as many snow-balls as I could make.

The competitive look on his face told me he didn't plan to lose. The cold seeped through my gloves, freezing my hands. I could barely move my fingers, and my poor aim became atrocious. I ran around the corner of a house trying to escape Slade. Someone yelled out their door for me to get off their yard. I lobbed a few more snowballs, but he still followed, gaining ground. I ran between two trees, knocking all the snow from the branches onto the ground. I screamed when he tackled me into a pile of snow.

"Give up?" he asked.

"Never!" I grabbed a handful of snow and shoved it down the back of his coat. It was his turn to shriek. We wrestled around until he was on top of me, his arms pinned mine to my sides until I quit fighting. "Ok, ok you win."

"Are you flirting or starting a fight?" Out of breath, we lay on the ground gasping for air. When he could manage it, Slade rose to his feet, took off his coat and gloves, shaking out the snow. He put his coat back on, flopping down beside me. "Dirty trick Charlie, I didn't know you were underhanded."

"Anything to win," I said.

"Are you sure you are not cold?"

"Only a little," I lied. I bent my elbow, resting my head down on my hand to look at Slade. All bundled up, the only things that uncovered were our faces. "So, how did an Elite end up working with the rebels?"

"It's a pretty brief story. Somehow, they found out I was digging into the past, searching for details about the experiments, among other things. They contacted me remotely through my security tag several times, but I ignored the messages. Then one of Zander's recruiters cornered me," Slade said.

"Cornered you, really!"

"It wasn't as ominous as I make it sound. The recruiter and I chatted a few times. Zephora was convincing but I didn't want anything to do with the rebellion. Then she introduced me to Zander."

"And Zander convinced you to help him?" I wondered who Zephora was. Was she from the Hollows or was she from outside? Was she pretty? Did he like her? Why was I thinking about this?

"Pretty much after the shock wore off. It started with him telling me about what he was trying to build on the outside. Then he convinced me to do one small favor for him. Which led to another..."

"How did he know he could trust you?"

"Because he's like you, he can tell who to trust."

"Why do you think Ajax joined?"

"That's easy. Boredom. He finds the bunker monotonous. He would do anything to get outside."

"You're kidding,"

"Part of it, the other part is his older brother, Atlas."

"I didn't know he had a brother."

"Yeah, Atlas, he was the shining star in the family, a natural leader. He always had the best grades in school, volunteered, excelled at everything he did. Ajax was invisible to his parents. They missed his school graduation to move Atlas into his own apartment. Nothing he ever did was good enough, so he stopped trying."

"Sounds rough."

Slade looked away. "Oh, my stars,"

"What?"

He pointed up at the night sky. I had been looking at him. The night sky cleared up and the stars sparkled brightly.

"Stars."

We shared a quick look. They were magical. A thousand stars danced, twinkling in the inky night sky. Within minutes, the clouds moved back in. We remained on our backs, hoping the clouds would part again.

"Amazing," Slade said.

I pulled the rebreather down off my face. "Unbelievable. I thought visiting the hot springs would be the highlight of my life, but this is so much better. No offence."

"None taken. I agree. I am so happy to be free of the bunker."

"Why were you so angry when we rescued you from the vault?"

"Um... because I knew Zander planned to release Ajax and the rest of his men from the vault. I figured I only had to stay there for a few days, maybe a week or two. I was mad you had all put yourself in danger when there was no reason to."

"Did you believe Zander?"

"Yes, of course, I did. He's never lied to me before. Why don't you trust him?" Slade's eyebrows drew together as he pondered the question.

"No reason. I'm just trying to get a feel for him. I don't know how much his word is worth. He says all the right things but . . ." I shrugged my shoulders, unable to explain how I was feeling. I couldn't shake off the impression things were not as perfect as they appeared. Whether it was my neurotic personality, cynical nature or Alpha powers kicking in, something felt off.

"I can tell you everybody here would jump off a cliff for him. That's how much they respect him."

"They would even have children for him." I scrunched up my face at the thought.

"I guess it hit you pretty hard. I saw the look on your face when you met all your sibling's mothers. Your jaw almost hit the floor."

"Can you blame me? It was horrifying."

"The women just want to have an Alpha child. I think it gives them status in the community"

"I think so . . . Three different women had his children, and one is pregnant again. I was just thankful to learn they did it in a lab and not the old-fashioned way." It was strange laying here in the snow chatting with Slade. Being with him had become more comfortable. "Since we are talking about fathers, what did you tell yours?"

"When?"

"At the assembly. When you left to plead for my freedom. Why did you?" I looked away from him, afraid his answer would be about Zander.

"My answer might horrify you."

"What's one more thing?" I laughed.

"I told him if he didn't let you go, I would tell my mother he was having an affair with his secretary. He didn't think I knew, but I did. He's more afraid of Elise than anything else." He laughed.

"Well, she is intimidating. I'll give you that." I shook off my mitts, dumping the snow out of them.

"As for the other question. Do you have to ask?"

Slade rolled me until I lay on top of him. His hand brushed the hair back from my face, tucking it behind my ears. He gently turned, then pressed his forehead against mine, hesitating a moment. I raise my hand and rest it on his stubbly cheek. He leaned in close. Our eyes met and held. My heartbeat sped up. He leaned in again, close enough to kiss me, but waited. I could feel his breath on my face. It felt like slow motion before his lips brushed mine. My hands wrapped around his shoulder to pull him closer.

"Thunder. Again! Could the two of you just... stop for a few minutes." Callahan covered his eyes with his gloved hands and turned his back. His voice sounded muffled by his rebreather.

Slade and I jumped apart as Callahan interrupted our moment. Standing, I replaced my rebreather and gloves.

"I thought you went to bed," I said.

"Couldn't sleep, right? Can I look now?" Callahan said.

"You know we are completely dressed, don't you?" Slade coughed a few times, then pulled his rebreather over his face.

"Memphis got called to go to a meeting. Couldn't sleep, so I thought I would look for you, Charlie," Callahan said.

"A meeting! Thunder, I wonder if I should have been there. Did you notice if Ajax left?" Slade bounced on his feet as if he wanted to run to the meeting.

"Didn't notice any lights on next door, but I wasn't really looking. Saw your... pet in the window before I left," Callahan said.

"You're neighbors?"

"Yeah, next door to each other. Six and seven Rose drive," Slade said.

"Blaze, Reese and I are at 14 Rose Drive, pretty close to you guys."

"Speaking of Blaze. I got a line on where she might be. They only have one building with electronics. I imagine that's where she is? Do you want to come with me? See if we can find her? I need to thank her for all of her help."

"Can Slade go too?" I was about to toss a snowball at Callahan, but he caught me. We wrestled for control like three-year-olds before it fell in pieces.

"Yes, your boy..." Callahan broke off as he noticed my murderous expression. He almost laughed before he remembered.

"It's okay, you can call me her boyfriend. I don't mind," Slade said.

"Let's get going," I said. We needed to leave before this conversation became more embarrassing. Slade and I had never defined this attraction between us, but it was nice to know his thoughts.

We located the communication center high on the mountainside of the village. We followed a narrow rock path looping around the mountain. Several footsteps imprinted on the snow showed that many people had traveled this way. The altitude made it hard to breathe. We had to stop to rest often. Callahan had the hardest time, dehydrated from crying and lack of food.

Rounding the corner, the communication center was straight ahead. One isolated house with solar panels, cables, and wires attached to the roof. There was an argument I could hear voices shouting. Something told me to be quiet. I put my fingers to my lips to quiet the others. *"Something is happening."*

"I can hear the General yelling."

"What's he saying?"

Crouching down, I moved closer, and they followed. Besides Zander's voice, I could pick out those of Memphis and Blaze.

"Blaze how close are you to replicating the technology from the restrainers?" Zander asked.

"I still need some time to—."

"You have until dawn," he said.

"What is the big hurry all of a sudden?" Jagger asked. When had he returned?

"Are you sure about this course of action, Sir?" Memphis asked tentatively. "They have resources in the Hollows we could use."

"General, I agree this is the best choice of action."

"Sir, we have enough explosives to blow the bunker to kingdom come"

"General, what about the children?"

"This is our chance to wipe them out once and for all. The commissions days of power are over. The flash drive gave us all the information we needed. First, we take out the bunker and then we take down their new city. We can thank Blaze for getting it to us safely. Anyone who is not in this room stays out of the loop... for now," Zander said.

I exchanged an uneasy look with Callahan and Slade. What was he talking about? What was he going to do? We had all risked our lives for the key in one way or another and now he wanted to destroy everything we had ever known with the information we had brought him. There were innocent people inside the bunker.

"Sir, they could be an ally for us against the Savages. There are attacks all the time. They encroach on our territory more and more every day," Blaze said.

The Savages must be the group of people Zander told me about. The other group living outside. I mouthed the word Savages at Slade and Callahan. By their confused expressions, they knew less than I did.

"General, we must proceed as planned."

"Enough. We have debated this long enough already. I want to destroy The Hollows, raze it from existence."

"Yes, General."

"First, we take out the power, and control center. We've pinpointed the locations from the schematics on the flash drive. Blaze, you have everything you need to reprogram the Authority. When you control them, we control the Hollows. We extract the Authority and other legends before we bury the others in the mountain. No one ever goes in or out again. There is no more hiding who we are."

27

———

The overcast sky Tuesday morning matched my mood. Gibson's funeral service, while brutal, was also beautiful. I was touched that most of the community took the time to attend, encircling my small group of friends in the sheltered graveyard. Gibson lay within a ring of stones; wrapped tightly from head to toe in white cloth. Flower petals and burning white candles surrounded her gravesite, along with fragrant pine branches. Torches burned along the edges of the cemetery.

Zander spoke first, then Jagger gave a quick talk about Gibson's life. Bristol sang a hymn while the others sang along with. I didn't know the words, or I would have sung too. Who was Grace, and why was she so amazing? They recited words from memory like a chant in a strange language. It must be a ritualized ceremony performed often by the community.

Someone in the clinic drugged Reese to the point where she didn't understand what had happened. Maybe it was better that way. I wanted to feel guilty for turning my emotions off, but I wouldn't be any help to anyone if I became a blubbering mess. Callahan held it together for the most part. I gave him my hand to hold during the service, and he almost crushed it. He tried to read the speech he wrote but cried too much to get out the words, so Memphis read it on his behalf.

The hardest part was covering Gibson's body with stones after the service. We all took turns until we entombed her beside her parents. Three graves among hundreds. Zander promised to have a marker carved for Gibson like the other names etched in stone.

Callahan and I sat together in shared grief beside Gibson's grave, long after everyone had left. Too numb to feel the cold, not a word passed between us for hours; we didn't need them. My best friend was heartbroken, and there wasn't a thing I could do to help him. It was past dark when Callahan and I reluctantly left her graveside.

As PLANNED, after the evening meal, Callahan and I walked to meet with Slade to discuss what we had stumbled upon the day before. We trekked to the far side of the village, choosing to meet out in the open, as if we were just exploring. Not knowing who we could trust or if there were listening devices in our homes, although everything appeared tech free here. It made me sick to think about the plan Zander wanted to enact. How could he be so callous? What could we do to stop him from killing those without powers in the bunker? There were a lot of innocent people there, older people, children.

"What is he doing here?" I asked Slade when he arrived with Ajax, who wasn't part of the plan. I bit the inside of my cheek, trying to hide my irritation.

"Presto Chango!" Ajax waved his hands as if he performed a magic trick. "Nope. You're still a —."

"Ajax . . ." Slade narrowed his eyes at Ajax. "Don't start something. Now is not the time."

"Ha, ha. You are so funny. You could have been a stand-up comedian in a past life." I don't know what it was about him that bothered me so much. Something about his smug face made me want to smack him.

"Stop it, both of you. We need all the help we can get." Slade flicked his gaze back and forth between us.

In the distance, I could make out a silhouette. Was somebody following us? Did Zander have someone watching me? I relayed my concerns to the others. We moved into the shadows, closer to the mountain wall where the snow wasn't as deep, and the trees could conceal us. This felt like being back inside the Hollows again. Hiding in the shadows.

"I don't like this." Callahan's eyes bounced from Slade to Ajax. *"I don't know you guys well enough to have faith in either of you. Don't trust them, Charlie."*

"Funny, that's exactly what Ajax said about you," Slade said.
"Why do I have to prove anything to you people?" A distasteful look crossed Ajax's face. *"I think* you *need to prove I can trust you."*

"Stop thinking so much it doesn't suit you." I regretted saying the words as soon as I saw Slade's face fall. I should just ignore the insults.

"Now who's starting something?" Ajax asked.

I raised my hands in surrender.

"How are we going to work together if no one trusts anyone? I trust Ajax with my life. His parents are in the bunker. He won't let anything..." Slade shook his head, unable to finish the sentence.

"Callahan, we can't do this alone. If Slade vouches for Ajax, I accept his word."

"Pffft, like you would say anything else, right?" Callahan glowered, pointing at Slade with his finger. *"Is this how it's always going to go now? You'll always be on* his *side?"*

"I am always on your side. Never doubt that. Never. We are family." I put my hand on Callahan's shoulder and squeezed. *"But... who else can we trust? Blaze and Memphis are under Zander's spell. Reese is in a narcotic slumber. Everyone here at the keep follows Zander. Give me an alternative because I don't see one."*

"Reese is devastated. Did you know the reason she kept her invisibility secret?"

"Nope. why?"

"Because she was jealous that we could all talk telepathically. When she discovered her invisibility, she just wanted to have something of her own. Then she waited too long to tell us, and she felt like she couldn't. The longer she waited, the more it snowballed and then—"

"She felt like she was lying to us."

"I can't believe I trusted every word Zander said. I thought he wanted the best for us. I thought we were starting a better world, an inclusive world where everyone could belong—." Anger crept into Slade's voice.

"Shattering someone's trust is the same as scrunching up a sheet of paper. You can flatten it, but it will never be the same." I crushed some snow in my hands.

Callahan ran his hands through his hair. His spikes were straighter now that he had access to his special hair goop and belongings Memphis had brought from the bunker. *"I guess so... we only have each other now."*

I tapped his forehead and smirked at him *"Keep that there as a given. You and me, always."*

Callahan covered his mouth to quiet his chuckle. His face fell as if he felt guilty for laughing.

"What can four people possibly do?" Ajax covered his yawning mouth. Were we boring him?

"I've only known you for a day, but all you ever do is whine. If you have nothing helpful to say shut up," Callahan said.

Ajax smirked. It was finally obvious to me he liked to provoke people to see how they would react. Like a game: if you reacted, he won.

"Four people rescued you and all the others from the vault," I said. Five counting Blaze. There was strength in numbers he wasn't wrong about that.

"You didn't even need to, daddy's girl. Zander would have liberated me," Ajax said.

"You're questioning my plan?" I asked. *"Zander's way involves a lot of innocent people dying."*

"I'm not questioning it; I'm saying it's stupid."

Callahan thumped his foot against the nearest tree, dumping snow from the branches onto our heads.

"Hey, watch what you're doing?" Ajax scowled as he wiped snow from his shoulders.

How were we going to get close enough to Joseph so he could order a mass evacuation? We still had to perfect the plan. Timing everything perfectly without getting trapped inside.

"Four people with powers can do a lot. Especially one who is an Alpha." Slade cleared his throat.

"An untrained Alpha." I touched the chain around my neck, the one constant in my ever-changing world.

"We are all on the same page, aren't we? We save them all, Subs and Elites," Slade said.

"I don't want my parents to die because they don't have power. I don't want them buried alive. I'll help, but I need to know everything before we attempt this. Including all the ways this could go wrong." Ajax's teeth chattered as he spoke.

"I hate to be a downer, but say we get everyone out: where would we go then? Your father won't let us come back here. We don't know how to survive outside. We don't know what the threats are. We don't know... anything." Callahan repeatedly rubbed at his eyes.

"I thought about that. There is the new settlement the TCC is building, the Silver Settlement. Maybe you can go there as a last resort." I rubbed my arms. The temperature dropped by the minute. We needed to wrap this up, get to a warmer spot.

"I don't think my parents would let us in even if we get everyone out alive," Slade said.

"True, your mother promised to ruin my life the last time I saw her. But... I thought if we saved her life, we could earn some good grace. Then she might let the three of you live in her city," I said. If we could get to the hot springs maybe we could survive until we could set up our own community. If Zander didn't destroy it first. *"We will figure it out."*

"Under the TCC's thumb, no thank you." Callahan snorted. *"What do you mean, 'the three of us'? Don't you mean four?"*

"I can't go there. I won't live that life again," I said.

"If we do nothing, are you prepared to have all those deaths on your conscience?" Slade asked. *"Cause I'm not. There are little kids inside the bunker."*

"I didn't say that. I just think we need to discuss what happens after. We need to be smart." Callahan rubbed his gloved hands together, trying to keep them warm. He was having a hard time with the frigid temperatures. *"If you haven't noticed, it's cold out here and we don't have any experience living outdoors."*

We will have to figure something out. The original group of exiles didn't have much either. I wish I could talk Zander out of this." Who was I kidding? I had no sway with him.

"You heard him last night. He seemed sure about his decision," Slade said.

"We have to do something," Callahan said.

"If we do this... we burn our bridges with Zander and his crew." Ajax rubbed his chin in thought. *"But it's the right thing to do."*

"I don't know what will happen next. I like it here," I said. *"I was looking forward to a clean slate. A new start. The old me would have just kept my head down, ignoring everything else, but I can't do that anymore. I wouldn't be able to live with myself if I sat back and did nothing. I would rather die doing something good than live forever knowing I did nothing."*

"You've changed. I didn't even recognize you when you entered the Nest. Long way from refusing to eat an apple the other day."

I glanced at Slade to see him watching me. Was he remembering the apple we shared at the hot springs? I looked away before the heat rose and reddened my cheeks.

"I just realize there is a difference between living and surviving. I don't want to just survive anymore. There is no point of return now; we may as well embrace our new future, whatever it is."

"The stars know my parents have done unforgivable things, but I can't leave them in there, to die," Slade said.

"Zander plans to strike at dawn, all we have is—." Ajax broke off when he heard the crunching of snow.

Whatever made the sound was heading towards us in a hurry. I scanned the area for somewhere to hide. Had a deviant overheard our discussion? I stood ready to create a portal.

A chorus of "baas" sounded moments before several medium-size, furry brown animals burst out of the trees, running for the mountain wall. Thick curved horns topped their heads, some horns were larger than others. We scattered in different directions to avoid being trampled as they ran through. I ducked behind a tree, falling to my knees. In the darkness, I couldn't see the others.

The animals reached the mountain walls, climbing them easily with nimble feet. Their clattering hooves reverberated against the mountain walls. Within a few moments, they completely disappeared, their hoof prints the only proof they had ever been here.

Laughter bubbled up from within. Another small reminder we were living a different life. Animals had survived somehow. I became excited at the thought of seeing more of them. How many types of animals had survived the devastation to the earth?

More crunching in the snow brought the sound of human voices. We hurried to stand in the clearing so we wouldn't look suspicious just as four soldiers rushed into the clearing with rifles in their hands, following the trail of animals. Three of them gave us quick glances and kept up their pace behind the animals. A tall woman slowed and remained behind, questioning us.

"What are you doing out here?" she asked, her voice scratchy. "There is a curfew."

"Us? Nothing, just walking... exploring."

"I need your names to report to the general."

Zander walked into the clearing with two of his soldiers. He had a rifle slung over his shoulder as did his companions; all wore orange, fluorescent vests over their camouflage clothing. "That won't be necessary, Hallie. This is my daughter and her friends. They aren't aware of all the rules we have in place for safety. I'll take care of this. Go ahead, follow the others in the hunt."

Hallie nodded her head and bounded off after the others.

"What are you doing out here?" Zander asked. He deliberately moved his head to study each of us. He had a way of looking at me with eyes that didn't seem to blink often enough.

"Nothing really. We were just out playing in the snow," I said.

"General, we were enjoying the fresh air. We haven't been outside before." Slade squared his shoulders, straightening until he stood at his full height.

"General, we are just exploring this tremendous community you built," Ajax said.

"I couldn't sleep," Callahan said.

We spoke on top of each other, making it impossible for Zander to understand what we were saying.

"I see," Zander rubbed his chin. "Listen, I know you haven't had time to memorize all the rules at Salvations Keep, but rule number two is that we don't allow people to wander around unarmed in the dark. You can visit at the lodge and one of my soldiers will escort you to your homes afterward."

"Um... sorry, Sir. We were unaware of the rules." Slade twisted his hands together as he shuffled his feet.

"Can I ask what rule number one is, Uncle Zander?" Callahan raised his hand.

Zander's eyes almost bulged out of his head when Callahan called him "uncle."

"What you can all do is go home and learn the rules. Each house has a list pinned to the back of every front door. Read them, until you have them memorized by heart, so we don't have this problem again."

"I don't understand. Aren't we safe here?" I asked. Had we exchanged one prison for another. "Why can't we walk around at night?"

Zander cursed under his breath. He spoke through his teeth with forced restraint. "Charlie, wild animals come out at night. They run through the village all the time. Plus, the other group I told you about, the Savages, attack after dark. My soldiers, Edwin and Bernice, will escort you back to the lodge."

I bristled at the tone of his voice. He talked to me the same way he talked to Bowie. Like a child. "No, take us back to our homes, then." I had to say something to stand up to him.

Our new friends escorted us back home. I asked for a moment to say goodnight to Slade after Callahan and Ajax said goodnight. Zander's men looked away to give us some privacy.

"You need a stool or vitamins to get taller," Slade said.

"I'll work on that." Standing on my tiptoes, I placed my lips beside his ear and whispered. "Tell Callahan and Ajax we are leaving at 2 am. Take anything you don't want left behind."

28

Early the next morning, I opened a portal to Slade's apartment in the Hollows. Slade rummaged through his closet for clothing to allow us to blend in easier with the Elites. Nothing he had seemed small enough to fit me, but I took one of his shirts, tucked it in and rolled up the sleeves. I held the collar to my nose, breathing in Slade's scent before I mentally scolded myself, hoping no one had noticed. Slade found a pair of Khaki pants that belonged to Toni. She was taller than me, so I rolled up the bottoms.

The butterflies fluttered in my stomach as I fought the nervousness I felt. If Joseph and Elise wouldn't help with the evacuation, we would have to come up with another strategy. There were only a few hours before Zander's promised attack. It felt like we were being watched, so I worried he would alter his plans if he knew we were missing.

"Slade lived here alone. Are you kidding? All this space for one person? This is incredible, right?" Callahan explored the apartment, inspecting the photographs and paintings in frames on bookcases and hung on the wall. When he noticed the silver dog dishes, he rolled his eyes. "Is that the Mona Lisa?"

"Nothing like this in the East End, eh?" I nudged him with my shoulder as I suppressed a yawn.

"You can say that again. They had everything and we had nothing." That haunted look flashed behind Callahan's eyes again.

"If you think this place is special. You should see mine." Ajax pulled at the tight sleeves of his shirt. The arms of Slade's shirt were too tight for Ajax's muscular build. It looked like if he twisted suddenly, the seams would rip. "I have a Monet and a Picasso on my... hey."

Slade swatted Ajax on the top of his head. Ajax followed Slade with his eyes. A fleeting look crossed his face before he resumed his normal visage. I knew that look. I looked at Slade the same way. Ajax was in love with Slade. No wonder he didn't like me. He viewed me as his competition. I wondered if Slade knew. Would he feel the same way about Ajax? They had so much history between them. I shook my head. Even if he did, he wouldn't break Code 5A-1526. Or would he? Now was not the time to worry about the future, since we might not have one.

We listened at the door for footsteps in the hall, wondering if someone still guarded the room. We heard nothing. Slade slid open the door carefully, poking his head into the hallway. He turned back to us and shook his head, blinking as if he couldn't believe what he was seeing. Then walked out, motioning for us to follow. What was happening?

The hallway in his building was littered with clothing, toys, bits of paper, and broken glass. Someone had tracked food onto the carpet, mushing it into the pristine gray fibers. The doors to the other apartments stood open.

"Thunder. What the hell . . . happened?" Ajax's entire body seemed to tremble.

"Your guess is as good as mine." Slade shrugged his shoulders.

"Wow, the East End is never this filthy. Right, Charlie?" Callahan couldn't resist the urge to take a poke at the Elites.

I rolled my eyes in response. "You guys, check out the rooms at that end of the hall. Callahan and I will check out this end."

We quickly walked through two other apartments and it looked like someone had ransacked them. The contents of closets and cupboards lay scattered around on furniture and the hardwood floor. Whatever had happened, the people who lived here had left in a hurry. Slade and Ajax came back and reported that they had found the other apartments in the same condition. We descended the stairway to the bottom floor, finding similar carnage everywhere we passed. Carefully, we exited the building.

"It's abandoned," I said.

"It's like a ghost town." Slade's hands carved through his hair, holding it back and then releasing it.

"Where did everybody go?" Callahan asked.

"This is unreal. I don't even see the Authority anywhere." I rubbed absently at my arms.

"Did somebody warn them, tell them what Zander was planning?" Ajax asked.

Ajax looked around for the guilty party. His eyes landed on me. I gave him my best "how dare you" stare. "Would it matter if someone did? Isn't this what we wanted?"

"It's possible they have a mole in Zander's camp?" Slade said. "Maybe the Elites have already gone to the new settlement."

"I need to check on my parents!" Ajax bolted away without looking back.

"Ajax, wait!" Slade kicked a pile of rubbish as Ajax continued to run. "Come on, let's go. I need to check on my parents, too. They live a floor above Ajax's."

"Umm . . . I have a grandmother, Laura-Jane Clark. Do you know her? Can we check on her after?"

"Absolutely, but by the looks of things she probably isn't here."

"You have a grandmother? That's new." A line appeared between Callahan's brows. "Is there something you want to tell me?"

"I know, sorry. I still have so many things I need to tell you. I am presently experiencing life at the speed of about fourteen thunders per hour, but I'm not trying to keep things from you, I promise."

He hadn't told me much about his experience at the Nest—other than he didn't want to talk about it. Whatever had happened changed him. I sensed it before Gibson's death, and more ever since. I couldn't wait to get some time alone with him to find out.

We followed Slade past a row of looted stores. Pieces of glass from smashed windows lay on the ground. The remnants of lives littered the paving stones: a doll, picture books, and a toy dinosaur. The piano somehow stood untouched in a sea of mayhem. It was eerie walking in an empty area that was normally packed with people.

Joseph and Elise lived on the top floor of the building. The door to their apartment stood wide open. We entered silently. Slade directed us to search in different areas with hand signals. Checking the kitchen area, I noticed something red and wet- on the floor. Was that blood?

Turning the corner by the island to investigate, I screamed. Covering my mouth, I spun away from Joseph Cutter's body, sprawled on the floor, surrounded by a slowly expanding pool of blood. The others ran to me. I felt like I would be sick.

Slade dropped to his knees beside his father. He put his fingers to Joseph's neck to check his pulse for life. Joseph's skin was sickly, his lips blue.

"They're all gone. Everyone. The West End is empty. Someone trashed my parents' apartment, too!" Ajax yelled loudly as he entered the apartment. Rounding the corner into the kitchen, he came to a dead stop, his mouth opened but his body didn't move. "Thunder. What happened here?"

"He has a pulse. Ajax, run and get me a pillow and some blankets. Callahan, call the medics—there is a list of numbers in the other room on the desk." Slade called out instructions in a matter-of-fact-voice. He drew his lower lip between his teeth.

"How can I help?" I dropped beside Joseph, feeling helpless. I bit down hard on the inside of my cheek. He had lost so much blood from the steak knife protruding from his chest. "Should we pull the knife out?"

"No, leave the knife, if we pull it out, he might bleed to death." Slade squeezed his arm. "Hang on, Father; help is on the way."

I held my hand out over the wound, palm side down, trying to heal him. The violet light refused to come. I tried again. Still nothing. Why didn't the healing power work?

Ajax came back with a pillow and a blanket, so I scooted out of the way. Slade slid the pillow under his father's head. Joseph's eyes fluttered open once or twice as he tried to focus on his son's face. Ajax covered him with the blanket, tucking it tightly around his body. Joseph was in shock.

"Is he going to make it?" Ajax whispered to Slade.

Slade gave a half shrug, his eyes filled with unshed tears. "Father, can you hear me?" Slade smoothed Joseph's hair back off his face. He tapped his fingers lightly against his father's beardless face, trying to wake him.

I noticed the similarities between both father and son's faces. The same high cheekbones, the same dark almond-shaped eyes. Joseph had heavy eyelids with an extra fold that came with age. His hair, while laced with gray, was still as thick as Slade's.

Joseph opened his eyes to narrow slits, as if they were too heavy to keep open. "My boy... you're back." His voice was weak and wheezy.

"What happened? How—"

"Joseph, who did this to you?" Ajax cut to the point. "Tell me who I need to kill."

"E... Elise..." Joseph gasped, fighting to speak.

Slade blinked rapidly as he tried to process his mother stabbing his father. "Mother—?"

"Elise did this?" I asked. It wasn't a stretch to picture Elise taking a knife to most people, but not her husband.

Joseph's eyelids closed.

Callahan sprinted back into the room, skidding to a stop. He bent over, trying to catch his breath. "There's no... one there... I called... a bunch... of numbers... on the list, no... one answered... anywhere. I ran down... to the front of the... building. There is no one to help. What do we do?"

"Don't bother, nothing... can do.... I don't have..." Joseph was weakening fast. "You need... to stop her."

"Who? Who do I need to stop?"

Joseph's lemon-yellow aura was fading. I knew there was nothing we could do for him. I placed my hands on either side of his temples, an easy way to hear his thoughts. He tried to speak, but I shushed him. "Relax Joseph, save your energy. Just think about what you want to tell us. We all can hear your thoughts."

Through his thoughts and images, he relayed his simple story. Elise received word of Zander's plan to demolish the bunker. Joseph wanted to evacuate everyone to the Silver Settlement, even though it wasn't quite finished. Elise only wanted the Elites extracted. She didn't want undesirable people in her brand-new beautiful city. No deviants. Logan Campbell sided with Elise. When Joseph wouldn't relent, she stabbed him. Elise's hands shook afterward in shock. She blinked rapidly, trying to process what she had done. Within minutes, she left with Logan and the dogs, leaving Joseph near death lying on the floor without a backwards glance.

"Save them." Joseph closed his eyes. Every word seemed to drain his life away.

Slade grabbed his hand, squeezing it tight. "Father, I'm here. I'm here."

"Then the Subs are still here. We need to get them out," Callahan said. "How much time do we have before Zander gets here?"

"Slade, sorry... should have... better father... failed to... protect you... love you." Joseph's head rolled back as he drew in his last breath.

"Charlie, we have to go. Now!" Callahan said. "Time is ticking away."

Callahan was right, but I was torn. Frozen with indecision, Slade needed me right now too.

Slade put one hand over the other and started pushing against Joseph's chest. Every few moments he checked for breathing. "Help me, somebody, please help me. Why are you all just standing there? Breathe, Father, breathe."

"He's gone, buddy. You can't help him now. I'm sorry." Ajax stood behind Slade, gripping his shoulders. Trying to tear him away from Joseph. Slade pushed Ajax away and continued CPR.

"Charlie!" Callahan shook me. "Wake up!"

Slade reluctantly stopped compressions. He wobbled to his feet; the tears that threatened earlier leaked slowly down his face. He wiped them with his sleeves. "He never told me he loved me before. Not once."

I could relate. I stood and threw my arms around him, trying to embrace his stiff form in an awkward hug. He hugged me back then after a minute before he moved away.

"I'm so sorry. I can't believe this happened. But we have to go, Slade. We have to go now."

Callahan covered Joseph's face with the blanket out of respect.

Ajax looked like someone had punched him in the stomach. Slade cleared the kitchen counter with his arm, sending everything flying.

"We have to go," I repeated, aware of how insensitive this was. "We have a job to do, there will be lots of time for grieving later." I tugged at his arm, trying to hold back my anxious impatience.

Slade rubbed his eyes with his left hand. "So what now?"

"We need to get the lay of the land, see what we are dealing with in the East End," I said in a voice softer than I felt. "If the Elites are gone, did they take the Authority? What about Uncle Jagger and the Kings? Would Zander warn them?"

Callahan shrugged his shoulders.

"The control center—." Ajax jerked up his chin.

"We would need my father's access card." Slade's eyes darted to look at his father's body.

"Ajax, you and Slade check the office, Callahan and I will check around here," I suggested.

I didn't want Slade to see me check his father's body for his tag. Callahan pulled back the blanket once they left the room. Gingerly, I pulled items from his pockets. Nothing of importance, keys, a pen, some poker chips. I tossed Callahan his wallet to search.

"It's not in here." Callahan tossed the wallet onto the island.

In the back pocket of his pants, my fingers touched the smooth metal of his security tag. "Got it," I yelled loud enough for Slade and Ajax to hear. Callahan re-covered Joseph with the blanket carefully.

THE TRIP to the control center didn't take long—a few flights of stairs and two turns down similarly trashed hallways. Slade led the way. We followed him in silence, stopping at a windowless double black steel door. A tiny, unobtrusive sign beside the door read 'Command Center'. It was unimpressive. Slade swiped Joseph's security tag through the card reader to the left of the door, then punched in a code. The reader blinked red.

A horn went off. I jumped. It was 6 am: time to start work.

"What the..." Slade tried the card again with the same result.

"Maybe he changed the code," Ajax said.

"It's always been 972107," Slade said.

"Are there any numbers he used a lot? Any dates special to him?" I asked.

"Try 123456, right?"

"It wouldn't be something that simple," Slade said.

"Try his birthday," Ajax said.

"Nope! Not it."

"Try your birthday," I said.

Slade swiped and punched in 111549. This time the light turned grey. "I can't believe he changed the code to my birthday."

Ajax barreled through the door without stopping to hold it open for those behind him. Slade grabbed it before it closed, holding it ajar for Callahan and me to enter. The door closed behind Slade with an unnerving click. I should be used to being locked inside but the little bit of freedom I had achieved made me tremble.

The command center was smaller than I expected, maybe forty feet square. Eight gigantic TV screens blanketed the walls. The softly dimmed light muted the blue-lit screens to reduce the glare. A diamond pattern of gray and black carpet covered the floors, giving the room a silent, solemn impression. Two rows of computers sat side by side on identical wooden desks. Orange lights glowed to show the computers were still active.

Four of the screens flipped through the empty corridors of the West end. The other side showed life as usual for those at the east end since the workday just started. There were more Authority than normal patrolling. Why hadn't the Elites taken them?

Slade walked over and punched a few buttons on the console hooked up to a microphone that squealed with feedback. Another switch and the video camera turned on.

"People of the Hollows, this is Slade Cutter speaking. I am here with Charlie Edge, Ajax Diaz, and Callahan Malone. An urgent threat has been made against the bunker. The West Side has already evacuated. Gather what you need and report to the assembly room immediately."

People looked up at the TV screens, confused and surprised. Would they believe a group of misfits?

The floor shook beneath my feet, vibrating with a deafening roar. Lights flickered before plunging us into darkness. The shaking threw me hard against the row of computer monitors before I hit the floor. Instinctively, I rolled under a desk and curled into a ball, protecting my head with my hands. Thunder, Zander was here, and we were in trouble.

29

Dust, dirt, and debris rained down on our heads. The walls screamed and groaned before everything quieted once more. A section of the ceiling had caved in, dumping a pile of rocks and rubble on the desks, tables, and floor. A beam had fallen and obliterated three desks to piles of kindling. Lights dangled, hanging out of their fixtures from what remained of the ceiling. The lights, still attached, blinked a few times before turning back on with a hiss. How soon until the next blast? Would the bolts hold the bunker together long enough for us to escape? The questions swirled through my mind as I crawled out from under the desk that had sheltered me.

The air was thick with dust. I coughed as the particles entered my lungs. "Everybody okay?" I croaked while scanning the room for the others. I located Slade and Callahan right away.

I had gotten lucky. The desk I crawled under was protected by another fallen beam. I scanned my body for damage, my left hip hurt, I pulled back the material of my pants to see a nasty bruise, probably one of many. There were various cuts and scrapes on my arm. Nothing to be concerned about.

Overturned tables, chairs, and computers lay sprawled on the floor. Papers and files dispersed everywhere, some still fluttered in the air looking for a place to land. An enormous crack ran down the length of the back wall. Another explosion within the walls would destroy the bunker. They didn't have sabotage in mind when they built it. Like fools, we had naively hand-delivered the schematics to Zander. I could kick myself; he had all the information he needed to destroy the Hollows because we had given it to him.

"Zander's early." Ajax crawled out from underneath the table he scuttled under when the shaking started. He dusted off his clothes like someone unaccustomed to being dirty. He sent a dirty look my way. "Someone must have tipped him off."

"If you have something to say, Ajax, just spit it out. Quit dancing around it."

"I think you told him what we were planning."

"That's ridiculous. Why would I?"

"Well, it wasn't me or Slade. That leaves you and Callahan."

"Believe what you want, but it wasn't me and it wasn't Callahan."

An electrical wire dangled from one of the destroyed lights sent sparks into the air. It hissed and snapped as it flung around without direction. I watched it for a moment, mesmerized.

"Thunder. Slade jumped to his feet. No worse for wear. He extended his hand to pull Callahan from where he fell.

"C ..." Callahan gasped. Debris covered Callahan from head to toe. A huge piece of the ceiling had fallen, pinning Callahan's torso against the floor. His spiked hair fell flat against his head.

"Are you hurt?" My heartbeat sped up.

Callahan tried to speak again but gave a stunted cough. The cement was compressing against his chest, pushing against his diaphragm. He couldn't breathe.

"I got you." Slade tried to use his powers to move the debris, but they didn't work. Neither did mine.

"What's going on?" Ajax asked.

I felt the tinges of panic but fought them off. What could we do without our powers? Think. I wouldn't let Callahan die, not after everything we had been through. Not after losing Gibson. I dug into the debris to help free him.

"This must be what Blaze was working on for Zander when he talked about replicating the technology from the restrainers." Slade grabbed pieces of wreckage and threw them aside. "She has nullified our powers."

I cut my hand on a sharp piece of glass from a computer monitor but didn't stop. I dug onward. Other pieces of rubble shifted to take their place, putting more pressure on Callahan's chest. We were back to where we started.

Ajax freed a piece of rebar, then jammed it in between two boulders. With Slade's help, he pried the largest boulder from his chest. Callahan inhaled loudly, coughing. He was still trapped but at least he could breathe. They continued until the large pieces had been removed from his body. I dug at the smaller pieces until finally he was free. Ajax helped him get to his feet.

Callahan grimaced as he stood but he could barely put any weight on his leg. He twisted, then turned his head until something snapped, and he sighed in relief. Blood poured down his leg from his thigh where his pants had torn. "Hanging out with you guys is hazardous to my health, right?" He coughed some more.

Always the clown. What would I do without him? "Can you walk? You're not up to this; you can barely stand."

"I'm fine." He waved away my concern taking a few steps to prove me wrong.

"Sit down before you fall down. Slade, hand me your belt." If things ever go back to normal, I vowed to learn how to use my powers to heal. Using his belt, I looped it around Callahan's thigh, tightening it above his wound to stop the bleeding, pulling it tight.

"I don't understand why Zander wants to destroy this place. There is so much we could take from here to help our life above ground." I shook my head at the thought of everything that would end up demolished. Senseless stupidity.

"Maybe he already took what he needed," Ajax offered.

"Charlie, try to open a portal to the assembly hall." Slade faced downward then ran his finger through his hair, shaking out pieces of ceiling.

"I tried a few minutes ago but nothing happened."

"Just try again."

I made the familiar motions to create a portal, but the white hazy swirl wouldn't appear. No matter how many times I tried. "What do we do now? How can we get out of here if I can't create a portal? If we can't use our abilities. We're trapped."

Callahan looked like a caged animal.

"No, we're not. There's another way out, but we have to hurry." Slade pressed his fingers against the keys on a nearby computer. It was dead. Most of the video screens blinked off and on. Some screens hung precariously, ready to drop at a moment's notice. The picture was snowy, fading in and out. Two of the screens lay in a tumbled heap on the floor.

"What are you thinking? The trap door!" Ajax rolled up the sleeves of his shirt past his elbows. He had a deep gash on the inner part of his forearm. The tight sleeves of his shirt soaked up most of the blood, limiting his bleeding.

"Ajax, rip off a piece of your shirt and tie it around your cut, so it doesn't get infected," I said.

Ajax looked at me strange and grumbled but followed my suggestion.

"We can climb out through the crawl space like we did when we were kids." Slade and Ajax exchanged a look. Was there a problem they weren't speaking of?

"Trap door? Explain." Had I missed the information on a trapdoor in my research of the bunker? "Where is it? Do we have time to get everyone out?"

"Maybe we should leave. If we turn back now Zander won't know we were here," Callahan suggested.

But we know all these people, Callahan! Worked with them, lived with them. I know losing Gibson was hard but..." I broke off, not knowing what else to say.

He wouldn't meet my eyes. Just turned away. Something was going on with him other than Gibson. His thoughts had been closed to me since he returned.

"It's in the North tunnel. If you didn't know it was there, you wouldn't notice it." A wound over Slade's left eye dripped blood.

"Let me look?" I took a step closer to check out the cut, but Slade waved me away. He wiped the blood away with his sleeve.

"Let's go. No telling how long until the next explosion." Ajax rolled his shoulders.

"Why hasn't he? Why is he waiting?" Ajax asked.

Slade pointed his head in my direction. "Charlie."

Callahan sat on a nearby chair, holding his head. An enormous goose egg had formed on his temple. "That was a warning. Otherwise we would be dead."

"I doubt it. Don't count on his "love" of me to stay his hand." I bunched up my face, rejecting his hypothesis, although there could be some truth behind it. He would have one less soldier in his army of Alphas if I died.

"He won't bring it all down until she is safe. I'm sure of it. We should have some time to fulfill our mission." A muscle in Slade's jaw twitched. He seemed worried, distracted. What was he hiding?

"I guess that could explain why he hasn't crumbled this place down on our heads already. He has the power." Ajax glanced warily at the ceiling, as if his words could come true at any moment.

I couldn't come up with another explanation, but it didn't matter. We had to save the Subs' and ourselves somehow. "Explain more about this trap door?"

"It's a fail safe." Ajax started then looked towards Slade.

"If the blast doors are unavailable because of... whatever reason, there is a trap door in the tunnels. A crawlspace to the surface."

"What are you not telling me?" I sensed they were holding something back.

"It's tight, tiny, and claustrophobic." Ajax went to open the door, but the mangled, bent frame made it impossible. "Holy Attila... now what?" He slammed his fist into the steel door before howling in pain.

Another problem. If we had our powers, we could rip the door open or teleport out, but without them, we were helpless.

Callahan solved the problem by picking up a piece of equipment and flinging it through the window beside the door. The crash was loud, glass splintered everywhere. He could have at least given us a warning first. I gave him points for creativity though,.

I needed to change my new mindset. Thinking I couldn't do anything without my powers was dangerous; I was a typical human first—my brain the most powerful weapon.

I grabbed a broom from the corner, using the handle to knock the rest of the glass out of the way. Slade and Ajax pushed a desk over to the window. Slade tossed a rubber mat across the bottom of the broken window for protection from the shards. Callahan went through first, followed by the rest of us.

Slade helped me down, although I could have made the jump. I took one last look over my shoulder at the crippled control center.

"Are you okay? You're trembling," Slade held on to me for a minute after I hit the floor. I could hear his heart beating as I rested my head against his chest. I wished we could stay like this forever.

"Well, Zander just tried to kill us, so there is that. This wasn't something I expected him to be overjoyed about, but not this?"

"Maybe he doesn't know we are down here." Slade offered.

"You know he does. My own father just tried to kill me." I told myself I didn't care, but Slade could see through me. He gave me a quick hug before we ran to catch the others.

Ajax led the way to the assembly hall. He said it was a shortcut, but every second felt like minutes as we raced through the empty corridors. I shook off how eerie it felt. We came to a pole with a hole in the floor. Ajax wrapped his arms and legs around the pole, then slid out of sight. Callahan followed him. I imitated their movements without hesitation, and Slade followed.

Two quick turns and we were at the assembly hall entering from the north side. The hall was empty except for half a dozen members of the Authority and Zander. I stopped walking as soon as I saw him, causing Callahan to run into the back of me. The Authority turned, pointing their weapons at us. Zander had control of them. I liked it better when Blaze was on our side.

30

———————

W
e raised our hands in surrender.

"Charlie, what are you doing? What were you hoping to accomplish?" Zander let out a gigantic sigh before looking upward. He stood in Joseph's place on the stage behind the podium. It surprised me how natural he looked up there. Memphis stood loyally at his side. "Were you trying to get yourself killed?" He sounded like any TV dad from the videos I streamed from the archive.

Every time I turned around, there he was. Absent for fifteen years and now he wanted to play father. It was insane. "That's rich since you are the person that set off the explosives that almost killed us. We're here to save human lives because you obviously don't have any respect—."

"Who told you of my plans?" Zander lifted an eyebrow. He spoke casually, but he looked at me with cold eyes.

"No one told us anything. We overheard you talking last night."

"It is impolite to eavesdrop."

Of all the things going on, I would think worrying about manners would be last on his list. "The human race is close to extinction, and you want to kill more people? Who gave you the right to choose who lives and who dies? You are not a god." My eyes raked him with freezing contempt.

"Maybe not God, but close." Zander laughed. He drummed his fingers against the podium. "I am an all-powerful Alpha, just like you will be in a few years. I want to create a colony of people with powers. A home for those of us who have been persecuted for years. A home where my children will be safe. Where you will be safe. Where you can live freely with your powers."

"Just for deviants like us, though, not the banals?" I toyed with lowering my hands, wondering what orders the Authority had.

"DO NOT USE THAT WORD. There is nothing deviant about us. We are legends, gifted. We were born this way. Thank the stars." Zander gripped the edge of the podium and leaned forward, as I had seen Joseph do many times before. "There are enough banals in the world without adding to their numbers. Not to mention the Elites escaped, thanks to you."

"You have already created a home and a new life why can't you just leave this place and these people alone."

"Because they'll never leave us alone."

"Sir, that wasn't us. They weren't here when we arrived," Slade spoke in a smooth, placating voice.

Whenever Zander was around, Slade fell under his spell. I elbowed him in the side to bring him back to reality. He looked at me, shamefaced. Ajax and Callahan were content to stay silent, their eyes trained on the Authority's weapons.

"Doesn't matter, does it? Your intentions were to free everyone, and I can't have that. I can't have my daughter running around behind my back causing chaos—."

"Your daughter... really... that's just a word. We're strangers... how can you justify killing hundreds of people? I don't even want to know anyone who could even contemplate such a thing."

"Charlie, we are all the same. We all have powers. You should be on our side," Memphis said.

"Really? How can you say that, Memphis? You know the people of the East End, worked with them, lived with them. They have always been our people."

"I don't have time to debate this further. This little stunt has already cost me too much time. Callahan, it's time to go."

Callahan lowered his arms, walking towards Zander.

"What?" I turned to Callahan, grabbing at his arm as he passed, but he pushed me away. "He's joking? Please tell me he's joking."

"I knew you were the bunker rat." Ajax said through gritted teeth. He stomped his foot on the floor, nearly cracking a tile.

"Callahan, what are you doing siding with him? Who are you right now?" I felt as if he punched me in the stomach. My head spun and threatened to explode. Memphis was too far under Zander's spell, but Callahan?

"I had to tell him, Charlie... tell him what we were doing."

"Why? You aren't even one of his people."

"I am though. I'm like him, like you. I have powers."

"I can't believe you sold us out," Slade said.

"Enough, Charlie. Callahan did the smart thing telling me. My guards will take you to the frozen fortress. Your friends will remain here to die with the others. I don't have any use for men who disobey my orders, not even men with powers. Don't even try to help them. We'll talk later."

"Callahan, you can't believe what he believes... everyone deserves a chance to live."

"I don't agree with everything, but he's right that we need to be with our own kind. I'm sick of hiding. Sick of being hunted," Callahan said.

"You don't believe that. I know you."

"Things have changed—." Something flashed behind Callahan's eyes. He clenched his fists so hard his nails cut into his skin. "Wake up Charlie, It's over! I tried to help you rescue everybody but it's too late now You can't fix everything. You can't make life perfect."

"And Charlie—don't go against me again. Next time I won't be so lenient," Zander warned, then spoke quietly into a small radio. Memphis opened a portal. "Callahan, now."

"Charlie, please come with us. You belong with us, not them." Memphis looked at Ajax and Slade with contempt.

"Don't do this. Don't go, Callahan!" I stepped forward to stop him from leaving, but a guard blocked my way. Another cocked his weapon. Callahan couldn't leave me.

"Let him go." Slade grabbed me around the waist, pulling me back. "You can't win this battle."

Callahan turned before he entered the portal. *"I'm sorry."*

Zander left without a second glance; confident his orders would be carried out.

A guard raised his gun and ordered us to follow him. I winced when he spoke. This can't be the way this ends. We can't leave these people to die. The thought of them being buried alive made me sick. What could we do?

Wait! If Memphis made a portal, the barrier to our powers must be down. How long did we have until it went back up again?

As the guard started towards me, I put my hands out in front as if to say stop. He stood in place, unable to move. Ajax sensed what I was doing and held the others in place. He was much stronger than I was with telekinesis.

"Let's go. Before they gain control again." I barged through the wooden double doors.

A couple dozen people lingered outside the door to the assembly hall, but not nearly enough. Where was everyone? There should have been at least three or four hundred people. Everyone scattered to the corners when we barreled through the door. I turned my emotions off before their fear overwhelmed me. I couldn't take any more emotions after Callahan's betrayal.

"Where is everybody?" Slade used his telekinesis to twist the gold-colored metal handles together to buy us some more time. He was strong with metals. What does the Authority do when they couldn't follow orders? Would their brains melt down?

A middle-aged man with a thin mustache swallowed hard before he moved forward and nodded a greeting. He carried a young child in his arms while another clung to his pants pocket. His wife held a tiny baby close to her chest. The baby was sound asleep, wrapped tight in a sling tied to her mother. They were both weighed down with bags of their possessions.

"Herb, where is everyone?" I recognized the man in the sanitation uniform. He worked with Callahan and Memphis.

"They aren't coming. Too afraid. They don't trust anyone." Herb glanced around uneasily. Dropping his voice to a whisper. "Is it true what you said? Have the Elites left? Is it safe outside?"

"Yes, they are gone, and they left quite a mess behind." Slade extended his hand to shake Herb's before realizing his hands were full. "Don't worry, we have a plan to get you out of here, but we have to hurry."

"Didn't they feel the blast?" Ajax's eyes rolled skyward. "How dumb are they to think they will be safe down here?"

"They are not dumb, they're scared." Slade raked his hand through his hair, still finding bits and pieces of debris.

"They have been safe down here their whole lives. We haven't offered them any proof to trust us. How can we expect them to believe us?" We were all such a disaster. How would we get people to trust us when we looked this bad?

"I felt the shaking, it's why we are here. The TCC promised we would never feel movement down this deep," Herb said.

"The blast was internal, not external." Slade kept his voice soft and low to avoid panic. "If you know where to set explosives, you can knock down any structure."

"They built this place to withstand natural phenomena, not deliberate acts of destruction." Ajax's lips were set in a grim line.

"You've been outside. Is it true we can breathe out there?" Herb bounced the child up and down as it fussed.

"It takes a bit to adjust to the air, but it's breathable. We have some masks we can share. We'll figure out how to make more." I pulled a mask from my back pocket to show him how it worked, then handed it to his wife. "Take this one. We'll figure out how to make more."

"It's safe outside. The jaunt has been a fake for years." Slade rolled his shoulders. "My parents and the commission have been making a fool out of us for ages."

"If there is even a chance to get my family out of here, I'll take it." Herb's hands clutched his children tighter. He shared a warm interchange with his wife, reassuring her. "Zander and his soldiers came through earlier. He tried to take my boy here. He has powers, you see. But I wouldn't let him go."

"I am so sorry..." I raised a hand to cover my mouth. That Zander tried to split up a family made me sick. What else should I expect from a narcissist?

"Trust me. Charlie and I are not like our parents, I promise you." Slade crossed his hand over his heart.

"You are in excellent hands now. We will get you out of here," I said.

"Or die trying if we don't get a move on," Ajax said. All eyes turned towards him. "What? It's the truth."

Over time, the others in the room drifted closer to the conversation. I turned towards them. "We need your help. Get as many people as possible to—"

"North Tunnel marker 29." Slade added in the information. "Don't bother bringing anything with you. The tunnel is tight, and we need to hurry. I hope none of you are claustrophobic."

"Some of them won't come," Herb warned. "They think they are safer down here than up there."

"They will if they don't want to die." Frustration crinkled Ajax's eyes. "We need some urgency here. Who knows how long until the next blast goes off?"

"Your father will wait until he thinks you are safe at the frozen fortress, but he won't hesitate long after." Slade glanced at his watch. "I wouldn't think we would have more than fifteen minutes."

"Then we have no time to waste. Maybe you and Ajax should go ahead to the tunnel. Make sure the trap door is still accessible."

"I don't want to split up." Slade frowned. The muscles in his face tightened.

"I don't either, but you know the tunnels and I know the East End, it only makes sense."

He hesitated before he nodded, kissing me quickly before leaving. "I'll see you soon."

"You'd better." My eyes shadowed him as he left.

I traveled to the East End with most of the others. Herb and his family went with Slade, along with those people with children. We banged on doors, yelled, and screamed. One man opened his door, listened for a moment, and slammed it shut. I moved on to the next room, determined to come back.

Remy was sitting in the hallway, surrounded by most of her belongings.

"Leave all that stuff and get to the North Tunnel."

She acted like she didn't hear me. What was wrong with her? Was she in a trance? I snapped my fingers in front of her face. When she didn't respond, I grabbed her by the shoulders and shook her. That got her attention.

"Remy, you need to leave."

"I don't want to. I'm scared." Remy clutched tightly at her possessions.

"Change is scary, I know, but you have to go if you want to survive. My father is going to decimate this place."

"Your father is dead."

"No, he isn't."

Members of the Authority streamed by us, weapons down as they passed us as if they were in a trance or something. If that didn't tell her something was wrong, nothing would.

Slade's voice came over the PA system, pleading with residents to come to the tunnel. It was pure chaos as people scrambled to follow his instructions. They cried and yelled, packing their pockets with what they could fit. This must have been what happened when the West Side evacuated.

"Remy, we have to go. You need to move."

Remy stared at me with vacant eyes, totally lost. I slapped her across the face to bring her out of her trance. Something I had wanted to do for years, but it didn't give me the satisfaction I had been hoping for.

She touched the point of contact with her hand. "What did you do that for?"

"Finally, pick yourself up and let's go."

Remy struggled to her feet. She bent to pick up her belongings.

"Leave them. There is no room in the tunnel for that stuff. Jumping jeepers, we don't have time."

Remy dug through her stuff, flinging the contents of her bag everywhere. She stopped once she located a small music box. I recognized it from our room. A present from her grandmother. She clutched it in her delicate fist with painted pink nails. "I'm ready,"

I nodded, "Just a few more rooms to check before we leave."

Remy followed me to another floor. After a few rooms, she got the hang of what I was doing and helped me spread the word. She had a natural way of sounding like someone of importance.

We returned to the room where they slammed the door in my face. I knocked again. Once again, the man tried to shut the door, but this time I stuck my foot out, preventing him from closing it. His face was the opposite of friendly. A woman holding a small young boy with curly black hair stood behind him. From the redness around her eyes, she had been crying. There were marks on her face. One eye swelled shut. What had we interrupted?

"You need to evacuate. There is a direct threat to the complex." I rushed the words out as fast as I could speak.

"Who are you to tell me what to do? Do you think I would listen to the daughter of Zander Edge? Yeah, I know who you are," the man growled. He jerked his hand towards his family. "They aren't leaving either. I am not falling for any of this. It's a trick. The Commission is testing loyalty and I won't fail."

I stood back and let Remy take over. The man wouldn't listen to anything I tried to tell him. I tried my powers again, but they didn't work. The barrier was back in place.

"Is this true? Do you want to stay here? I can assure you it's not safe here," Remy said.

She wiped her hands on her green uniform, shifting her eyes to her husband's once before answering. Her voice trembled. "Y... yes"

"Remy, we can't risk missing our window. If they don't want to listen, there is nothing we can do. This isn't the first group of people refusing to leave." I scrubbed my hand over my face.

"We're leaving. Come if you want, or stay here and die. I really don't care which," Remy said.

The woman's eyes held mine for a split second before she stepped in front of her husband, thrusting her child into my arms. She slammed the door behind her. Remy banged on the door, but they refused to open it again.

Remy and I took off running. The boy screamed in my ear, almost bursting my eardrums. At this moment, it was more important he was alive than happy. Slade waited in the tunnel. There were still several people ahead of us in line.

"What are you doing here? You should be outside." I wanted him to be safe.

"Ajax is at the top, guiding everyone. I waited for you. Who is this little guy?" Slade asked. He stuck out his hands and the boy practically threw himself into Slade's arms, immediately stopping his squealing.

"A recent friend."

"What's your name, little guy?"

The boy stared up at Slade with the saddest expression I had ever seen. His thick lashes soaked with tears. He wiped at his eyes before he tucked his thumb into his mouth.

The corridor ceiling rattled before it rocked. The noise was ear-splitting, loud enough to drown out the surrounding screams as the ground shook violently.

"Not again." Remy dropped to her knees, making herself small.

Slade slid as close to the wall as possible, using his body to shield the boy. Cracks appeared on the walls and floor. The few people remaining in the corridor stumbled and wobbled, falling to the ground, crawling to the sides. The force of the explosion caused the bolts to break, chunks of rocks fell from the sky. I threw up my hands before the lights went out, plunging us into darkness.

An invisible shield covered those of us in the corridor. Within the bubble, it was pitch black. Rocks and boulders fell around the void I created. They bounced off the shield, clanking, crunching, and grinding. It was terrifying. The only home most of us had ever known was falling around us. Did my powers work again? Had Zander removed the barrier?

"I... I can't hold it much longer." The pain from holding the shield was excruciating. I dug as deep as I could, bending at the knees.

Slade handed the boy to the man standing beside him and stumbled towards me. Wrapping his arms around my waist, he tried to keep me steady on my feet. *"Take my strength,"* he said.

I couldn't take his strength. I didn't know how. Then I remembered what Zander taught me, transference. I closed my eyes and inhaled. Mentally reaching towards him, I felt it. His strength poured out of him. I absorbed it, finding a second wave. A reserve I desperately needed. I pushed upward, raising the shield higher.

Once the shaking stopped, we were safe inside the void I created. The pressure of holding the shield had taken a toll on my body. I rested my hands on my thighs, fighting for breath. Remy maneuvered her way to the opening of the tunnel after checking on me. I waved her away.

Slade stood up beside me. "Can we get out of here now?"

EPILOGUE

I lay on my back on the grass. It was cold, but warm enough with my hat and coat. The smell of pine from the nearby trees was a welcome new pleasure. The sky was cloudy, but now and then a beam of light would touch my face, warming me with its glow. I ran my fingers through the blades of grass. Someone told me the brown would soon turn green. I didn't question how he knew. I was just happy it wasn't rock, concrete, or steel.

I heard a rustle before Slade dropped behind me, pulling me closer so I could use his chest as a pillow. He rested his chin against the top of my head. The warmth from his body felt good. It was odd how quickly I became accustomed to his embrace. "Here you are, Charlie. I caught you taking a break."

"I deserve it." I smiled up at him. "How is Cuddles? Is she starting to like her new home?"

"Not yet, but she'll adjust. It is starting to come together, isn't it? What are we going to call our new home?"

"Maybe you should run a 'name the town contest'," I joked.

"I'll add it to my to-do list."

Down the hill, the others we rescued milled around the stream talking, building fires, gathering wood, cooking, and fishing.

Construction on the temporary shelter was complete and the framing of two log homes had begun.

We picked this spot in the valley for our new home. Close to water and fertile farming land. Used to hard work, and interminable days, this location would feel like home in no time. Everyone seemed full of enthusiasm since we were building this place for ourselves.

Remy and Ajax come closer. They were having a lively debate about something. From their faces, it was a friendly discussion. They lowered themselves to the ground when they arrived.

Remy lay flat on her back. "I'm exhausted."

"Look around. All these people are alive because of you," Slade said.

"Because of us, all of us."

He paused a moment, as if deciding something. "Do you think Zander will come after us here?"

"Your guess is as good as mine, but I hope not."

"What about your friends?" Remy propped herself up on her elbow. "Memphis, Callahan, Reese, and Blaze. Are they welcome here?"

"Can we trust them?" Ajax asked.

"I don't know, we'll figure it out... together." My stomach rumbled.

"Ajax, can you grab my knapsack over by the tree? There's some food inside."

Ajax groaned but pulled himself up to retrieve the bag, tossing it in Slade's direction. Slade dug through the bag. "Charlie, catch!"

Instinctively, I reached up to grab the object he threw to me. An apple. Without hesitation, I sunk my teeth into the tasty, tart treat.

ACKNOWLEDGMENTS

Writing a book is harder than I ever thought it would be.

My writing group, The WRITE NOW Club, has been wonderful helping this first-time novelist finish her book. From accountability sessions, to writing critiques, to beta reading, to blurb crafting, they have helped me at every stage of this journey. A big thank you to Piyushi Dhir and Darcy Herring for reading an early draft of *Hollow Edge*.

Jackie Brown, my editor, has been a wealth of information taking me through the self-publishing process step by step. She helped to tighten up my novel and deal with sensitivity issues.

My pug who wrote every word with me and my husband, who keeps asking me if this book is going to make any money.

My daughter, Brittany, has been an enormous help, providing beta reading, grammar checks, and emotional support when needed. Thank you for the encouragement, and for simply being you.

My parents, who took me to the library for the first time and encouraged my love of reading. I wouldn't be who I am without them. My brother is not a reader, so please don't tell him this book isn't dedicated to him.

www.ingramcontent.com/pod-product-compliance
Lightning Source LLC
Chambersburg PA
CBHW071410200726
48294CB00002B/347